SLEEPWATER BEAT

KATHRIN HUTSON

Books by Kathrin Hutson

Gyenona's Children (Dark Fantasy)
Daughter of the Drackan
Mother of the Drackan

The Unclaimed (NA Dark Fantasy)
Sanctuary of Dehlyn
Secret of Dehlyn
Sacrament of Dehlyn

Blue Helix (Speculative Sci-Fi/LGBT Thriller)
Sleepwater Beat

Cover Design by OliviaProDesign

https://www.vecteezy.com Free Vector Art by Vecteezy

ISBN: 978-1-7322016-5-1 (Exquisite Darkness Press)

 Exquisite
Darkness
Press

For those who believe in the power of words, even when they don't seem to be enough. Convince yourself, and that's all that matters.

Acknowledgments

A special thanks goes out to the Charleston Writers Group. Without the hours of workshopping spent on the original *Sleepwater Beat* and their phenomenal questions and suggestions, this would never have become more than a wildly disjointed attempt to startle readers with a short story.

Thanks to those who read this book before publication, especially Jason Pere and Roy Daman, who got the whole thing chapter by chapter while I slaved away. And to Gretel Dougherty, who caught the "meat" of it.

As always, I must and forever will thank my husband Henry, who puts up with my one-track writer's brain and makes it possible for this to be my sole focus.

Part One

1

GODDAMNIT, HE WAS tired. Tired of hiding, tired of looking over his shoulder, tired of working with the underground class of society on nights like tonight. And still, he wasn't tired enough to put an end to it. Part of him wanted them to catch him—the same part of him that always felt guilty for the crime he never committed.

Karl gripped the steering wheel of his station wagon. He'd parked across the street from the gas station, planning on grabbing a bottle of liquor to open instead of the beers at his place. It was just one of those nights. He looked through the window and caught the flash of blue and red lights unaccompanied by a siren.

The cop pulled over on the other side of the road and headed toward the gas station. The door flew open with a jingle, and a skinny girl with a ratty nest of dark hair barreled out. The clerk followed, baseball bat in hand, but stopped when the cop intercepted the girl. One hand clutched her scrawny arm underneath the folds of a denim jacket, the other hovered over his gun. That hand did not shake.

The girl spun around in her trap, trying to both shoulder her backpack and escape.

"What's in the bag?" the cop asked.

"She's been stealing from me," the clerk put in, jumping from foot to foot.

"Is that so?" The cop never took his eyes from his prey. "I tell ya what. I'll give ya one chance to tell me what's in your bag, then I'm going to check it, and we'll go from there." The cop's smile was sharp—predatory.

The girl scowled. "You really want to know everything?" She managed to jerk her arm free, giving no chance for an answer. "I'm an upstanding citizen just like everyone else. I paid for a candy bar and tried to leave. *This* guy"— she nodded toward the clerk—"likes to make trouble. I did *not* steal anything, and there's no reason for you to search my bag, let alone be here in the first place."

The cop and store clerk glanced at each other, faces slack in a blank confusion. The clerk tilted his head, and the cop's mouth opened and closed without sound.

"I still..." he finally managed to say, then glanced toward the rooftops, as if he'd find his words there.

"You don't still need to check my bag," the girl spat. "And I think the two of you owe me an apology after these bullshit accusations." Her indignant smirk seemed out of place on her tiny frame.

"Sorry," the store clerk said. His chin drifted toward his

chest, like he would fall asleep where he stood. "I must have forgotten that you paid."

"Thank you"—the cop blinked—"for your... time. Now that that's settled, I'll be on my way." His words came out like molasses, and as he turned around, his footsteps fell with a robotic jerk. The clerk shoved his hands into his pockets, searching for clarity, and returned to the shop with the same sleepy, bowed head.

The girl shouldered her bag again and stalked off into the newly dark night.

Karl watched all this through the open window of his car. The cop and clerk would be all right. Later confused, but he'd seen the symptoms before. He removed what looked like a Bluetooth headset from his ear, grateful that he'd forgotten to take it off before what he'd seen, and put it in the glovebox.

The girl was one of them. It was a gut instinct, a pinprick of certainty in his life's haze. There was so much he could teach her. He'd sworn years ago he'd never use the beat again, but maybe with her under his wing, he could redeem himself. To redeem himself to anyone—this dirty, stubborn girl, even—was better than the daily pit of his conscience. He could help her do what he never could, though helping did not come naturally to a man like him anymore.

The girl hadn't walked too far away. She sat against the front window of a cell phone store, running a hand over her tangled hair. Karl stood from the driver seat, locked the door behind him, and stepped into the pools of ruddy lamplight, fingering his lighter. After all, if she didn't like him, she could just make him believe anything she wanted. He had just watched her do it.

Leo sat beneath the awning of a cell phone store, rubbing her wrist where the cop had grabbed her. The sun had set while they were arguing, but the clouds still hung low, dense, blocking any light. The streets and sky were dry, but it smelled like rain.

That had been stupid, shoplifting without a plan. Her head hurt, her mouth was dry, and her heart fluttered, more now in relief than anxiety. She needed a cigarette. She kept them in the inside pocket of her denim jacket, and when she brought one to her lips, a pair of scuffed work boots crashed her private party. She looked up, and the guy squatted in front of her. They stared at each other, and a flame produced itself from his lighter. Her lips were puffy when she blew out that first breath—a girl's best nicotine friend.

"Thanks."

He nodded, tucked the lighter away, and casually glanced down the street. "You got anywhere to stay to-night?"

"This was gonna do it," she answered and brought her knees up to her chest. Her back rested against the window. The cigarette threw a thin cherry reflection against the dark.

The man rubbed his fingers through his beard, bouncing slightly in his squat, and looked her up and down. "Naw," he started, rising to his feet. "I got a couch. Car's parked across the street."

"Great. Go drive your car." Who did this guy think he was?

He took a deep breath and squinted down the sidewalk. "You know, I've seen a lot of cops out tonight. I'm willing to bet some of them remember you. I'm also willing to bet it would be a nice change for you to have a roof and four walls for a night."

It was extremely difficult for Leo to argue. In a minute, this man had sized her up and offered her exactly what she needed. To turn him down would be stupid. Good Samaritans were hard to come by; taking off with total strangers was also stupid. And yet, the idea of shelter after weeks without it was almost worth it. When she only responded with a glare, he turned toward the street, giving her a wide view of his back.

She watched him until he pulled keys out of his pocket. "What do I have to do?" she called, ready to run.

The guy flipped through his keys, opened the car door, and didn't look back. "Eat my cooking." His head almost scraped the roof of the car as he folded himself into its belly and closed the door.

Leo kicked against the wall and jogged across the street. A car honked at her, barely slowing. She raised a middle finger, opened the passenger door of her new friend's car, and hopped inside. The un-flicked ash of the cigarette fell and warmed a place for her on the seat before she smothered it and shut the door. The old station wagon rattled when she moved and coughed when the keys were turned.

If she didn't know better, Leo would have thought the guy was ignoring her as he shifted into gear and coaxed the old car onto the road.

It was completely silent. She flipped out another ciga-rette; he lit it without looking at her. The ride lasted maybe ten minutes, and she touched him with her eyes. Prodding, poking, looking for soft spots or rotten edges. Once, he glanced at her quickly, looked her over from dirty hair to stripped-down sneakers, and still said nothing. His fingers were loose on the steering wheel, the way a man rested his hands on a woman's leg. When he pulled into the driveway of what looked like a burned-down garage, Leo sniffed and sucked on her lip.

She had one bag only—big enough for another sweat-shirt, a newly acquired carton of cigarettes, and the rest of her money. At one point, she'd had quite a bit. Not so much now, but it would have bothered her more if it had been clean money. She got out first, testing the dusty ground with her feet, waiting for his slow lead to the front door. His steps might have made him seem dumb, but she thought better of him. Sometimes, people chose to be slow.

He thrust a solid hip into the rusting door and flipped the lights on behind him. Leo followed, popping her lips, approving of the place. It looked like the back end of a trailer that had been sawed off and separated from its head. A short rectangle, only slightly longer than it was wide, with no other walls than the four. On the left were a small fridge, industrial plastic sink in a short countertop, and a micro-wave. A three-legged wooden table completed the circle, weighted disproportionately by an open camping stove. The opposite wall stood backed by a long brown couch, maybe once orange, whose end cushion sunk like the corner of a stroke victim's mouth. It was the end closest to the twenty-inch television. On the right side was a mattress on the floor—boxes mixed with clothes, paper scraps, a lone shoe without the laces. Between the bed and the couch was an end table, adorned by a bowl of lighters and two picture frames. At a glance, she felt at home. She smelled old socks that had been removed but forgot to take their stink and wondered if the tangy, red-sauce scent had baked itself into the walls or if he just hadn't washed the dishes.

"So…" she started, rubbing a hand along the unpainted wall. "Uh…"

"Karl."

She nodded. "So, Karl, how long you been here?" She wasn't going to sleep on a couch without first knowing exactly what the offer meant. She made her way slowly into the center of the one room, stopped, glanced at him.

"Long time." He turned his back again and headed toward the tiny fridge. He moved with the ease of a man who had nothing to hide, or whose secrets were buried too deep to find.

He sorted through the jumble of pots and plates, opening and closing the refrigerator as though he were forgetting something. Leo took a deep breath, noticing the thin film of dust on the chair. She had grown up in small, dirty places where everything was out on the table, nothing swept under the rug. Her eyes landed on the pictures by the bed. One of them was of an Australian Shepherd, obviously not around anymore. The other was of a sweet, fresh-looking redhead, late twenties, her hair blown about her shoulders as she laughed underneath the shade of a large tree. It was a great picture, the kind people paid good money to have manufactured. The rumble and hiss of the water through the tap filled the place, and Leo handled the photograph.

"Who's this?" she asked after a few seconds. The smile played on her face until she turned around to lock eyes with Karl.

He stood by the table with a handful of dried pasta. His wild beard had acted like a mask and would have continued to hide any emotion if it were not for the sudden rigidity in his movement. When he reached her, he took the picture, looking down at it when he held it by his hip.

"That's my wife."

"Where is she?"

Karl placed the picture back on the side table. This time, though, the laughing face was buried against the peeling wood. He cleared his throat and returned to the round table. "I'm making spaghetti."

Leo sat at the table and bored holes into his back as he cooked. She hadn't eaten real cooking in over a month, but she didn't want him to see the glisten on her lips when she licked them or hear her swallowing in silent hunger. She hoped her stomach wouldn't start growling with the smell of meatball sauce and garlic.

They ate in complete silence, sharing an occasional glance over dinner. The man mostly focused on her fork. He graced her with a beer from the minifridge, and she found herself downing it faster than she would have liked. Finally finished, finally full, she wiped the red from around her mouth and sighed contentedly. It took him over a minute to finish the rest of the spaghetti, wipe his mouth, chug another beer. Then he met her gaze and held it for the first time.

"Thanks for dinner," she told him, and his only response was a raised eyebrow. "So, what now?" She rubbed a hand through her hair, pulled out a cigarette, and he lit it for her. Her bent elbows met on the table, and she inhaled smoke from atop the cradle of her hands.

"There's a reason I brought you here, you know." He cleared the table. His back was to her as he washed dishes in the industrial sink, and Leo sat against the chair. He had not spent more than ten seconds actually looking at her.

"What, it's not that I'm dirty and hungry and look like I need a place to crash?" She blew smoke into the light above the table.

"You're really bad at flirting," he said over the running water.

Leo swallowed, took a drag, folded her arms. "What makes you think I'm trying to come on to you?" He was remarkably uninterested, yet she knew he wanted something from her.

"Your smile."

She choked on the smoke. "What's wrong with my smile?"

"It makes you look like you have the flu." He turned from the sink just in time to watch her put her cigarette out on the flimsy tabletop. "I'll remember that." Rubbing his beard, he returned to his seat and folded his hands.

"Why am I here, then?"

"I watched you. With the cop and the store clerk."

"Yeah." She felt her frown border on a headache. "I handled it."

Karl's mustache moved. "You made them believe you."

"I'm very persuasive." She stood abruptly from the table. "Apparently, I've managed to persuade you into some pretty fucked-up conclusions." She shouldered her pack. His hints hit far too close to home, and she never let herself get close. Her secret had been protected for this long, and she wasn't about to spill it all to this fucking hermit. She was three feet from the door when he spoke again.

"We both know it has nothing to do with the actual *words* coming out of your mouth."

She froze.

"You have a special… talent," he said softly, and she turned again to face him. "Go ahead." Karl sat back in his chair and folded his arms. "Do it. Tell me what you want me to believe."

She swallowed. "Why?"

"To prove me right." This time, he met her eyes and held them fiercely. "Which you know you really don't have to do. I know exactly what your secret is."

She took another drag of the cigarette, only now her hand was trembling. "How?"

He lit his own smoke. "I can do something similar." The pipes clinked as the sink finished draining.

"What do you make people do?" The words were dry and stuck in her throat.

"There are a lot of us out there who can change people with our words," he replied. "More than you'd think. I'd like you to meet them."

"You know them all?" Her heart was racing now, a sheen of sweat building at her hairline.

"I know where to find them. How about I show you?"

Leo returned to the chair, her backpack slipping from her shoulder to the floor.

"We call it spinning a beat, when your chest burns and the words come out," he said.

"Like what I do."

"Like what you do. But first, you know my name…" He offered his hand over the table.

"Leona. I—Leo." They shook briefly. His hand was calloused and firm but warm. A hot flash went down her back, and she sucked hard on the cigarette. She stared intensely at his mouth, now understanding the difficulty in eye contact.

"Leo. First then, Leo, tell me about yourself."

A nervous laugh burst out. "What, you want me to tell you my whole life's story?" Her foot tapped on the dusty floor.

"Just enough so I know what I'm working with. Another beer?"

She took a deep breath. "Yeah."

2

"DADDY, ARE YOU okay?" The bunny heads on the tops of her slippers still kept her toes warm, even though Rex had chewed off the noses.

Daddy unrolled the string on the top of his arm, sighed, and leaned back in his red reclining chair. "I'm fine," he whispered, then realized who she was. He twitched and turned his heavy head toward her. His eyes were dark and watery, and he looked sick. "Leona, you need to go back to bed."

She stood there, tugging at the bottom of her night-gown.

"Did your night light go off?"

Nothing.

They stared at each other for a few seconds, her huge

brown eyes swimming in tears. The goosebumps raised up on her bare arms, but she stood still.

"You cold?" he asked, fighting to keep his eyes open. The corner of his mouth drooped, but to her, it looked like a smile.

She shuffled toward him and turned around. Reaching his bony hands under her arms, he pulled her up into his lap. The chewed brown blanket covered them both now, and he brought the edge of it up to her chin. He rubbed her arms for a short while until she felt his hands go slack around her and heard his breathing slow.

The clock ticked away above the hole in the wall, and she let herself glance across the room. Another man, younger than Daddy, uglier than Daddy, lay sprawled out on the couch. His arm hung over the edge as he sucked in a rattled, sleepy breath, and an empty needle lay on the floor below his bruised elbow. Sweat glistened on his pale skin, soaked in the moonlight slinking through the rip in the curtains.

"Daddy?" she asked, leaning against him, feeling him stiffen as he noticed her again. "Who's that?"

Daddy grunted, sniffed, and brought his mouth close to her ear. "That, baby, is a junkie." His breath was sour, like pickle juice and cigarettes. His arms around her melted the goosebumps. "Take a good, long look, Leona. Never forget the sight. Those junkies will do anything for their next fix."

She stared at the needle on the floor, thinking it looked a lot like the one next to Daddy's chair. It was probably a good idea not to say anything about it. Pulling the tattered blanket farther up toward her face, she kicked out one foot and then the other, watching the bunny ears of her slippers flop up and down.

Daddy gave a little jolt. "What is it, baby?" He gave her elbow a weak squeeze.

"When's Mommy coming home?" Daddy was never sick like this when Mommy was home. Mommy could put him to bed, wipe his forehead with a cool towel, and rub his tummy. And sing a song. She always felt better when Mommy sang her a song.

Daddy's eyes opened a little when he craned his neck to look at her. "You miss her, don't you?" She nodded, watching his eyes move in a dizzy circle around her face. "I miss her, too. Let's go back to bed. I'll tuck you in."

He patted her shoulder, getting ready to sit up. She shifted in his lap to look at the scruff on his cheeks and waited. He took a deep breath, then out came a muffled snore. She watched a pool of saliva gather at the corner of his mouth and topple over the side in a lazy string towards his chin. Sniffing, she pecked him on the cheek and slipped off the chair, making sure to tuck the frayed blanket back into place.

Her bedroom was at the top of the stairs, and she only tripped once on her nightgown. The door squeaked when she pushed it in, and she shuffled sleepily to the mattress in the corner. Her sheets had ponies on them, but the ones closest to her head had faded to smudges. Plucking her slippers off, she slipped under the sheets and pulled them tight around her. A small weight settled behind her legs. Rex never left her bedroom when Daddy's friends came over. She didn't like them much either, though they acted like she wasn't there.

"Hi, Rex," she whispered, and the wiry brown mutt nuzzled her legs. She reached down to scratch the top of his head, and he gave a short, concerned whine. "Thanks for tucking me in." She grabbed one of the slippers and nestled it between his legs. "Sleep tight."

3

IN OTHER NEWS, the FDA released a new drug last month. Produced by Laleopharm, Pointera *targets the superior temporal gyrus in the brain, responsible for morphosyntactic processing. That's the process of forming speech, sentence structure, and word choice. This medication is proven to improve the directness of thought and speech. So for those with Attention Deficit Disorder or severe anxiety disorders, this is an incredibly helpful tool for people to gather their thoughts quickly and to speak with a much higher level of ease. Studies by the FDA show an overall decrease in the time it took research participants to answer questions, and to even explain ideas or techniques, by an average of five point three seconds. That doesn't sound like much time, but imagine thinking about something for five seconds. When you're on the spot, that seems like an eternity.*

Maybe I should try Pointera, *John. Sometimes it takes me longer than five seconds to get my thoughts together.*

Well, Brenda, you'll have your chance next week. The pill will hit pharmacy shelves across the country, and you can talk to your doctor about a prescription for Pointera. *For more information, check Laleopharm's Facebook, Twitter, and Topper pages with updates on this fast-thinking, smooth-talking pill.*

4

THREE BEERS IN, the talking came easier for her. It wasn't her natural state—the buzz or the conversation—but Karl had pulled the trigger of curiosity, and it was impossible to escape the crossfire.

"So you've been on the streets for how long?" he asked.

"Six years. It's not so bad if you know where to go, who to see… the right things to say." She had finished almost an entire pack from the carton in her backpack but lit another cigarette anyways. Karl closed his eyes and shook his head. Leo leaned her elbows on the table, the warmth of alcohol in her head and food in her belly adding to her sense of comfort here—opening her almost non-existent social interaction.

"Go ahead," she said. "You got something to say. Say it."

"It's not always that easy. The way I see it, you're running out of the right things to say." He fiddled with the tin ashtray, tapped his own cigarette against it.

Leo laughed. "Cops are idiots. That was nothing. I've been in way worse trouble, and I'm still here." Spreading her arms, she sat back in the chair.

"You're pretty cocky for someone who looked pretty scared." He brought them each another beer, and Leo felt the lump in her throat stick. "Why don't you show me personally how you handle your *trouble*?"

She realized the flush in her face was not entirely due to the beer, and she instantly wished she had kept her mouth shut. She eyed the bottle in front of her.

"Go on." He nudged it closer to her and drank his own. "Little badass like you can keep up with me. You're so proud of yourself, show me."

The smell of yeast and hops made her lick her lips, but her stomach hardened anyways. "I can't."

"Why not?"

"This is like, my fourth beer. It doesn't work... when I drink."

She sounded crazy. She sounded like a phony. She hit her cigarette and breathed the smoke in through clenched teeth.

Karl placed the beer directly in front of her. "Well, you know more than you let on. At least you figured that much out for yourself. What else screws with your words?"

She grabbed the beer and stared at Karl's upper lip peeking beneath the mustache. His eyes had never left hers, and she felt them probing more deeply now that she was aware of her mistake. He knew way more than she did, and she was about to prove him right, no matter what she said.

"What is this, fucking therapy?"

"You want to know what I know?" he asked and crossed a scratched leather boot over his knee. "Then I need to know what you know. Answer the question." He didn't raise his voice, didn't clench his fists. He barely seemed affected at all by the beer, and yet Leo had matched him drink for drink.

"When I get pissed off. When I get scared. When people ask me too many questions." She gave him a pointed glare. "I can't always choose when to make people believe me. Sometimes I can't stop it." She shook her head, flicked the cigarette with unnecessary force.

Her heart beat faster through alcohol-thinned blood, and she was momentarily surprised by the lack of burning in her chest. Her mouth tasted the same as ever, without the spicy, metal tinge that always led the way for her really powerful words. She tasted beer and cigarettes—nothing else. She had given up spending her money or "talent" for alcohol years ago, once she realized what it did. Every time she drank and the burning never showed, the disappointment was as harsh as the first time it happened. So was the panic of realizing she couldn't talk her way out of rash decisions. That made drinking a liability on the streets. But when it was offered freely, and she didn't feel threatened, it helped to relax a bit. She regretted that now, but there was no way out. Karl held the wild card of information, of something resembling answers, and she had already accepted the invitation.

"Is that what you wanted to hear?" She wanted the sting of her words, but drunken sarcasm would have to work.

Karl made a noncommittal noise of consent, and the back of Leo's neck burned hot in the next few seconds of silence.

"What happened to your mom?" he asked.

"Seriously?"

He spread his arms, reminding her of the necessity to talk. Tit for tat.

An irritated laugh escaped her. "She's gone." She gulped on the beer and wiped her mouth. "I was four when she walked out. My dad was one of the first to use Pointera as a career-booster." She tried to focus on the strips peeling from the underside of the table. "She called him a robot, but she had no problem leaving me there with him."

"How long did it take him to…"

Her smile felt sour and twisted on her own face. "I spent my sixth birthday burying Rex in the backyard alone. Turns out a kid can survive on peanut butter and Twinkies. A dog really can't."

"And after your dad?"

"Nothing. If she was still alive, she didn't come to the funeral. I stopped giving a shit way before that." The grinding of teeth in her head was the only sound for a moment, and she gave up a silent death wish for the woman. That, at least, she didn't have to share.

"I'm sorry, kid." He drained his beer, stood, and cleared his throat. "Well, I'm turning in. The couch is all yours."

She smashed her cigarette out and watched him click the lights off. "That's it?" He said nothing.

The yellow street lamp filtered through the cheap blinds, falling on half of his mattress. Through the lit smoke, she watched him undress. She didn't mean to stare, but he was right there. Down to his boxer shorts, his chest lit up in the streaks of dim light, showing surprisingly less hair than his beard and head would suggest. He sat on the mattress, and his eyes met hers for only a second.

He had caught her watching him, without invitation, or shame, or humor. Her mouth went dry, and when she drained her own bottle, he buried himself in the blanket and turned away from her.

She lay on the couch, its old age no doubt responsible for the odd, lumpy comfort. The toes of her shoes caught the street light, and she stared at them. The man's acknowledgment had left her bitter and rejected. She couldn't remember the last time she'd slept in someone's house on the couch. Alone. With her clothes on. But through that sting of silent denial, she knew this wasn't just another way to get through the night. She folded her arms and let the dizziness beneath closed eyes spin her down into sleep.

His place looked different in the morning—sad. The one window opposite the door lit up the cracks in the walls, the frayed ends of the couch, the stains in the rug, and the duct tape on the table leg. The light washed everything out, made it feel empty when the night before, it had held the dark mystery of something new.

A part of her had still expected him to try something during the night. Even after their conversation, her reason for staying, she still wasn't convinced. Even after he met her eyes with a silent no, she had wanted it to be a yes.

Karl was frying bacon on the portable stove, and she

watched the rhythm of his moving arms, the way he stood with his feet wide, legs straight.

"Breakfast smells good." He didn't say anything. She stood from the couch and walked toward him. "Hey." He made a noise in his throat but didn't look at her. Her face went hot. She deserved his attention. He had fed her, shared his booze, given her a place to sleep, and no matter how rare those things were for her now, they were hardly equal to what she had given him. If he expected her to admit her secrets, to listen to him and open this door, it wouldn't be for free. She was fed up with being invisible. She placed a hand on his arm, and he froze. He met her gaze with calm detachment. Her need flared into anger, and a white-hot pressure burst in her stomach.

"Kiss me." The words burned in her chest, up her throat, out of her mouth, and his eyes relaxed. "You want to kiss me, because I'm more than some homeless-girl freak show."

Karl bent toward her, gently grabbed her face below the ear, and his mustache was surprisingly soft against her mouth. The fork clattered onto the table, and she pulled him closer. He was a good kisser, but when her breathing got heavier, when she pulled him tighter against her body, her enthusiasm went unmatched. He kissed her, but that was all.

She pulled back, held him around the waist. The anger melted into a pool of guilt in her diaphragm, and she clenched her eyes to shut out his face. "That was fucked up." She whispered it through clenched teeth, and the heat of his body melted through his shirt to appear as sweat in her palms. Her heart was beating faster now at his silence. She looked up.

His eyes moved from lazy slits to round awareness, the color flashing in his irises like the flare of a stricken match. "Are you done?" he asked.

She could have kissed him again if she wanted, he was so close. Her hands washed in a new wave of clammy anxiety when she realized that that would be his only response. Anyone else would have been shocked, maybe angry. She tightened her grip on him, hungry to find the tension of a loaded spring. She could pick that tension out anywhere, so used to the aggression that always followed. The kind she expected. Karl's breath was a steady hum of warmth on her face.

She dropped her hands from his hips, fighting back the urge to push him over. The only reaction she would ever get out of him was that flash of intelligence returning to his eyes. The awareness in them alarmed her more than any harsh words or heavy hands. She wiped her hands on the back of her neck and focused her attention on the door.

Karl retrieved the fork and continued with the almost burnt bacon.

He knew exactly what she had done. He was the one person who knew, who could put two and two together and hold her accountable for the childish ways she used it. He had ignited her latent need to be known. She couldn't turn back now. And whether or not her interest in him was physical, whether it stemmed from her need to finally be seen, it still scared the hell out of her.

He didn't have to tell her not to do that again.

He asked her if she wanted to meet others who used the *beat*, as he called it. She said yes. It wasn't necessary at all for her to say yes. They both already knew she wasn't going any-where, didn't have anything better to do, that this was the closest thing she had to a purpose. Without any words at all, she now felt both free and trapped. If she had told Karl to go fuck himself, if she had stormed out of his place as she'd planned, would she really forget about all the things he'd already told her, no matter how vague? She knew there were things you never, ever forgot. Since she'd taken to the streets, completely on her own, Karl's invitation might have been the first thing she could not make herself forget.

They got into his station wagon after a strained break-fast, and that too looked the worse for wear in the daylight. Leo noticed he didn't lock his garage of a home. She was willing to bet the door didn't even have a lock. It felt too soon to ask. That steely gaze of his was a better deterrent than any other punishment. The control he had over his emo-tions was enough to make her hands slick with sweat as she pulled on the handle to the car door. She couldn't get his apathy and that kiss out of her head. He acted as though it never happened, which was probably for the best. Still, she doubted she'd touch him again anytime soon. There was no great lay in their agreement, but what she was about to learn was far more worth it. It was impossible to imagine what Karl was getting out of the deal.

Cigarette smoke snaked through the open windows. They drove silently in the scent of burnt ash, and Karl pulled over beside a payphone on the downtown main road. She tried hard not to watch him as he stood with his back to her. She heard the lilt of his voice through the open window but couldn't make out the words. He seemed completely at ease, standing squarely with one hand in his pocket, but Leo found herself searching the street.

What was she looking for? As far as she knew, it wasn't illegal to use a payphone. She felt watched, like she had come out of hiding and been spotted in the middle of a hunt. Now that her secret was out, the world would change around her. But the cars heading their way passed without slowing. The barking dogs were only chasing squirrels. Nobody cared about them and the beaten station wagon.

Just as she started to laugh at her own idiocy, Karl opened the door and scared the smile right off her face. She coughed on the smoke in her lungs.

The softness of the smile he gave her washed out her momentary paranoia. "Jumpy?" he asked and started the engine.

It was the first thing he'd said to her since before breakfast. She realized she'd been hoping this whole time that she hadn't seriously fucked up. She wanted him to like her for who she was, not what she could do. That feeling was surprisingly uncomfortable.

"Hey," she started and fumbled with a new cigarette. "About this morning—"

"We're good." He glanced at her quickly before lighting her cigarette with one hand and steering them onto the highway with the other.

His curtness cut right through the weight of that discomfort. She felt her shoulders relax, realizing how long she'd been so tense. She was not used to the rationality of other people or the compassion of anyone in the same boat.

They were good.

Karl took them out of downtown and into the limit of the suburbs. There was a dividing line between the grittiness of the city and the white picket fences and manicured lawns. Leo had learned early on not to cross that line. These people who seemed to live on a different planet, who relished in the scandal of the homeless in their neighborhood, had nothing good to offer. More often than not, the police got involved, and while Leo had always managed to get herself out of it, the trip was more trouble than it was worth.

Something vaguely familiar picked at her from the cleanliness on the other side of the line, from the lack of chaos and the routine of the American Dream. It pulled at a memory she couldn't quite retrieve, threatening things she thought she knew but tried to forget. Her mother, so long gone, came to mind amid these HOA-prescribed hives of the middle class. Had her mother come from places like this? Or perhaps she'd escaped *to* them, leaving the dirty, worthless, scandalizing family of hers behind. Whatever the connection, Leo ran from the line, dreaded crossing it, and wondered what on earth kind of business Karl had so close to it.

Some people lived *on* that line, the limbo in between, and if one picked the right person, it didn't make the area all that bad. Karl pulled into the drive of a ranch-style house, the yard full of fallen leaves spilling onto the porch. He put the wagon in park, and Leo stared out the window.

"Who lives here?" she asked.

"Her name's Bernadette. She's a pretty important person." He opened the door.

"Is she the leader of the 'beat people' or something?" She instantly cursed herself for the stupidity of that question and flushed when Karl laughed out loud.

"She's a storyteller, and she's a friend of mine."

"Is she the best?"

He glanced up at the house with a tiny, nostalgic smile. "Maybe once. Come on."

5

"EVERYONE TAKE OUT their vocabulary books." The classroom filled with the rustling of backpacks and paper, of half-chewed pencils falling onto the linoleum floor. "You had pages sixty-seven through seventy to fill out last night for homework. Turn to page sixty-seven."

Leo sulked in her elementary school desk, the never-used vocab book shining like a beacon on the laminate wood. She slowly opened it to the right page and stuck a pencil in the crease. The book wouldn't even stay open. Ms. Gambrone asked the other students to recite their answers, and Leo felt like she was sinking into the floor, out of the chair, into a world of shame beneath the foundation of the school.

"Leona," the skinny teacher called. "What did you get

for number eight?"

"I didn't get anything," she mumbled and slipped a ragged fingernail between her teeth.

"I'm sorry, what did you say?" The scent of rosewater wafted toward her before the teacher. The other kids stared and tried to hide their smiles.

"I said I didn't get anything for number eight." Her voice cracked as she strained not to yell.

Ms. Gambrone laid a single index finger on the edge of her desk. "Did you not do your homework last night?"

The vocab book was still closed, the pencil peeking out its black and yellow nose. Leo glanced down at the book and back up at the teacher. "My... my dog ate pages sixty-seven through seventy."

A few sniggers came from the other kids surrounding her, and Ms. Gambrone made a hushing gesture. "Leona, do you expect me to believe that your dog specifically ate just the pages you were assigned to do for homework last night?"

"Do you even have a dog?" one of the kids hollered, followed by explosive giggles. Ms. Gambrone shushed them again.

"Yes," Leona whispered. Something clicked into place inside her then, a tingling in her chest that made her feel both peaceful and chaotic at the same time. When she opened her mouth, the burning in her chest rode the wind of her words. "Yes, my dog ate just those pages. My dad and I were walking home from the store last night, and this mutt started following us. He wouldn't leave us alone, so we brought him inside after he stood by the door crying for a while. He seemed like a good dog, but when I took out my vocab book to do the homework, he jumped at me and ripped the pages out of my hand. He's really a good dog. I just forgot to feed him, and he was hungry."

It was the most ridiculous thing she could have possibly said. She couldn't stop it. She expected the outburst from her classmates, the apprehensive and disappointed frown from her teacher. Instead, Ms. Gambrone smiled, eyes wide and glassy, and tapped her finger once on Leo's desk.

"Of course, Leona. Some stray dogs are hard to train. But if you work at it and feed him, your new friend should have plenty of time to learn to stay away from your homework. Leave the dog outside your room while you do your work next time, okay?"

Leo froze, staring back at the teacher. After a few seconds of silence, she managed to ask, "You believe me?"

"Of course I believe you, Leona. Why shouldn't I?" Ms. Gambrone's voice was a level drone, but the tilt of her head and her smile suggested something entirely different. She didn't seem quite like Ms. Gambrone.

Leo very slowly turned in her chair, eyeing the other students. They all looked back at her with half smiles and glassy eyes, but nobody laughed, nobody joked. Tommy Cooper sat behind her, and she bet he was the one who made the comment about her having a dog. She stared at him now, and his frown was the most sympathetic thing she'd ever seen on his scowling face. It looked so strange to her, but if anybody was going to tell it to her straight, it would be Tommy. Even if it embarrassed the hell out of her.

"Is this weird?" she asked him. Something essential was missing from his eyes.

"No. I like dogs too."

Her hand shot up to her hair, and she considered pulling it out to wake herself from this ridiculous dream. What was going on? She spun back toward Ms. Gambrone. This had better not be a giant prank. "And... you'll mark my grade like I did my homework?" She couldn't help herself from the tingling breath rising through her throat and into words.

"Well, I—"

"You *will* mark it right," she amended, clasping that strange power like a flitting bug in her hands.

Ms. Gambrone nodded. "Absolutely." Then she returned to the front of the room and continued the lesson without another question. She did not ask Leo again what she got on her homework; she barely looked at her.

Leo had been cleaning the puke off her father the night before, dragging his sweaty body as far as a ten-year-old could pull, dabbing his face with a wet cloth as he babbled incoherencies. Homework had seemed relatively inane then until faced with Ms. Gambrone's judgmental, passive retribution. But she had believed the story. They all had.

There was no possible way she could sit in class like this. How was she supposed to focus on anything resembling school when this awesome thing had just happened?

She raised her hand.

"Yes, Leona?"

She had to force a frown onto her face, pretend to be serious, and put the raised hand onto her stomach. "I don't feel very good," she groaned, feeling the tingle rise again, watching the reaction on her teacher's loose features. "I think I should go to the nurse and go home."

A few seconds passed, and Ms. Gambrone's face softened even more if possible. "Of course, Leona. Go straight to the nurse. I'm sure she'll see you need to go home sick."

Leo made sure to put the un-eaten vocab book in her backpack and slung it quickly over her shoulder as she scrambled from her seat. No one said a word.

The burning in her chest was a powerfully intoxicating sensation, the sound of her own words no different than normal. But they *tasted* different coming out, danced off her tongue with an unknown grace and confidence. She jumped toward the door, forgetting in her haste that she was supposed to be sick.

She picked up a stick on her walk home at 11:30 on a Tuesday, swinging it against the fence lining the sidewalk. What in the world *was* that? It couldn't have been a joke. The school would never let her just walk out of there. She didn't even actually go see the nurse. It had to be something she said, had to be something real.

The neighborhood park was just around the corner, and she threw the stick toward the small creek running under the trees. A shout came from behind her, and she froze. The shout repeated, and she turned, poised to run. She'd been noticed before at the gas station in the middle of the day, either returned to school or escorted home. She liked outrunning the police, though. They never chased her very far if she ran.

A blond head and black sweatshirt jetted around the corner. "Leo! Hang on!"

Leo laughed and slid the backpack off her shoulder so

it skirted the ground. "I didn't know you were skipping to-day."

Alex shrugged and kicked up a patch of grass with a worn sneaker. Her smile meant trouble—the smile Leo had wanted so badly last year to make her friend. And she had.

"I didn't know you were, either. I was at the nurse with a stomachache." She exaggerated a grotesque vomit, that dangerous smile sweetening the motion. "Then you ran out, and nobody followed you, and I had to see what happened. Is everything okay?"

Leo felt the excited, anxious knot tighten in her stomach. "I think so."

Alex shoved her hands in the baggy pockets of her hoodie, and her face went blank. "Is it your dad?"

It was Leo's turn to kick up a chunk of grass and dirt. "No. He's probably still at home."

Alex was the only person who ever asked about her dad—who ever knew. She had met him a few times, but Leo tried as hard as she could to keep her friend away from the house. Alex lived with her grandparents, who spent most of their time and worry looking after her uncle with some advanced thing called M.S. Sometimes, Alex brought Leo over, and they were left to do whatever they wanted in the house and the neighborhood. Alex's grandma said that as long as she took a shower every morning, went to school, and was home by 9:00, she was doing her job as a kid. That was more than anyone ever asked of Leo, but she liked going to Alex's because sometimes her grandparents would make them dinner without being reminded.

"How did you get out?" Leo asked.

"I told the nurse I felt better and could go back to class. Then I left. They're all so dumb." Alex pointed a finger gun at her head and pulled the trigger.

Leo laughed. Alex always made her laugh. "Yeah."

"So… what happened?"

Leo puffed out a sigh and gripped the top strap of her backpack even harder. "I'll tell you what happened. If you *promise* to keep it a secret."

Alex put a hand on her hip. "Well I already have tons of friends to tell *all* your secrets to. So…"

"Whatever." Leo bumped her shoulder into her friend's, picked up her backpack, and they walked toward the creek with secrets and dangerous smiles.

6

WE HAVE SEEN some incredible results with Pointera *on the market in just the last six months. The AST—Association for Social Technology—in coalition with the FDA, has published several studies of people who began taking and have been on* Pointera *at least one month after its release to the public. They've found that productivity in the workplace, specifically the corporate positions in companies owned by or in affiliation with the AST, has increased dramatically. We have one story here of a social media manager at Mind-Blink, Marcus Tieffler, who started* Pointera *just two weeks after its release. He tells us that the company has had some major breakthroughs in internal media downloads and idea output.*

For those of you who have been slower to jump on the technology train, MindBlink is one of the world's leading Quick-News Social Media Companies. They release news, entertainment, stock tips, any information you could want, personalized to your individual tastes and interests. They made their mark two years ago when they were the first to release complete Infodeos less than two minutes in length. Now Mr. Tieffler has given us only pieces, but he hints at MindBlink's new Infodeos coming out at less than one minute in length each. And he says that his team working on this project have all been taking Pointera *and owe their breakthroughs to this new drug.*

That is just incredible, Brenda. It amazes me how far our technology has come in such a small amount of time. I can't wait to hear more from Mr. Tieffler and his team, who are working extraordinarily quickly with the help of Pointera *to bring us to the next level in our technological advancements.*

7

A BREEZE LIFTED and pushed at the windchimes on the front porch. The house was modest in size, normal in every facet, and Leo felt like an intruder. It had been a long time since she'd been invited to a home as nice as this. A large orange tabby stared up at them from a wicker porch chair, licking its whiskers. Leo stared back.

"What exactly can she do?"

Karl knocked after opening the screen door. "Something pretty unique. She falls into her own category." The slow shuffle from within seemed to take an awfully long time in greeting them.

Leo peered into the window, finding only a wall of blue lace curtain. "Why won't you tell me?"

"That's not my story to tell," he answered, and the door

opened with a groan.

"Karl," the woman exclaimed, followed by a cough that smelled of cigarettes. "You got here faster than I expected." She was a large woman in her sixties, wearing a flannel nightgown that pinched up under her sagging breasts. Her greying hair was short, ruffled before its treated time in curling irons, but her smile was warm. "And who have you brought?"

Leo raised her eyebrows and tried to smile pleasantly. Her introduction stuck in her throat.

"She's a new friend in town," Karl answered for her. "She may have something to offer, and I thought it would be nice for her to meet you."

Bernadette touched a hand to her cheek and sighed. She shared a long look with Karl, then pulled out of it with an excited gasp. "Well, come in, then." Her blue eyes glittered, and for the second time in twenty-four hours, Leo's icy caution melted a little more.

Light filled the house even with the lace curtains against every window. The living room and kitchen were lined wall to wall with dark wooden bookshelves—expensive-looking shelving and cheap-looking books. They were used cookbooks, the covers worn right off, stuck in between textbooks, worn volumes of Poe, and foreign novels in languages Leo didn't recognize. A stack of loose papers cluttered the table centered in the kitchen, and Bernadette sat down there to a sticky bowl of something mostly eaten.

"Make yourselves at home." She flitted a hand around the kitchen in invitation. Leo sat across from her, and Karl brought them three glasses of tap water. Bernadette plucked a pair of rimless reading glasses from her pile and used them to stare Leo up and down. "So Karl thinks you have something," she said. Leo shrugged. "Has he told you what I do yet?"

Karl slumped into a chair, slid the glasses all around, and sat back. "Of course I haven't told her," he replied. The thinnest trace of a smile danced beneath his mustache. "That would ruin the entire point of our visit."

"Well, not entirely." Bernadette grasped the frame of her glasses and held them there. "Let's get started, then." She squinted and leaned forward. "Leather," she whispered.

This was a game to them, and Leo felt like the ball bounced between players. Being the object of this strange interest was enough to wipe her mind clean. She couldn't think of anything to say, how to find her voice at all.

Karl watched them, holding his glass of tap water like another man would hold his own tobacco pipe. She stared at Bernadette, waiting for the rest. The long silence found her tapping her fingers on the table. Karl gulped his water. The clock above the kitchen stove ticked.

"No," Bernadette decided. She sat back in her chair and folded one thick leg upon the other. "It's not leather. We'll go with the crunch of autumn leaves."

The minute the words hit her ears, Leo felt a warm stir of excitement bubble up from between her legs. She shifted. It felt like someone *touched* her. Last time she checked, she wasn't a nympho, but the feeling paid no attention to her logic. There it was, the *touch* again below the belt, and she held her breath.

Bernadette nodded once, grinning, and folded her arms.

"Yes, that's it. The leaves."

Leo had to breathe out, to look away from the older woman, and she glanced at Karl instead. If he'd kicked his shoes up onto the table and fingered a glass of brandy, he couldn't have looked smugger. He enjoyed this. She opened her mouth to protest that realization, but the look he gave her said to sit still, to pay attention. Tit for tat. She bit her frustration and felt her face flushing as hot as the rest of her body.

Bernadette's words came effortlessly in a soft, slow tune, and Leo was never able to remember exactly what was said. The story overtook her, caressed her, Bernadette's voice as much a part of the story as the words and the order in which she expelled them. The heat rose from the bottom of Leo's belly, trailing goose bumps along her inner thighs, brushing the soft skin around her ribs, bringing her nipples to hard, cold points. She licked her lips, gripped the arms of the wooden chair until her knuckles burned white. No matter how ridiculous she told herself this was, she could not stop Bernadette's story.

It was a simple thing, a tale of walking down a worn country road in mid-autumn, bare feet brushing through the dusting of dried leaves covering the path. The wind through the trees, birds maybe, that spent their last days in the nest before the flight south. Nothing whatsoever sensual about the story, about the tone of the teller's voice. Bernadette could have been Leo's grandmother, for all the story-time feel she portrayed in her posture and absent smile as she wove the images into the picture. But nobody's grandmother ever made Leo breathe this heavily, her chest rising and falling with increasing speed as the words struck her nerves.

She was building up, burning, electrified by the touch of a lover existing only in sound. She was suddenly afraid she would do something humiliating. Her hips moved forward, and she popped from her seat. It was no longer time to pay attention.

"Stop!" she cried. She collapsed into the chair in surprise, sweat beading down the back of her neck. Her teeth ground each other down into self-restraint.

Bernadette closed her mouth and took a long drink of water. Karl cleared his throat and tried to hide his own smile with a sip. Leo felt her harpy's clutch on the chair loosen. She swallowed and tried to slow her rapid breathing. Without looking at her, Karl slid her glass closer, and she attacked it with shaky hands.

"Sorry." That was all she could think to say. The water was not enough, her voice still hoarse with yearning.

"Oh, don't be silly," Bernadette said. "You're not the first, my dear, and you certainly won't be the last." She chuckled and removed the reading glasses.

Leo smoothed a sweaty strand of hair from her nose back up onto her forehead. She glared at Karl. "Is this for real?" The old woman answered by throwing out a few more words about leaves and walking. Leo's toes curled, and she nodded furiously. "Okay, I get it," she said under her breath.

Karl let out a raspy chuckle, and as Leo slid a fraction lower in her chair, she couldn't help but smile at the sound of his laugh. And at how ridiculous she must have looked.

"Bernadette has had her own run with the beat, haven't

you?" His glass was now empty, and he twirled it around his hand on the table.

"There's still a demand for certain words," Bernadette said. "But this old bag doesn't have quite enough energy to keep up with the rising generation of thrill."

"Thrill," Leo repeated. "That fits." She felt mostly back to normal, but her palms were still clammy. She rubbed them on her jeans. In the short silence, she met the gazes of each of her new *friends* and knew it was time for a decision. Here was proof, right in front of her, that Karl wasn't bullshitting her. This new world actually existed. Exploring it was completely up to her now. After making it through Bernadette's experiment, she figured there couldn't be anything much more humiliating waiting for her.

"My name's Leo." She extended her hand, and when Bernadette grasped it with a grin, she knew the test was over. "I'm really fucking glad to meet you." Again, words she hadn't said in such a long time. Getting them out was a relief. An embarrassed laugh followed, and she ran a hand through her hair as Bernadette sat back again.

"So am I, Leo. You handled that very well." Amusement rode the words, and suddenly, Leo felt like a player in the game. And not just one who did what she was told. A player who actually got to choose what to do with the ball.

"More water?" Karl asked. His smile was not nearly as obvious, but Leo felt a surge of courage.

"You just liked watching me squirm, didn't you?"

He reached for the glasses and collected them carefully in his giant hands. "I can't say no."

If Leo had ever had close friends in her adult life, she

would have recognized the banter. The comfort was new, the playing was new, but she realized that whatever she thought she'd fucked up with Karl was definitely okay. She'd held her own, she'd passed their test, and this sense of belonging was settling in without a name. She pushed the feeling aside before she could grasp too hard and crush it.

"Has Karl told you what I can do?" she asked.

Bernadette reached toward Karl for her glass and wiped a trickle of water off the side. "He did not. Leo, the ownership of the beat goes both ways." Karl returned to the table with a getting-down-to-business frown. "He would not tell you what I do, nor would he share your gifts with anyone else. It is for each of us to show at our own discretion. I hope the importance of that will become clear very quickly."

The mood had dropped, and Leo felt responsible now for these secrets she didn't even know. She supposed that was the point. It was definitely not a joke. "Sure."

"Good. That's the most pressing thing for you to know right now. Next in line. You get to show me just what you *can* do."

"You mean… use my words?" She had expected this, but the pressure now had her feeling a bit cold. Any other day, she would have laughed at her own varying temperatures.

"We call it the beat, Leo," Bernadette said, her intensity burning through an unwavering stare.

"I explained that to her," Karl said.

"I'm sure you explained what you could, Karl. I'm sure you also can remember how difficult it once was for you to understand all this." The patience in Bernadette's voice was something Leo thought didn't exist.

Karl crossed one old boot over his knee. "Yeah. I remember." He spread his hands out across the table, and the small smile under his bowed head was meant to be private.

"And whatever you decide to do after today," Bernadette continued, reaching out to cover one of Leo's hands with her own, "is your own decision. We'll give you as much information as we possibly can, but no one is forcing you to do anything."

Leo's first thought was to pull her hand back into her lap, but she didn't. Karl had not expressed the same gravity Bernadette obviously felt. But with that gravity came an understanding, a connection with something that reached far beyond what she had always known—just Leo, on-her-own Leo, fighting-for-life-every-day Leo. She could have more, even if it was just two more people who knew about her words. She had wanted to share the secret again for so long.

"Okay. You want me to do it now?" Bernadette patted her hand and nodded.

"You can tell a story on command, can't you?" Karl asked. There was no hint of spite in the question. They were genuinely curious.

"Well, yeah." She felt like the witness to some extraordinary event, expected to give truthful and correct answers. Expected to be an upstanding citizen. "It's just been a long time since I've done this for... fun." Her honesty surprised her, and she shrugged.

"That will get easier." Bernadette sat back, folded her hands in her lap. "Fire away."

She took a deep breath and imagined herself backed

into a corner. "My name is Anthony." There was the spark, the familiar burn deep in her chest. "I'm thirty-four years old, and I was born on Mars." The fire rose, filling her lungs and her throat, and she imagined this was how dragons felt before spewing fire. "There are dragons on Mars, you know. They raised me." Yes, it was incredibly ridiculous. She could only take random thoughts and piece them together under the pressure, but it really didn't matter what she said. Nobody would question her. Nobody ever did.

The last time she'd "spun a beat" just for entertainment was so long ago. There was a silliness to it now, a game-like quality that reminded her of being fourteen. She'd spent so many nights sitting in the gravel of the playground under the dirty yellow street lights washing them in hazy circles. Most of the time, she would tell funny stories, adding in the right words that forced Alex to laugh. Alex had laughed so easily, never cared that she was too loud, and once Leo finished, Alex would laugh some more about how funny she had *thought* it was.

The memory caught the words in her throat, and she paused. Karl's eyes were closed. Bernadette looked at Leo, but her blue eyes seemed to stare right through. A thin film of hazy white covered those eyes, shielding them from reality. It was almost impossible to detect, but Leo had spent years causing that milky film in the eyes, the blank stares. Sometimes, the people she used her words on would freeze, start drooling, go slack as if they were sleepwalking. Others looked like they heard someone calling their name from far away, trying to locate and recognize the voice. Once Leo started talking with the fire in her chest, nobody was ever completely clearheaded. However misted Bernadette's eyes were, she smiled in alert amusement. Like she believed Leo completely and also knew it wasn't real.

Leo kept it to a few minutes more. "And that's how I became President of the United States." Ridiculous. Listening to herself made her flush hot with embarrassment. She was shaking. Chewing on her lip, she watched the fog clear rather quickly from Bernadette's eyes. Maybe ten seconds, and the old woman flashed her a wide, nicotine-stained grin.

"Very good," she said and clapped once. Leo forced a smile. "Why do you look so uncomfortable, sweetheart? That was very good. Mars." She chuckled and reached for her water.

"I'd like to see the scale you use for grading people on this," Leo said and managed a laugh of relief.

Karl opened his eyes and cleared his throat. "Most people struggle through their first interview. A lot."

"Interview?" Leo's heart skipped, and she couldn't decide whether it was excitement or fear. "You didn't say anything about a job." There it was, her old friend, desperation. She knew how to fight her way out of a corner, out of something she didn't want. If anything went her way—well, that happened so rarely, she hardly knew how to handle it. Good things were not a part of her existence. They felt cheap and patronizing. A carrot on a stick to nowhere.

"Not that kind of interview, my dear." This time, Bernadette must have sensed her panic. She did not move again to touch Leo's hand but spoke with controlled calm. "More of a first initiation."

"Into what?" And if they wanted her to be in a cult, they

could fuck off right now.

"Our way of living. Like I said, all your choices are your own, Leo." She glanced at Karl. "Grab me the ashtray off the stove, will you?" He stood to obey, and Leo followed their lead to pull out her own pack of cigarettes. Bernadette held an open flame toward Leo first.

She had been so incredibly out of her already thin element that she hardly noticed how bad she wanted a smoke. And she forgot how tense she'd been around Karl just earlier that morning. That all seemed like another lifetime. Focusing on the burn of nicotine in her lungs, she took another deep breath and steeled herself. "Okay." She nodded for the other woman to continue.

"There are certain things that we as beat-spinners have to keep to ourselves. A sort of brotherhood, if you will." Leo was aware again of how thinly veiled her thoughts were when Bernadette burst out laughing. "No sacrifices, no chanting, and this is not a cult. Nothing like that."

"Think of it as a family," Karl put in. Bernadette hummed in agreement. "A big family with a lot of big secrets."

Even more inviting than his smile was this new idea that she could be part of something big. The word "family" had always been a trigger, and she'd crushed the end of her cigarette into a flat, fuzzy filter. She fiddled with it, trying to roll it back into shape. "I'm not new to keeping secrets." If that was the price for meeting others like herself, for learning how to belong, paying it would not make her poor.

"No," Bernadette said through a mouth of smoke. "I'm sure you're not. We choose who we share our stories with very carefully. You know it can be incredible, and more difficult than anyone else can imagine, to live with this gift."

Leo swallowed her discomfort. Her automatic reaction to touchy subjects was rage, but this tired-looking woman had seen through her with x-ray vision. For the first time, being appropriate felt like a necessity. "So what do I have to do?"

"Meet the family."

Leo tried to hide her smile and the accompanying hot flush up the sides of her neck. "Right. No sacrifices."

"No sacrifices." Bernadette's nightgown bounced with her laughter. Leo's own chuckle sounded foreign, buried under a pile of dust. But it felt good to give her face a bit of life again. "I'll make some calls, and I'll get in touch when it's time to meet everyone."

This part was all too familiar. The tension broken, the deal made. Bartering, keeping her cool. Doing business. While her heart beat just as quickly, while she hid the shake of adrenaline in her hands, this kind of business did not come with the guilt. This kind of business did not warn of destruction. She looked forward to this.

"And of course, if you're looking for a job, Karl can set you up with another interview."

Leo tilted her head at him. "Is it anything like this one?"

He grinned and sucked in a breath through his teeth. "Not quite."

"That never was my area of expertise," Bernadette said and rose from her chair. "Leo, before you leave, would you mind bringing my mail in for me? I'm hardly dressed to neighborhood code."

Leo only glanced at Karl, who gave a tiny nod toward the door. "Sure. Be right back."

She obviously hadn't passed all the tests. This was her cue to give them privacy. Although she hated the feeling, it was almost a relief to leave this dark fairytale that had been offered her. Make sure it was still real. She walked quickly to the front door but took her time getting to the mailbox at the corner of the yard.

"She has no idea what's going on, does she?" Bernadette watched the skinny girl through the living room window.

"She's been on the streets for the last couple years," Karl said. "I doubt watching the news was very high on her list."

Bernadette chuckled and patted her disheveled hair. "Good. We've not had someone who can do what Leo can. She has a lot of strengths we can work with."

"Yeah, and a lot more weaknesses. She's like an entire Achilles Leg."

She slapped his shoulder and laughed. "Karl, don't say that. Did you completely forget who you were when you found us?"

He gathered the glasses from the table and took them to the sink. "No. I'll never forget that."

"We'll just have to be extra careful with her, like we were with you." She watched Leo respectfully take her time in coming back to the house, pausing to look up into the trees around the yard. "I'll call Sleepwater, see what they have going on for the next couple days." She turned to point a playful finger at him. "You make sure she has everything she needs."

Karl folded his arms. "Trust me, that's not going to be very hard."

8

"OH, MY GOD. That was a good one." Tears streamed down Alex's face, and she wiped them away with her shirt-sleeve. "Where do you come up with this shit?"

"I don't know. It just kinda comes out." Leo picked up a pebble from the concrete steps they sat on and chucked it at the chain-link fence.

"Yeah, no kidding." Alex threw a pebble to match. "That dinosaur thing, though." They burst out laughing, and Leo found tears in her own eyes.

She'd gotten used to the ridiculous things that came out of her mouth when she told these kinds of stories. The game had changed around the beginning of the school year. It was a relief that Alex knew what she could do. She was the one who prompted Leo to do it more, to practice, to stretch out her words and find out what could happen. Then Leo started telling the funny stories, ridiculous things she realized would make her friend die with laughter even with the filmy haze in her eyes and the weird look. Alex's expression would be a little blank, a little far away, but that laugh never changed a bit. Then they always talked about it because Alex wanted to talk about it. She remembered the things Leo said, and Leo took it as a good sign. Now she did it just for that laugh.

They skipped school almost every day, sometimes half an hour early, sometimes meeting at the park in the morning and never going in the first place. It was a lot easier in high school. Just two dirty-looking girls in baggy t-shirts and scuffed-up Chuck Taylors. A couple of cops found them at the park a few times and tried to make them go back to school. Leo used her words on them too, the image of seriousness. Then they'd walk away, Leo trying so hard to choke back a hiss of laughter until Alex opened her mouth to the sky and let out a cackle of triumph. "Did you see their faces?" she squealed. "You should have seen *your* face. I think you believed *yourself*!"

It didn't take them very long to find a place the cops just didn't give a fuck about—two streets down from Leo's house, between what Alex called "the Crack House" and an abandoned building that had given up trying to be a gas station or a fast food joint. No one was there to care that they weren't where they were supposed to be. No one to bother them.

The street stayed fairly quiet, even on a Saturday. They sat on the steps at the back of the brick building, staring through the fence into a lot of cracked concrete and toppled cinder blocks. Someone had given up on that spot too.

An older black man shuffled by with a cardboard box full of loose feathers that kept escaping and sticking to his clothes. His mismatched pair of shoes—one red, one neon yellow—elicited a sharp bark of laughter from Alex. She clapped a hand over her mouth. The man glanced at them and stopped in surprise. One feather flittered up to land in the hair he hadn't lost yet. Leo shrugged at him, and they broke into giggles again, faces red with the attempt to contain it. The man hurried off, a trail of feathers flying behind him. Leo had to bury her face in her arm, shaking with laughter, and Alex leaned against her shoulder and hissed giggles through her teeth.

Recovering, Leo wiped the corners of her eyes. Alex sat up again, and for a minute, they just stared at each other. Leo watched those blue eyes, sparkling with sunlight and something else. Then Alex leaned her elbows on her knees and grinned.

"Do another one," she said.

"What? Come on," Leo said and smiled at the stairs again. "We've been here for like an hour. I've done nothing but vomit shit to you."

"No, come on. I like it." Alex nudged her with her shoulder. "Do another one."

Leo looked back up at her and swallowed, feeling the smile leave her face. Her ears burned hot, and then her chest, and she felt the words come up and stopped thinking altogether. "Kiss me," she said. The world was suddenly quiet. "Because you like me, and you're the only person that's ever liked me."

Alex leaned in, and Leo met her in the middle, putting a hand up to the blonde hair that had grown long over the summer. It lasted only a few seconds, and then Alex pulled away. Leo watched the haziness clear from the blue eyes. She hadn't expected it to actually work.

A tiny frown, and then Alex stood and walked away, hands in the pockets of her sweatshirt. "Fuck," Leo whispered and stood to follow her. "Wait, Alex. I'm sorry. Hey." She followed her around the fence and into the narrow alley between two brick buildings. "Alex, come on."

Alex stopped and turned around. The frown had grown to darken her face, and Leo realized she'd never seen her friend this upset. This angry. "I'm so sorry," she blurted. She felt like her head was going to explode. The other girl folded her arms against her chest. "That was stupid, and I shouldn't have done it, and I wasn't even thinking. We can just forget it ever happened." Her hands felt like water, and she shoved them into the back pockets of her jeans. She wished her legs would stop shaking. It was all seriously fucked up now because of her stupid words. She couldn't imagine what she'd do if she didn't have Alex around anymore. But she couldn't say that, not after what just happened.

Alex shook her head like she was trying to clear something out of it and closed her eyes. "You don't have to do that," she said.

"What?"

"You don't *have* to make me believe things."

"I know. I know, it was stupid—"

She was cut short when Alex took her face in both hands and kissed her again. Without the words. Without the fog. Leo's brain scrambled for something to hold onto, and she managed only to pull away a few inches. "Really?" No way was this real. But her heart pounded anyways, and she bit her lip.

Alex laughed, the echo bouncing off the close walls around them, and pulled her in again. Leo's arms slipped around her waist, fingers inching up the back of her shirt. She felt the curved muscles of Alex's back in her hands and the sharp sting of the bricks as they pushed up against the wall. The only actual thought she had was that now she could call Alex's smile her own.

9

JOHN, LET'S TURN again to the miracle drug, Pointera.
It's working for hundreds of people already, a leading phar-
maceutical phenomenon especially in the Social Media and
Digital Information industries. Topper has moved to the top
of the list in Social Media, with almost three billion users
worldwide logging in for friends, updates, photos, market-
ing, global connection, and the news.

Last week, Topper released their official partnership
with MindBlink in an effort to improve the availability of in-
formation and the current styles of media involvement we all
enjoy. Months ago, we introduced Marcus Tieffler and his
team of technology experts at MindBlink. They had quite the
task ahead of them but have successfully shown us the future.
The team has created full Infodeos under one minute in

length that inform the viewer with complete and relevant content. How-To videos are just the start, and our sources say they're now working on current affairs. MindBlink mentions even moving into educational videos for online courses. This may replace school textbooks altogether if done correctly.

It may replace the news, Brenda, if this gets big enough.

Oh, don't get ahead of yourself, John. We won't have to find new careers just yet. The genius of MindBlink comes with a catch. As of right now, the new Infodeos are only successfully significant to those who have been on Pointera *for at least two weeks. Already, hundreds of people in the U.S. are taking the next step, but for those of you who haven't yet, we have a clip of what you're missing.*

Wow. Uh, I'm not sure I understood all that.

I guess it's time for Pointera, *John. We have a statement from Leonard Cobeler of Sacramento, age fifty-six, who has been taking* Pointera *for two months.*

"I get it now. Before, I didn't know what the world was about. Now I do. I can see everything out there and I understand. I worked construction all my life, but I think I can be an engineer."

Oh. Wow.

That's right, John. Mr. Cobeler is currently designing the plans for a building to house the AST's new corporate branch in Los Angeles. So for you viewers out there who are ready to open the door to our new Information Age, talk to your doctor today about Pointera.

10

"SO WHAT EXACTLY is Sleepwater?"

They sat on a public bench and ate chili dogs from the street stand. Karl's mustache churned as he took his own sweet time in chewing.

"That's the group."

"What, of the beat people?" She swallowed her food and wondered if he could hear it.

"We voted no on The Association of Beat People. Wasn't as catchy."

She choked on a laugh and felt her ears grow warm. "When do I get to meet them?"

"When Bernadette finds a good time. They're a little busy right now." He wiped a massive glob of melted cheese from his beard.

"Doing what?"

Karl's head swung down to meet her gaze next to him. "You'll see."

Okay, enough questions.

It had been a long time since Leo had eaten food in a public park without feeling protective of it. A blonde woman pushing a stroller jogged past them in tight leggings, and while Leo watched her for a few extra seconds, she noticed that Karl didn't.

"I'm guessing you don't eat out a lot," she said. His stoic observation of nothing in particular creeped her out.

"Not really a big fan of paying for something I can do myself." He crumbled the foil bag into a ball, sucked the bread from his teeth, and focused on the trashcan a few feet away.

They'd pulled over by the park after a few last goodbyes with Bernadette. Leo wanted to ask why the sudden stop and splurge on chili dogs—wanted to be a smartass. Then she thought of an annoying kid in the back seat on a long road trip and didn't.

"I could have gotten us a free lunch," she said. "Easily. I used to do it all the time." She sucked on her soda, wiping away the drops sweating on the paper cup and dripping on her jeans.

"Yeah, that's probably not the best way to use your words right now," he said, taking aim. "I think I know someone who'd go pretty crazy over your beats."

"Why?" Were there seriously more groups out there besides this Sleepwater? She was finding it harder every minute to keep up with him and all this new shit.

Karl looked at her and raised his eyebrows. "For money." He turned back to the trashcan and launched the wrapper in a tall arc.

He actually set up a real interview for her the next night. She didn't have any nice clothes, didn't know what to do for a real job, so she'd brushed out her hair. Looking good had been as easy for her as licking her own elbow.

"Good thing you're not trying to impress him with looks," Karl said, flashing her a quick glance as he came around the side of the car.

She made a face at him. "Thanks? Why's that?"

"He's gay." He ran a hand through his hair. Apparently, looking good was more important to him. He'd abandoned his stained t-shirt for a flannel button-down and maybe his only pair of jeans with no holes. She choked on a laugh.

She flicked the cigarette behind the station wagon and hurried to catch up. A bouncer stood at the door and glared in every direction. He recognized Karl and stood aside, opening the door to let out a blast of music and neon lights. Leo reflected the bouncer's scowl as he stared her into the club. She didn't like being looked at for too long, especially like that.

"Got a problem?" She had to almost yell it over the music. The giant, bearded man turned away from the parking lot to frown down at her. She was at most half his size.

"I got it, Ed," Karl said. His hand went around Leo's wrist, and he pulled her and her challenge of a stare into the hall. "Let's not start trouble first thing in the night, okay?" he yelled. "Save that for later." He didn't look at her but guided her through the first wave of people. She would have yanked her arm back if he hadn't dropped it first.

The last time she'd gone to a club was in high school, using her words on the bouncer to let her and Alex inside. They'd made a time of it for a while. Cocaine, booze, toying with the strangers on the dance floor. But that was when they could still convince themselves that everything was just fun and games. It had been a long time since Leo felt the need to drown herself in pleasure. Clubs seemed pointless now. Bodies moved around them, sucking them in, dissolving them into the crowd of sweat and skin and lights. She stayed two steps behind Karl. He was one of those people who wouldn't stop and wait for someone to match his pace, but he kept turning back to make sure she was still there. She could barely hear her own thoughts but had a brief vision of Karl grabbing her hand to yank her through faster. She shoved her hands into her pockets.

He sidestepped and retracted his arms from a good number of girls who grabbed at him to dance. He didn't smile, didn't even look at them. If she hadn't seen the picture of his wife, she would have thought he had no interest in women whatsoever. Leo wouldn't have minded at all if one or two of them reached out for her like that, but no such luck. His square shoulders made a path, and she kept up before the bodies filled the hole.

The door looked like an exit—plain, metal, with no sign or signal. A back bar had been placed by it, manned only by a skinny Asian in a suit who looked like he couldn't lift a pistol. No bouncer, no bodyguard. Karl knocked once, and they waited. She had time to let the music and her nerves sink in, and with one eye on Karl, she sidled to the bar.

"Shot of whiskey," she told the Asian.

He looked her over, flashed a smile of straight, ice-cube teeth, and pulled out a shot glass. "Who you here with?"

"Not you." Karl's big hand grabbed her arm and yanked her away. "I told you, no stupid shit," he whispered, his lips tickling her ear.

"I can have *one*. What's the big deal?" she hissed, struggling against his grip. He only let her go when she was back beside him in front of the door.

"You're gonna spin a beat for Louis, that's the big deal. Even one drink, and he'll know you're not straight. Then he'll kick you out on your skinny ass, and I'm fucked too." He glared at her, his eyes darting between her and the door. She folded her arms and stood back against the wall. "We have one chance. If you really don't give a shit, tell me now and we'll leave."

Leo bit the inside of her cheek and finally glanced at him. "You afraid of this guy or something?" She regretted that, but she didn't like being told what to do.

He looked down at her, gave her the briefest hint of a smile, and then the door opened from the other side. "After you." He smirked and waved her in first.

The door pulled open into what some might call the VIP room. Black leather couches lined the walls, soft lights glimmered on the hard surfaces, the stainless-steel corners of the tables, the grey walls with gleaming runners. It was full of people. Groups had broken off into different areas, huddled around one or two in each group who commanded full attention. Leo watched their faces. Some listeners hunched forward with eagerness, others sat back in contentment, smiling, as though they were soon to unbutton their pants after a full meal. A few faces soured with discomfort, but all eyes centered on those who spoke. The low hum of indecipherable conversation made it easy for her to take in the view, but she couldn't hear anything. The club music drowned out the laughter, the sounds of dancing and drinks, and this room vibrated like a quiet motor underneath her feet.

A hand on her lower back brought her back to herself. Karl leaned toward her. "Eleven o'clock." She looked. It had to be Louis. His blazer might have been purple velvet, somewhere between pimp and Italian Mafia, but with a flare he somehow pulled off. He had a thin nose, long but delicate, as if he could pull her thoughts out of the air by sniffing. Two beady black eyes plotted some mischief underneath his generously oiled and coifed hair, a few curls drifting down over his forehead. A manicured hand stroked a short, full goatee, and his smile seemed made of candy. Sweet, but too much of it would make you sick. He was listening to one of the speakers—a beat-maker, Leo assumed—with forced indifference. He failed to notice them until they stood directly in front of his armchair.

Louis sighed, tilted his head, and formed a slow path with his eyes to their faces. Leo had to force her mouth into a tight smile when she felt it threatening a grimace. The fucker was stuck up. The beat lord pursed his lips.

"Karl," he said, one corner of his mouth curving up with a flip of his gelled hair. "You're back. With a pet."

Karl lowered his head but would not break the gaze. "I

told you we were coming."

"Yes, you did." Louis clapped his hands. "And look, there's room for both of you." His hand came down on his neighbor's knee, then fluttered it toward the other end of the room. Two of the listeners picked up and moved without a word. Louis grinned, teeth and eyes flashing alike, and motioned to the empty seats.

The speaker in Louis' group must have drawn his story to a close as they took their seats. Karl made sure to seat himself between Leo and the master of the backroom beat. Louis eyed him with something between hunger and craving. The group around them was quiet, and she noted the look in the listeners' eyes, like a foggy mirror clearing after opening the bathroom door. A few of them blinked, and most tried not to meet each other's gazes. Karl cleared his throat, and Louis clapped once.

"Yes, well, that was certainly entertaining," he said flatly. He turned his gaze toward her, and one eye twitched. "You, uh…" His hand flittered like a frightened bird.

"Leo," Karl added.

"Leo?" Louis' smirk made her want to throw her chair into the center of the room. "Right. You have one chance. Twenty minutes."

She quickly glanced at Karl, who nodded once. Taking a breath, she began.

At first, there were only a handful of people in their small group, the ones more easily amused by the last storyteller. After five minutes, the group doubled, then most of the room stood around the circle of chairs all aimed in her direction. They were enraptured, satisfied, gasping, laughing, and sighing in all the right places. But none of them looked directly into her eyes or at each other. Like eye contact would contract a venereal disease of the mind, not to mention more discomfort than the room was pumping out on its own. Louis stroked his goatee, nose pointed toward the ceiling, the smug corner of his mouth upturned.

She tried to go for the absurd again, to trump the beat at Bernadette's, because this time, she was somewhat prepared. A childhood fairytale, complete with witches, magic wands, spells, and flying things. Nonsense. The first few words made her feel like a child again, hoping that whatever wandering adult passing by would believe the embellished lies. But like the end of her childhood, people started believing the lies, no matter how far-fetched. When more listeners moved to her circle, she gained confidence and even changed a few of the details, adding some tiny oddity that from anyone else would have ruined the story completely. She made sure nobody could ever have taken her seriously.

No one scoffed, or rolled their eyes, or got up from their seats. Captivated, they followed her story like breaking news, like they could be next on the journey of her make-believe hero. When she finished, the lounge was silent, all eyes aimed toward her but not on her. Gripping the arms of her chair, she leaned back and tried to melt into the leather seat.

Karl was bent over with a fist to his forehead, frowning. Louis untwined his fingers from his beard and blinked at the ceiling. Then he clapped once and fluttered both hands toward the gathered crowd. "Get back to your boring lives."

The spectators dispersed throughout the room. A good handful left the lounge, faces not yet cleared of the same fog. Louis barely turned his head toward her, trying to ignore a beggar in his court. "That was twenty-three minutes."

She sat up straight, ready to stand. "But I—"

Karl grabbed her knee so tightly she thought he meant to throw her.

"Karl," Louis continued, pulling lint from his jacket sleeve, "that was a bit overdone."

"She's raw."

"Naturally." He tilted his head. "But there's use for a beat that can draw the entire room." Again, that sticky-sweet smile flashed briefly in her direction. "You can handle her, if you want."

"I do." Karl would not meet her gaze.

"I need a certain… talent. To deal with the world outside my kingdom." Louis' lips curled. Leo almost grabbed her own eyeballs to keep from rolling them. "We'll start with some pesky flies who have been buzzing around my club for a few days. Looking for something they won't find, of course." He rubbed the corner of his eye and surveyed the tip of his finger. "Nevertheless, it affects business." His eyes flickered toward Leo. "When you're finished, I want a story too. A beat. Make it good, make it entertaining, worth the trouble you'll cause."

"Fine."

"And I will pay you."

Karl stood, and Leo followed his lead. Louis fixed her with an unblinking stare. She couldn't decide whether she wanted to stare him down or get the fuck out of there.

Then the door blasted open like it could no longer stand against the bass on the other side. A man entered, and the door clicked quietly shut behind him. He stumbled to the closest group of listeners gathered around a thin, mousy girl with a rash across her chest. She glanced up at the newcomer and took a sharp breath. Her audience tensed in community wariness, and the magic of the beat slowly faded, the fog clearing from their eyes. The man's heavy breathing held company with a dark flush up his neck, across his cheeks. He chuckled, and even from where they stood by Louis' chair, Leo could see he had broken the first rule. He was wasted.

"You think you're good at this?" the man asked the mousy girl. She shrank into herself, both the magic of her words and the confidence it brought fading into nothing.

"I... I don't know," she started, and the man laughed.

"Sure you do! You sit back here in a room full of the best, right? So obviously you... you're better than most?" The flush darkened on his face, and his sneer betrayed just how pissed off he was. "I'll show you," he said and spun around the room, raising his voice. "I'll show all of you a *real* beat!"

The other circles that had formed after Leo's beat had now all died down to watch. One man rose from his seat and approached the newcomer. "Come on, man," he said and put a hand on the other's shoulder. "You look a little rough to-night. Maybe now's not the time—"

"Now is *my* time," the intruder roared, pushing the well-wisher away.

The entire room was quiet, broken only by the dull

thump of the bass, and the man cleared his throat. His words were watery, halting, glistening with a film of inadequacy, but that was all. The listeners looked at each other, all thinking the same thing. You couldn't spin a beat if you were fucked up.

It took only half a minute for the center of attention to come to this understanding as well, and the words of his story cut off abruptly. "Fuck!" he growled and pulled at a chunk of his hair.

A mixture of annoyance and pity floated through the air, but no one made a move. Leo felt Karl by her side and wondered why he wasn't doing anything. Her skin crawled in that silence made of pity, but she didn't know how anyone was going to stop it. Karl had told her that Louis threw out the idiots who stepped into his world under any influence, so where was the guy to do that? She couldn't imagine Louis even attempting it himself. He wouldn't want to wrinkle his coat or break a nail.

The man cursed again and spun about the room, locking onto any eyes that brushed past him, daring them to do something. Then he found Louis, snarled, and stormed toward them.

"You fucking faggot," he spat. "I am so tired of your pathetic games."

Louis remained seated in his chair, crossing one leg gingerly over the other.

"You promised me everything I wanted, and where the fuck is it, huh? Answer me!" It was amazing that the man's spit landed everywhere but in Louis' face. The Lord of the Beat stared up into the man's eyes, and a tiny movement at the corner of his mouth spread into a white-toothed, feral grin. "You think you fucking own me, don't you? I'm gonna wipe that shit-eating grin right off your—"

"Go home," Karl said. The man looked up at him as if just noticing he was there. Leo had to look at him too. A part of her wanted to see just what the pissed-off guy was going to do to Louis, wanted to see if there actually was anything that could remove his smug authority. She thought now that maybe Karl was the one who dealt with the breakers of Louis' rules.

"I bet he thinks he owns you too," the man said to Karl, eyeing him up and down. "Does he make you the same promises when you're sucking his dick?"

Leo's face burned. Louis might have done something to deserve the asshole's threats, but Karl definitely fucking hadn't. She couldn't take her eyes off Karl, off the stoic mask of his beard and the still awareness burning in his eyes. Was he really just going to let the fucker get away with that?

"Don't worry," the man said. "I can fix that for you." He reached into his pocket and pulled out a switchblade, flicking it open.

The very real metal click shattered something inside her. She didn't have time to think about it, to tell her instincts they didn't belong in this room, and her fist came up to connect with the man's hot, blood-red cheek. He half turned, collapsed on his face, and the knife clattered to the floor and spun under a table. Wide-eyed, she stared at his body and shook her fist. She hadn't felt that kind of anger in a long time.

Looking up, she realized that all eyes were on her—

some surprised, some appraising, others amused. A feather chuckle broke the silence, and the rush in her ears and the heavy rhythm of her breathing started to fade.

"Well handled," came Louis' sugary voice from the chair beside her. She had actually forgotten he was there. He flitted a gesture, and a man removed the unconscious form of the night's depressing distraction. "Everyone has their limits." Leo couldn't tell if he referred to the unconscious man on the floor or herself. His flighty hands clapped against each other three times, and he stood.

The room reluctantly went back to its storytelling. Like nothing had happened. But Louis was locked on her now, flashing a sickly impressed grin. "Karl did tell me you were something else."

Karl. She turned to look at him. Why hadn't he done anything? She felt her ears get hot, felt like she should apologize for stepping in. Karl folded his arms and didn't smile, but then he nodded. She realized suddenly that only half of the interview had been about her stories.

Apparently, she'd passed the second test, because Louis was now five times more interested in her. He gently touched her elbow, leading her back to the door, making her feel strangely dirty. She hadn't done it for him. "I've heard your beats," he said in a low voice. "And now I've seen what you can do. I have a very specific job opening I think you will fill perfectly." His breath, so close to her, was just as cloying as the whisky fumes, though sugared and soft—cotton candy against her face.

11

ALEX'S GRANDPARENTS HAD taken her uncle to the doctor. Not an emergency, she'd said, just some routine thing that he needed once a month now. But they'd locked all the doors, told Alex they'd be gone for hours, and suggested she "go to her little friend's house." They liked Leo well enough, but she didn't think they quite trusted her either.

"We can go to your house," Alex said through a mouthful of popcorn. She swung the plastic bag of snacks and Gatorade Leo had weaseled out of the gas station. It wasn't technically stealing if the guy behind the counter gave it to them. Even if he didn't realize then that they actually hadn't paid.

"I don't know," Leo said, staring at the cracks in the

asphalt as they walked down the street. "It's pretty fucking messy."

Alex grabbed her hand and stopped. Leo had to look at her then, biting her lip. "Do you really think I care?" Alex's smile was meant to make her feel better, but it only made Leo feel guilty.

"No," she said slowly. "I just..." She winced.

"Your dad?"

She tried to look at anything but those blue eyes. Alex never asked her for much, but when she did, it was ridiculously hard to say no. She knew Alex didn't give a damn about dirty houses or shitty parents, but her dad was just fucking embarrassing. Leo sighed, felt like she was about to jump off a cliff.

"He said he was going out this morning. He doesn't really... ever do anything he says. If he *is* there, he's gonna fuck with you." She tried to smile, but it felt dry.

"Okay," Alex said. "Well, if it's really bad, we can just leave."

"Yeah." Leo nodded and watched the clouds for a second. It had been a long time since anyone else had been in her house, even the men who called themselves her dad's friends. Those men with the sunken eyes and ribcages poking through their thin shirts. She knew she couldn't keep Alex away forever. The girl got what she wanted, and now she wanted to know more about Leo's life. To see it.

Alex squeezed her hand, kissed her on the cheek, and they turned the corner. She went back to swinging the plastic back.

The dirt-spattered, peeling house matched the others on

the street. No one had bothered with landscaping in the last fifteen years, and the yard was a maze of dying weeds and mud puddles. Alex's eyes lit up like they were in fucking Disneyland, and she gave Leo a sideways smile that said, *I knew it wasn't that bad*. Leo pulled the lopsided gate closed behind her, but it bounced back open like it always did.

"Dad?" The house was dark, its natural state. The bathroom light was always on, though, and it lit a path of dirt and dust in a triangle on the floor. Leo had thrown away the splintered broom the week before and hadn't gotten around to getting another. At least the dirty dishes were in the dishwasher.

"Dad, I'm home. And Alex is here." There was still no answer. Her dad didn't have a clue who Alex was. Even if Leo had told him about her, he wouldn't have remembered the conversation. It took a lot of repeating herself to get him to remember anything, and she didn't want to talk that much about the things she felt for Alex. She thought that would lessen it, somehow. But she used her name anyways, because "friend" wasn't quite right, and "girlfriend" was something she didn't think she could say yet.

"Uh, wait here for just a second?" she said.

Alex shrugged and opened a Gatorade. "Sure." She wiggled her head, the same excitement on her face as if they were headed on some impossible adventure, the same as when she waited for Leo to use her words. That excited smile, that energy, seemed too big for this house. Too bright. Leo hissed an embarrassed laugh and eyed the dirty floor.

"I'll be right back."

KATHRIN HUTSON

She went to the stairway, casually glancing into the living room just to make sure. She'd found her dad passed out almost everywhere at one point or another, but he had his favorite spots for ignoring the responsibilities of being alive. One of those was at the foot of the couch, his head and sometimes an arm shoved under the coffee table. But he wasn't there.

She checked the bathroom floor beside the toilet, the chair wedged against the back door, then upstairs in the hallway and both bedrooms. The house was empty. Her feet felt light even as the stairs creaked beneath her. Alex had slumped onto the couch, chomping away at handfuls of popcorn. Like she was watching a movie.

Leo laughed at her. "What are you doing?"

"Getting comfortable." Alex smacked her lips and grinned. "Your dad here?"

"No." Leo suddenly felt like maybe it was okay to smile for real, to relax a little and enjoy the fact that Alex was on the couch and her dad wasn't ruining it. She sat next to her and plunged her hand into the popcorn. "I guess he actually did go out." It probably wasn't a good idea to say that that meant he was out working the streets with full pockets and an eye for customers. For people like him. Not now, anyways.

"So we have the entire house to ourselves." Alex's blue eyes were wide, swimming with mischief, and she laid her legs across Leo's lap.

"Looks like it." Leo grabbed a pack of cigarettes off the ash-strewn table and lit it. Her dad had stopped trying to hide his smokes when she was twelve. The house was small, and his head was never clear enough to find an effective hiding spot. She held the pack out to Alex.

"Don't mind if I do."

Leo loved the way she accepted every smoke like picking her favorite out of a box of chocolates. They sat there with the lights off, smoking cigarettes and looking at each other. "This is weird," Leo said.

"What?"

She put a hand on Alex's leg, played with a fraying seam of her jeans. "You here, my dad somewhere else. Anywhere else. I mean, it's good. Just weird."

"Do you know where he went?"

"Fuck no. And I don't care." Leo knew exactly where he was, and the lie was sour. But it tasted better than digging up that body right now. She wanted to keep everything as it was in that moment for as long as she could. "I just hope he stays out." That was more truth than she wanted.

Alex sucked on her lip. "Should we go to your room?"

Leo grinned and flicked ash onto the floor. "Why?"

The bag of popcorn was flung onto the table, spilling over the side, and Alex climbed into her lap and kissed her. Leo tasted salt, and smoke, and something sweet that had nothing to do with what she ate. Something very Alex. She held her around the waist with one hand and her cigarette over the arm of the couch with the other. Alex's fingers were in her hair, mixing with the dusty stink of nicotine and the murmur of breathing that still tried not to be too loud. Too fast. She didn't think anyone in the world was this soft.

She probably would have taken Alex to her room if they

got further than a few hands up a few shirts. It was margin-ally cleaner than the couch and fortunately lacked things that reminded her of her dad. Of the fact that she had no idea when he'd be back. But before she could mention it, there were two sharp knocks on the door.

Alex leaned away from her and took a drag of the ciga-rette she hadn't put down. "So, your dad's out of the house. You expecting more people?"

Leo rolled her eyes. "Ha, ha." She bit at Alex's shoul-der, then looked back toward the door. It wasn't her dad. He never knocked, and he never answered the door. She didn't either. "Who is it?"

The door opened, and a short, stocky Mexican carefully lifted his feet over the tattered welcome mat. He was any-where between thirty-five and forty-five, clean-shaven, wearing an unbuttoned cotton polo and khakis. The only thing expensive-looking were his shoes—a pair of leather-capped Forzieris. Leo only knew what they were because her dad called the man Forzieri when he talked to himself in a drugged temper. The man's name was Carlos, and two larger men in button-downs who might have been brothers squeezed through the doorway after him. Leo had never been able to tell them apart, but she knew the names Mario and Aldo.

"Hola, Cariña," Carlos called.

Leo met Alex's questioning gaze and squeezed her leg. Alex very slowly slid from her lap back onto the couch.

The trio stepped farther into the room until Carlos stood in front of her so she had to look at him. He spent a few seconds watching Alex, who puffed on the cigarette and glared at him. Then he tilted his head at Leo. "Do you know where is tú papa?" His smile was shadowed by silent disapproval.

"He went out." She glanced up at the maybe-brothers. "You guys should be able to find him."

"Sí." Carlos sighed and clasped his hands behind his back. "We found him. Tú papa is in the jail."

Leo closed her eyes, trying to keep her hand from shaking as she brought the cigarette to her mouth. She should have fucking known. Alex leaned gently against her, and she couldn't have been more grateful for that small weight on her shoulder.

"Pero, he owes me dollars still. You no have it?"

She stared at the coffee table, unwilling to look at anything else, and plucked another cigarette from the box. "No. He keeps it on him, when he has it."

"Yes. For this I was afraid. I cannot get my monies if tú papa is in the jail."

Leo blew the smoke toward the floor and swallowed.

"He cannot sell what he sells if he is in the jail." His eyebrows rose languidly as he glanced up at his companions. Leo turned briefly to follow his gaze, but the giant Mexicans wore empty masks of expression.

"Last I heard," she said, "he had around eight hundred dollars."

Carlos chuckled once, like it was funny she seemed to think eight hundred was a lot. Like she expected it to be enough. "He owes me three thousands. And for getting him out, la policía wants ten."

Fuck, that was a lot. Her heart pounded furiously, but

she clenched her jaw. She couldn't afford to be a child, so she did not beg. Carlos spoke like he owned her dad, which for all intents and purposes was probably true. He knew what kind of man her father was, had watched him become that man over time. Leo had the sudden disgusted feeling that Carlos had used the same meticulous observation on her and that likely he was here for something other than her dad's money.

"Bueno." Carlos gave a nod, and the sound of a paper bag slid above the roaring in her ears. "How many years are you now?"

She suddenly wished she had a baseball bat. If they gave her time to breathe her burning words, more than likely they would just leave. But if one of them grabbed her first...

"Sixteen." She raised her head.

"Eres muy bonita." His smile was softer, and he glanced at Alex again. "And your amiga too, I think." He sucked something out from between his teeth, and the sound made Leo want to punch him.

Alex took another cigarette, lit it, and handed it to her. It was better than grabbing her hand, than looking at her, than the weight of her leaning against Leo's shoulder. It grounded her, and she was finally able to look him in the eye.

"Tú papa is no more good at selling. He loves las drogas more than the monies, eh?"

There was no point in answering.

"You work for me. You pay me back the four thousands—" he held up four fingers "—and tú papa is sitting in his good chair." He nodded toward the recliner.

She felt frozen, dry. The cigarette filter stuck to her lips, and she noticed how the tension had made them crack.

Carlos took a step toward her side of the couch, hiked both pant legs up at the thigh, and draped one leg over the armrest. He sat there and bent toward her to meet her gaze full on. "Leona," he said softly, and she wanted to run away from both the compassion in his voice and the pang of guilt shooting through her. It had been so long since someone had said her name with such sincerity. "Tú papa can no do what a man should do for his família. You know this. You want more. Is no just a favor to me. We help each other, no?"

A slew of possible answers raced through her mind, all the things she could have said to this man who had walked through that door hundreds of times. But this time, her father wasn't here.

"Okay," she whispered.

"Okay."

One of the large men leaned over the couch to offer the paper bag. She clenched it tightly in the fist at her side. It felt a lot heavier than it looked.

"I get him out," Carlos said. He winked, stood from the armrest, and briefly touched his belt. "La policía no knows you are here. I pay them to no know. Tú papa is coming back tonight, and I come back Saturday for you monies." He pointed a fat finger at the bag in her hands.

She nodded and swallowed. Carlos led his men out without another word, his fancy shoes clicking on the front step. The door was shut, the lights were off, and the setting sun trickled through the battered blinds. The light played in a haze of smoke as she took the longest drag ever, letting it out when her entire body shook.

It took a long time before she could look at Alex, and even then, it was only for a second. She stared at the coffee table with a dry, sour mouth.

"Holy fuck," Alex whispered. "You okay?"

The laugh escaped her like a splash of hot grease. Her eyes were warm, felt wet, but she wasn't quite sure yet that that meant tears. "My fucking father."

Alex put a hand to the back of Leo's head, ran fingers through her hair. "What's in the bag?"

It crinkled when Leo opened it, and they stared into the brown hole with their heads together.

"Is that…"

"Yeah." She turned her head to look at Alex, searching her face for the things she felt herself.

"And your dad was…"

"Yup." She quickly rolled up the top of the bag and tossed it on the coffee table. "See? This is why I don't let anyone come over." Leo slumped against the couch and dragged her hands down her face. The back of her neck hurt, her face felt tight and hard, and she wanted to rub it off.

"Hey," Alex said. "I would have rather been here for that, with you, than not."

Leo couldn't let go of her own face. The sweat in her hands almost felt nice.

There was a long silence. "You're not actually going to do it, are you?"

Through the cracks of her fingers, Leo shot the girl a pointed stare. Then she gestured toward the door. "Did it look like he was giving me a choice?" She didn't mean to snap, didn't mean to sound like a bitch, but she couldn't contain the mix of shame and hatred that was meant for her father. Alex was the only one here. And she couldn't apologize, because it would have come out the same way. She wanted to mean it when she said she was sorry.

The look Alex gave her said she understood all that. Alex stuffed her cigarette into the overflowing ashtray. "You don't have to. You're not a drug dealer, and he can't *make* you do anything."

Leo rolled her eyes at the ceiling. "Really? And what am I supposed to do, just tell him sorry, I changed my mind? I've known that man a long time, and that doesn't work." She grabbed a fistful of her hair.

"Use your words on him. Make him believe this never happened."

"Yeah, that would work once. And not for very long." Her voice was harsh, getting louder. Alex didn't know how any of this worked. The legal system, the foster system, the drug-ring system. The system of Leo's words. "I can make him leave, but in like an hour, he'll remember what actually happened. And then he'll come back. Or he'll stop paying off the cops and I'll go to a fucking foster home."

Alex's eyes shimmered, her cheeks growing red. If she cried, Leo didn't know if she would put an arm around her or scream. She didn't think she had it in her to make that decision, too. But Alex held it together and grabbed her hand.

"We'll figure it out."

"You got a way to find four thousand dollars in a week?"

"Well, not yet. But the impossible doesn't stop you." Alex laughed, but it wavered in uncertainty. There was no hint of its normal, boundless ring.

Leo flung her head back to glower at the ceiling. She rubbed her fingers over Alex's hand for a few minutes. They were alone again in the house, but this time, it didn't seem like such a good idea. It probably hadn't been in the first place.

"Your grandparents are probably home," she said.

"Yeah, probably." Alex laid her head on Leo's shoulder. "You want me to stay?"

Leo breathed in the smoky-sweet scent of Alex's hair, then shook her head. "No, you should go. My dad's gonna be home soon. After all that, I have no idea what he's gonna do."

Alex sat up and nodded. "Okay." The kiss she gave Leo should have felt better. Then she stood with a grimace of concern and a deep breath. "We'll take care of this. Just promise me you won't start selling that shit."

"Yeah." Leo bit at the cracked skin of her lip. "Okay."

"Okay."

She pictured Alex walking through the house in her mind until she heard the gate swing open and bounce back on itself. Then she let herself think. Running a hand through her hair, she briefly entertained the image of killing the man she called Dad. It made her feel a little better, but it wouldn't actually fix anything.

The paper bag waited on the table like a poisonous snake. She pulled her knees up to her chest. A part of her knew she was up shit creek, that the only way to get out was to keep fucking paddling. The bigger part of her wondered what would happen when she took the bag out on the streets. She couldn't turn down the chance to do something else, anything else. As long as it wasn't what she felt in that moment.

12

A WOMAN IN Heber, Utah, was found dead yesterday morning in her home. Thirty-four-year-old Alice Wallace worked as an Information Specialist in Topper's Midwest Headquarters building just outside her hometown.

Her neighbor had called 9-1-1 when she attempted many times to both call Ms. Wallace and knock on her door, stating that the dog had been barking all night from inside the apartment. When police arrived at the scene yesterday morning, they found what at first appeared to be a suicide. Police Chief Robert Cain reported finding Ms. Wallace at her desk with an open bottle of pills. Upon further investigation, they discovered that Alice Wallace had in fact received a prescription from her doctor for a higher dose of Pointera.

"This is not an issue of Pointera *being dangerous,"*

Chief Cain explains. "Ms. Wallace overworked herself and was both a very driven and stressed individual. Even though she had a new prescription, she consumed far more than the prescribed dose, which we believe resulted in the accidental fatal overdose."

Both the police department, Topper's publicists, and the company itself want to stress the importance of taking Pointera, *and any medication, only as prescribed by a doctor.*

As a valued employee of one of the top social media companies, Ms. Wallace had been the team manager of a project, yet to be released, that would make MindBlink's Infodeos more accessible to people who have not yet decided to make the switch to taking Pointera. *Topper and MindBlink partnered seven months ago in this new endeavor, and the goal of Ms. Wallace's project was to offer a downloadable program to all smart devices that would write itself into the user's apps.*

But Ms. Wallace's employer also admits that she was having trouble in getting the new program to work the way she wanted. Topper's Sarah Bennett tells us that Wallace's project will not be abandoned.

"Our teams are working around the clock now to ensure that Alice's passionate, ground-breaking ideas come to fruition. No matter what it takes, we will see that what Alice wanted for Social Media and Information Technology users becomes a reality."

13

THIS, APPARENTLY, HAD become Leo's new job—the first she'd had in a long time. Louis paid her twenty-five dollars an hour to stand in the back room of his club, The Purple Lion, Thursday through Sunday nights. All she had to do was stay in the corner and watch the beat-spinners and their listeners from afar in search of any "trouble". Louis had made it perfectly clear that she was not to get close enough to the storytellers to actually hear what they said; he needed her to retain a clear mind. Leo still found the whole premise of the back room pretty difficult to believe, that there were so many others who could do what she did with their words, and even far more than that who would pay to listen.

She definitely didn't mind that non-engagement with Louis' customers was a job requirement. And it helped her keep an eye on the subtle changes in mood throughout the room. Among the other skills living on the streets for years had taught her was the ability to read people when shit started to get nasty. That ability had gotten her out of trouble more times than she could count, and now she was actually getting paid for it. Of course, it was harder to read the suckers who paid to have their realities turned upside-down through words—their faces ranged from slack-jawed ecstasy, to raptured engagement, to laughter, terror, pain, and some just merely blank, emotionless oblivion. But Leo felt those changes in the room, the prickle of electric anticipation before a beat started, the sigh of cathartic release or resigned disappointment when it ended. Apparently, her having handled the last situation with a punch to the drunkard's face had given her more credit for knowing when to punch someone than she'd expected.

In that first week, she'd realized that Louis kept regular beat-spinners in his back room, at least Thursday through Sunday. The mousy girl with incredibly dry, stick-straight hair was Rebecca, whose words made everyone around her seem infinitely more attractive, including herself. Evan had the peculiar skill of spinning himself into any animal he chose. The man seemed to particularly hate making his listeners think he was a dog—they'd fawn over him and scratch him behind the ears, some even planning for the experience by bringing dog treats and chew toys with them before paying to hear his beats. Leo tried not to watch his face. It twisted into a perpetual grimace of disgust when he used his words, jerking away from those who reached out to touch him. At first, Leo wondered why the fuck he'd subject himself to such a disgusting display until she learned that he made a ridiculous amount of money from the clients who paid to think he was a dog.

These were the two beat-spinners who sat farthest back in the room, those on whom Leo could most easily keep an eye, and the only ones to which she'd had at least one opportunity to introduce herself and learn their names. Louis had told her—in his oily, sugary way and in not so many words—that he didn't pay her to make friends with his other employees, so even meeting Rebecca and Evan had been short-lived experiences.

Karl was always there with her at the Purple Lion, though she had a hard time figuring out exactly what he did there. He never told a story, never had any clients come to pay for his beats, but just sat and occasionally listened in on some of the others. Leo had a hunch that Louis might have been paying Karl to be her "handler", or something along those lines. Maybe he got a commission just from having brought her to Louis' attention, but she hadn't managed to work up the courage to ask Karl about it. Every night that week, they'd gone back to his one-room garage of a home around four in the morning, had a few beers in almost complete silence, and gone to bed. Leo still slept on the dying brown couch, and she promised herself that when she got paid enough money, that couch would be replaced by a futon, or a pull-out sleeper, or something that actually laid flat and didn't make the blood rush to whatever end of her body happened to sink into the pocketed cushions overnight.

That Friday, her second night in the back room, Louis

had put her at an empty table with only two chairs halfway through her shift. He said he had a client in need of her services and that she was to meet the woman in a few minutes. Leo sat at the table, arms folded, and glared out over the room of storytellers. It wasn't hard to miss the lavish display Louis made of meeting the woman at the huge door to the back room and fluttering her over to Leo's table.

There was no introduction of names, no pleasantries in the transaction. The woman was probably in her early thirties and wore a black fur shawl and sequined dress to the place, making her flamboyantly purple-red hair seem like it shot irritatingly fiery flames in all directions. She was hard to miss, even without the fucking fur.

The woman sat at the table and focused the entirety of her attention on the gold nail-filer she'd pulled from her leather purse then used for a self-manicure. Leo hadn't known anybody actually *did* that shit in real life, and she scowled. If the woman wasn't going to say anything, Leo sure wasn't going to be the sucker to try to break down that wall. Louis then leaned down to whisper in Leo's ear, telling her what the woman had requested for her beat. The feathery curl of his moisturized lips against her ear sent goosebumps running up Leo's arms even under her sweatshirt, and she had used every ounce of strength she had not to cringe away in disgust. The last words of Louis' whispered secret, though, made her glad she'd kept her aversion to personal contact at bay. "You'll make three hundred dollars for thirty minutes." That was more than she made in a whole night, so she couldn't very well tell the woman to fuck off, no matter how much she wanted to.

It was pathetic, really, what the woman wanted in her story. Louis had told Leo the name of the woman's husband, Ricardo, and that she was to spin a beat about the passionate and vigorous sex life the woman shared with her spouse. So much for a first paid beat. Leo had absolutely no idea what the woman wanted to hear, so when the words burned in her throat and formed around the various sexual positions that came to mind when looking at her, she was only met by the woman's delicately haughty scowl and upturned nose. Leo had gone through another uncomfortably explicit list of activities, and when the woman showed no sign of enjoying what she heard, Leo realized that maybe the problem was the woman just didn't enjoy a good lay in the first place, period. So then she'd had the bright idea to add, "And you liked it," in various forms, after each explanation. That had seemed to do the trick, and when her half hour was up, Louis appeared like a specter dressed in silk pastels out of nowhere.

The woman had stood quickly from the table, all her composure re-collected after its momentary lapse in judgement, and gave Louis a small nod, her eyes fluttering closed as if blinking for too long would ruin her makeup. She exchanged an almost contact-less embrace with Louis, air-kissing him first on one cheek then the other, and shimmied briskly from the room. Louis stared after the woman and placed his manicured hand upon the table. When he removed it, Leo found three hundred-dollar bills fanned out before her. Without giving her even the courtesy of a glance, Louis had told her, "Good girl," in a lilting sigh, then patted her on the head.

Leo had almost grabbed the man by the hand and torn his arm from its socket at the treatment, but then she locked her burning eyes onto Karl, who stood against the far wall as he always had with arms folded across his chest. He eyed the bills on the table in front of them and gave a tiny nod in their direction. Leo had swallowed her anger then, hearing nothing for a brief moment but the sharp grinding of her own teeth against each other, and put the money in her back pocket. She couldn't afford, after only her second day, to lose this job, and something about the way Karl interacted with Louis told her that her employer was the last person she should piss off.

Louis had clapped once, then fluttered the hand in front of her face and twittered, "Get back to work." So she had, hoping that the next sack of shit who paid Louis for "her services" would at least want something remotely exciting.

Sunday night, she stood in her normal spot, with Karl just opposite the room, watching her and everybody else. Everything had gone well, no mishaps or emergency stories for Leo herself to tell, and she was looking forward to having the next three days off. For years, she had roamed the streets of the city, using her time as she wished, and having worked almost a full forty hours all of a sudden had her itching for her space again. She couldn't ignore the money coming her way, but she needed a break.

It was almost two in the morning when a man bulkier than Karl walked into the back room and directly to Louis. Leo watched the guy in his tight black t-shirt and black jeans. He seemed rather full of himself, and she wondered why the hell she was back here pretending to be a bouncer when Louis obviously had somebody much more suited to the job. The man bent over Louis to whisper something in his ear, then turned right back around and stalked through the door.

Leo frowned, having momentarily forgotten who she was supposed to be watching. She quickly stopped staring at Louis and took a sweeping glance of the room. With just over another hour left in the night in the Purple Lion's back room, beats were still booming.

"Leo," Louis called, twirling his hand in the air. She swallowed, stood from against the wall, and walked to stand beside him. "One of those flies I mentioned is buzzing around outside. They always show up repeatedly where they're not wanted. Take care of it."

That was all he said, and Leo almost laughed at the skinny, flamboyant club owner playing mob boss. She nodded quickly, and when she looked up, Karl met her gaze. She also noticed the glance Karl threw Louis, and she blinked very slowly to keep from rolling her eyes. It was her job, so she'd have to go deal with it.

When she walked through the door and onto the club's dancefloor still writhing with drunken, sweaty bodies, she found Karl had followed her. She stopped to wait until he stood beside her, and then she yelled up at him. Karl leaned over and tilted his ear toward her without looking at her.

"Do you know who it is?" It hurt her throat trying to be heard above the pumping bass and electronica.

He shook his head slowly. "No idea."

"Then why are you coming with me?"

"I'm here to watch." He gestured toward the dance-floor, and Leo rolled her eyes and stepped in front of him.

Trying to make her way through the gyrating bodies around her, feeling Karl closely behind her but still taking his time, felt rather like reverse déjà vu. Louis made sure she never had time to get out of the back room while the Purple Lion was still in full swing, so Leo never had to make her way through the crowd of sparsely dressed and overly sexed dancers. Not since the first day Karl had brought her here. Even this time, trying to push her way through the crowd, she couldn't help but notice that, while she led the way, she was still the clueless one. How the hell was she supposed to know what to expect?

The giant bouncer in black sat on a stool at the other side of the dancefloor, and he nodded to her when she passed. The same guy who hadn't spared her a glance when he spoke with Louis—how could he possibly know who she was? She tried to give him an eyebrow raise in response, but she frowned so much with curiosity and a bit of nervous anticipation, she felt it came off more like complete confusion. At least she hadn't shrugged at him.

The dancefloor was separated from the front door by an absurdly long series of hallways. Apparently, Louis thought it added to the suspense and excitement of getting into the club just to get drunk and hump other people in public, but Leo thought it was ridiculous. There was no back door at the opposite end of the club, only Louis' back room, so the only way to get in and out of the place was to walk the tiresome hallways and cross the dancefloor.

When she stepped out into the parking lot, the street

lamps there almost seemed bright. The front door swung shut behind her, but she heard Karl catch it and step out behind her. Then the pumping of the music inside was abruptly silenced by the thick click of the door shutting completely.

Leo didn't have time to ask whether or not the guy chugging then smashing beer bottles in the parking lot was the "fly" she was supposed to "handle". He beat her to it.

"Oh, fuck…" The man laughed at his own words and turned to face her square-on. He swayed in the circle of yellow light cast by the streetlamp, then spread his arms wide. In one hand, he held another bottle of beer, already half-empty.

He was short and stalky, with a flop of black hair that looked like a guinea pig hanging down the front of his face. It only took him a couple seconds to focus on Leo, look her up and down, and flash a shit-eating grin. He stepped a bit closer to her then, but only so he could peer around her and take a look at Karl.

"So, you're the joke he sent to send me away, huh?" he spat.

Leo spun around quickly to look at Karl, who just stood against the front door with his hands folded over his chest. She turned back to the man and walked toward him.

"Fucking Louis and I," the short guy hollered, "still have business to take care of. I'm only coming back for what's mine, and I'll stop hanging around when I get it."

Karl said nothing, and Leo was glad he was there just to watch. As much as she didn't prefer Louis over many other people, this guy already seemed like a pain in the ass. When she was just a few feet away, she snapped her fingers at the guy and said, "Hey."

He hadn't looked at her as he yelled to Karl, but finally his eyes fell on her. The man staggered back a little, eyes opening in surprise at finally having noticed she was closer than before, and then he scoffed. The tiny smile turned into a frown of annoyance, and he squinted at her. "Beat it, sweet cheeks. I'm in the middle of something."

That was it. Leo was sick of being fucking ignored with Karl around—with anyone around. She was sick of having to do shit like this when nobody would take her seriously. Then she felt her throat get hot, felt the burn of her words about to make the guy shit his pants first and then get off the property.

"Fuck you," she started in a low voice. "Look, buddy, you need to get out of here and—"

"No!" the short man hollered, and before Leo could process it enough to react, he sprang toward her and connected his fist with the corner of her mouth. Leo didn't go down, but she quickly wiped her mouth with the side of her hand, eyeing the smear of blood there. "Don't fucking use your bullshit words on me!" the man shouted, shaking out his fist. "I'm not gonna listen to whatever it is you—"

Leo barreled toward him and brought her fist up under his chin. There was a loud thud, the short man cried out in surprise, and then he stumbled backward with flailing arms and landed on his ass beneath the streetlamp. She'd never before been interrupted once her words started to come out, whether they began by choice or out of anger. It felt like having the rest of her dinner snatched away after only taking two bites, like getting tossed off the bed right before an orgasm, and instead of taking the time to process the sudden severing of the link with her burning words, she took the easier road of unleashing her rage.

She bent over the man on the ground and took another swing at his face. She heard his head crack against the asphalt, felt the bite of the blacktop tear through the knees of her jeans when she threw herself down to straddle the guy's chest. Karl called out her name in a harsh bark, and she definitely heard that too, but it meant nothing. The man struggled weakly under her, and she pummeled his face, left, right, left.

The sound of gravel crunching under tires traveled to her, but it didn't register until she heard the whoop of a siren and saw the man's face below her fists flash blue and red.

"Leo!" Karl called again. He didn't sound very far away, and she heard his footsteps rapidly getting closer.

"Hey. Hey! Police!" came a new voice, and then a pair of hands gripped her roughly by the arms and pulled her off the short guy.

Leo felt her heart racing, heard her heavy breathing, and suddenly felt so incredibly tired. She slumped against the hands holding her arms behind her back, then caught herself on her feet again and stood there without struggling.

The cop turned her around, spewing legal words that didn't quite make it to her brain. The cold embrace of handcuffs clicked around her wrists, and she looked up to see Karl inches from her.

"Don't say anything to them," he whispered harshly into her ear. "I'll get you out later today. Just don't fucking let your words burn."

She struggled to understand why saying anything would be an issue, especially since the cop had watched her mashing in the face of the guy who now lay bloodied and groaning in the parking lot. She'd always been able to talk her way out of trouble before, so why not now?

"Sir, step back," the cop hollered. Karl took one step back and locked onto Leo's gaze through strings of hair falling across her eyes.

"Don't," Karl whispered to her with wide eyes.

"Sir." Leo felt one of the hands gripping her wrist let go and heard the clink of what must have been the cop putting his hand on the gun at his hip. "Sir, I need you to step back."

Karl raised both his hands into the air and nodded, walking backward as he stared at Leo. "Okay, okay. Sorry, officer. I just wanted to make sure she's okay."

"Yeah, well, you can check on her in County."

Leo followed the cop's lead as he opened the car door, bent her down with a hand on the top of her head and the other still on her wrists, and shut the door behind her. Sitting on the plastic back seat of the cop car, the handcuffs cutting into her wrists as they rested between the seat and the small of her back, she listened as if through a tube to the officer mumbling into his radio.

14

THE DISAPPEARANCE OF her mother had essentially marked the end of Leo's childhood. That had been so long ago, she almost didn't remember the stabbing pain of disappointment every time the little girl of her past had woken in the morning with still no sign. Now, almost three-quarters of the way through her high school career, she was acutely aware of the upcoming tedium of having to spend a whole extra year there.

The April sunshine warmed her back through her thick sweatshirt, and she leaned back against the wall of the gas station. From her perch here, she could see the entire front of the school, both sets of double doors, and the entrance to the gym. The teachers had to park in the front, and she watched them, too. If anyone were to approach her here, she'd see them first.

Earlier in the year, she'd traded skipping the last class of the day to spend time with Alex for skipping the last class of the day to man her post across the street, watching until the bell officially rang. Her counselor had decided to automatically schedule her free period during the last hour and a half of each day until she graduated. She obviously never made it until a quarter past three, anyways. Leo never put up an argument, never suggested the plan, but it worked just as well.

The muffled scream of the bell bounced off the street, and she raised her head, watching. The double doors spit the students out like rotten fruit, and they swarmed across the parking lot. Most couldn't wait to get off the grounds. Leo stayed and watched. Waited. Like clockwork, the usual small groups broke off from the rest, huddled together as they lit their cigarettes and made a split-second decision. She knew it was a decision they'd been pondering for the last twenty-four hours—that was how it always worked—but they liked to pretend it was last-minute. And she was always there waiting for them.

When the groups made their lingering way across the street, careful not to interfere with each other, Leo crushed the cigarette beneath her boot and reached into both of her front pockets. The hard, round packages assured her, reminded her she'd be walking away with a handful of cash in a couple hours, that she could grab dinner and maybe a new jacket.

The first two kids approached her, hands stuffed deeper into their own pants than she wanted to see. The boys shared a glance, and she nodded at the one closest to her.

"Forty," he said, his voice threatening to break as he met everything but her eyes. He pulled out two twenty-dollar bills and stared down at them like they would transform into what he wanted. He sniffed, bounced, pulled up his saggy pants, and looked across the street.

Leo rolled her eyes and popped two tiny bags from her left pocket. They went into the kid's hand, and she took the money with the other. He rubbed his nose on his sleeve, nudged his friend, and they swaggered in whatever direction they had chosen. Leo slipped the money into the back pocket of her jeans, enjoying the way the bills crunched as she stuffed them against each other.

These kids thought they were so cool, the bad boys on the block with a handful of their new favorite drug. They'd go off to some abandoned lot, much like the one in which she and Alex used to spend so much time together, she thought, and enjoy for a few hours their supposed newfound intelligence. Then they'd do more and more of the shit, thinking they'd discovered a new awareness of themselves, and come to see her more often. Eventually, she'd have to meet them at their homes, or the next street down, where their high would have turned them into drooling, brain-dead hulks of need. Those were the worst cases, she knew—she'd seen it in her dad.

The students at her school weren't her only customers. The same things happened to the working moms who couldn't afford to see a doctor, or the thirty-three-year-old burnouts living in their parents' basement. But the school, full of seniors struggling to pass their college entrance exams, would give her a new pop of desperate kids every year. If they stopped to think where a sixteen-year-old, quiet girl from homeroom had gotten her side job in the first place, they'd be even more afraid.

She lit another cigarette, leaned back against the wall. Another group had started to cross the street, a few cheerleaders among them this time. One of the football players caught her eye, and she nodded, exhaling the warm smoke through her nose. Carlos would take a cut when she met him on Friday, would tell her how pretty she was and ask if she wanted to start moving up the chain. She'd smile and tell him no, wonder how much longer her boss would agree to civilly hold out, maybe bring something home for her dad so he would stop vomiting long enough to eat a few bites.

The transaction with the football player took longer than it should have. Leo almost had to tell the two girls in short skirts and too much makeup to fuck off so she could talk without being interrupted by giggles, gum smacking, and the intolerably un-intimidating dirty looks they shot her way. The kid's cocky smile wavered when she glared a warning at him and told him to just come by himself next time. They left her without another word.

A scrawny kid in a plaid button-up, who clutched his laptop briefcase and blinked at her from behind enormously round glasses, only managed to catch her eye for an instant before he stared at his moving feet and flushed a bright red. Leo smirked, gazing out over the parking lot in search of anyone who might have seen this guy and found him as embarrassing as she did. Instead, she saw Alex, who slugged the other strap of her backpack over her shoulder and trudged up the hill toward the street. For a brief moment, their eyes met, then Alex quickly looked away and walked faster.

The kid with the glasses finally made it to where Leo stood against the wall, and he stuttered out a request.

"Sorry," she said, staring after Alex. "I'm all out. Find me tomorrow." She gave him a brief once-over before kicking off from the wall, smashing the cigarette into the ground with her toe, and stalking away from the gas station.

Leo shoved her hands into the pockets of her hoodie and bent her head, trying to match Alex's speed up the hill. Alex acted like she didn't know Leo would come after her, and when Leo finally caught up, she was treated that way. "Hey," she huffed, trying not to sound as out of breath as she felt when they stepped onto the sidewalk.

"I don't have anything to say to you," Alex said flatly. The sun was warm outside, but not warm enough to cause the red flush high on her cheeks. She tucked a piece of blonde hair behind her ear and stared straight ahead, holding the straps of her backpack as if it made her feel better.

"Alex, I know I've been busy, but that—"

Alex stopped and spun toward her. "You haven't been busy, Leo. You've been stupid." The scowl on her face looked as if the spite in her words tasted as bad as they sounded.

Leo forced herself not to look away from those blue eyes, tried to hide how far the pit in her stomach had fallen. "Look, I know you're pissed at me," she said, giving a weak smile and willing her voice not to shake. "And I should have tried to talk to you earlier, but that's what I'm doing now. I miss you." She took a step closer and gave Alex's shoulder a gentle squeeze.

The girl's thoughts seemed to fight her eyes and lost when she glanced down at Leo's hand. Then she quickly looked away at nothing in particular, dipped her shoulder out of the way, and stepped aside. "Great. Now you can quit doing that shit."

Leo shrugged and tried to laugh. "Come on. I can't just... stop."

"Why not?"

Someone else might have thought the fire behind Alex's eyes was anger, but Leo knew it was sadness—a sadness she hadn't ever seen there before. "Because I can't," she said. "It's not as easy as you think." But it was far easier than telling Alex she'd made a deal with Carlos to work for him, much easier than saying that in some deep, buried part of her, she actually enjoyed it. Leo pulled her pack of cigarettes from her hoodie—only three left—and offered one to her friend.

Alex pulled a smooshed pack from her back pocket, took out one of her own cigarettes instead while staring at the sidewalk, and turned away from Leo to light it herself. When she turned back, she sighed through a thick cloud of smoke and closed her eyes for a deep breath. "So, we couldn't come up with a way to get that money for your dad," she started. Leo tried to hide the wince; she knew what was coming. "Okay, fine. It was what you had to do for... that much money. Whatever. But we talked about it. It was just supposed to be to clear things up for your dad. You promised me you'd walk away, and then you decided to shit all over that promise. This is *not* who you are. Until you stop, you're probably gonna be missing me for a while." She shifted her weight and spread her hands to the side, waiting for Leo to say something.

Leo put a hand through her hair and sighed. She knew she would lose this battle, but she couldn't make Alex another promise now just to break it later. "It's not that bad. I don't see what the big deal is."

"You're hurting people!" Alex shouted, then looked around to see if anyone had noticed and put a shaking hand to her mouth for another huge drag.

The dry lump in Leo's throat made her swallow against her will, and her mouth felt glued shut. "No, I'm not."

"Really?" Alex said, her eyes wide now. "Take a look at your dad. I'm pretty sure he hasn't had the flu for the last ten years."

Leo's forehead suddenly exploded with the pressure of a need to cry, or scream, or punch something. Instead, she only glared at the girl in front of her, the only person in the world she had actually wanted to make happy. "Fuck you."

Alex gave a sharp bark of a laugh, tossed the cigarette into the street, and dropped her hands to her sides with a sharp slap against her jeans. She looked at Leo for seconds that felt frozen in time, searching her eyes. Her smile was tinged with an acrid twist. "Yeah." Then she rolled her eyes and walked away.

Leo twirled her tongue inside her mouth, wanting to shout something after her but knowing that would only make it worse, though it probably wouldn't matter at that point.

She realized her body shook as her heel bounced repeatedly against the sidewalk, and she couldn't for the life of her figure out what to think. She inhaled the cigarette and stormed across the street with her head bent low, flipping off the car that honked at her to get out of the way.

15

THIS WEEK, THE FDA officially released its ruling that the drug so many Americans have been using for the last few years, Pointera, *is now a Schedule II controlled substance. While it still has accepted medical uses when prescribed by a doctor,* Pointera *also has an extremely high potential for dependence and/or abuse. It now ranks among controlled substances such as Oxycodone and Adderall, and its medical use and dosage are now regulated through the FDA and any pharmacy. Laleopharm has not commented on this ruling so far.*

Today, we have with us Dr. Harold Laney, psychiatrist at Duke University's Department of Psychology and Neuroscience, to talk about the effects of Pointera *and how the decision has been made to so drastically change the drug's classification. Hello, Dr. Laney. Thank you for joining us.*

Thank you, John. Good to be here.

So, Doctor, over the past year, we've seen an explosion of Pointera-*related deaths across the country, some ruled as overdoses or suicides, some completely accidental. Can you explain to us how this drug, so helpful to those who struggle with high-performance and attention issues, has become such a dangerous substance so quickly?*

Absolutely, John. First of all, Pointera, *in low doses and monitored by a doctor and pharmacist, is still perfectly safe to use on a regular basis. This drug affects cognitive functions in the brain, targeting the superior temporal gyrus, which is used for processing information and language. The chemical makeup of the drug that targets this portion of the brain acts as both jumper cables and a battery with a very long life for the electrical impulses created there. The problem is that the other two components in* Pointera *act as both stimulant and suppressant at the same time. It activates and binds to the endorphin and dopamine receptors in the reward circuit, reduces metabolic activity, and also surprisingly constricts parts of the thalamus, which gives the drug an analgesic, or pain-killing, affect.*

Now, the combination of all these qualities of the drug leads to a) a potential for increasing one's tolerance of the drug, b) a great potential for dependency where the dopamine receptors are concerned, and c) a sort of painless, always stimulated state of being. However, when the tolerance for this drug increases, there's a certain ceiling effect happening, where the synapses in the reward circuit of the brain start to actually die. It's almost like when lightning strikes a house and all the power goes out, only it happens over a long period of time using Pointera. *The superior temporal gyrus gets to the point where it* only *responds to the chemicals and can no longer function on its own. So we see people who have become addicted to* Pointera *no longer able to form thoughts or sentences much longer than those of young children. I've worked with a lot of patients who are professionals in the Information Technology industry, working for companies like MindBlink and Topper. They had to be able to package and deliver information in such small, sudden doses that taking* Pointera *over a long period of time, in order to be high-functioning within their workplace, eventually turned off completely all other modes of thought process in the brain.*

The majority of these sad cases we've heard about over the last year have concerned highly productive, highly ambitious people who initially started Pointera, *with a doctor's prescription, in order to improve their productivity in the workplace, balance busy and hectic schedules, or merely to branch out of social anxiety. Unfortunately, as with most Schedule II controlled substances, even being prescribed these medications can result right away in dependency and, as of yet, there really has been no alternative discovered to combat or compete with* Pointera's *effectiveness in the realm of increased morphosyntactic processing. For right now, if your doctor prescribes* Pointera *or you have contemplated starting the drug, it's the only pharmaceutical on the market that targets these issues, but it has to be monitored accordingly.*

Thank you, Doctor. For our viewers watching right now, can you describe the potential side-effects of Pointera dependency?

Absolutely. The main signs of Pointera dependency are trouble forming sentences over just a few words, little to no appetite whatsoever, reduced movement capabilities, and decreased sleep or chaotic sleep patterns. In some of the more extreme cases, we see heart palpitations, dry, flakey skin, and an increase in saliva production. But again, these are extreme cases, and make sure to tell your doctor about any adverse reactions the moment you note them when taking Pointera.

So, Dr. Laney, I can't help but wondering if we've come across another 'black market' scenario with this drug, now a controlled substance. Is there a possibility that we may find an increase of Pointera being sold on the streets without a prescription, like heroin, cocaine, or oxycontin?

Absolutely, John. There's always that possibility. The first step to decreasing the demand for that, however, is to make sure that doctors prescribe patients only the safe doses of Pointera, and that we start working on a way, chemically or psychologically, to help those already dependent on Pointera safely stop taking the drug and help rebuild some of their normal functioning.

16

THEY SAT ON the couch, beers in hand, and let the silence fight for them. Karl had picked her up from the police station only an hour before, and though he hadn't said a word, she knew he was annoyed with her. He rarely spoke anyways, but he hadn't met her eyes once, nor could she find the hint of smile under his mustache that she had learned to track.

Leo winced as she lit a cigarette, the knuckles on both her hands already bruising and swollen. The cops hadn't asked her too many questions, hadn't really cared that a scrappy girl managed to rough up a guy who apparently was drunk in public more than he was anything else. She'd been in a holding cell for eight hours, and then she'd been let out to meet Karl in his anemic car. It had been an abnormally difficult eight hours; not only did it piss her off that she could have avoided the whole thing altogether if she'd just used her words, but she also hated the fact that Karl felt he could tell her what to do as she was carted away to County. She'd only gotten maybe two hours of sleep and spent the rest of the time wondering why the fuck she made so much money using her words only to be ordered not to, especially at a time when they would have been far more helpful than not.

"I was doing my job," Leo said, looking at the man beside her and hoping he'd acknowledge her presence somehow. Karl grunted. "And I didn't say a thing to the cops."

Karl only chugged his beer and lit another cigarette. They started early at just before noon, but Leo wasn't going to complain. She just wanted an explanation for the silence and what so obviously felt like blame. When another few minutes passed, she realized she had either fucked something up really bad, or Karl was in another world altogether.

"What the fuck did I do wrong?" she asked.

He leaned over and held the beer bottle between his legs. "Nothing, Leo," he sighed. She could hear his heavy swallow when he looked up at the ceiling. "You didn't do anything wrong. I know you didn't talk to the cops, didn't use your words. It's just..." He stopped to run a hand through his hair, his head hanging almost between his own knees. Leo thought he looked really fucking tired. "This happened in front of the Purple Lion. We just have to be careful about our connections with people... and how they're made."

"With Louis?" she asked. Karl leaned back to give her a short-lived but pointed glance out of the corner of his eye. "Why?"

A loud knock rapped on the door. Leo stared at Karl, hoping he'd give in and tell her *something*, but whoever their visitor was had already distracted him too much. He still didn't return her gaze when he stood from the couch.

She didn't find any recognition on his face when he answered the door. As soon as it opened, a giant chest barreled Karl out of the way, followed by the gaudy velvet and over-indulgently slick hair of Louis. The Lord of the Beat retained his usual, flippant composure, but he wore a scent Leo thought smelled like fear. His eyes burned as he caught sight of her, though that was his only giveaway.

"Had a lovely visit with the city police, did you?" His voice was as silky as his clothing, though it failed to conceal as much. His companion, a giant of a man, wore a shiny silver vest over a dark blue oxford shirt, the buttons of which strained to hold in his chest and giant belly beneath. He seized a metal folding chair, jamming it upon the floor in front of Leo, and Karl was left to close the door behind them. Louis approached the chair, swiping at the seat with a manicured hand before setting himself upon it like a dainty housewife.

Leo glanced at Karl, who leaned against the rim of the sink, arms folded across his chest. Then she noticed the knife there, at his left elbow, just in case. He didn't say a thing. She took another drag of her cigarette and met Louis' gaze again.

"Something makes me think you might enjoy their friendship more than mine." Louis plucked an invisible hair from his shoulder, sprinkling it to the side. She didn't respond. Louis tucked his already plastered hair behind his ear and met her gaze with purpose. "Tell me." He spoke through his teeth. "Tell me that you and I are still friends."

She took another drag, letting the smoke out toward their visitors. She'd cater to the man at his club, when she worked for him. But she was off the clock, and this was where she fucking lived—for now. "I tell stories, Louis," she said, and the sound of her voice instantly triggered the fog in his eyes. "But I don't talk to cops. And I did my job. You and I are square."

A lopsided smile split his tidied face, and he nodded. Then he took a deep breath, smoothed his oiled hair again. "Yes." He sniffed. "You and I are right with one another." His bodyguard shook his head, her short beat having affected him as well. Louis turned very slightly in his chair. "But Karl and I are not."

Karl's eyes widened only a little, and he raised his head. Nothing else.

"Karl and I have unfinished business, left unattended for quite some time. I believe you, Leo." His eyes did not leave Karl's face as he addressed her. "Your... mentor, however, must also clean up the mess you've made. How many drinks have you had today, Karl?"

Karl only nodded at the half-empty beer bottle beside the couch, his jaw flexing in defiance.

"Not enough to keep you quiet this afternoon." Louis crossed his legs. "Let's hear it from you, too."

Karl uncrossed his arms and stood straight. "Hold on, now." He glanced at Leo, discomfort and guilt flashing in his dark eyes. "You know the reason I don't—"

"I know the reason," Louis said. "But your girl here has

put me in quite an uncomfortable position, dogs on my trail and all. You owe me, Karl. Spin a beat for me now, for the sake of Leo's loyalty, and I will continue to pay you, let you work for me. Refuse me, and I will turn you both in. How long have you been running, exactly?"

Karl swallowed, his beard bristling as his jaw worked in anger and forced composure. He glanced at Leo again, who could only frown at him. She couldn't do a thing, had absolutely no idea what Louis was talking about. Leo hadn't done anything wrong, except for maybe taking her job a bit too seriously the night before. Sometimes she snapped like that. Rarely, but it still happened. But that had nothing to do with Karl, and she'd already been turned in and released. So what the fuck were they talking about? She stared back and forth from one man to the other in the next few moments of silence.

"I got the call from Melissa earlier this afternoon," Karl began, glaring into Louis' face as his words took hold.

Leo had never felt anything like it, the warm sensation blooming in her stomach, spreading through her shoulders and arms, tingling in her feet. Sighing, her head drifting backwards, she sank into the couch. She heard the lilt of Karl's voice, his short pauses, but could not place the words. All the world had become a warm fog, melting her, and she was vaguely aware of the beer in her hand tipping out of her grasp. The lived-in garage faded away, and all that existed was Karl's humming voice and the magic in her veins.

When he finished, there were a few long minutes of silence before the light returned to Leo's eyes, and she sighed. The fog lifted, the warmth faded, and she felt it leave with a sweet longing. She opened her eyes to find Louis smoothing his oiled hair back onto his head, wiping a single bead of sweat from his brow.

"Oh, yes." His voice was a sigh, and he straightened his jacket. His eyes were still hazy when he opened them, but his toothy smile was sweeter than usual. "Karl, I have so missed your words. It's a pity you're so adamant about keeping them to yourself." He leaned his head back, breathing deeply through his nose and shaking his oiled curls.

Karl leaned against the sink again, knuckles white at his sides. His nostrils flared as he stared at the back wall, never looking at Louis, or at Leo. The bodyguard by the door snorted, shook his head, and a thin, dopey smile spread across his dull lips.

"Leo." She swallowed at Louis' voice. "Your friend has won you back my trust. You owe him for what he's just done." He stood, again brushing imaginary dust from his sleeves, and nodded at his companion. The giant man swung the door wide and waited for Louis to skirt through it, who called over his shoulder. "I'll see you two soon."

Karl's home felt quieter than usual, despite the hum of the minifridge. Leo remembered her beer and righted it. Half of it had drained away, leaving a sweet stain on the cushion beside her. "I had no idea that you—"

Karl's eyes caught hers in a flash of anger and pain, cutting her off with their knifelike intensity. His lower lip trembled, and for a moment, she thought he was going to tell her everything. Instead, he shouldered his way through the door, pulled it firmly shut behind him, and left her alone in the yeasty smell of beer.

17

"HOW WAS SCHOOL today?" It sounded like he tried to care.

Leo put her backpack on the kitchen table, scattering paper plates onto the floor, gauging his lucidity. He sat in the armchair, a half-smoked cigarette dangling from his cracked lips, one arm hanging over the armrest—a single thread of dried blood on his forearm.

"Same as every day, Dad." She grabbed a can of coke from the fridge and cracked the top. He didn't move.

"That's good, that's good." His eyes were closed, head sinking into his chest until it popped back up, and he drew on the cigarette. She plucked it from his limp fingers before he dropped it, took a long drag, and put it out in the crowded ashtray. She sat on the couch and watched him, holding her knees to her chest. He fumbled with the pack of cigarettes in his lap, lit another, and leaned his head back.

She rolled her eyes, watching the new cigarette burn dangerously close to his bathrobe. "I'm failing science and math," she said.

There was a ten-second lapse. "Why?" He dragged on the cigarette, eyes still closed.

"I just don't get it." She sipped the coke.

"Well." His voice was rasping and dark. "I never... never got it, either. Until I tried..." His head drooped, popped up, and he shifted. "Harder."

"Yeah."

"You've got a good brain," he continued and croaked a few coughs before inhaling more smoke. "You need to finish school."

"Yeah." She clicked on the remote. The TV light swirled in the smoke.

Groaning, he leaned forward and grabbed the closest needle. She watched him, not daring to hide her disgust, but he never looked at her.

"I'm gonna take a shower." She stood, chugged the rest of the coke, and picked up the cigarette he'd set down on the armrest.

"Okay, baby." He lazily combined spoon, needle, and water.

Throwing a fit never helped, begging and pleading for him to stop never helped. Her quiet disdain was all she could manage anymore. She sighed and walked off. A thirty-minute shower would give him enough time to settle into the high, and maybe she wouldn't have to watch it again tonight.

She came back in her pajamas and a sweatshirt, wet hair in her face. The freezer had a few frozen dinners, a half-full bag of peas, a pizza. "You want anything for dinner, Dad?" The only response was the squeal of a car chase on the TV. "I can order Chinese. Kinda feelin kung pao chicken."

Another cigarette smoked alone on the coffee table. His head had fallen below his chest, resting at an awkward angle against his arm. She turned off the TV. "What do you want?"

She placed a hand on his shoulder, but his head never popped back up. "Dad?" She shook him gently, and a slime of white dribbled from his chin. She felt his pulse, moving his head in search of what wasn't there. "Dad?"

She stepped back and picked at her lip. She counted to fifty, hoping she'd see some sign of life as she watched him. The only movement was the smoke from the cigarette, still burning on the coffee table. Instead of reaching for it, she pulled the phone off its cradle and punched in the only numbers she could think of.

"Hello?"

"Alex, it's me."

Waiting for the long pause to end made Leo dizzy.

"Hi."

"So, I know you probably don't want to talk to me… that's cool. I just didn't know what else to…"

"Leo, are you okay?"

The lump she swallowed felt like a rock wrapped in gauze.

"My dad's gone."

"Where'd he go?"

"Well, he's right here in front of me, but… he's not…

um. He's gone." Leo realized she clenched her free hand into a tight fist, and even though she hadn't cried in a really long time, she couldn't help but wonder why her eyes were still dry.

"Oh... oh, my god," Alex said. Leo couldn't understand why she sounded so surprised. "Do you want me to come over?"

"I think so." She heard Alex take a deep breath.

"Okay. I'll be right there. Did you call 9-1-1?"

Leo couldn't take her eyes off his lips.

"Leo?"

"Yeah?"

"Did you call 9-1-1?"

"No."

"Okay. Call them right now. I'll be there in like two minutes."

"Yeah."

Her hands felt so heavy. The dial tone echoed out, and she only just remembered she still had the phone. Swaying, she punched in the three numbers.

"9-1-1, what's your emergency?"

"I think my dad just overdosed."

"What do you think he took?"

"Pointera."

"Is he breathing?"

"I don't think so. I couldn't feel his pulse."

"Is there anyone else in the house with you?"

"No."

"What's your name?"

"Leona."

"How old are you, Leona?"

"I turned eighteen yesterday."

She'd walked outside to sit on the drooping step of the tiny front porch. The thought of stepping outside had seemed like a good idea, but the image of his face had come with her. She just wanted to be able to see something else when she closed her eyes.

Her breath steamed in the cold night air; the cherry tip of her cigarette glowed brighter than she thought it should have. She was only halfway through when she heard the crunch of footsteps on the sidewalk. Alex stopped only briefly at the rotted, slanted gate before pushing it slowly open with a creak.

Leo wished suddenly that she hadn't called her at all. They hadn't talked in months, and she hated the fact that Alex showed up now only for an emergency. It wasn't *really* an emergency; nothing could be done now, anyways. That was probably why the ambulance wasn't there yet. Did they even send an ambulance when… this happened?

All she could do was drag on the cigarette and watch Alex's boots. She couldn't look up at her face, didn't want to see the pity there. Pity didn't serve a purpose, and Leo wasn't actually sad—was she?

Alex sat beside her on the porch step, tilting her head forward to try to meet Leo's gaze. Leo thought she smelled like cinnamon, and it made her sick to realize how much she'd missed that smell.

"I hope you weren't busy," she mumbled.

"No," Alex answered, and it sounded a bit overly enthusiastic. "No, I wasn't busy. Even if I was, there's nothing more important than this."

Leo put her head in her hand and turned to look at Alex for the first time. She couldn't look at her for very long, but she couldn't stay away from those bright blue eyes for much longer, either. How could Alex be here, now, after all the shit Leo had pulled? She suddenly felt more ashamed of her pride than she had ever been of anything else. The girl sitting next to her, the person she wanted next to her forever, had swallowed her own pride to be here at a moment's notice, whether Leo needed her or not. She couldn't tell if the phone call had been because she'd needed her, or wanted her, or just didn't know what else to do. Alex only sat there and looked at her, waiting patiently for Leo's anxious gaze to calm and finally settle.

"I'm so sorry," Leo whispered, finally able to drink in the sight of Alex's face without having to look away. She felt a pressure at the corners of her eyes, a burning in her nose, and she wondered if she was finally going to cry.

Alex's eyes brimmed with tears, reflecting the light from the streetlamps, and she gave a heavy sigh. Leo tried to find something else to say, anything to break that silent tension, but she didn't have to. Alex leaned in, grabbed her face with both hands, and kissed her. Leo felt like she'd break if she moved, the kiss was that fragile. It seemed to say everything all at once—*It's okay. I love you. I'm sorry. I'm here.* She squeezed her eyes shut, wanting to breathe in the smell of the moment forever, and when she covered one of Alex's hands with her own, she felt a hot tear slip out from between her lashes.

They pulled away from each other, sniffing with weak smiles beneath heavy frowns. If either of them had anything else to say, they didn't have a chance for it in that moment. The shadows flickered and bounced between red and yellow lights, interrupting them. The girls stood slowly as two cop cars pulled silently up to the house. Alex slipped her hand into Leo's and gave it a squeeze. Whether or not Leo actually needed her here for this, she couldn't have been more grateful.

18

MARCUS TIEFFLER, THE man who brought us the one-minute Infodeo just shy of two decades ago, passed away late Thursday evening in his home. At the age of thirty, Mr. Tieffler left his position as Social Media Manager at Mind-Blink after making his mark on the world of Information Technology. Unfortunately, officials say Mr. Tieffler's untimely death at the age of forty-two was, in fact, due to a Pointera *overdose. Mr. Tieffler's toxicology report showed incredibly high levels of the controlled substance, and it seemed an accidental overdose. We have no comment from his family or friends at this time, but our condolences go out to them.*

19

KARL DIDN'T COME back to his place until much later that night, and even though the last thing Leo wanted to do was talk about what had happened, she knew that something had changed in him. Something, maybe once held together by a weak scar, had been broken open again. He acted again like the first night they'd met—nonchalant, apathetic. But this time, he wouldn't even talk to her, let alone look her in the eye.

She couldn't figure out what she'd done to make him act like she wasn't even there. Something knotted in her stomach, itched to be let out, and her face burned hot when she realized she wanted to yell at him. She could have used her words to make him tell her what had really happened earlier that day, why Louis had forced Karl to spin his own beat. In his snobbish, manipulative way, the owner of the Purple Lion had said he'd turn them both in if Karl didn't do what he wanted, had asked how long Karl had been running. That, above anything else, made Leo want to leave. She wondered just what exactly she'd walked into when she'd followed Karl into his boxy home that first night. The thought crossed her mind that she never should have accepted his hospitality, never should have told the man anything about herself. Any trouble Karl might have been in was more than she could afford to keep in her life.

Still, the memory of her first meeting with Bernadette, of Karl promising he'd introduce her to Sleepwater, kept her quiet. Years of learning how to be patient in order not to lose everything had taught her that just when things got too uncomfortable to bear, something else always showed up to make it worthwhile.

It happened a lot sooner than she'd expected. Leo had the next three days off work—three days of freedom that didn't include Louis and his bourgeois bull-whip—and she was almost afraid of having to find something with which to occupy her time. She woke up Monday morning on the couch, the sun shimmering in through the cheap slatted blinds, and Karl was already gone. She waited a few hours, not bothering to eat anything but going through a pot and a half of coffee.

She sat outside on the gravel in front of his place when the station wagon slowly rolled up, and Karl unfolded himself from the driver's seat. Looking up at him, she didn't feel like standing, like saying anything at all as she cradled the tin mug in her hands. But she watched his face, and his eyes finally met hers as he stood beside the car.

"You been up long?" he asked.

"Kinda." She didn't want to push the sarcasm, but the way he'd acted around her the day before seemed worthier of her resentment at the moment. She drained the rest of the coffee, then looked up at him again. When he glanced down at his worn boots, she grabbed the pack of cigarettes beside her and lit one.

"I just talked to Bernadette," he said softly, and she only raised her eyebrows in response and blew her smoke in his direction. Karl grunted, like he agreed with himself, and came to sit down next to her. "She said Sleepwater's expecting you, and they want us to meet with them tonight."

Leo finally let herself look up at him, at the worn frown beneath his mustache and something like pleading behind his eyes. She still couldn't figure him out, couldn't decide what his less-than-varied expressions meant, and she suddenly realized it pissed her off. Staying with him because he knew about what she could do with her words was one thing—sticking around with him if he planned on playing some fucked-up emotional head game with her was something else entirely.

"You sure you still want to take me to them?" she asked and didn't really care that her voice sounded hurt and mean all in the same breath. Karl swallowed and shifted his body completely toward her, staring at her. She had to bite the inside of her cheek to keep from saying anything else, something that might have been bitchier than she intended.

He pulled out his own cigarette and lit it with a vengeance, then finally seemed to pull his brain and his body into the same space. "Yesterday... that wasn't your fault." He took only a moment to launch a mouthful of spit across the gravel. "That didn't have anything to do with you. Louis would have found a way to blackmail me, one way or the other, whether it was now or later... with you or someone else."

Leo found herself suddenly and with no warning wishing that Karl's reference to "someone else" was only a figure of speech. She couldn't imagine that he'd had anyone else sleeping on his couch nightly, eating his camping-stove food, and taking up the passenger seat of his dying station wagon. She wanted to think that she was the first, that she'd be the last. Karl definitely wasn't the savior of all homeless orphans with beat-spinning powers, but she still didn't enjoy hearing the phrase from his lips.

"If it's not my fault—" she started.

"We can talk about it later," he said and turned to look at her again.

She glared at him, wishing he'd be open enough to let her finish a sentence, even though she recognized and sympathized with the exact level of discomfort she saw in him then. She didn't like discussing her own shit any more than he did, and it was pointless to want him to be anything more than she was capable of herself.

"We *will* talk about it later," Karl added. Leo gave him one slow nod, understanding that this was the closest thing to a promise she was going to get. "I want to leave here around two. Sleepwater's waiting for us, and we've got a couple hours' drive to get there."

"You're not going to tell me where we're going, are you?" Leo asked. If he hadn't still been stony and detached from whatever the fuck had happened the day before with Louis, Leo thought she would have seen the twitch of a smile under his mustache. But today, he only flicked the cherry of his smoked cigarette out across the gravel and stood. "I'm going for a walk," she added, and the only response she got was the door closing from the inside.

They drove out of the city, past the gleaming suburbs, and north into what served as the mountains out here. They were more like rolling hills, the winding road glistening with short bursts of sunlight falling through the trees. Karl had taken her to grab a sandwich and a few packs of cigarettes, and their drive was silent. Leo found herself wishing she knew how to talk to him, how to approach any topic of conversation without making it seem like she pried him for information. But with Karl, she didn't know a single goddamn thing. Everything was new information.

It took them almost three hours before they finally turned off the highway and another twenty minutes of poorly kept gravel roads before they pulled in and stopped. Leo wondered how many more trips the dying car could make, especially if Karl planned on bringing them out here more than once. A newer-looking Jeep and an old Ford pickup were the only other cars in the front lot, though it could have comfortably fit at least four more. Tall pines rose around them in all directions, casting flickering shadows against the brown-red roofing of the house. The only houses Leo had ever seen in the mountains were those visible from the highway, or those dilapidated old things she'd come upon once or twice just on the outskirts of civilized towns, sitting only a mile or two back from public parks or open spaces. This was more like a lodge, tucked away behind winding roads and the seemingly endless forest.

When they stepped out of the car, Leo heard the rush of water a short distance off. A sudden, overwhelming sense of vastness hit her, and she placed her hand on the car as she looked up toward the tops of the trees. That made her feel dizzy, and she gave a little kick at the gravel underfoot. The air smelled sweet, warm despite the breeze, and she felt small and mechanical surrounded by so much wilderness. She couldn't quite understand why anyone would want to live out here, so far away from everything.

Karl shut the driver-side door and stepped toward the house. "Come on," he called, and the grumble of his voice pulled her out of her anxiety-inducing view of the place. She wondered if she would have felt less hesitant about meeting the so-called 'Sleepwater' group if they'd have chosen a place to meet in the city.

Her sneakers made a low, wooden echo when she followed Karl up the front porch stairs, and they only waited a few seconds after he knocked for the door to open. The woman who answered was almost as tall as Karl, with luminous green eyes and a head of thick, dark hair, curls piled high on top of her head. A gathering of scarves wrapped around her neck, falling in different lengths between long, beaded necklaces against her patchy-colored skirts. A huge grin spread across the woman's face, and she gently pushed the door open wide as far as it would go.

"You're early," she said to Karl, and Leo thought she'd never seen someone smile so much through their eyes. Then the woman looked at her. "I'm so glad you made it," she said, her low voice flooded with genuine gladness and understated enthusiasm.

Leo felt her face go hot, her hands covered in a sudden clammy chill, and all she could do was nod. The close-lipped smile she gave the woman seemed out of place and incredibly lacking after being met with such compassion by a complete stranger. Karl stepped inside and embraced the woman, who then ushered them in and closed the door behind them.

"We the first ones here?" he asked, taking a brief minute to wipe his boots off on the doorway rug. Leo had to keep herself from laughing at the sight of him suddenly showing symptoms of a well-trained houseguest. But then she realized that she did the same thing, feeling ridiculous but at the same time not wanting to track anything onto the shining wood floors of the hallway.

"No," the woman answered, leading the way and glancing back with a grin. "Bernadette beat you."

"Of course she did," Karl muttered, distinctly the type of aside meant for others to hear.

Leo followed them through the short hallway, passing a staircase on the right, then found herself unable to keep from staring with wide eyes at the giant living room opening up in front of her. The entire back wall was made of windows, looking out behind the house onto a wide expanse of more pine trees. She caught the glimmer of sunlight on water, surprised to find just how close the river must have run behind the house. The left side of the living room housed a tall fireplace made of dark, smooth stone, and a few candles burned on the mantle. They had to have been for show, because sunlight spilled through the back windows and lit up the wooden floors like they, too, had been set on fire. Couches, armchairs, and a few benches lined with pillows filled the room, one of which was currently occupied by Bernadette.

"Hello, Leo," the old woman called, setting her cup of tea down on the side table and leaning back with a warm smile. She was a lot more put together than the last time Leo had seen her, complete without curlers in her hair and wearing a jean skirt and coral-colored sweater.

"Hi," Leo replied, unable to find any other words. She'd never been welcomed anywhere with such warmth and comfort, let alone in a house that looked like this. She realized she'd been clenching her fists, and she shoved them into the pocket of her sweatshirt. She felt a warm hand on her shoulder, and she tried not to jump as she looked up into the green eyes of the woman she didn't even know a little bit.

"My name's Mirela," the woman said with another smile.

"Leo."

Mirela removed her hand from Leo's shoulder, then spread her arms wide for a hug. Leo didn't have a chance to say anything before she was embraced by clacking beads, the smell of fruit and flowers, and what almost turned into a mouthful of thick, curly hair. "It's wonderful to meet you, Leo."

Just managing to clear her face from the bedding of

scarves around the woman's neck, Leo brought her hands up to pat Mirela's shoulders a few times. She glanced at Karl, who stood behind Mirela now and watched the exchange with a smirk. Leo held her breath in the woman's hug but couldn't stop a sigh; she wondered whether it came from Mirela's hospitality or the fact that Karl seemed to finally be coming out of his stupid mood.

"Would you like something to drink?" Mirela asked.

"Beer?" Karl asked.

The woman turned to give him a gaze that, had it not come from such a loving, compassionate face, would have made Leo feel like she'd just killed the woman's cat. "Brad is supposed to pick up drinks on their way back."

Karl grinned and held up his hands in surrender. "I can wait."

Mirela laughed and walked past him into the kitchen. Leo followed her movements with her eyes, noting the bundles of drying herbs hanging from the ceiling, the jars of different-colored liquids flooding indiscernible matter, the surprising amount of colorful bowls holding even more colorful produce on almost every surface. She thought it looked weird, a little kooky, but the feeling of comfort in the house and the way Mirela seemed like she wouldn't care what someone else thought one way or the other gave Leo a willingness to look past all the dead plants *inside* the house.

"Would you like some tea, Leo?" Mirela didn't look at her but clanked together some jars and lit the stove beneath a bright green teakettle. Her skirts swayed with almost every single movement.

"Okay." That was all she could think of to say. Once

again, she'd been thrust suddenly into a stranger's house and made to feel as though she'd skipped the scene in her life where she'd met everyone the first time. No one acted like they'd just met her, like they needed some time to figure her out. Leo wondered if this was what it felt like to have amnesia. People didn't generally take a first look at her and decide she could use a hug, or a cup of tea, or whatever the fuck else was headed her way now that she was here.

"Make me another cup, too, will you?" Bernadette called from the living room. Mirela turned from the stove to grin at Leo, who only then realized she'd been staring. "Leo, come sit down for a minute."

Leo turned and gave the old woman a shrug of a smile. Karl had already taken the armchair by the fireplace, even though a fire hadn't been lit there yet, and Leo walked across the wood floor to take a seat on one of the other couches. She wanted more than anything to pull her knees up to her chest but wondered whether or not having feet on the furniture was against the rules. It had been a long time since she'd been in a house where that might have even been an option.

Bernadette chuckled and leaned back against the cushions. "I still don't bite," she said.

Chewing on her lip, Leo folded her arms and couldn't help smiling back before she glanced quickly at the floor. This old lady hadn't bitten her, no, but she seemed to have a lot more bark stored away in there somewhere.

"What have you been up to the last couple days?" Bernadette asked.

Glancing at Karl, who gave her a tiny nod, Leo sighed and let herself lean back into the surprisingly soft couch.

"Karl helped me get a job…"

"Doing what?"

"Watching, mostly. Sometimes I make a little extra money spinning a beat, but mostly I just keep an eye on people." The phrase 'spinning a beat' sounded like she'd just babbled in a different language, but when she looked up and saw Bernadette's shining grin, she couldn't help but feel like she'd caught on to something important.

"Where's this?" Mirela walked toward them with three mugs of steaming tea, handing one across the space toward Bernadette before sitting directly next to Leo on the couch. Leo would have stared at the woman, would have maybe inched away toward the armrest, but Mirela offered her the mug with a shining smile and wide eyes, and it took her completely off guard. She accepted the tea, found herself smiling back into the woman's round face, and holding onto a warm cup in her hands felt more comfortable than anything else.

"The Purple Lion," she answered, leaning forward to take a whiff of the steam from her cup. She almost spilled the whole thing in her lap when Bernadette burst out laughing. Leo glanced up sharply at her, then shifted briefly for a look at Karl. He had one long leg crossed over the other, his scuffed boot swinging in lazy circles, and he reached a hand up to scratch the back of his head. It looked like he tried to hide some form of embarrassment, though his beard covered any would-be blush.

"I'm so sorry," Bernadette finally said, waving her hand in front of her face as though she could swish away the laughter. She shook her head and brushed some thin pieces of hair behind her ear. "That's Louis' club, isn't it?" When

Leo nodded slowly, Bernadette shot Karl a pointed look masked by her persistent smile, then glanced up at the ceiling and put a hand to her cheek. "Leo, I'm glad to hear that Karl helped you find work, and I'm sure you're very good at it. I just... Louis." Another fit of giggles gripped her before she finally let out a shaky sigh. "That man is *something*, and I've never been able to take him seriously."

"How do you know him?" Leo asked. The question surprised her, and she wondered how much of her comfort in asking it came from the warm welcome these women had given her and how much had come from seeing someone else laugh at Louis' expense.

"Oh, I've met with the man once or twice," Bernadette answered, dabbing at the corner of her eye with the sleeve of her sweater. "It's been a long time, but he tends to leave an impression—"

The sound of tires on gravel reached them, and they all looked up toward the front of the house. "They're back," Mirela said with a grin and stood from her chair. Karl cleared his throat with a smile, and Bernadette leaned toward Leo with a conspiratorial pat on the cushion beside her.

"We can talk about all that later," she said.

Leo nodded, and her attention was drawn suddenly toward the entryway, where the sounds of boots, people shuffling through the door, and loving greetings floated into the living room. At least half a dozen people filed in, met by Mirela's open arms and an exclamation of how good it was to see everybody. Someone moved quickly into a side room with an armload of what looked like duffel bags, then closed the door and joined the gathering.

The first man into the living room was hidden behind a giant bush of red beard, wearing all black beneath a leather jacket and wool hat. "Hey," he called through a laugh, catching sight of Leo, Bernadette, and Karl sitting there. Karl rose and took two long strides toward the man, who ripped off his hat to reveal a thick shock of the same flaming red hair. He rubbed a hand vigorously through it and held his arms out for a rough but warm embrace from Karl. The man only came up to Karl's shoulders. "Look who's making themselves at home," he added. Karl hit him on the back and stepped back.

"Brad," Bernadette called.

Brad approached her, saying, "Don't get up," and leaned down to give her a hug.

"And this is Leo," the woman added after their embrace. Brad glanced up at Karl, then back to Leo.

Still holding Bernadette's hands, he nodded and grinned from within the ruddy facial hair. "First time here?"

Leo didn't know whether she should stand or stay seated, but then she caught Bernadette's wink. "Yeah," she said and rubbed her clammy hands on her jeans before jerkily getting up from the couch.

Brad clamped a rough hand on her shoulder, standing barely a few inches taller than her, and nodded. "I'm Brad. Welcome." Then he stuck his hand out in front of her, and she had no choice but to shake it.

"Thank you." Since when did she suddenly become so polite? But the joy was infectious as she watched Brad return to Karl and punch him in the shoulder. They headed into the kitchen, where someone had placed a case of beer, and Leo realized she'd never seen Karl smile quite like that—without a hint of darkness around him.

20

THE SICKLY SWEET smell of the funeral parlor made her stomach fold. It came from the flowers lining the aisles, from whatever stale air freshener they'd used, but the only thing she could think of was his body. They must have used formaldehyde on it—didn't they do that with every embalming? She'd paid attention on the day they dissected frogs in science class her sophomore year, and the only thing she really remembered was the smell and the name of that damn fluid.

Leo's mouth felt dry, but whenever she thought of standing to get a drink of water, the image of his mouth—dry, empty, dead—stopped her. His mouth must have smelled horrible, and she wondered whether or not the embalming fluid would have masked it. She couldn't walk up to the open casket, no matter how much she told herself that was what people did. The possibility of smelling him kept her in her seat.

They'd told her that family sat in the front row, where those paying their respects to his coffin could then easily make their way toward her and offer any condolences they might have felt appropriate. She turned slowly to look at the people behind her as the funeral director stood at the podium and said a few words about her father. They all went right through her head, nothing sticking to her memory. The man didn't fucking know her father. What made him the expert on crappy eulogies?

Nine. That was the number of people who felt it worth their time to show up. Three of them had introduced themselves when they arrived early, telling her they had worked with her father years before and were so sorry for her loss. One was their neighbor across the street, Mrs. O'Neilly, who looked like this funeral was the highlight of her year. Leo hadn't spoken to her since she was very young and didn't know how in the world the woman knew her father had died. She hated the bright light behind the woman's eyes, shining beneath thinning eyebrows even though the hunch in Mrs. O'Neilly's back almost folded her in half while she sat. A man and a woman, both remarkably skinny with dark, sunken eyes, had chosen to sit in the very back row. They looked too much like junkies to her, and she was glad they never made an attempt to speak to her, never met her eyes when she gave them a few seconds' stare.

The other three people in the bare-walled room were the last three she'd ever want to be here. Leo didn't want to be here herself, and while six people willingly attending her father's funeral was way more than she expected, she couldn't care less about any of them. Except for the man sitting discreetly in a chair by the back door, his leather Forzieris betraying his wealth beneath the striped polo and jeans. Two men, square, stoic, and remarkably similar, shared a bench on the other side of the door, staring at the funeral director with no trace of expression.

Carlos had paid for the entire event—she knew it. The funeral director had showed up himself at her house, explained that he normally didn't make house calls without an appointment, but he didn't have a phone number. Leo didn't have a phone. She'd told him that she couldn't afford a funeral and asked what would happen if she just left her father's body at the coroner's. The funeral director had merely shaken his head with a tiny smile and told her the entire service had already been planned and purchased, then offered her a fucking flier with all the details. Leo's initial thought had been Carlos, and seeing him here with his stupid, shiny shoes and his twin goons only solidified the truth. But she wouldn't say anything to him about it—she couldn't. She hadn't wanted a fucking funeral service, even if she'd had the money to pay for it herself. What had her dad been to her when he died? Forget that day—what had he ever been for her? The relief of finally having him gone mixed with an unknown terror. What the hell was she supposed to do now?

She glared at the funeral director behind the podium, trying hard not to imagine the things they'd had to do to her father's body to make him look even remotely acceptable for an open casket. It was so quiet in the room that the squeak of the back door opening almost drowned out the funeral director's words. Leo's heart fluttered, and for a brief instant, she imagined the newcomer might be her mother. Had she heard the news? Had she come back from wherever she'd escaped to to pay her own respects to the father of her only child? To look her daughter in the eyes and tell her she was sorry for her loss?

The thought was stupid, and she almost cursed aloud at herself for being such a baby. Her mother hadn't thought of her in fourteen years. If Leo's childhood, anything in her entire life, hadn't brought the woman back to her, the death of her father sure as hell wasn't going to do it. The bitch probably didn't even know—or if she did, she was laughing and wishing the man a happy stay in Hell.

Leo turned around and watched the door open, seeing long blond hair peeking through first, followed by Alex in a black dress. The sight didn't make Leo's heart beat any slower. But she didn't have the chance to meet Alex's gaze, because Carlos stood from his chair and put a hand on the girl's arm, stopping her. Alex barely flicked her eyes up toward him before immediately staring at the floor as the man whispered something in her ear. He was too damn close. Alex's face flushed a light pink before Carlos gave her shoulder a little squeeze.

That piece of shit. Leo instantly turned back in her seat, wishing she sat at least one more row back so she could prop her feet on a chair in front of her. Instead, she stuck the legs of her black jeans all the way out, crossing one foot over the other, and folded her arms. The funeral director kept talking, though he glanced down briefly at her movement.

Alex came to sit next to her, pulling her long dress down beneath her legs before settling in the chair. "I'm so sorry," she whispered. She leaned in toward Leo, who didn't move. She couldn't stop thinking about Carlos' hand on the girl's arm. "Leo," Alex repeated, worry in her soft voice.

Leo couldn't look at her, didn't want to. Her ears burned, and it seemed everything she heard now floated through a thick haze. She clenched her teeth.

"I locked myself out of my apartment and had to break back in to get the directions." Alex put a hand on one of Leo's folded arms, pleading.

Leo felt her gaze, knew there were tears in Alex's eyes from the sound of her whispers. She took a deep breath and turned slowly to look at her. Alex looked great in black, her light hair pulled into a half ponytail, wearing more makeup than Leo had seen on her even though it was only mascara and some blush.

The soft smile Alex tried to give looked more like a grimace, and her eyes held a wet shimmer. "I wish I'd been here sooner," she added.

"It's fine," Leo whispered back, staring at the far wall. Then Alex cupped a hand to her face and kissed her softly on the lips.

Leo found herself able to breathe again, and she gripped Alex's hand in hers when she pulled away. As she stared at the funeral director's mouth moving in a blur of sound, then at some employee who sang a song she didn't recognize, the only thing she could think about then was whether or not Mrs. O'Neilly had had a heart attack from seeing two teenage girls kiss in public. That, at least, would have made the whole pitiful ordeal a lot more bearable.

When the service was finally over and everyone had put a hand in detached deference to the coffin—everyone but Leo and Alex, and only then because Leo held her back when Alex had started to stand—an empty silence filled the funeral parlor. It only lasted for a few seconds, and then the singing employee pressed play on a CD-player, and the low sound of cello tunes bounced around the empty walls. Leo felt the anticlimactic exhalation from those gathered around her; everyone had already addressed her, expressed their sorrow, and now what was there left to do? She stood, pulling Alex behind her by the hand.

"I want to get the fuck out of here," she muttered, ignoring the curious, concerned frown on Alex's face.

Mrs. O'Neilly opened her mouth and pointed at them. "I want—" she started, but Leo marched forward, head bent low, and headed toward the back door.

She didn't have to talk to anyone, even the funeral director. What was she going to say to him? It didn't make sense to thank him for a service she didn't fucking want in the first place. She'd only come because Alex had said she might regret not going, but she knew now that never would have happened. What a pathetic way to waste a Tuesday afternoon.

Carlos stood beside the back door, guarding the entrance into the foyer that would lead them outside. The brothers stood beside the bench, nodding in stoic apathy to whoever happened to meet their gaze. Leo slowly moved Alex to walk in front of her—she wanted to bring up the rear in case someone tried to say something else. Alex would have turned to acknowledge anyone who spoke. She didn't want to allow the opportunity.

Alex walked through the back door, and Leo made the mistake of looking up at Carlos' face. He stared after Alex, looking her up and down, and the final straw broke whatever was left of Leo's reserve when she saw him lick the fucking smile on his lips. She stopped, dropping her hands from where they had gently guided Alex's back.

"Hey, are you—"

"Go on," Leo said, then glanced at Alex and gave her a short smile and a nod. "I'll be there in a second. Just wait outside for me." Alex stared at her, then briefly glanced up at Carlos. But she finally nodded and walked through the foyer and outside.

Leo glanced up at Carlos, feeling the hatred warm her ears and tingle in her tightly clenched fists. He smiled at her. "What are you doing?" she hissed. The men who had introduced themselves as her father's past coworkers brushed by her, giving her sympathetic looks and nods. She only briefly glanced at them, ignoring them, and stepped to the side in front of Carlos to get out of the doorway.

"Leona," he said calmly. "Lo siento mucho for you loss."

"Fuck you," she spat. The lack of reaction on his face only made her angrier. The last time he and Alex had been in the same room was the day he'd come into her home and offered to return her father if she worked for him. That was over a year ago, but she knew Carlos had recognized Alex the minute she'd walked into the funeral home.

"I know you are angry, and you father death is a very

sad—"

"What did you say to her?" She'd put up with so many things from him over the years. He held her father's debt over her head like a monstrous carrot, tried to bribe her with money, a life of luxury, never failing to express his attraction to her and whatever fucked-up, manipulative emotions he thought it induced. She'd done as much as she could to keep Alex out of the picture entirely, had cut her out of her life because Carlos was so closely tied to it. And Alex was off limits.

"I tell her she is beautiful," he answered in his calm, overly soothing voice, and Leo felt the seal of all her logic crack right open.

The burn started in her belly, fired up in a column of rage that made her want to cough. Instead, she embraced that itch and spewed her words out at the one man she'd never dared touch with them before. "You stay the fuck away from Alex. She will *not* become a part of your world. And if you ever lay a hand on her, approach her in any way, even *look* at her from across the street, I'll fucking kill you. I know you believe me, and I have everything I need to destroy you. If you even think about her, I'll bring you down."

Carlos blinked, wide-eyed, the full force of her burning words having now enveloped him in that familiar fog. She knew he believed her—in that moment, at least. She knew he'd remember what she'd said, and she knew he wasn't going to let it go. He was the kind of man that didn't let something like that go—ever. But she didn't care.

The room was deathly silent, and she wondered if the world wiggled around her because Carlos shook in fear or because she herself shook with her rage. Then she barreled out into the foyer, burst out of the glass double-doors into the sunlight and fresh air, and turned down the sidewalk.

Alex whirled around and stared at her, then quickly caught up and tried to match Leo's pace. "Whoa," she said, and Leo reached out to grab her by the hand. They trudged on for a few minutes, and Leo realized that Alex had tripped twice already in her platform heels, but she couldn't slow down. "Hey, what happened?" Alex asked, clutching one of Leo's arms with her other hand.

"What did he say to you?" Leo growled.

"Is that what you're mad about? It's nothing—"

"Tell me right now." She couldn't stop walking, couldn't quite swallow the burn back down her throat.

"Hey!" Alex called, and stopped dead. Her hand ripped out of Leo's.

Then Leo had to stop. She glared at the sidewalk, fuming with heavy breath, and reached a hand up to her forehead to find sweat running down her face. She blew out a giant breath and bent her head up to the sky.

"Calm down," Alex called, then stepped up toward her and a put a tentative hand on her shoulder. Leo turned to her, lost in the beauty of this girl having dressed herself in Leo's own tragedy. "He told me that if I needed any help, or wanted any extra money, I should talk to him." Alex's words were a whisper, angry in their own right and tinged with embarrassment.

"Fuck," Leo said, but she felt herself finally calming down. The information didn't surprise her. She reached out for Alex and pulled her into an embrace, feeling her tangible, thin form against her own, and buried her face into Alex's neck for just a few seconds. Then she pulled back and made sure Alex met her eyes. "If he ever talks to you again, tell him to fuck off. Tell him you want nothing to do with him and don't let him get to you."

Alex's half smile broke her heart. "You don't have to tell *me* that," she whispered.

Leo couldn't help but smile back, and then she took Alex's hand again, and they continued up the street. Her heart still pounded furiously; the realization of having just used her words on Carlos, of all people, hadn't quite sunken in yet.

"Move in with me," Alex said after a few more minutes.

Leo felt like she could have buckled right there on the sidewalk and cried. After all this—the last year, the last week, the past twenty minutes—Alex still fucking wanted her? She looked at the girl, feeling her nose burn with what could have become tears.

Alex's smile wavered a little, but she laughed to cover it up. "I mean, if you want to. There's no reason to stay in that house." No, there sure as shit wasn't. Not now that she'd be completely on her own in that carcass of a home. "And... I miss you."

If she gripped Alex's hand any tighter, she felt like she'd break it. Alex had moved into her own apartment six months ago, with the full blessing and first and last months' rent paid by her grandparents. They knew she had a decent job waiting tables downtown but had apparently been so thrilled with the idea that they supported the chance to only have to focus on their handicapped son from there on out.

Leo had spent the night there with her after the ambulance and coroner had left, but she'd never expected this offer. She took another deep breath.

"Okay."

"Really?" Alex immediately asked, like she'd expected Leo to tell her to fuck off, too.

Leo tried to suppress the grin cracking through her tension. But it won, and she laughed. "Yeah, really. It's a fucking great idea."

The sunny laughter flying from Alex's mouth was contagious, and Leo wondered what she'd said that was so funny. "Yeah," Alex said. "Yeah, it's the best idea." They stopped, and Alex turned toward her and threw her arms around Leo's neck. "I love you."

Leo couldn't help the sharp intake of breath. "I—" But she didn't get anything else out, because Alex grabbed the back of her head and kissed her in a way she'd almost forgotten.

The cotton of Alex's dress was soft, warm from her body, and Leo's hands found her waist, sliding toward her back, until she wrapped the girl in her arms and spread her hands beneath Alex's shoulder blades as though any minute this beautiful thing might fly away. She breathed in the smell of her, sighing, and a car honked briefly as it passed them on the road. Alex giggled, kissing her over and over, managing to push down the panic that fluttered just below the surface of Leo's joy.

21

LAST NIGHT, THE body of a woman in Sturgis, South Dakota, was found within her suburban home. Twenty-eight-year-old Tracy Daleheart, who worked at Pioneer Bank and Trust, lived with her husband right outside of downtown Sturgis. Police report that concerned neighbors heard a commotion in the early afternoon but didn't think anything of it until a loud scream, a crash, and the sounds of squealing tires filled the quiet, family neighborhood at around 8:00 p.m. When police arrived on the scene, they uncovered the gruesome sight of what they believe to be a murder. They are still investigating the crime and have told us that eye witnesses stated having seen two different vehicles fleeing the house shortly after the loud disturbance.

The driver of the first car is believed to be Mrs. Dale-heart's husband, Karl Daleheart, age thirty-one, and the second man to flee the scene may have been Jackson Warner, who had been employed by the Dalehearts for the last six months as a contracted landscaper. Mr. Daleheart drives a black 2004 Ford Expedition, and the second car was described as a tan-colored, four-door sedan, possibly with Nebraska license plates. Both Daleheart and Warner are being investigated as suspects, but police have yet to find any sign of either men or their vehicles.

22

TEN PEOPLE SAT gathered in the living room. The five others who had arrived with Brad were the same strange mix of people, none of whom Leo would have ever expected to spend time with each other. Randall was a tall, gangly man in his early forties with unframed glasses, a bleached mop of hair, and one of the longest noses Leo had ever seen. Despite the chill in the weather, he wore a pair of red, Hawaiian-themed swim trunks that looked far too big on him and a fleece zip-up jacket. Next to him on the largest couch, where Leo had sat before, were Tony and Don, who seemed maybe a few years older than Leo. They were very obviously twins, a trace of Italian showing through their dark eyes and hair, and Leo wondered for a moment whether or not they both held magic in their words and how exactly that would work.

On one of the benches was a man named Cameron, who had the most plain-looking face Leo had ever seen beneath the bushiest pair of dirty-brown eyebrows. He sat in a sort of slump, legs spread wide and arms resting on the cushions at his sides, and he stared out from beneath those eyebrows with his head hung low. It made her want to laugh every time she looked at him, and it was hard not to look at him because Leo couldn't take her eyes off the woman sitting next to him.

She'd been introduced as Kaylee, but so far, she hadn't said a word. Leo couldn't figure out how old she looked, because her face wavered in and out of what seemed like well-masked pain. When the girl glanced around at each person in turn, her eyes shone with excitement, but her mouth was permanently drawn in a thin line, and Leo didn't once see it curve up into anything even remotely resembling a smile. She was tiny, smaller than Leo, and must have been part Japanese. Her black hair hung down in a flat, shining curtain across the side of her face, and her eyes were almost round, a lighter brown color than Leo expected. Dressed all in black, Kaylee sat next to Cameron with her legs pulled up and crossed beneath her, her arms folded. Apparently, there weren't any rules against putting feet on the furniture, but Leo couldn't pull her knees up to her chest like she'd wanted, because someone had already done it first.

Karl sat in the same armchair with a beer in hand, and beside him, Leo shared the other couch with Bernadette, whose cup of tea had also been refreshed one more time. Leo felt too anxious to have accepted anything else to drink. The house had filled with laughter, the sounds of hugs and greetings, and just as Brad had introduced himself, Leo got a brief introduction from everybody except for Kaylee. Even Cameron had stared down at her briefly and given a stiff nod of acknowledgment, but Kaylee had just breezed past her without so much as skirting around Leo before slumping onto the bench. Now, with the house having calmed down and a warm silence soaking in, Leo wondered just what exactly she was about to be a part of and what exactly she might have to do.

"Everybody's got what they need?" Mirela asked. There were a few smiles, nods, and grumbles of agreement around the circle of chairs and couches in the living room. "Good." She walked from the kitchen and squeezed in beside Brad on the dark purple loveseat, handing him another beer and holding her own cup of steaming tea to her chest. Brad put his thick arm around her, and Leo thought they looked like the oddest couple. But their wide grins mirrored each other.

"Well, we've had a day, huh?" Brad asked with a grin. Randall let out a high-pitched giggle and scratched the side of his face, while the twins smirked and Cameron huffed a laugh. "But it went well. And our friends—" he shook an open hand toward Karl "—have made it up here." Brad shifted his bright smile toward Bernadette, who gave him a not-so-subtle wink.

"Yeah, why the hell's it been so long?" Don, or Tony, asked. The only thing that distinguished him from his brother was that he wore a blue shirt instead of a green one, and at that point, Leo couldn't find anything else to tell the difference. She reminded herself that she'd have to find *something,* if she ever ended up seeing them again. That thought made her almost too anxious, and she tried to forget about the future.

Karl, having taken Brad's mention of him as an opportunity for a long swig of beer, stopped himself short with a pop of his mouth coming off the bottle, and he licked the bubbles from his mustache. "I've just been really, really busy."

"You fucking liar," Cameron said in a deep voice, but the corner of his mouth turned up. Karl's sarcasm hadn't exactly been thinly masked.

"Yeah…" he started, then glanced at Leo and gestured toward her with his beer. "I've been helping this one get set up."

Leo felt like dying. He really had to call her out like that, paint her as some pathetic creature who needed all the help she could get? She glared at him for a few seconds with a hot face until the conversation continued.

"Leo." It was Randall, who leaned forward with his skinny elbows on his bony legs and smiled at her. "What are you doing now?"

The guy had never met her, never said two words to her beyond their immediate introduction and handshake, and his sudden, genuine interest caught her off guard. The thought, completely random and unnervingly unfamiliar, floated through her mind: Randall was just *nice*. That was it. Leo swallowed, wishing she'd accepted Mirela's offer of a glass of water, something, as her throat went dry under the sudden attention.

"Karl got me a job—"

"At the new Mexican restaurant downtown. The one on

Deland," Bernadette cut in.

Leo turned quickly to shoot Bernadette a questioning frown, realizing Karl was the only one sitting at the right angle to see her expression. Bernadette only smiled warmly at her, like she didn't even understand the surprise. Leo's glance at Karl only lasted a second, but the flare behind his eyes struck the immediate memory of the way he'd looked at her when she'd been arrested the other night—communicating the same intensity.

"Yeah," Leo added and turned again to force a smile at Randall. "I still don't know the city very well." She shrugged, and the responses of smiles, the lack of blank and confused faces, and the nod from Randall made her realize she actually sounded convincing. Without thinking about it, she glanced over at Kaylee, who met her gaze and made her eyes big beneath raised brows, as if asking what the fuck Leo wanted from her. Leo felt her face flush, but she looked back at Mirela and Brad cuddling on the couch and gave them a 'that's all' smile.

"Has he told you anything about us?" Brad asked.

"No," Leo said. She had the sudden feeling that if she were to say she'd heard the word 'Sleepwater' tossed around without an explanation, it would make her look even stupider than just saying she was completely clueless.

Brad barked out a laugh and leaned forward in his chair, resting his cheek against Mirela's arm. "This fucking guy," he said, grinning and pointing toward Karl like he couldn't hear them, "likes to pretend he has all kinds of secrets." Mirela butted his face with her shoulder, and he sat back, glancing up at the woman with a huge grin.

"So you haven't heard a thing about us?" Mirela asked after making a face at her partner. Leo shook her head.

"The blind leading the blind," Cameron muttered, but the corner of his mouth turned up.

"I guess," Leo said, knowing her face flushed again and feeling like an idiot.

"They're messing with you," Randall added, nodding at Leo like he understood exactly what she felt. "It happens every time we meet somebody new. And I'm sure there's more to you than just working at a restaurant."

If it had been anyone else but Randall saying this, Leo would have thought the guy was coming on to her. But the skin-and-bones look of him and his ridiculously cheesy smile beneath his glasses almost made her laugh at the idea. "Maybe," she told him, because even her working at a restaurant was a lie.

"See? She'll fit right in," Brad exclaimed, raising his beer in the air.

"Wait 'til the twins get at her," Cameron said. The twins, still silent, mirrored each other perfectly as they met Leo's gaze and smiled slowly out of the right side of their mouths.

"Give her a couple days, at least," Mirela cut in, shaking her head with a soft laugh. "You'll scare her off before she even gets to make a decision."

"A decision we can talk about later," Brad declared, then stood from the loveseat. "We've had a long day as it is. Anyone want another beer?" The twins raised their hands.

"Offer accepted," Karl said. "And bring Leo one, too."

When Leo looked at him, he gave her a single nod like

it was nothing before returning his attention to Brad in the kitchen. Apparently, she wasn't going to be doing any beat-spinning tonight, or Karl wouldn't have offered her drinks. Not that it was an offer anyways, but she was grateful for the fact that she didn't have to ask anyone for anything right then. Still, she couldn't help but wonder whether her discomfort was that obvious to everyone else, or if Karl just wanted her to loosen up a bit.

Mirela glanced around the room, taking note. "So, anybody not drinking tonight want to share a little bit about themselves?"

What the hell did that mean? Leo accepted her drink with a soft, "Thanks," when Brad delivered them around the room. She caught a quick memory of the first night she'd met Karl, when he'd asked her the kinds of questions she'd never wanted to answer, and she hoped he hadn't dragged her into some other kind of sobby therapy circle. Even if these people had the same kind of power in their words that she did, she wasn't about to sit patiently and listen to a bunch of bleeding heart whatever-the-fucks.

Randall leaned back in his chair and stretched his arms out wide, looking like a starving pterodactyl about to take flight. "I can start," he sighed.

"Great, I haven't eaten yet," one of the twins remarked. The other folded his arms and nodded.

"Yeah, make it something good, will ya?"

Randall ignored them, and Leo felt her stomach drop. She hoped this wasn't about to become some kind of gruesome description, some terrifying thing that usually made people sick to hear. She wasn't in the mood for being grossed out, especially if it was somebody talking about themselves.

As soon as Randall started talking, she realized she'd been expecting the wrong thing entirely. She ran her tongue over her lips, noticing a difference about the taste in her mouth. It took her a moment to recognize the flavor of garlic bread drenched in butter, and she immediately took a gulp of her beer. But the flavor returned. She smacked her lips, glancing around the room. She heard the sound of Randall's voice but couldn't quite make sense of the words. Most of the others just leaned back in their chairs, listening with their eyes on the floor, the wall, or, in Brad and Mirela's case, each other.

The garlic bread was replaced by some kind of bean soup—maybe lentils, because Leo thought she might have known what lentils were. The ghost of texture floated around in her mouth, but the flavor was there completely. She lifted a hand and licked her finger, but of course there was nothing there. Then she glanced at Karl, who grinned through his beard at her, laughing silently. She frowned back at him but couldn't keep her own smile away. Was Randall's beat actually making everybody taste food? A splash of wine followed the soup, warm and rich down the back of her throat.

"Fuck, come on!" Cameron shouted. The twins burst out laughing.

"Sorry," Randall said. It was the only word of his Leo could hear, but it didn't sound very genuine.

Next came the rich aftertaste of pesto, something that might or might not have been pasta, and then something sweet and creamy—maybe cream cheese, with a hint of chocolate. And then it was over.

This time, when Leo drank her beer, she tasted nothing but beer and wondered what the hell kind of use a beat like that could possibly provide. It took her a moment to realize the room was completely silent, and the others seemed to come out of their own haze of listening all at once.

"Every fucking time," Cameron grumbled, shaking his head and glaring at Randall.

Randall pushed his glasses back up on his nose, shrugging. "I like wine. It's not my fault you have such an unrefined palate." The twins mimed holding glasses, bumped their empty hands together, and offered Cameron an imaginary toast.

"Fuck off," he said.

"Why don't you go next, Cameron," Mirela said, hanging an arm around Brad's shoulders.

"Okay." He hadn't moved from his position on the couch, legs spread out wide in front of him with his head hung low as he looked out at everybody.

He spoke in such a low voice, Leo had to lean forward on her knees to hear what he said. She caught something about a boat, and then she thought she saw something move across the floor in front of the couch. Glancing at it, she didn't see anything, so she turned to look at Cameron again. But before she could focus on his moving mouth, something flashed across the window in the kitchen. It looked, from the corner of her eye, like a light had come on somewhere outside the house, but when she actually looked, the night around them still hung dark through the window. She started to wonder if anyone else had seen it, then completely forgot about the light when she thought she saw something shiny glinting on top of the mantelpiece. It could have been a reflection from one of the framed photos of Mirela and Brad, but...

She glanced at them and briefly noticed their confused faces before...

The sound of Cameron's voice caught her attention again. Something about a blue fish ... she'd never gone fishing. Her dad ... her dad was dead. She'd been to his funeral, surrounded by the flowers that— Were there any flowers growing outside the house?

When Cameron finally stopped speaking, it took her a moment to remember where she was and who was there with her. "Whoa," she whispered. It came out without her even realizing it, and she heard Brad clear his throat.

"Yeah," he said, shifting in the chair and putting a hand on Mirela's thigh. "That one takes some getting used to."

Leo looked at him, feeling the fog clear all the way and grateful to finally be getting her brain back. She hadn't felt anything like that before—completely unable to keep herself focused on any one thing, constantly distracted by the tangled webs of memory tucked away over time. She gulped down her beer.

"It's not that bad," Karl added with a smirk.

"Yeah, well, you can handle anything. Can't you, Superman?" Brad said. He ran a hand through his blazing red hair again and patted Mirela's leg a few times. "Why don't you follow up on that one, babycakes? Lighten the load."

Mirela laughed and finished the rest of her tea. "Why not?"

The minute the sound of Mirela's voice carried across the room, Leo felt herself breathing deeper than she could ever remember, like something had been squeezing her chest her whole life and she never even knew it. Now, it let her go. She sat back against the couch, feeling warmed and enveloped by the soft cushions. She sighed, realizing her breathing had slowed, and turned to chance a look at Bernadette. The woman turned to meet her gaze, gave her a warm, loving smile, and put her hand on Leo's arm, rubbing it up and down a few times before returning it contentedly to her lap. Leo had no issue accepting the comforting touch, wouldn't have minded if Bernadette had reached out to hug her.

She looked to Mirela. The woman's face glowed a healthy pink, her green eyes shining, face illuminated by a smile that didn't just exist in the lines of her mouth alone. Brad leaned his head on her shoulder, and she briefly glanced at him while she spoke. Leo thought she heard the words "love", "compassion", and "peace" thrown around in there somewhere, but she couldn't be sure. It could have just been the words floating around in her own head, sinking into her like a tonic meant to physically illicit such things. She glanced around the room, noting Karl with his eyes closed, Randall with his hand placed over his heart. The twins both leaned their heads back over the top of the couch, sighing in unison, and even Cameron had his head tilted upward, the way a person did when they relished the feel of the sun on their face. Leo had a sudden desire to reach out to each and every one of the strangers around her, tell them how connected she felt to them, how grateful she was to be in this place of open love. And then her eyes fell on Kaylee.

The tiny girl hadn't moved or spoken a single word since she'd arrived at the house. She sat in the same position, knees pulled up to her chin as she wrapped her arms around them and leaned against the armrest of the bench. Her face was the only one among them that didn't show outward signs of content, of feeling the encapsulating blanket of Mirela's powerful words. Kaylee seemed to be experiencing something else entirely, some deeply hidden pain that hadn't expressed itself before. She blinked, and a tear slid down her face, sparkling out against the contrast of her dark hair. Leo wanted to go to her, to put her arm around the girl and tell her that everything was okay. But then Kaylee looked up, right at Leo, and held her gaze for what seemed far longer than only a few seconds. Leo found herself completely unable to move, caught by the heavy plea behind those light brown eyes. Then Kaylee struggled to swallow, looked away, and Leo instantly became aware again of the silence of the room, the peace floating around everyone else.

"I always look forward to that," Bernadette said softly, and the spell was broken.

"I snagged the best woman in the world," Brad said, kissing Mirela on the temple.

"Couldn't let you get your hooks into anyone else, could I?" she replied.

"Thank you," Randall said. Then he gave another comical stretch and slapped his hands on his knees. "Well, I gotta be getting back home. You guys need a ride again?" he asked the twins.

"That would be cool."

"Sure." Randall stood. Mirela followed suit to embrace

him in a warm, scented hug, and he reached out to shake the hand Brad offered from his seat.

"Great work today, buddy," Brad called.

"I hope it worked. Let me know if you need anything else," Randall replied, then turned to address the rest of the room. "See you guys next week. Karl, Leo." He gave Leo a huge grin. "It's good to see you here."

"You too, Randall," Karl replied.

"Nice to meet you," Leo added. Before meeting Bernadette, she couldn't remember the last time she'd said those words, or even the last time she'd appreciated the sentiment behind them. She saw Karl look at her out of the corner of her eye, and she gave Randall a small smile.

"Later, suckers," one of the twins said. The other turned to Leo, pointed two fingers at his own eyes, then pointed at her. She suddenly remembered the beer in her hand and finished it.

23

"I FUCKING HATE this place," Leo whispered. They stood just inside the doorway of her father's house, staring at the living room and the ratty armchair that would always be empty.

Alex gave her hand a little squeeze. "I know."

Leo hadn't tried cleaning up a damn thing in the last five days. There was no point in picking up after a man who wasn't there anymore. The ashtray still overflowed with cigarette butts, blankets still scattered around the living room, and sometime during the day, the crumbling blinds on the living room window had fallen off the rod. They now hung to one side like a drooping eyelid. She'd slept in her own bed the last few nights, but she hadn't done a thing otherwise.

"Is there anything you want to grab in here?" Alex asked.

Leo felt Alex looking at her, but she couldn't bring herself to look back. She swallowed. "Just in my room."

They headed up the stairs, the creaking steps feeling ridiculously loud now. There was no mumble of TV noise from below, no sounds of her father propping his feet on the coffee table and maybe knocking a beer onto the floor. Just silence.

They stopped outside her door, and Alex took a deep breath. "Well, you already have boxes."

She had two, actually—one for her books and the other for a bunch of hats and scarves. She'd meant to grab herself a bookshelf when she started making money with Carlos, but somehow, it never seemed that important. It definitely wasn't now.

Alex walked to her closet and opened the sliding door to peer inside. "Do you want me to grab some more?" she asked.

"No," Leo said and joined her in the room. "I can leave most of these books. Everything else will fit."

"Sure." Alex turned around to take in the entire room.

Leo knew it was bare, hadn't given a shit about making it her own space. She'd always expected that when she moved out, she'd be able to start completely over, get a bunch of new stuff, and put some time into making it look decent. The timing of having that opportunity now threw her off.

"Hey," Alex said, walking to the other wall and wiping her hand over a giant Beatles poster. "Can we take this too?"

She spun around and raised her eyebrows, biting her lip in excitement.

"Sure." Leo laughed shortly, then pulled out the clothes on their hangers from her closet. There weren't very many, and she managed to fit most of them on top of the scarves and hats in the one box. Then she glanced at the shelf and took down the green shoebox. She hadn't touched it for years and really didn't know whether or not it was important enough to bring with her out of this shitty house—and the shitty life that came with it.

"What's that?" Alex asked.

Leo just held the box and looked down at it, not turning around. "Some old stuff," she muttered.

Alex flopped down on the mattress on the floor and patted it. "Bring it over here." Leo didn't move. "You don't want to show me?"

With a wincing frown, Leo turned around and looked at her. "You really wanna go through this shit?"

"It's a box, Leo. I'm not afraid of anything in there." Her smile said it better, her blue eyes sparkling as she laughed out the words.

Leo shrugged. "Okay." She walked over to the bed and sat down next to Alex, who crossed her legs and peered over them into Leo's hands. The lid came off, and Leo realized she'd been holding her breath. It was just a bunch of paper, things she knew she'd wanted to keep at one point or another. Nothing really important, and she'd forgotten about most of it. She took the first thing out and laughed.

"Is this from Ms. Bellini's class?" Alex asked, her grin widening.

Leo grabbed the few stapled-together papers and held them out for them to see. "Yup. First B I ever got. As in, my highest grade in middle school." Alex lifted her head back and laughed, then put her hand over her mouth like she was trying to pull the laughter out and squeeze it in a fist. "What? It took me a while."

"You got better, though," Alex said, playfully rubbing Leo's arm.

"Sort of." They laughed and sorted through the other things in the box. A poem about emotional freedom she'd stealthily ripped out of a poetry book in high school. A flier she'd picked up off the street for a concert she couldn't afford at the time. A hate note from Rachael Terrinson sophomore year.

"Why the hell did you keep this?" Alex asked, reading through it and grimacing at the expletives, which had been punctuated by annoyingly perfect hearts beneath each exclamation point.

"Because she pointed out all the best things about me," Leo said, flicking the paper in Alex's hands and almost tearing a hole through it. Alex cackled and shoved Leo's shoulder. Smiling, Leo remembered the day she'd gotten that gift from one of their high school's tennis players. She'd loved the fact that, by doing absolutely nothing and never talking to the girl, she'd managed to make Rachael hate her so much that writing about it and shoving it in her locker seemed the bitch's best option.

"What's this?" Alex said as she picked at the corner of a Polaroid at the bottom of the box.

"I don't—"

But Alex pulled it out, shaking the other papers off it, and held it with both hands. "Is this you?" she asked, rubbing a finger over the photograph.

Leo swallowed, then finally let herself look down at the picture. "And my mom, yeah," she whispered.

"She's beautiful." Alex put her hand on Leo's leg and looked up at her. "Do you remember very much about her?"

"Not really." She didn't want to talk about this, had never talked about it with anyone, but this was Alex. She still just couldn't say no if Alex wanted to hear about it. "I tried, but my dad got rid of all her pictures. Then I stopped imagining what it would be like if she ever came back to get me."

"That's rough, I know," Alex said with a sigh. Her own parents had died in a car accident when she was seven, which was how she came to live with her grandparents. Leo knew they shared that similar experience, but she doubted that Alex's pain had lasted nearly as long. She hadn't been left on purpose. "How old are you here?"

"Probably three." Leo tried really hard to hide the shaking in her voice, but it didn't work at all. Her palms turned clammy, and she had to try two times to swallow.

Alex looked up at her. "Hey," she said, her voice soft and full of concern now. "Hey, it's okay."

Leo bent over the box, hanging her head between her knees as she gripped it with both hands. "Can we just get this shit packed? I really want to get the fuck out of here." She opened her eyes and watched a tear drip onto the carpet.

"Okay," Alex said. She put a hand briefly on Leo's back and rubbed it. "Okay. Come here."

Leo didn't move. She watched the tears falling from her own face as she hung her head and didn't want to look up. She didn't want Alex to see her crying, not when their whole reason for being here was supposed to make them both happy. In a few hours, she'd be living with Alex, living with that gorgeous smile and those blue eyes and the girl who knew all her secrets. Especially now. So why was she fucking crying?

"Leo," Alex whispered. She slid the box out of Leo's lap, placing it on the floor, then kissed her on the cheek. "We'll get everything in the boxes." Her breath fluttered into Leo's ear, and she kissed her cheek and the corner of her mouth between words. Leo felt one of Alex's hands in her hair, the other sliding up her thigh.

Was that really going to work? Leo couldn't imagine that happening, couldn't get the image of her mother's smiling face in that picture out of her head. She hadn't expected any of that—she hadn't prepared for it.

Alex pushed Leo's shoulders back, forcing her to sit up. Then she pulled the bottom of her black dress up over her knees and slid one leg across Leo's lap, straddling her. Leo finally looked up, biting her lip. "I don't—"

"I promise," Alex added. She cupped Leo's face in her hands, staring at her with a mix of love and determination. "Shut up." Leo had no other choice but to obey.

She felt the tears running down her cheeks, one after the other in hot rivers as Alex kissed her. She still couldn't believe this girl still wanted her, still cared about her enough to try to ease her pain. Leo had never really told her how much Alex meant to her, how much she wished she could take back all the shitty things she'd said and all the stupid shit she'd done. Alex's fingers slid through her hair, giving a small tug, and Leo finally wrapped her arms around her and slid her closer into her own lap.

The sound of Alex's sighs only stopped briefly when she pulled back. Reaching down, she grabbed the bunched waist of her dress and lifted it up over her head. Her blond hair spilled down her chest, barely covering the twin points of her nipples, and she tossed the dress aside.

"God," Leo whispered. She was perfect.

Alex grabbed her face again and kissed her. Leo wondered if anybody else could ever have such gentle lips. She tasted some unknown sweetness on Alex's tongue, breathed in the milky taste of her hot breath, and pulled the girl to her with a hand on her back as she traced a finger around the curve of her breast. Could anyone ever be softer? She heard herself breathing hard, felt the ridges of Alex's ribs beneath the skin as she slid her hands down Alex's sides to her waist. And then she lost herself.

Alex let out a soft moan when Leo pulled her out of her lap and turned, laying her on the bed beneath her. Leo felt like her body had been set on fire, and she didn't think about anything except how beautiful this girl was, how much she loved the mole just beneath Alex's left breast on her ribcage—how much she wanted to stay here and never let go.

Starting just below her jaw, Leo's lips trailed down Alex's skin, over the curve of her collarbone, onto the thin skin above her breastbone. Alex's chest heaved. Leo moved lower, wishing she could touch every piece of skin in every place all at once. She lingered at the dip of Alex's belly, slid down to nibble the curve just inside her jutting hip bones. Alex raised her hips in response, in invitation, and Leo slid off the tiny piece of black lace, running her hands down from hip to thigh and up again. The harsh taste of her tears gave way to the sweet, salty taste of hot skin on her lips. She felt Alex's fingers in her hair again, felt the sharper tug of wanting, and she brought her mouth lower—hungry, burning. This was home, the only place she ever wanted to be.

It was an odd feeling to realize there was nobody downstairs to hear them, no reason to quiet Alex's sharp gasps. But it didn't stop her.

"Did you ever think we'd end up here?" Alex asked.

"In my bed?"

"Shut up. I mean here in time. Did you ever think we'd be moving in together?"

Leo lay on her side, staring at Alex's naked body as she lay on her back with her hands sprawled up over her head. Nothing else existed then, and she had to take a few seconds to think about the question. "I'd thought about it. Hoped for it. But after a while I started to think you'd never... forgive me." She swallowed, and instead of going down that road, she leaned over and kissed the middle of Alex's chest.

"For what?"

Leo hovered over her, then looked up into those blue eyes. "I really fucked up," she said.

"And then you fixed it." Alex propped the back of her head on her hands to get a better view. "If you're not convinced yet that I love you, I'm running out of ideas."

Leo slid a hand beneath Alex's back and kissed her

softly. "I'm convinced."

"Good." Alex sat up and grabbed Leo's face. "I'm gonna go get my grandparents' van. There's no way I'm carrying those boxes all the way to Pinnell."

"It's not that far."

"Right…" Alex stood from the bed and bent over to grab both her panties and the black dress.

Leo lay down again, propped her head on her hands, and just watched. She loved the way Alex's hands moved, like tiny, fluttering things with too much energy. The rest of her, though, seemed perfectly put together. Minus the sex hair, but Alex smoothed that down last.

"What?" she asked, turning toward Leo with a smile and a tiny shake of her head.

If Leo didn't know any better, she'd have thought the girl was embarrassed. "Nothing."

Alex looked her up and down, biting her lip. "I'll be back in, like, half an hour." And then she walked out.

Leo rolled onto her back and stared up at the ceiling. She felt like this whole thing was completely unreal, some dream she'd created to take herself out of the hell she'd lived in for so long. But the mattress was firm beneath her, the hot, sweaty smell of the last hour still in the air. There was no way it *wasn't* real.

What had she done, what right step did she finally take, to get here? For so long, she'd wanted nothing more than to get out of this place, to be able to lead some sort of normal life with somebody she actually cared about. Alex had been the only one, always, and now she finally had this chance. But she knew she didn't deserve it.

She'd said she'd fucked up, and Alex really thought things were better. She really thought Leo had 'fixed it', had cut out all the remaining decaying parts of her life in order to move on. And it wasn't fucking true. The night her father died, the night she'd spent with Alex in her new apartment—in the apartment that was about to become hers, too—she'd told Alex she was done selling. She'd told her she was done with Carlos, done with Pointera, done with hitting the streets. The whole fucking deal. She'd lied and said she'd stopped weeks before her father died. And she did it because she knew Alex would never have spent another second with her if she knew the truth.

Fuck. The truth. Leo sat up in bed and grabbed her head. The truth was that she was still a fucking dealer. The truth was that Carlos held so many things over her head, keeping her tied to him with his little puppet master's strings—like her father's debt. She'd paid it in full, but the fact that Carlos had given her the opportunity in the first place was something he wasn't ever going to release from his fucking claws. And she'd used her words on him.

"Fuck!" Leo screamed and scrambled from the bed, looking for her clothes. Why had she been so stupid, to pull some shit like that? Besides Alex, she'd never used her burning words on anyone she knew, anyone who had been to her house, anyone who kept tabs on how much she owed them. Anyone who knew her girlfriend. Carlos had had his beady fucking eyes on Alex the first day he'd seen her, in this house. The cocksucker had asked Alex to work for him, had played the good guy for whatever reason, and Leo just hadn't used her fucking dumb-ass brain.

She didn't doubt he'd absolutely believed every word she'd said to him—that she would kill him if he ever touched Alex, that he needed to remember she knew all his little drug ring secrets. But once it wore off? Once he realized that he'd believed her then, but didn't anymore, and all he could think about was how that little idiot of a girl had threatened him, would she be safe? Had she just dug herself a fucking hole with her stupidity?

He would come after her. It might take him a while to form some story of his own about what had happened, but he'd find her. He'd approach her about it, and while she wanted to think he liked her, that he held some soft spot for her in his heart, she knew he wasn't the kind of guy to take that type of threat lightly. She had essentially told him she would end him, even knowing he had more than half the town police in his back fucking pocket.

She almost ripped a hole through her shirt as she pulled it over her head, tripping on her black jeans when she shoved her feet through in panic. Even if she somehow managed to make good with him again, convince him she was loyal—and what reason could she possibly give now?—she'd still have to keep working for him. And Alex would find out. She couldn't hide that from her forever if they lived together, wouldn't be able to explain away the lie that had started it in the first place. And if she kept working for Carlos, he'd find out so fucking easily where they lived.

Leo gripped her hair, realizing she'd been pacing across her bedroom since she'd put on her clothes. Her foot tapped the green shoebox, skidding it briefly across the carpet. She froze for a minute, staring down at it, then picked it up and hurled it at the wall. The impact was far less than satisfying as the box bounced off the wall, shedding fluttering paper in all directions. She shouted with desperate energy, then shoved her feet into her sneakers. What the hell was she supposed to do?

She couldn't get Alex involved in this, and she couldn't fight off Carlos for very long. Maybe at all. She had, what? Twenty minutes until Alex came back? Tears ran hot down her face, almost unnoticed against the heat of her skin. She'd really, *really* fucked this up now, and the only thing she could think to do was run. Her hands shook as she knelt by the box of her clothes, throwing the top layer of crap behind her and dragging out her backpack. Another pair of pants, two shirts, her jean jacket. Shit, a hat. She crammed it all inside, then jumped to her closet and fumbled with the old pair of boots in the back corner. Ten thousand dollars. That was what she'd managed to save up in the last year, and it was all she had. Fuck, she couldn't do this. She had to.

Ripping the wad of bills out of the boot, Leo shoved it deep into her backpack, then slung that over her shoulder. Was this what it felt like to flee disaster? She'd lived in the eye of a dying storm her whole life, but she never ran away from it. What the hell was she doing? She wiped the sweat from her forehead and rushed out of the room, flew down the stairs and to the back door. It slammed shut behind her, making her flinch, but she only walked faster. Hurry. She had to hurry and get as far as she could before Alex got back. There was no other fucking way—she couldn't do anything else. She tried to convince herself that she'd never really wanted to be with Alex anyway, never wanted that danger of intimacy in the first place. She wouldn't even know what to do with it.

She was free.

Two blocks down, she felt the burn of cold air sticking in her chest, drying the tears on her face. It only briefly occurred to her that she buried her dad, buried her debt, buried the future she might have had, all in the same day.

24

AT APPROXIMATELY 2:15 a.m. on Wednesday morning, the Salco Genomics research facility just outside Decker, Montana experienced a series of large explosions that authorities suspect were the result of radical terrorist activity.

Salco Genomics was initially founded six years ago after entering a partnership with Laleopharm, who offered funds for the buildings' construction, equipment, and genetic research proposals. In CEO and Research Director David Aberrol's press release just this last spring, he mentioned that one of Salco Genomics' many projects included the chemical reworking of the commonly used drug Pointera, *which would prevent the potentially destructive side-effects some people experience on the medication. This is one project on which Laleopharm's research specialists specifically teamed up with the professionals at Salco Genomics, and the updated findings on this life-changing project were scheduled to be published within the next year.*

Now, with the recent attacks on the laboratory facilities in Decker, Aberrol says the forthcoming status reports, not to mention the much-anticipated results of the project, have been pushed back at least until 2027.

"We've put a lot of time, effort, and money into this project," Aberrol states, "and the majority of our data was lost in the explosions. We've got a team of professionals working as hard as they can to retrieve whatever remains, and Salco Genomics will be sure to update the public when we have a more thorough inventory of what was lost."

A few rumors have circulated over the last week about the facilities at Salco Genomics being targeted in response to a public view of the company's 'secret experiments'. This is completely unfounded, and Police Chief David Melbourn assures us these rumors will be put to rest.

"This attack was initiated by what Big Horn County Police believe is a small, local terrorist group," Chief Melbourn says. "These are left-wing radicals, who have unfortunately found some fantastical, illegitimate reason for targeting a research facility dedicated to improving medical technology and advancements for the betterment of humankind. The explosives were mostly home-made, using hardware manufactured in the US. We can only speculate as to the motives of this terrorist group, but we want to assure the residents of Big Horn County that these people are amateurs. They don't seem to know what they're doing, and they're sloppy."

Authorities also report having discovered what seems to be a symbol painted on one of the laboratory's exterior walls, depicting a vague double-helix design. This could, of course, be merely a product of passing vandalism, but police are asking anyone who has seen this symbol before to please step forward and contact the Big Horn County Police Department. Any information will help the capture and prosecution of this radical terrorist group.

25

IT TURNED OUT that Cameron and Kaylee lived there with Brad and Mirela, too. They obviously weren't all related, and Leo wondered just how many bedrooms they had in this house. After Randall and the twins left, Leo found herself craving a smoke, surprised by the fact that she hadn't even thought about it since they'd arrived. Bernadette stood to go with her, and they headed through the sliding glass doors off the kitchen.

Lights had been strung through the railing of the large porch running from the kitchen to open up onto the back of the house. Leo jumped when the lights flashed on after they opened the door, and Bernadette chuckled, following her out. "Motion sensors," she said.

"Yeah," was all Leo could say. She'd had a momentary

flashback of police lights cutting on in the darkness, illuminating her in a place she wasn't supposed to be. That had happened more than once, long ago, before she'd gotten used to avoiding the worst places to spend the night. But Bernadette's laughter had dissolved the momentary panic, and Leo found herself smiling despite the small embarrassment.

A metal table with an umbrella through the center and a scattering of chairs filled the expanse of the porch, and Leo moved past them to lean on the far railing. She couldn't see anything beyond the lights, but the rushing of the river was a lot louder out here. Bernadette came to stand next to her, and they lit their cigarettes together.

"How close is the river?" Leo asked. She didn't quite have to raise her voice above the sound, but her words sounded just a little swept away to her own ears.

"The house is built on the ravine," Bernadette explained, "and the porch hangs over it just a little. The river's just a couple yards away. It's not very big, but the sound really echoes in this valley." Leo nodded, exhaling the smoke and wondering how much of it was the mist of her breath in the chilly air. "They picked a good spot," Bernadette added.

That last remark sounded to Leo like it held the possibility of adding what the 'good spot' was actually for, but when she waited for Bernadette to continue, she realized that was all the woman was going to say. "Is this Sleepwater, then?" she asked.

"Some of it." Bernadette turned to look at her, flicking her cigarette over the railing. "What you saw tonight was just a tiny piece. You'll get to experience more of it. It just takes some time." She laughed. "Everyone seemed to like you, and that's a very good start."

Leo immediately thought of Kaylee and how Bernadette's statement didn't seem to really apply to everyone. "What did Mirela mean when she said I had to make a decision?" She'd thought these people would be the ones to make some decision, if there even was one to be made. That was why she was here, wasn't it? She didn't like the fact that she had so many questions rolling around in her brain, but this one seemed the most appropriate for the moment. If Karl had been out here with her instead of Bernadette, it might not have been so easy to ask.

"You'll know when that happens," the woman said, putting the cigarette to her lips again and propping her elbow up with the other crossed arm. "We can't bombard you with everything at once, now, can we?"

That answer infuriated Leo. She would much rather know exactly what was going on than be kept in the dark about whatever it was she was walking into. The first time she'd met Bernadette, they'd told her that her meeting would be a sort of interview. Why would she have to make some kind of decision during an interview? She was still here, though; they hadn't kicked her out or shown her anything but welcoming kindness, as uncomfortable as it had made her. Was that it? All she had to do was sit quietly, listen to the others spin a beat, and make small talk? She doubted it, but she didn't think anything else she could ask Bernadette about Sleepwater right now would make the woman answer her any differently.

The sound of the sliding doors opening from the kitchen were barely heard above the rumble of the river. Leo turned around and leaned back onto the railing, and Karl rounded the side of the house to join them.

"Brad's making sandwiches," he said with a grin. He fumbled with his lighter a few times before finally managing to light his own cigarette. Leo had never seen him act even remotely affected by the number of beers she'd seen him put away since she'd met him, not to mention just past the drunken line as he seemed to be now. He smiled even through a puff of his cigarette. "Anybody hungry?"

"Maybe not as hungry as Brad," Bernadette said, ashing her cigarette in the glass bowl on the table. "Or you, for that matter. But I haven't eaten yet." She walked toward him and patted him on the shoulder. "Having fun, are we?"

Karl giggled and backed away from her like her pats tickled him. Laughing, Bernadette gave him a wink and headed toward the kitchen door. Leo could only stare at Karl. She'd never seen him act like this—smiling, joking, friendly. He looked at her, the grin still on his face, and she tried to hit her smoke again to distract herself but realized it had already gone out.

"What?" he asked, raising his eyebrows at her.

"Nothing," she said, finding it impossible to hide a smile and wondering what the hell had gotten into her. Where was all this happiness coming from? She knew Mirela's beat had worn off, that it couldn't possibly last this long. She didn't even know what she was doing here, didn't even know these people or what they wanted from her. The ease in this house felt unnatural, and her first reaction had been thinking the whole thing was fake. But she felt something—some different part of her existing in a place where not all people were dirtbags and liars. Was this what it felt like to just be okay?

"You enjoy that?" Karl asked. He stuffed one of his hands into his pockets and swayed a bit to the side.

"Sure. You?" Was there something else she was supposed to say?

Karl chuckled. "Go eat something," he said, then leaned back and gazed up at the star-studded sky.

It didn't sound like a command, or a dismissal. It sounded like an invitation, which didn't make any sense to her. She stuck the rest of her dead cigarette into the bowl and headed back inside.

Brad certainly attempted to make sandwiches. He stood at the island in the kitchen, huddled over a stack of bread slices, all out of the bag, smothering mustard, mayonnaise, and peanut butter on a few of them. Leo also saw some cheese and meat slices next to a plate of poorly sliced onions. Mirela stood in the kitchen beside him and looked up when Leo walked back inside.

"You like peanut butter?" she asked with a grin.

"Not on a ham and cheese sandwich," Leo said, raising an eyebrow.

Brad laughed and slopped a bit more on his own piece of bread, not even looking up at her. "You don't know what you're missing," he said and took a long drink of the almost-empty beer in front of him.

"Here," Mirela said and handed Leo a plate with a sandwich that looked far less sloppy than whatever Brad attempted with his own creations. "No peanut butter."

"Thanks," Leo said, grabbing the plate. She got herself a glass of water and turned to find a seat in the living room.

Cameron and Kaylee sat next to each other on the bench, not looking at each other or speaking. Leo glanced at the girl and tried a flimsy smile. Kaylee met her gaze, stared back at her for a few seconds, then grabbed her own plate from off her lap, stood, and headed down the hallway toward the stairs. Leo found herself staring after her, wishing she could get some kind of reaction—other than Kaylee's avoidance—that went completely beyond simple apathy. Had she done something wrong?

"What the hell are you staring at?" Cameron asked from the couch, knocking Leo out of those thoughts.

"Nothing," Leo answered, looking at him. "I just—"

"Leave her alone, and you'll be just fine," he said. He voice was so low, a whisper of a growl, and he took a pointed bite of his own sandwich, staring at her as he chewed.

"Is she okay?" Leo asked.

"I said leave her alone."

Leo felt herself burning from the inside out with a mixture of embarrassment and anger. She hadn't even done anything. Kaylee had seen Leo looking at her more than once, had stared back but never said anything, and that somehow pushed the girl's buttons? She turned back toward the kitchen, but Brad and Mirela apparently hadn't heard Cameron's warning. The thought occurred to her that she should just go outside and eat on the porch, if it meant avoiding whatever bullshit game Cameron was playing.

"You can sit down and eat," he added, as if reading her thoughts. "I don't bite."

"What the fuck?" she asked, glaring at him. All she wanted to do was throw the fucking plate at his face now, sandwich and all.

A small smile cracked Cameron's lips. "I like you," he said, then took another bite.

Leo rolled her eyes and took a seat on the couch where she'd sat with Bernadette, putting the other couch between her and Cameron's bench just so she didn't feel like she sat next to him. The bathroom door opened in the hallway, and Bernadette came out, yawning.

"Sandwiches any good?" she asked, looking at Leo and Cameron.

"Always," Cameron said, and Leo nodded.

"Where's Kaylee?"

"She went to bed," Cameron answered.

Bernadette just nodded and headed to the kitchen, and Leo couldn't help but feel like she was missing something big here. What was up with that girl? Karl came back through the kitchen door, leaning heavily on the wall, and Brad looked up with a flashing grin.

"You look rough, buddy," he slurred.

"You're seeing things," Karl answered with a lopsided smile.

Brad handed him a gooey plate overflowing with what looked to Leo like the worst meal ever, and Karl grabbed himself a glass of water, too.

Everyone came to sit again in the living room with their late-night snacks, laughing and throwing jokes between mouthfuls of food. Leo set her empty plate on the coffee table and pulled her legs up toward her chest on the couch, which only made her think about Kaylee again. But she didn't care at that point.

"You enjoying yourself, Leo?" Mirela asked. She sat on the couch between Leo's couch and Cameron's bench, as Brad now lay sprawled out in the loveseat, obviously on the verge of passing out with his plate in his lap.

"Yeah," Leo said, glancing around the room. "Thanks for having me here," she added, biting her lip. She wanted so badly to get a minute with Karl to talk to him about what this whole thing was, but she knew now wasn't the time. His eyes hovered on her briefly before lazily swinging downward, and he buried his face in his glass of water, taking large, loud gulps.

"It was a great way for these guys to celebrate," Mirela said, laughing at Brad when he hiccupped. "We haven't seen Karl around here in a while."

"Too long," Brad grumbled, rubbing his head.

"I've had a lot going on," Karl said, wiping his mustache on his sleeve.

"Well, we've just been sitting on our asses here, man." Brad's words were thick with sarcasm, and he lolled his head to the side to look at Karl. "It's not like we have anything to do."

"Yeah, yeah, I know." Karl waved a large hand and leaned back in his chair. "I'm sorry, man. I'll be around more often."

"We know, Karl," Mirela said. "We're glad you're here. And hopefully you'll be spending more time with us too, Leo, huh?"

"Yeah, sure," Leo said. She didn't know when she'd be here again, if Karl ever wanted to bring her back, or what the hell they were even doing here besides hanging out to listen to beats and get drunk. Nobody had told her a goddamn thing yet, and being asked whether or not she'd come back felt like a question to which she should have known the answer. But she didn't.

"Good," Brad grumbled, pointing a limp finger in her direction. "We need you guys." He closed his eyes, and his head dropped back onto the armrest.

Leo laughed at that, at the fact that everyone knew why she was here except for her. "For what?" she asked, the words falling out with a chuckle. She looked at Bernadette and caught the tail end of a look the woman shared with Mirela. Bernadette didn't smile or look back at Leo.

There was a really long silence, Brad and Karl almost passed out in their seats and Mirela and Bernadette not meeting her gaze. Leo would have thought it was an awkward silence if she knew what the fuck was going on.

"'Night," Cameron said, shattering the pause. He stood abruptly from the bench and headed toward the hallway, where he walked into one of the rooms off the front hallway and closed the door.

"Yeah, bed," Karl added, making a few attempts at standing before he finally got out of the chair.

"Leo, I'll show you your room," Mirela said, and the smile she gave looked remarkably forced compared to the ease of her comfort up until that point.

"Okay. But what—"

"It's late," Bernadette said softly beside her, putting an arm on Leo's shoulder. "They've had a long day. We'll talk about everything later, okay?"

Leo took a moment to look at Bernadette, wanting to explode and scream at everyone that she had no idea what was going on. It didn't look like anyone had had a rough day, that anything was wrong here besides the fact that nobody would talk to her. She wasn't some child who could be dragged around and kept in the dark. What was this? She thought of Louis putting her up for display at the Purple Lion, charging ridiculous people even more ridiculous amounts of money to listen to her beats. Was this something like that? Were these people going to try to pimp her out? She realized she was clenching her fists, but she finally let out a big breath when Bernadette just nodded at her, urging her silently to just go with it.

"Sure," she said.

"Come on," Mirela said and headed toward the hallway. "Karl, you've got the same room upstairs," she added, and Karl waved his hand while he steadied himself with the other on the back of his chair.

Leo followed Mirela into the hallway, then turned behind her to walk up the flight of carpeted stairs. "I know this might seem a little strange," Mirela said, her hand on the railing and her skirts waving with every step up. Leo didn't know how she didn't trip on them. "There'll be plenty of time for us to explain everything. We just have a lot going on right now. Really, we're so glad to meet you, and Karl couldn't have brought you up here at a better time. I hope you don't hold the vagueness of everything right now against us." She turned back briefly to look at Leo, smiling with a tilt to her eyebrows that made her seem a little embarrassed.

It caught Leo completely by surprise. Mirela exuded patience, kindness, and love, reflected by the house and the way everyone had been so welcoming, not to mention the way she existed with a seemingly unshakable sense of confidence and self-ease. The expression on her face now, though, looked like an apology, and beyond all the joking thrown around through the night, Leo suddenly thought that maybe there was way more to this whole Sleepwater thing than just what she'd seen. She felt the odd sense of guilt over having been so angry just minutes before. She didn't like the way it felt in her stomach, and she blinked back her surprise.

"No, I don't," she replied and swallowed. "It's been a long time since I've felt this... okay around people." God, that sounded pathetic, but she couldn't think of anything else to say.

"Really?" Mirela said with a chuckle. Then she nodded and turned back to finish walking up the stairs. "That's good to hear."

In the upstairs hallway, they passed a bathroom on the left, and Leo peered into the doorway on her right. That, apparently, was Kaylee's room. The girl lay on the bed against the back wall, her small face made to look even smaller by a pair of huge, bright green headphones over her ears. She held a book, but Leo couldn't make out what it was before Kaylee looked up and gave her that same, unwavering stare. Leo couldn't tell if it was a threat, an invitation, a rebuke, or anything besides a blank-faced gaze.

"Right here," Mirela said, opening the door to a room just on the other side of the bathroom.

Leo passed her to walk inside and felt the lump grow in her throat. It was a small room, with just a twin bed in the corner, a desk, and a window in the far wall, but the bed was made with clean sheets and the room was warm. She hadn't seen a real bedroom in so long, and while she didn't at all mind sleeping on Karl's couch as she had been, the idea of having her own room—a real room, with a door that closed—was overwhelming.

"Thank you," she whispered.

"You bet. Good night." Mirela gave Leo another wide smile that seemed to have recovered its original energy, then turned and walked back down the stairs.

Leo turned to close the door behind her and caught sight of Kaylee through the open doorway on the opposite side of the hall. The girl still stared at her blankly and didn't move at all. Leo wanted to ask her what the fuck was wrong with her, but she didn't want to ruin the way the night had come to a close. She didn't think Kaylee would have said any-thing, anyways, even if Leo had stepped into the girl's room and ripped the headphones off her head. So she just closed the door silently, feeling like she'd stumbled into a dream when she pulled off her jeans and crawled into the bed.

26

TWO MONTHS, AND no one had been able to find her, if anyone was even looking. Leo wondered who might have tried harder—Carlos, because she'd threatened him, or Alex, because she'd broken all her promises. Still, it didn't matter. If anyone ever *did* catch up with her, the only thing she'd find would be more lies, more anger, more shit. She couldn't go back to any of that now. She was free in a way that scared her with all its possibility.

Being essentially homeless was its own world. It had its own rules, and already, she'd learned where she fit and where she didn't. She wasn't one of those drug-addled bums, scrambling for change, half-smoked cigarettes, or the last drop in an abandoned liquor bottle. No children hung by her side, gripping her by the hand and crying over their starving bellies. She hadn't lost her home or her job, and she refused to go to a shelter. No, she wasn't a stagnant homeless girl, with no prospects and nowhere to go. Leo could do anything she wanted, and she held in her hand something none of the others had been dealt—her words.

She'd rushed out of the city in the first three days, putting as much distance between her and her old life as she could. But after that, she moved from town to town however she wanted. It didn't take her long to realize that she didn't have to keep her burning words buried down in the pit of her stomach. Sure, Alex had loved them, but Leo didn't need anybody to fucking love them anymore. She didn't need anybody to love her, either.

The owners of convenience stores were all too easy; she could grab from then whatever she needed. The pedestrians on the street with the silver spoons up their asses proved a little more difficult. She'd talked one of them into emptying his wallet for her and almost shit herself when he returned three hours later to where she'd camped under the overpass, threatening to call the cops if she didn't hand the money back. It wasn't hard to use her words on him again, get him to fuck off, but she didn't make that mistake again. She kept moving.

People weren't friendly to the homeless, but Leo already knew that. She'd spent her fair share of time around junkies, homeless, and desperate, lost souls alike, and she knew how they operated. She'd never had a chance to see what the rest of the world thought of them, though, because she hadn't ever given a shit before. There was a hell of a whole different world out there, things she never thought existed before, and people who sometimes terrified her more than the useless sacks her dad used to have over at the house. But it didn't take her long to learn how to make this different world her own, how to navigate the grimy pits, the clubs and bars that served as hot-houses of desperation and longing, and the people within them.

She didn't miss her home, didn't miss the terrifying future she'd left behind, and she never once found herself wanting to go back.

27

WELCOME TO WWC, the World-Wide Conspiracy show on KWMR Springfield, Missouri. I'm Donald Havish, your host, and today with me I've got a very special guest I'm sure none of you listeners have ever heard of.

People are still talking about the small riot that broke out two weeks ago outside of Laleopharm's headquarters building in Minneapolis. Of course, this was only one of the company's central buildings, but it still got a lot of attention from the press in almost every state. For some reason, the majority of the American population still believe the conglomerate that is Laleopharm is a leader in both the Information Technology and the pharmaceutical industries, working diligently day and night to improve the quality of life, both in entertainment and medicine. How more people don't see this as a ridiculous combination of specialties, not to mention an attempt on Laleopharm's part to corner two incredibly lucrative and not-so-user-friendly markets, as it stands, I will never know. But that's America, isn't it?

Anyways, this little riot outside their building in Minneapolis was such a huge deal, because it turned into a case of police using brute force against just under a thousand rioters, which, as I said before, isn't very much. You'd think these people were standing outside the frickin' White House. Many of these rioters' names had been signed on a petition they planned to bring to the Supreme Court, of all places, to demand an investigation into the company's "nefarious and illegal dealings", as it states in the petition itself, with the following charges: human experimentation, mass mind control via pharmaceuticals, planned assassination of the president, and world domination. These are just my favorites on here, but there were others.

Yeah, I know, it sounds crazy, and these people probably are. If Laleopharm ever went to court with this, the petitioners would be crushed in no time flat. But that'll never happen, because first of all, a Supreme Court petition needs way more than eight hundred and seventy-seven signatures. Secondly, the legal system just doesn't work like that. These people obviously have no idea what they're doing, trying to go straight to the Supreme Court with something ludicrous like this, without going through any of the proper channels. I don't even know what proper channels there are for the kinds of claims these people are making, and I'll eat my chair right now if somebody can prove these guys even have a lawyer.

I'm getting ahead of myself. Now, everybody knows how I feel about Laleopharm and their partners in crime, mainly MindBlink and, surprisingly, the FDA. No, I'm not saying I condone what these idiots outside the Minneapolis building are doing, or that I agree with anything they claim. They're crazies. However, anybody bold enough to stand up to Laleopharm like this, however idiotic their methods, also catches my attention. I can't say I think there's mind-control, assassination, and world domination involved, but you guys have heard me wonder about this company's true intentions for the last few years. I've never been able to find a single positive thing about what they've done, what they plan to do, and who they partner with, even though I try as hard as I can to look at this from every angle. That, I just can't get past, so when I was contacted by this man sitting beside me here today, who told me an incredible story about the riot in Minneapolis, I invited him to be on the show with me. And you're gonna love this.

This is Darius Kimbell, and I'm not going to say where he's from, but he doesn't live in Illinois. Yes, I bought the man a plane ticket. Say hi, Darius.

Hello, Donald.

I was really, really intrigued by the email you sent me detailing your experience, and I've brought you on the show today so you can share this information with all my listeners. So, what is it you do for a living?

I'm a high school chemistry teacher.

Hear that, folks? This guy knows science, the scientific method, the difference between hypotheses, theories, and fact. A perfect guest for this show. And what were you doing in Minneapolis during the time of the riots?

I'd just gotten into town for a cousin's wedding, which was two days after the riots.

Well, your weekend certainly got a lot more entertaining than a wedding, didn't it?

Yeah, Donald, you could say that.

You laugh, but it's true. So, you told me you didn't take part in these riots...

That's right.

...but you spoke to people about them.

I did.

This is the part where you tell us, Darius.

Okay. Well, it was that Friday night, the day after the riots, and I was at a bar downtown. You know, family reunions. They can make a man want to drink. I'd only had two beers at this point, and they had the news playing on the TV, covering the events from the day before. I really couldn't believe what had happened, all the information they were giving. It was pretty ridiculous, the whole thing, but I hadn't heard about it yet because I'd spent the night before with my cousin and her fiancé's family. These rioters were crazy, and I couldn't help laughing.

I'll give it to you there, Darius.

Right. Anyways, this guy sitting a few spots down at the bar must have seen me laughing, because he asked me what I thought about the whole thing. I told him it was just people being stupid, as seems to happen more often than not these days, and he agreed with me. He bought me a shot, and we started talking about the whole Laleopharm thing, some of the crazy stuff MindBlink and Topper have come up with in the last few years. There are a lot of other people out there who don't agree with their businesses model.

That's one way of putting it.

Yeah, among other things. This guy, he said his name was Hank, seemed to agree with me on everything, and he told me that, even though the people who caused the riot were completely uninformed, there was still a lot of information about these companies that they'd kill to keep secret.

He said they'd kill people?

Yeah, and I don't think he was joking. He meant like seriously top-secret stuff.

Did he mention anything specific?

No, that's the thing. We were having a good time, and I joked around, asking what he meant by that. The guy got all serious and said there are some people, people like him, both these companies and the government would kill to keep a secret as well.

People like him?

Yeah, I thought he was just making a point about all the stupid people out there. I'm really not much into conspiracy theories myself, though I've streamed some of your podcasts and I love the way you approach things. Anyways, I asked him what he meant by people like him, and you know what he told me? He said there were people out there who could change you with their words, make you think, hear, see, or feel things that aren't there. I started to get a little freaked out by how intense the guy was, but then he said he'd prove it. He wasn't drunk. I hadn't seen him order anything but diet coke the whole time, and I can definitely handle more than three beers and a shot. I know I wasn't seeing things.

Anyways, before I could leave him right there and forget about the whole thing, he opened his mouth and started talking. I swear to God, it was the weirdest thing. I heard this buzzing, kind of far away, like a helicopter somewhere. I tried to listen to what he was saying, but the sound got louder. I looked around, trying to see if anyone else heard it. Maybe a few people stepped outside, but nobody noticed anything. The sound wouldn't go away, and I realized I was the only one who heard it. Then all of a sudden, I swear, I thought there was a plane flying right above the frickin bar. I heard more than one helicopter, the sounds of gunfire. I fell off my stool at one point, thinking something had exploded right outside. Then, when I stood up, the man had stopped talking and the sounds had all gone away.

I mean, I was embarrassed as all hell. I threw myself on the floor with my hands over my head when nobody else had even moved from their seats. A few people were staring at me, and the bartender asked if I was okay. This guy who called himself Hank, he just ordered me another drink and stared at me.

So, did it occur to you that maybe you'd hallucinated? That something happened and you thought you heard sounds?

Oh, yeah, that was the first thing that went through my mind. I was pretty terrified, and, Donald, I normally don't doubt myself like that, but I thought I'd gone crazy. I just sat there, trying to decide whether or not to get out of the bar and go to a hospital or something, and the guy just stared at me. Then he asked me, "You heard planes and gunfire, didn't you?"

He asked you that, specifically?

Yes. And then I asked the bartender if I'd said anything before I fell over, like maybe this Hank guy had heard me talking about what I'd heard and I didn't remember saying anything. The bartender gave me a weird look but told me I just ducked a lot and then tried to bury myself under the stools.

Why don't you tell everybody what you think happened?

Well, I think the guy was right. I thought about this a lot before I emailed you, Donald, and I couldn't come up with any better answer. I think this guy actually made me hear those sounds from whatever it was he'd said, and he knew exactly what it would do to me. So I stayed. And he told me that he wasn't the only person who could do that, that there are a whole bunch of people, all over the country, who can do the same thing with their words.

Did he say what they're called?

No, I don't think they're called anything. I've never experienced anything like this. But I believed him, and I asked him why he was showing me this and what I was supposed to do with it all.

What did he say?

He just told me somebody needed to know. And then he left.

Wow. What did you do?

I stayed at the bar and got hammered, that's what I did.

Did you ever see this Hank guy again?

No. Haven't heard from him or met anybody else who could do this weird thing. I know it might sound impossible, but there was something even weirder about it.

What's that?

When the guy handed me that last shot, I saw the tattoo on his forearm. It was a blue double helix.

So, I already know the answer to my own question, and I'm sure most of my listeners do, too. But just in case somebody new is listening, trying to open their mind and enter the underworld of secret knowledge here, why was that the weirdest part?

Well, remember that bombing of the genetics research lab, the one seven months ago that the media kept saying was a radical terrorist attack?

Yes, the Salco Genomics building.

Right. Well, all the news stations kept talking about the symbol that was painted on the outside of the buildings after the explosion. The double helix.

There it is, folks! This is why this story has grabbed my

attention, and why I have this insightful, observant man on the show today. He made the connections, and he came to me. Do you think this Hank guy had anything to do with the bombing of the Salco Genomics research facility?

I don't know. I don't know, Donald, that's why I emailed you. Maybe, maybe not, but I couldn't not talk to anybody about this. The whole thing with this guy, the noises I heard, his tattoo, the Salco Genomics attacks, I wasn't sure. But then, once I got home from Minneapolis and I heard even more about the riots outside Laleopharm's building, something clicked. It feels like it's connected, but I have no way of figuring out how.

Part Two

28

LEO WOKE UP to the sunlight shining on her face through the window blinds. She sat up quickly, throwing the quilt off and taking a moment to orient herself. The door was still closed, her backpack untouched on the floor, and she was alone. In a room. In a house, where other people slept and didn't expect anything of her.

She pulled on her jeans and slowly opened the door, looking out into the hallway. Kaylee's door was closed, but she heard conversation coming from downstairs. Walking toward the bathroom, she reached out for the doorknob and almost jumped against the opposite wall when the door was thrown open.

Kaylee stood there in the bathroom, glaring out at Leo

like she'd known she would be there. She just stared at her, and as soon as Leo opened her mouth to say something, the girl brushed past her in a blur of black and headed down the stairs.

"What?" Leo whispered. She blinked and shut the bathroom door behind her, wondering what the hell the girl's problem was. She hadn't said two words to her, had figured that Kaylee had just pegged her as the target of whatever bullshit anger she kept locked behind that curtain of dark hair. Part of Leo wished the girl wasn't there, that she could exist in the house without constantly feeling like an ass for no reason, and the other half of her wanted to make Kaylee say something, anything, that would make her feel like a real person.

Walking downstairs, she was greeted with a warm smile from Mirela and a chorus of good mornings from almost everyone else. "How did you sleep?" Mirela asked, working on the stove with something that smelled like eggs and bacon.

"Great, actually. Thanks," Leo said. She had to admit that breakfast smelled better than anything Karl had cooked for her so far, though she didn't think she'd find the guts to tell him that. Then she saw him, lying spread out on the largest couch with an arm flung over his eyes. "You look rough," she said, and he only barely moved his arm so he could roll his eyes toward her briefly.

"Just waking up," he grunted. His voice sounded like gravel under boots, and Leo thought he might not have slept at all. Not with the way he'd been throwing back beers the night before.

"I've got something for that," Mirela said from the kitchen. "A good breakfast, and a little something I created myself. Most of it's from the garden." Leo glanced at her, realizing that maybe all the weird-looking plants hanging from the ceiling had some kind of useful purpose. "Coffee's ready, Leo," she added.

"Thanks." Leo grabbed a mug and made herself a cup, then turned to find Cameron hovering behind her.

"What did you do to her?" he said in a low voice.

Leo blinked. "Who?" She glanced quickly behind him to see Kaylee sitting on the padded bench in the living room, a plate of eggs in her lap, staring at her again. "Kaylee?" Cameron just glared at her. "I didn't do anything to her." What the hell was up with these two?

"Good," he said, then brushed past her to pour himself a cup of coffee.

She found herself wondering why she put up with this shit, and she couldn't help herself. "What the hell's your problem?" she hissed at him, watching him stir his drink and take a calm, collected sip.

"I'm not the one with the problem," Cameron replied, turning around slowly and briefing flicking his eyes up to meet hers. Then he walked past her and headed toward Kaylee on the bench.

"What did I—"

"I smell bacon!" Brad's voice boomed from the stairwell, cutting her off. He rounded the corner with a dopey smile, passing Leo to sweep Mirela up in his arms and kiss her head. Mirela swatted him away with the spatula, and Leo found her glare on Cameron's back distracted. Whatever it was with that mopey, rude, pissed-off duo would either quit eventually, or she'd make it.

She grabbed herself a plate of food, taking it with her to the armchair Karl had claimed the night before. She almost burst out laughing when Mirela brought Karl a thick, frothing green glass of something that smelled like it couldn't possibly help his hangover. He glanced at Mirela with a mixture of pleading and disgust, and she only patted him on the head.

"Bottoms up," she told him.

"I blame you," Karl said, pointing at Brad, who only shrugged and took a quick bite out of a piece of crispy bacon.

"Where's Bernadette?" Leo asked.

"She left early this morning," Mirela said, grabbing herself breakfast and joining them. "She had some work to do, I'm sure."

"What does she do?" Leo realized she'd never actually figured that out, either. For that matter, she didn't know what any of them actually did. That thought alone made her pause, and she stared down at her place.

"All kinds of things," Mirela answered, but the look Leo got from Karl, who slowly sat up on the couch, told her it was the only answer she would get right now.

Karl drove her back into town, and they spent most of it in silence. Leo still couldn't understand why the hell he'd taken her to that house in the first place. It couldn't possibly have been just so she could hear other people spinning beats, however eye-opening it had been, but she hadn't learned anything else.

"That wasn't it, was it?" she asked him after finally working up the nerve to get it out.

Karl leaned on his elbow against the driver's door, flicking his cigarette out the open window with his other wrist flopped casually over the steering wheel. His sunglasses were dark, but she caught the flicker of his eyes behind them. "What?"

Mirela's hangover cocktail had either cured him or made him worse. She couldn't tell, but he was back to his normal, quiet, stoic self. Did it really take getting smashed to make the guy open the fuck up?

"The whole Sleepwater thing," she said, staring at him. He didn't answer. "Seriously. You guys made it sound like it would be the answer to all my questions, and I only have a million more. It's great, sitting around and listening to everybody spin their own beats, fine. But that happens at the Purple Lion anyways. I know where to find other people who can do this, so what the hell's so important about this Sleepwater? You haven't told me anything." She surprised herself with the outburst, realizing she'd been thinking this for the last twenty-four hours and wanting to shout at somebody. It felt way out of line at Mirela and Brad's house, but now, in the car, alone with Karl, there weren't any kind smiles or light-hearted joking to make her hold her tongue. Only Karl's fucking silence, his lack of emotion, and that pissed her off even more.

"I'm not the right person to answer those questions," he said. He didn't look at her, didn't offer any kind of explanation. He only stared out at the road, dragging on his cigarette like he owned the world and didn't give a shit about anything else.

She glared at him, feeling her face flush. "Why not?" Was he planning on dragging her around in circles forever, never explaining anything and waiting for her to stumble onto some solution for the both of them?

Karl cleared his throat. "Because I made a promise."

"Oh, so it *is* like a cult. Some kind of secret society that I have to kill a cat to get into? You can tell me it exists, but you can't talk about it, right? What the fuck is so scary about this?" Her face burned in frustration, everything pent-up and targeted toward the man who had plucked her off the street, from a life she'd preferred over what she'd left behind, and shoved her into a place she didn't fit without caring about how much it beat her up. What the fuck was she doing with this guy? "Tell me!"

They were lucky nobody else was on the road, because Karl slammed on the breaks. Leo jerked against her seatbelt, her own cigarette flying from her fingers onto the station wagon floor. She picked it up, cursing, then glanced out the front and back windshields, looking for any cars sure to be flying right at them. "What the fuck are you doing?" she asked. "You can't just stop on the highway."

"No more questions about this, Leo," Karl growled, snatching his sunglasses from his face. His eyes burned from within his flushed face, and Leo forgot entirely about the cigarette she'd just picked up.

She swallowed. There were a lot of sides to Karl she hadn't seen before, but this was what she'd seen behind his eyes all along—the wild, furious, all-knowing mixture of terror and determination that he now didn't try in any way to hold back.

"You know so fucking little about what's going on, and I can't blame you for that, knowing where you come from." His voice was steady, eerily so, but his eyes never left hers, and she couldn't tell if he'd blinked at all. "But the things I've done, the promises I've made, are more important than you can even imagine, and I'm not going back on my word just to make you feel better." They stared at each other for what felt like eternity, and then, calm and in charge once again, he put the sunglasses back on his face and started back down the highway.

It was only a few minutes until he spoke again. "I'm not doing this to piss you off, Leo. You'll figure everything out when you're supposed to." He grabbed his pack of cigarettes and pulled one out with his teeth.

Leo could only glare out the front windshield with her arms folded, feeling terribly childish and fed up, even though she knew she couldn't go back to the life she'd led before this. "Fuck you," she muttered.

Karl glanced up to check through the rear-view mirror, lighting his cigarette with one hand. With it hanging from his lips, he said, "Yeah, fuck me."

She hadn't expected to feel any more comfortable when they got back to his place, any less pissed off. But she didn't expect to find, when they pulled into the gravel lot in front of Karl's garage, that her anger was suddenly the least of her worries.

The thin, metal front door had been ripped from its hinges and crumpled, like a giant robot had stepped on it, lying feet away from the gaping hole of the doorway. Karl sat in the driver's seat for a few seconds, like he needed the extra time to make sure it was real, before he pushed the door open and grumbled, "Wait here." He didn't, however, take the time to turn off the engine.

"No fucking way," Leo answered and stepped out of the old station wagon.

"I said wait," Karl called, not bothering to turn back to her. "We don't know who's in there."

Leo glanced around the empty lot, taking in the site of the mound of gravel that had been pushed up in a half-circle, probably left by whatever car had sped away. "It doesn't look like anyone's still here," she said quietly. It made sense that whoever had been here was gone now, but she didn't quite find enough courage to say it any louder. No way was she just going to sit in the car with her thumb up her ass without getting a look at what had happened.

Karl stood next to the doorway, peering in at an angle. He slapped his hand around the inside wall, and she heard the switch flip, but the lights didn't come on. It was nearly sunset, and the ratty blinds above the back window just barely gave them enough light to see by. Karl just gave her one expressionless glance, then took a slow step inside. Leo followed and froze.

The place had been trashed. The small, round table had had its remaining three legs broken off. The sink had been pulled down from the wall, and a thin stream of water still arced out from the pipes. Clumps of foam covered almost everything, having been ripped free from the giant gash running the length of the brown couch's cushions. The few boxes of things Karl owned had been torn apart, the contents strewn everywhere. Someone had taken a knife to the mattress in the back, its surface now covered with holes, like open sores, bursting with the filling beneath. His clothes had been cut, too, and lay in a heap by the bed.

Karl took one step after the other into the small room of his home, his eyes roaming across the damage and taking it all in with very little reaction. Leo took a step forward, then immediately withdrew her foot as she heard the crunch of glass. She looked up and saw that even the single light in the ceiling had been shattered. Who the fuck had been so angry they had to smash the lightbulb, too?

"Are you missing anything?" she asked. It was the only thing she could think of to break the sad, crushing silence. It looked like everything was still here, but Karl owned so few things anyway.

He stood over the broken end table and lifted one side, stooping to move aside the broken pieces of glass, metal, wood, and whatever had been on the table before. He picked up a wooden picture frame, dropping the table, then quickly opened the back of the frame and removed the photograph. A piece of broken glass fell out of the frame to join the ruin on the floor. Karl carefully folded the picture and stuffed it in the back pocket of his jeans, then sauntered out of the garage again. "We need to go," he said, breezing past her without so much as a glance.

"What?" she said, turning on her heel. "Go where? Who the fuck did this?"

"Come on," he growled. He ducked down into the car, and she barely had a chance to close her own door before he spun out of the gravel lot.

"Karl, what's going on?" she asked, feeling her face flush. Her first reaction had been that someone had finally found her. After all this time, she'd slipped up in covering her tracks, and they'd actually come looking for her. She wanted him to tell her he didn't know, so she at least could know what to expect. "Is somebody after you?" She surprised herself by how angry she sounded at him, by how easy it was to make it about his problems.

"That was a warning." His voice was flat, low, stuffed deep back in his throat like if he changed the way he spoke, some nameless thing would come pouring out.

"A warning about—"

"I said no more fucking questions, Leo. One more, and I swear I'll leave you on the side of the road, and I won't come back." He didn't yell at her, didn't slam on the brakes again to stare her down. Leo swallowed and glanced at his hands on the steering wheel, which he gripped so tightly she thought he'd rip the thing in two at any minute. His voice had taken on that all-knowing, level-headed, patient ferocity she'd heard the morning she'd made him kiss her with her words, and she suddenly felt like the last week hadn't even happened. That resolve of his terrified her, and she'd forgotten about it after all the things he'd done for her, after she'd seen a different side to him at the Sleepwater house. "We're going to Bernadette's."

What the fuck could Bernadette do? Leo wanted to ask that next, but she didn't think Karl's words were a threat. He was absolutely serious, and she suddenly felt herself clutching at the fact that she didn't want to be left … anywhere.

So she shut up.

She turned her head when Karl rolled her window down, and when she looked at him, he'd pulled out his lighter to hold it out for her. Why the fuck not? She took the lighter and lit her own cigarette, then handed it back so he could do the same. As the sun set over the mountains, they drove to the other side of town in silence.

The street lamps in Bernadette's neighborhood seemed almost too bright, the yellow-white glow forcing Leo to look around for shadows. The garage light was on at Bernadette's, illuminating a paper bag with what looked like an open carton of broken eggs and a few cans of food strewn hastily in the driveway. All the other lights inside were on too, and the front door was wide open. Karl had only slowed down briefly in front of the house, took one look at it through Leo's window, then sped up again down the street. "Fuck," he said through his cigarette.

Leo found herself turning back in her seat, trying to get a better look at the house. She didn't see anyone inside, couldn't tell if the place had been hit just like Karl's, but he was gunning down the residential street too fast for her to even know for sure. "She could still be in there," she said quietly, then turned around again to gauge his reaction.

The sharp, jerky shake of Karl's head could have been a twitch for how much he moved. "We're looking for a bright red Jeep," he said, turning the corner onto another residential street with a short squeal of tires.

Leo realized she clutched the armrest on the door, positive the station wagon would just fall apart at any minute if he didn't slow down. But no matter what she said, she realized, Karl wouldn't listen to her. She winced when they jumped over a speed bump, then shot him a hateful glance.

"Don't look at me! Look for the fucking Jeep," he growled, and the seriousness of the situation suddenly hit her.

She leaned forward to look out the windshield, feeling dizzy as the street lights whizzed by and wondering how the fuck he expected her to see anything going this fast. She heard a few dogs barking in the neighborhood and tried to keep from blinking as she scanned the right side of the road. They barreled out of the suburban neighborhood and onto a frontage road, where the street lights were suddenly far fewer. A few restaurants were scattered here and there beside the road, but mostly it was just open space ahead of them. Where was he going? How did he know where to look in the first place?

"There! Fuck, there," she yelled, pointing ahead where she saw the back end of a red Jeep, its front tires just turned off the bend in the road and resting in the small ditch. She almost puked when Karl pulled the station wagon to a jolting halt behind the Jeep. She thought he was going to break the door off the side of his car as he fumbled to get it open, then he rushed toward the driver's side of the Jeep, almost tripping in the ditch.

Leo watched from her seat in the station wagon, too stunned to move. Karl opened the Jeep's door, and when the dome light turned on, she saw a plume of smoke trailing out. She thought at first that the car had caught fire, but then she heard Karl's sharp bark of laughter, immediately cut off by him saying, "Shit." He leaned into the car, then struggled back out with a mostly limp Bernadette in his arms. Her head wobbled on her shoulders, but she managed enough strength to keep the lit cigarette between her fingers.

"Leo, open the back door," Karl yelled.

She scrambled out of the car and yanked the back door open. Karl stooped to lay Bernadette in the back seat, and Leo just stood there, staring. The right side of Bernadette's face was covered in blood, dripping down her neck and onto her chest from a horrifying gash in her head. Bernadette half raised herself up and offered Leo a weak smile. "I thought this would be my last cigarette," she choked out, taking a weak drag. "But I guess I'll need to buy some more, now." Her head swung low and then back up again, and Leo could only blink. What the fuck had happened?

"Come on," Karl shouted, and it brought Leo back to her senses. Both doors slammed shut at the same time, and they sped off again down the frontage road, eventually coming back to the highway.

Leo glanced around, realizing they'd already made this drive today in the opposite direction. "Are we going back to Brad and Mirela's?" she asked.

Karl glanced at Bernadette through the rear-view mirror, then nodded toward Leo. "Take her smoke before she burns herself," he said in a low voice.

She glanced back toward Bernadette, whose eyes drooped as her head lolled. But the older woman still had some of her wits about her, and with a slow smile, she held her cigarette out for Leo to take. This was weird. Leo took a drag on her cigarette, wondering what the hell was going on.

"No, toss it," Karl said. The tone of his voice left no room for her to question him, so she flicked the half-smoked cigarette out the window.

Leaning back in her seat, she turned to look at him, trying to figure out if there was any way to form the question that wouldn't piss him off again. She opened her mouth, and then Karl started talking.

Leo felt herself sinking into the chair, the dizzying lights of the highway passing them by in a blur. She was vaguely aware of the large sigh coming from the back seat, and she swallowed. It was so hard to keep her eyes open, and she drifted into the heavy warmth of whatever Karl's words happened to be. Her last thought before she stopped thinking altogether was that if she'd still held that cigarette in her hand, she wouldn't have been able to keep herself from dropping it.

29

SHE WOKE UP with a start, wondering where the hell she was. Jolting upright, Leo cursed when the seatbelt cut into her chest, and she realized she was still in Karl's station wagon. He'd fucking left her there.

Bernadette wasn't in the car either, though she'd left behind a smear of blood on the already dirty back seat. Leo looked up through the windshield and realized they were back at the house in the woods—at Mirela and Brad's. Everything came back to her then. Karl had obviously used his words for Bernadette, who had looked pretty badly beaten up just in the few minutes Leo had seen her. But the bastard hadn't thought to warn her, to tell her what he was going to do. Leo had been in the car, so of course she'd been affected too. Damn, though, it was a useful beat to have.

The lights were on in the house, and when Leo got out of the car, she noticed a few more cars parked outside in the gravel. It wasn't quite dark outside, but it would be in a few hours. She got out of the car and stormed up the stairs to the front door, hoping for Bernadette's sake that everything was okay and pissed as all hell at Karl. He'd used his words on her and didn't even bother to wake her up after she'd passed out.

She walked into something she hadn't expected to see in that house. Bernadette was laid out on one of the couches, Mirela kneeling beside her with what looked like leftovers from bandaging her head. Karl, Brad, and Randall stood by the island in the kitchen, arguing over something. Randall had obviously returned with the twins, because Tony and Don stood just behind Mirela, trying to get a better look at Bernadette. And Kaylee and Cameron just sat on their bench, like fucking always, watching everyone silently.

"Do you think it was him, though?" Brad asked. Leo rounded the corner to get a better look at the group huddled there. Brad clutched his cell phone, and she hadn't seen him look as angry as he did then.

"No. I don't know," Karl answered and put his fist on the kitchen island.

"He's made threats before," Randall said. "Someone could have told him. You know we can't get to everyone before they start talking."

What were they talking about? Did they know who had ransacked Karl's house and then obviously gotten to Bernadette? "Hey," she said, but nobody paid her any attention. Flustered, she walked toward Bernadette on the couch. The woman was asleep, hopefully, but the bandages around her head were already soaked through with crimson. "Is she okay?" Leo asked.

"Oh, Leo, hi," Mirela said, distracted by her charge. "Can you get me a jar from the kitchen? It's red, about this big, with a white flower on the lid."

"Sure." What the hell would flowers do for an injury like that? But she walked into the kitchen, passing the twins, who gave her a second's glance before staring again in concern at the unconscious Bernadette.

"We already did that," Randall said again, carrying on the conversation in the kitchen.

"What's going on?" Leo asked, glaring at Karl. He seemed not to even hear her. Nobody seemed to hear her.

"That was last week," Brad added. "He had to have heard about that. It's still all over the news."

Leo walked to the sink, glancing around at the shelves until she found the red jar Mirela had requested. Unscrewing the lid, she took a quick whiff of something that smelled like no one would ever want to use it. Making a face, she put the lid back on and started back through the kitchen.

"No, I don't think it's him," Karl said. "He wouldn't do that. I've been over the terms with him. He and I both knew what was at stake. It's not him."

"Well, whoever it is," Brad added, "things are going to get really dangerous now. We might have to move to the houses in Colorado or Utah."

"Let's not get ahead of ourselves," Karl said, putting a hand to his head. "I can at least talk to him, see if he knows anything—"

"But if somebody already knows how to find you and Bernadette, it's only a matter of time until they find us," Randall put in, adjusting his glasses with a shaking hand. "Do we have enough time to wait around and figure that out?"

What the hell were they talking about? Leo felt a cold ball of fear fall into her stomach, realizing she had no idea what was really going on, what she'd really gotten herself into by being here with these people. If whoever was trying to find them actually did, would 'they' come for her, too?

"Hey, can somebody tell me what's going on?" she asked, trying to lift her voice above the already strained arguing in the room.

Brad briefly glanced at her. "Leo, just... go help Mirela."

What? She couldn't help herself. Her hands flew up in confusion, the red jar tumbling from her grasp, and she only glanced at it. It was plastic; it wasn't going to break, anyways. "Yeah, well, I was—"

"We can talk about this later," Karl growled, and Randall turned around quickly just to give her a look.

That was it. She was in this house, trying to help with something she didn't understand, and nobody would give her the fucking time of day. What was she even doing here? What kind of shit had they pulled her into? The words burned up through her throat before she could stop them, and she didn't even try.

"No, fuck you," she yelled. She was vaguely aware of everyone else in the living room turning their gazes to her, too. "Listen to me! I've been dragged into this shit, Bernadette's hurt, your place has been torn apart, and you guys are talking about people coming after us. I'm sick of being told to wait, that we'll talk about it later, because no one ever talks to me later. I haven't gotten any answers to any of my questions, and you're going to finally fucking answer them for me. I'm not invisible, and I won't be invisible, and you're all going to pay attention to me. I need that!"

It took her a moment to realize that the only sound was her heavy breathing, and she felt her face flushing hot. She'd used her words on all of them, had told them to listen to her, told them to pay attention. And they were. Now, though, she didn't have anything else to say.

The fog behind Karl's eyes cleared quickly as she glared at him, just the way it had that morning not so long ago when she'd used her words on him the first time. She swallowed, expecting that cold, calculating awareness. Instead, a small smile cracked beneath his mustache, and he nodded.

"Okay, Leo," Brad said, looking at her with an open grin and wide eyes, the fog clearing away from them, too.

Were all these people just so used to hearing beats that they didn't last very long on them? She turned, seeing everyone else staring at her, and she swallowed. She expected to be met with angry glares, expected to be stared at with hatred like the outsider she most definitely felt she was. One of the twins let out a little giggle, and as she looked at each of their faces, she realized that everyone was smiling at her. Everyone but Bernadette, who had missed the whole thing, and Kaylee, who Leo didn't even think *could* smile at this point.

Cameron stood from the bench and walked towards her, keeping her gaze. He had an idiotic grin on his face, the kind that made her think he was going to try something stupid. Leo glared at him, feeling her fist ball up at her side, and her gut reaction was to punch him in the face if he made a move. But he just stood there, staring at her, and she couldn't break his gaze. What the fuck did he want to mess with her about this time?

His hand came down on her shoulder before she realized it—not hard, but just heavy enough to relay the fact that he meant it. "Welcome to Sleepwater," he said.

The twins burst out laughing, and Leo turned to glance at Karl, Brad, and Randall behind her. Randall gave a laughing sigh, pushing his glasses back up his nose again. Karl just folded his arms and smiled, looking smugly proud in a way she didn't recognize.

"What?" she said, completely caught off guard by the reaction.

"Yeah, well, this one definitely wasn't planned," Brad said, flashing her a grin. "But it's as good a time as any."

"What is?" What was this, some kind of joke? She hadn't done anything but completely lose her shit on them, and they all looked some weird version of impressed.

"Bernadette would say that this is what we needed to see," Brad added, and he rubbed his hand through his bright-red hair. "It's important for us to make sure you're committed to this, that you want to know what we're doing and actually have something invested in this, even though you have no idea what's going on." The twins kept laughing. "We never would have asked you to spin a beat for us, Leo. That was your choice, and you made the right decision."

"That's what she was talking about?" Leo asked. Everything Bernadette had said that first time at her house came rushing back to her, that she'd have to make the decision when she met Sleepwater. Of course, nobody ever fucking told her what that would be, and she'd thought she was completely stepping out of line. "Was this whole fucking thing a test?"

Brad's face darkened, and Karl paused. "Well, not really," he said, glancing at Brad. "We would have found a better way to give you the chance, but you picked the perfect time without us. This problem is real, though. There's something—"

"Leo," Mirela called from beside the couch, her voice calm and pleasant but with a hint of urgency. "I really do need that jar."

"Oh, right." She stooped to pick up the red plastic jar, inching past Cameron to take it to Mirela. "Sorry," she told her, handing out the container.

"That's perfectly okay," Mirela said with a smile. She paused with her hand on the jar, gazing up at Leo. "You did well."

"I need a cigarette," Leo whispered, and one of the twins guffawed again from behind her.

"You should have seen your face," Don—she thought—said, pointing at her while his brother flashed a cartoonish mock of anger on his own face.

"Go ahead and step outside," Mirela said, ignoring them. "Brad can answer any of your questions."

"Yeah. Yeah," Brad replied, almost jumping to attention at the mention of it. He gave Leo a sheepish grin and nodded toward the sliding glass door in the kitchen.

"I'll come too," Karl said, and the two of them started toward the door.

Leo gave Mirela a small smile, though her face still burned hot. She felt like she wanted to say something, like she owed some kind of apology, but Mirela just shook her head slowly, wordlessly telling her otherwise, and returned her attention to Bernadette.

She took a big breath, taking in the sight of everybody else around the room, who just stood looking at her. She glanced quickly at Kaylee on the bench, who didn't even act like anything had happened. The girl just stared back at her, and Leo stuffed her hands into the pockets of her sweatshirt and stepped silently outside.

Karl leaned against the railing of the patio, gazing out over the valley that dropped almost straight into the rushing river below. Leo gingerly picked a cigarette out of her pack, noticing just how sweaty her hands were. She lit it and took a moment to soak in the view she hadn't seen before in the dark.

The sun had gone down already on the other side of the mountains, but the sky lit up in hues of orange and red, casting golden glows through the branches of the pine trees. It would have been peaceful, but the roaring, sweeping river almost beneath the deck lent a wild air to the place. She'd never seen a river quite like that, out here in the woods, and it felt like something violent and predatory waited just below the churning water.

Brad sat in a chair by the glass table, studying her with a small smile. "Really, you did great," he said.

She turned to him, feeling almost like Brad's thorough attention was stronger now than when everyone had stared at her inside. "Thanks." It sounded like a question even to her own ears.

"That has to be pretty useful," he added, and Karl turned around to look at them. Leo shrugged. "Come sit down," Brad beckoned, and she habitually glanced at Karl before taking a seat opposite Brad at the table. Somehow, she felt that from here on out, she wouldn't need Karl's permission for anything. She wondered why she'd felt she ever needed it in the first place. "So, what do you want to know?" he asked.

Leo blinked, then looked quickly down at her jeans. She'd gotten their attention, all right, and she had no idea where to start. Now that answers were being offered willingly, she couldn't figure out what damn question she wanted to ask first. "I don't know," she whispered.

"There may not be a lot of time after tonight," Karl added, puffing on his cigarette like he didn't really want to be a part of this conversation. But the openness behind his eyes, the tiny lift in his eyebrows, showed he wasn't threatening her. He just stated the facts.

She nodded. "So, what's actually going on tonight? Is there someone after us?" *Us.* They'd accepted her into Sleepwater, whatever Sleepwater was, and she was now suddenly tied in with them more than she'd realized until that moment. It also occurred to her that she might not ever find another place where she felt okay being tied to others.

Happy, maybe, if she took the time to pick things apart, but now didn't feel like the right time to actually feel happy. She felt like a whole bunch of shit was about to come raining down on her.

"Probably," Brad said with a frown. "Trashing Karl's place is one thing. If that had been it, I'd say he deserved it." Karl grunted and flipped Brad the finger, and Leo couldn't help a small smile as she watched the exchange. "But Bernadette's something else entirely. They went after her, and only someone who knows her connection with us would try to hurt her."

So a connection with Sleepwater was a bad thing? A storm went off in Leo's stomach, but she pushed it down. "Do you know who it is?"

The men exchanged another quick glance, and Karl chewed on his upper lip. "Randall thought it might have been Louis—"

"What?" Louis? The frilly, coiffed fuck who'd been her employer for all of a week?

"But I don't think so," Karl added, holding up a hand for her to let him finish. "Louis has had some issues with Sleepwater in the past, but I really don't think he'd go after Bernadette."

"Really?" Brad asked, frowning up at Karl.

"Maybe you and I can talk about this later," Karl said.

"No," Leo said, and they both glanced at her. "I want to know. If you're answering my questions now, why do you need to talk about that without me? Did I fuck things up with that guy?" The guy whose face she'd pounded in outside The Purple Lion.

"No," Karl said, shaking his head. "That was you doing your job, and you didn't talk to the cops. This doesn't have anything to do with that night."

"Louis came to your place, though. He made you spin a beat for him..." She noticed the surprised look on Brad's face and thought maybe she'd said too much.

"Karl..." Brad started.

"He was being his usual shit self, holding our deal over my head. That's all, man." Karl eyed Brad down. "I swear. After that, he and I were even again."

Brad rolled his eyes and shook his head, sighing. "Okay..."

Leo felt like this chance to get her answers only made things worse. Turned out there was way more to all this than she'd thought, and whatever her opinion of Karl had been was changing into something completely different. "What kind of deal?" she asked, feeling her heart pounding in her throat.

"I guess we should probably start from the beginning, huh?" Brad said, rubbing a hand through his orange beard.

Leo raised her eyebrows. "That'd be cool." It sounded pert, but she was really fucking confused.

Brad leaned his knees onto his elbows. "You remember that first bombing, the one of the genetics research lab in Montana a few years ago?" he asked.

"Uh... no." Where the hell was this going?

Brad flashed Karl another huge grin. "You really did find her under a rock, didn't you?" Karl just snorted laughter. "You haven't heard any of the news around this?" he asked, turning back to Leo.

She felt her face flushing hot. "I don't have a TV," she snipped.

"Some kind of lifestyle choice?"

"Yeah, being homeless. I don't give a shit about TV."

Brad's eyes widened. "Seriously?" She just stared at him. Karl chuckled. "For how long?"

"A few years."

Brad sat back in his chair and seemed to find her confession oddly amusing. "Well, that makes a hell of a lot more sense, now."

"What are you talking about?" she asked softly, hoping the annoyance in her voice could be plastered over with her even stronger curiosity.

"Tell me you've at least heard about Pointera and Laleopharm's partnership with MindBlink," Brad said, locking her gaze.

Leo felt sick. If these assholes planned on taking her for another ride with that bullshit, the whole thing that not only had ruined her life but her parents' marriage, she was out of here. Her voice shook when she opened her mouth, and she didn't even think she had the willpower to stop it. "My dad worked for MindBlink, and that fucking shit killed him."

Brad's eyes were wide. "I'm so sorry, Leo. I've talked to a lot of people who feel the same as you do. Who was your dad?"

"Marcus Tieffler," she whispered.

Brad almost jumped out of his chair, gripping his knees tight, and frowned up at Karl. "Holy shit." He looked back at Leo, and she wanted to puke. "Marcus Tieffler was your dad?"

"I didn't stutter," she said and took a long drag of her cigarette. She really didn't want to go down that road again, and she didn't see how any of this could possibly matter.

"Having Tieffler's daughter with us could make a really big statement," Brad said to Karl, who just nodded slowly.

"What the fuck does my dad have to do with anything?" Leo asked, realizing she was close to yelling.

"Hey, sorry," Brad said, and he put out a hand as if to comfort her, but they sat too far apart. "I'm sorry. I'm getting to the point. You know what Pointera does, right? The good *and* the worse?" Leo nodded, and she really didn't think her meaning could be misinterpreted. She knew that poison inside and out. "Good," Brad continued. "It may have started out honestly enough, but it didn't stay that way for very long. The company who makes the drug is Laleopharm, and they've done their damnedest over the last two decades to get their hands on everything and everyone. They practically have the FDA in their pocket, and even companies like Salco Genomics, the research lab that... was bombed a few years ago. They gripped the Information Technology industry by the balls, Topper and MindBlink, where your dad worked... Jesus. If the Devil owned a company on Earth, that's it."

"When are you gonna get to the point?" Leo asked, feeling her nose start to burn with what she knew could turn into tears. She couldn't figure out why the hell she'd start crying now, other than from confusion and frustration.

Brad glanced at Karl, like he couldn't figure out how to answer her. Karl gazed down his nose at her and said in a soft voice, "Leo, behind everything this company does, they're experimenting on people."

Was she supposed to care? Pharmaceutical companies experimented all the time—that was how they figured out what their drugs did. She almost laughed. "Like drug trials?"

Karl shook his head, and it was almost invisible. "No, like off-the-record experiments. On people like us."

Leo stared at them, and then she did laugh. "What the fuck?" Neither of them smiled back, and she knew they'd pull out the punchline sooner or later. "You're telling me some secret government lab has a bunch of guinea pigs running around spinning beats?" She laughed again, dragged on her cigarette, and stared at them. They had to be messing with her, putting her through some kind of initiation. But the second shoe never dropped. She stared at Karl, feeling the smile fade from her face. "Come on."

"Louis is the one who managed to get us most of the information," Karl said, taking a huge step across the porch to crush his cigarette out in the ashtray.

Leo suddenly remembered that Bernadette was, in fact, just inside, lying on the couch with a nasty bash in the head and on the verge of some serious damage. Her smile completely vanished, and she thought about what she'd just heard. "What does that guy have to do with any of this?"

"He used to do what we can do," Brad said. "With his words."

She tried to imagine what kind of ridiculous beat Louis might spin if he could—probably making everyone bow down before him to worship him as a god. The laugh about to escape her died abruptly when she thought about what that meant. "And now he can't?"

"They took it from him," Karl said. A shiver went up Leo's spine.

"He owned a place in Chicago before The Purple Lion," Brad said. "Same kinda thing he does now, only he was spinning his own beats, too. And it wasn't illegal back then."

"The Purple Lion's illegal?" Leo asked. That thought brought a whole new level of understanding, why the whole place was so disgustingly hush-hush.

"No," Karl said. "Spinning beats is, though."

"What?" she said, putting out the last of her cigarette and rapidly lighting another one. This had to be a joke too, right?

"You really haven't been paying attention to the world, have you?" Brad asked with a pitying frown. She glared at him, blowing a cloud of smoke towards his face, and he nodded. "Yeah, sorry. Right. Almost five years ago, the federal government made 'storytelling' illegal, though it's not really public knowledge and you can't really put a label on 'storytelling' if you don't know what you're looking for. They buried it pretty deep in all that political voting bullshit. Karl," he almost shouted, looking up at the man. "I need a smoke, too, now." Karl grunted with a half-smile, gave the man what he wanted, and Brad made a face when he took the first drag. "I haven't smoked for three years," he said to Leo with a sheepish grin. "Mirela's gonna kill me."

"I think she has her hands full inside," Leo said, knowing how Brad felt and thinking that, if there ever was a time to smoke after quitting, it might be now.

"Yeah," Brad said through the smoke, then ruffled his hair. "Anyways, Louis wasn't the first, but he was at the top of a long list of people who got taken. He told me probably half of what they did to him in there, and I'm not gonna repeat it."

Leo frowned. "You know him?"

"He was part of Sleepwater, once," Brad said.

"In Chicago."

"Yeah, sort of. We started in Sparta. Sleepwater was the name of one of my buddy's ranches." He looked up at her with a flash of red blooming in his face.

"Sleepwater was a farm?" Leo asked. Half of this story scared the shit out of her, and the other half sounded like some kind of childhood fantasy. What the hell was this?

"Yeah, well, the name stuck," Brad said, making a face again when he hit his cigarette. "Louis was part of our group. We met a couple times a month, spinning beats and busting each other's balls. He moved our 'meetings', I guess you'd call 'em, to the back room of a club he'd just opened." His face folded in on itself. "The place got raided a couple months later. The cops said it was for drugs, but they'd already hit a few other businesses run by some people we knew who had… words. Like us. They took him the weekend I married Mirela." The notes of bitterness and regret hung heavy on his words.

"Who's they?" Leo asked.

"The government. Fucking Laleopharm. Could be one and the same thing, at this point," Brad said. "The legislation started in DC, like it does half the time." He gave a biting laugh. "Illinois is a hell of a lot closer to DC than Wyoming is. Mirela and I watched our friends disappear on us, then we booked it. I quit smoking when we bought this house," he added, glaring down at the cigarette in his hand before hitting it again.

"And you started Sleepwater here?" Leo asked. So she was getting into some kind of illegal crime ring, only with actual words now instead of drugs. Perfect.

"Oh, no," Brad said. "We left a trail across the country." He grinned at her. "Sleepwater's just about everywhere."

Leo frowned, shaking her head. "Fine," she said, glancing up at Karl. "So now there are people—government dudes, or scientists—bashing up Karl's place and going after Bernadette because spinning beats is illegal?" This seemed like some kind of crazy war on … beat terrorism, and she didn't see what the big deal was.

"Not really," Karl said in a low voice.

Brad glanced at him, then sucked air through his teeth and let out a long sigh. "Yeah, we didn't exactly make it easy for anyone." He fixed Leo with a cold stare overlapped by what she thought might have been embarrassment. "Louis wasn't the first person who found us after he'd been… released. He wasn't the first person who told us what they'd done to him, but he remembered a lot more than most of the others. We'd heard some names of the facilities where they took people like us, and Louis brought us not only a name but a location and detailed layout of the buildings. I guess he'd been moved around a lot, but Salco Genomics was the place he wanted fucking destroyed."

Leo felt both sets of eyes on her as she looked back and forth between Brad and Karl, and then it hit her like a frying pan to the face. "And you fucking blew the place up?" she yelled. This was what they did? She was hanging out with some violent crazies, smoking on their back porch like nothing else mattered. What the hell was she supposed to do with that information? "This is bullshit," she spat. "Tell me it's bullshit." Both Brad and Karl's faces remained blank slates of deadly seriousness. Leo burst out laughing and instantly shut herself up. This was insane.

"We didn't want to," Brad answered, avoiding what seemed like her hypothetical question altogether. "But we didn't have a choice."

"You absolutely had a choice," Karl said, his voice low and menacing as he leaned toward Brad from against the deck railing. "I told you not to make the deal, and you could have listened to me."

Brad stared up at him, his beard bristling as he sucked on the cigarette like it had gone out. The lit end burned brighter, illuminating his face. "Brother, there wasn't a choice to be made. You're part of this, one of us, and I love you. I wasn't going to let him take you away."

Karl swallowed hard, his Adam's apple seeming to stick on its way back down. "And I can't thank you enough," he whispered.

"The deal to blow up a lab had something to do with Karl?" Leo asked. She almost felt guilty for interrupting the strangely emotional exchange—she'd seen Karl acting happy the night before, and now she'd just witnessed him about to choke up—but her curiosity got the better of her.

Clearing his throat, Brad said, "It wasn't so much a deal as it was blackmail. When that fucker got out of Salco and found us, he told us everything. I'm not gonna lie, it was terrifying. And then he demanded we destroy the place. I can't imagine the things he must have gone through in there to change him like that, but no matter what they were, we didn't want to go blowing shit up."

No shit. Leo thought these people were okay—a little eccentric, but okay. It made no sense why they'd blow up government buildings and research labs.

"Louis hated us," Karl added, "for reminding him of what he'd had taken from him. He wasn't the same guy after they took him, and he turned into even more of an ass in a matter of months."

"Hard to believe," Leo muttered.

"When we told him we couldn't pull any Rambo shit on that lab, it gave him the push he needed to hate us completely. We'd been his family, and I guess he thought we'd betrayed him, too."

"So he gave us an ultimatum," Brad continued. "Take down Salco Genomics, or he'd spill all our secrets and bring the cops to break down our door. No matter what Karl says, none of us were going to give him up."

"Give him up for what?" She didn't understand what Louis could have possibly held over their heads. Even if he hated them for still being able to spin beats when he couldn't anymore, she didn't think he'd turn them in for it. He owned his own club just to surround himself with people like her; it might have been illegal, but he wouldn't willingly put himself out of business.

Brad glanced at Karl, then stubbed his cigarette in the ashtray. "I'm gonna go see how Bernadette's doing," he said warily, shifting his gaze toward Leo before standing from his chair and walking toward the kitchen door. "You two can finish this conversation without me."

30

THEY HEARD THE kitchen door sliding shut, and with an unexpectedly heavy sigh, Karl left his place by the deck railing and took the chair Brad had just left. Leo watched him, her stomach knotting with both apprehension and guilt. She'd obviously touched on something Brad must have felt was a private matter. Some secret, like he'd said. The worst part was the look on Karl's face—a sad, dark, chaotic visage in his wide eyes. The curiosity drove her nuts, and she still couldn't help thinking Karl was about to put himself through hell just to answer her questions. Leo couldn't decide what she wanted more—to hear everything explained or to avoid putting Karl through whatever shit he was about to lay down.

"You're gonna tell me what happened, right?" Leo asked. She couldn't help it; she had to know what was going on, what she'd walked into. What she had coming for her if she stayed with these people whose pasts both scared the shit out of her and made her feel right at home.

Karl glanced down at his hands, having pulled from his back pocket the folded picture he'd taken from his ransacked home. "Yeah," he whispered, tracing a finger over the photo. Leo caught only a glimpse of red hair from where she sat, but she remembered the picture of the smiling woman all too well. "But I'm only going to tell you this once, because tonight's the night you get answers from me for free."

What did he mean by that? Leo frowned at him, but she held her tongue and repeatedly told herself to keep her mouth shut. It felt like Karl was made of glass right then; if she pushed too hard, he'd crack and shatter into a million pieces. And broken people were even harder to put back together than glass.

"That's your wife, right?" she asked jerkily. Her voice sounded like trying to close a door on a rug.

"Her name was Tracy," he started, his voice gruff with suppression. No tears, no frown, just that low, scratchy hiss of air and sound. "She worked as a banker. Handled our money pretty well. More than anything, she loved to dance outside." His mouth twitched, and he lit another cigarette, cradling the picture in his lap. "We had a huge backyard, had a little row of trees she went crazy over. She convinced me to hire a landscaper to take care of the place." His eyes flicked up to meet hers, and Leo held her breath. "You know what I do when I spin a beat," he added.

Leo remembered vividly the high of floating out of her own body, both during the beat Louis had so cruelly forced from Karl only days before and during the drive back to Sleepwater with a wounded Bernadette. She nodded.

Karl cleared his throat. "We didn't have enough money to actually pay a maintenance guy, so I paid him in trade. With beats. Like any drug, any high, the guy got hooked. I had no idea that would happen. I'd never spun beats that many times for the same person before. The guy would show up three, four times a week, begging for work so I'd tell him a story. He even brought a tape recorder once, tried to take it home with him. That was before anyone figured out recordings don't ever work."

Leo found herself wondering at that last bit. She'd never thought of it before, had never tried to record a beat herself, and hearing there was an apparent limit to the power of her words sent a shiver rippling underneath her sweatshirt. She wanted so badly to ask him more about recordings, about what that meant for them, but interrupting him now would only set her fifty steps backwards. This wasn't the time, but she'd bring it up later. She looked up at Karl and saw that he'd been staring at her, somehow aware of her having lost her focus for a few seconds. She nodded, and he continued.

"When he found out he couldn't record it, the guy lost his shit. Broke into our house while I was out, tied Tracy up, and gagged her. When I got home, he gave me a choice. Agree to give him an endless supply of my beats or lose my wife. The guy was sweaty, twitchy, like he was on crack or something. But it was me. He was... high on me."

Karl's mouth twitched again, but down this time. He stared at Leo's knees, and his nostrils flared. "So I did it. I told a story. I gave him what he wanted. He stopped twitching, eyes cleared up like he got his fix. He killed her anyway. Slit her throat. She was smiling, foggy, not in her right mind. She had no idea what was going on in the end, because I got her high, too. Too high to be afraid." He leaned back in the chair and blew smoke up towards the sky like a man enjoying his freedom. But when he looked back at her, Leo saw the wetness in his eyes reflecting the lights wrapped around the porch.

Her breath had pretty much stopped in her chest. She didn't know whether to scream or cry, but it was harder to think of something to say. His admission was the last thing she'd expected, and she felt a wave of nausea. Maybe this hadn't been important for her to know. Maybe she'd asked the wrong questions and could have gotten everything she needed without dragging Karl back down this road. She swallowed the sharp, dry razors in her throat and held his gaze. It was the most he'd ever said to her, and she didn't want to make him stop.

"I wanted to kill him," Karl continued. "I would have if I ever caught him, and I chased the motherfucker out of South Dakota. By the time I realized he'd fucking vanished on me, Tracy's death was all over the news, and they'd named me as a suspect. I couldn't go back, didn't have any family to answer to or worry about me. So I kept running. That was about a year before I met Sleepwater here in Wyoming, and I swore I'd never use my words again. Louis was already... back, but he hadn't made his choice to blackmail us yet. I was there when he told the others about his own hell, and he heard the version of mine."

"He threatened to turn you in if Sleepwater didn't blow up some fucking lab?" Leo's face burned, and she wanted to get her hands around the flaming fuck's goddamn neck.

"Yeah, as a wanted murderer," Karl replied. "We all have our secrets, our legal shit, but I don't think anyone else has been wanted for killing their wife." He grabbed the back of his head with both hands and rubbed vigorously. "I pretty much had to do whatever he wanted after that. Keep him happy."

When Leo had been arrested outside The Purple Lion, she'd put Karl in serious danger. And she'd forced Louis, in whatever twisted way he justified it, to come to Karl's house and blackmail him into a private beat session. A tingling wave shot down her legs as she realized her inability to keep her fucking temper in check had forced Karl to break his promise to himself. He'd done it as much for her as he had for himself, and it all made sense. Louis had mentioned Karl 'running', had waved that threat right under his nose like a flippant, puppet-master flag. Karl had obviously agreed to work for Louis, as much to bring new beat spinners to The Purple Lion as to stay under the man's watchful gaze. To do whatever else Louis might have wanted…

Karl looked up at her and must have read the horror on her face. "When I said I had to do whatever he wanted, I meant in a business capacity. I haven't been in a room alone with him, if that's what you're thinking."

A mortified spray of bile hit the back of Leo's throat, and she swallowed hard, having to look away from him. She couldn't imagine what he'd been put through, but she realized that even through his wife's death, Karl wasn't a victim.

She felt ridiculous for having thought he would have whored himself out to Louis, of all people, just to keep good on a deal. "Right," she said, her voice like sandpaper.

"Leo," he called, forcing her to look up at him again. "Some of these guys have no idea I've been working for Louis. They felt the terms were settled when we went after Salco Genomics, and they didn't want anything else to do with him. Making that deal for me had been a group choice, and they all felt responsible. I think it's better not to bring up that either one of us has seen him lately, yeah?"

She nodded. That was why Bernadette had changed the story when she'd met everyone the night before. Now she was the one who had to keep secrets. Thinking about Bernadette suddenly brought the whole day back to her mind, and she welcomed the less tragic change of topic. "So they think Louis trashed your place and went after Bernadette?"

"Right. But we kept up our end of the deal, and Louis didn't have The Purple Lion when we made that agreement. He's got too much to lose now to even think about a legal spotlight. I really don't think it's him."

Right, spinning beats was illegal, and that was still the governing force of Louis' world. No, Leo didn't think the man was that stupid, either. "So who do you think it is?" she asked.

A wry smile twisted the corners of Karl's mouth. "Like Brad said, it could really be anyone. Salco Genomics was the first, just a few years ago, and we haven't really stopped. The number of people joining the different Sleepwater houses exploded when the beats became illegal, and while they got their shit together and realized they had to keep it under wraps, we still got a few people coming back from those fucking... places. Experimented on, like Louis. We, uh... we couldn't keep watching it happen. There are a lot of people with a lot of money out there, and Sleepwater has pretty much pissed them all off—government, Laleopharm, MindBlink, probably a few military branches, for all I fucking know. Anybody who had money tied up in the research we've destroyed is just as much of a possibility."

"Jesus," Leo whispered. She'd had no idea this shit was happening in the world, that anything as grotesquely conspiratorial could ever be a reality. And she'd been dropped in the fucking middle of it.

Karl gave a sarcastic huff. "They're kidnapping people, Leo. People like us. You think Sleepwater's making the wrong choice?"

She sat back in her chair and folded her arms, staring at him. Maybe, all along, *this* was the decision Bernadette had told her she'd have to make. And it really wasn't that hard.

"No," she said. "No, I fucking don't."

31

SHE LAY IN the bed she'd stayed in the night before, staring up at the ceiling fan. Leo had gotten her answers, or at least the ones they gave her in response to the questions she could think to ask. The biggest question, though, of who had actually gone after Bernadette, didn't have an answer. No one knew. But they all agreed they had to be careful.

The image of Bernadette lying asleep on the couch with a bandage wrapped around her head was the one thing convincing Leo they weren't fucking with her—or that they hadn't completely lost their own minds. She'd wanted to tell them all to get a grip, to look around and open their eyes to the fact that conspiracies like that didn't exist in the real world. But they didn't have a reason to lie to her, did they? Keeping secrets as Sleepwater had done, however briefly, wasn't the same as pretending to tell her the truth with a ridiculously detailed lie. She didn't think it was a lie. Karl had opened up to her in a way she'd never expected, had told her about his wife without seeming to leave anything out, and had given one more person the truth of his past to hold over his head, if she chose. Leo couldn't ever see herself doing that; she'd only ever threatened to rat out one other person, and that fuck-up had left her with no choice but to run. Karl's secrets were a lot different than Carlos', and she even saw Louis in a different light, now that she knew what he'd done.

Part of her wanted to pity him, wondering what it would be like to have her words taken from her, unable to spin her beats to get through life like she had. That was all she had going for her, really, when she looked hard enough at herself. The other part of her, though, wanted to string the man up by his dainty fucking toes and pound his face in while the blood rushed to his head. Blackmailing a person to save someone you cared about was one thing—she could understand that—but stringing an innocent man along by his past to get what you wanted just didn't fucking fly. Leo didn't care that Karl seemed to have resigned himself to that 'deal' or that he'd found a way to 'make it work'. Nobody deserved to be squeezed dry like that, especially someone who'd gone through the things Karl had been forced to put behind him.

Like watching his wife die in front of him, convinced it had been his own fault.

Leo cringed at the sudden memory of that first morning at Karl's place. It had barely been over a week ago but seemed like months. She'd seen so much more of Karl since then, what existed of him behind the stoic mask and his bristling social interaction. She'd thought, that first morning, that there had to be another reason he'd offered her a place to stay under his roof, and she'd been stupid enough to think it was something physical. She'd used her words on him to make him kiss her, to make her feel she was fucking worth something, when she knew nothing about him. On top of that, she hadn't even cared about what his past looked like, what he'd experienced to get him where he was; the thought had never crossed her mind. Now, when she looked back on the terrifying awareness she'd seen behind his eyes, the fire of both knowledge and restraint, she knew what had created it. The fact that he never mentioned it and didn't hold it against her, that despite her apathy he'd still brought her to Sleepwater and introduced her to a world she quickly found herself appreciating, convinced her this was real. And, she realized, perhaps it was a world she also wanted to protect.

That thought carried both hope and a twisted, guilty anxiety. It made her want to run. Leo had never known what to do with hope, only having experienced it moments before something ripped it away from her completely. No warning, no explanation. Hope was the herald of despair, a reminder that all she could depend on was the knowledge that it never lasted.

And still, here she was, spending her second night in a house full of strangers, people who considered each other family and might now be offering Leo the opportunity to join them. Yeah, she wanted to run, but she didn't. Not yet.

She lay in this bed in her t-shirt, having thrown off her jeans for the comfort of the clean sheets, and folded her arms behind her head. After she and Karl had returned from the porch, Mirela had told them Bernadette seemed to be doing fine. She'd be slow, a bit disoriented, maybe taken out by headaches now and then, and they'd have to keep an eye on her. But she'd be okay. Leo hadn't realized how heavily Bernadette's injury had weighed on her mind until it was lifted by relief. She didn't even know the woman. Then again, Bernadette had been partly responsible for getting her to Sleepwater, for understanding what she could do and thinking she'd find a place to belong with these people.

Everyone else but Brad and Mirela had gone to bed already, Randall and the twins having agreed to stay until they figured out what to do. She guessed a few people had to double up in the bedrooms, but no one had said anything to her about it. Maybe they didn't think they knew her well enough to ask her to share a room. A prickle of guilt had shown itself at that, but she pushed it down. She couldn't remember the last time she'd had a whole room to herself, the previous night notwithstanding.

The bedroom door creaked open, and Leo turned her head lazily to look at it. She didn't expect to see Kaylee, of all people, standing there in an over-sized Metallica t-shirt that draped to her knees. She stared at Leo, never taking her eyes off her as she stepped into the room and closed the door behind her. Her hand rested on the doorknob, like she wanted to make sure she could step out again as soon as she found something she didn't like. Leo didn't know what the hell to think; the girl hadn't spoken to her, had barely acknowledged her existence. What the fuck was she doing here?

"Marcus Tieffler was your dad?" Kaylee finally said, her voice low and sounding way too big for a body that size. But it fit the darkness radiating from the girl.

Leo's ears burned hot. The first thing Kaylee said to her was to ask about her damn father? If she thought she could come in here and start some kind of sleepover bonding bullshit, Leo had no problem telling her to go screw herself. When the tiny girl by her door didn't say anything else, Leo realized she wanted an answer. "Yeah," she said.

Kaylee blinked and slowly slid her hand off the doorknob. She kept Leo's gaze, locking her into those light brown, almond-shaped eyes, and walked barefoot across the carpeted floor toward the bed. Leo sat up and crossed her legs under her. Did this girl have no concept of personal space? Kaylee's unchanging expression told her nothing. She looked at Leo the same way she had every other time before, eyes wide, her mouth set in a thin line of apathy. This time, though, when the girl sat on the side of the bed next to Leo, she saw Kaylee's jaw working in a repetitive clench. Had she pissed her off again somehow?

Gazing quickly back and forth into each of Leo's eyes, Kaylee added, "And he's dead now." She nodded once as she said this, as if she only wanted to confirm what she already knew.

Leo returned the blank stare, wondering what the hell was going on. She swallowed, vaguely aware of the fact that she wasn't wearing pants, and cleared her throat. "Yeah."

Kaylee's eyebrow twitched upward, like she agreed Leo had told the truth. It felt like the girl was searching for something, trying to read Leo's mind or find some buried thing Leo couldn't possibly guess. She had a feeling this tiny girl with the dark curtain of hair and the blazing eyes wasn't going to tell her what she wanted. And she didn't—she just grabbed the bottom of the giant t-shirt, ripped it over her head, and threw it on the floor, revealing gray cotton underwear and nipple piercings on tits that almost weren't there. Almost.

"What—" Leo started, then turned to stare straight ahead at the bedroom door. She'd had no idea that was coming, no idea what to do or say, but she had the feeling Kaylee would have ripped her apart if she stared at her body instead of the door. She had to chalk it up as one of the stranger interactions she'd had in a bedroom and found herself blinking rapidly at the door. She cleared her throat. "Look—"

"I don't want to hear it."

She turned again to look at Kaylee, not sure whether to be amused or insulted. Then the girl rose on her knees, leaned over her, and kissed her.

Yeah, that was one way to avoid talking, but what the hell? Leo took a minute to run through all the possibilities—Kaylee didn't smell like alcohol, Leo didn't have anything she might have wanted, even if it was money, and she hadn't done anything remotely resembling a favor to warrant something like this in return. A cold hand slid up her thigh, and that was what it took to snap her out of the feel of Kaylee's lips on hers. She stopped Kaylee's hand with her own and pulled back to look at her. "What are you—"

"Seriously," Kaylee said, staring at her from beneath thin eyebrows, their foreheads almost touching. "Don't talk." No hint of embarrassment, no hesitation, just pure determination swirling behind the girl's deadpan stare. She moved her hand farther up Leo's thigh, completely ignoring her, and kissed her again. She must have been four or five inches shorter than Leo, tiny in comparison, but when she pushed Leo back onto the pillow, she was all power—lean muscle and humming with dangerous energy.

Leo's hands went to Kaylee's waist as the girl leaned over her, hiking up Leo's t-shirt just above her ribs and leaving a trail of hot, hard kisses down her neck. If it had been anyone else, Leo might have thought she'd break the girl— she seemed that small. But despite her size and her obvious lack of finesse, Kaylee was a bomb waiting to go off. Her body quivered with tension that didn't quite seem to stem entirely from excitement.

It occurred to Leo then that she hadn't physically been with someone "for no reason" in a long time. The last few years had brought her a long list of experimental partners, all of whom she'd thought she'd been repaying in some form at the time. The decision to really just lay back and enjoy this tempted her more than trying to figure out what the hell Kaylee wanted, and she closed her eyes and sighed as Kaylee slid a knee up between her legs.

The sudden image of Cameron entering her mind, face twisted in that threatening grimace, almost made her bolt upright. Sure, she'd been "accepted" by Sleepwater in some way, with whatever else that entailed, but she didn't think it extended to Cameron's warnings of leaving Kaylee alone. He'd seemed more than serious about that. Leo couldn't push aside the thought, and she took her hands off Kaylee's body.

"Isn't Cameron—"

Kaylee grabbed Leo's wrists and pinned then down to the bed by her head. Something like a growl came out of the girl, low and frustrated, and she reared up as much as she could while holding Leo down. Her cheeks were flushed, lips wet and glistening after almost having completed her line of kisses to Leo's chest. "I swear to God," she said, "if you say one more fucking thing, I'll just hurt you. And then I'll leave."

Leo recognized immediately the power in Kaylee's words, feeling her head swim just a little. It wasn't like any other beat she'd heard. It seemed the beginning of one—one over which Kaylee must have practiced gaining a lot of control. But she felt a twinge on her nipples beneath her t-shirt, like Kaylee held them tightly between her fingertips instead of grasping Leo's wrists by her head. The pain couldn't be ignored, bordering the lines of pleasure and just strong enough to threaten an excruciating experience.

A tiny echo of shocked laughter escaped Leo as she stared up into the girl's burning eyes. A few strands of straight black hair stuck to her lightly freckled nose, but Kaylee did nothing to wipe them away. She wasn't fucking playing. Okay. If Kaylee wanted her to shut up, fine—this chick obviously meant business. Leo lifted her knee, brushing it against Kaylee's leg still between her thighs in a gesture to continue.

Apparently satisfied, Kaylee leaned down again and bit Leo's bottom lip in what seemed another warning to do as she was told. She ran a cold hand up Leo's raised thigh, sending a river of goosebumps all the way up to Leo's shoulders. She sat up, grabbed fistfuls of Leo's t-shirt, and yanked her upright, ripping the shirt over Leo's head. Then she pushed her back down on the bed with surprising strength, hissing out a sigh. When she brought her mouth over Leo's nipple, flicking it with her tongue, it was completely without the harsh sting of pain she'd inflicted with her words. That, at least, was gentle enough.

Leo buried her fingers in Kaylee's hair and reached down to play with the cold metal of the girl's nipple piercing with the other hand; Kaylee seemed to give her few other options, and Leo was almost afraid to do much more than that. At this point, it felt too good to risk either making Kaylee stop or forcing her to make good on her threat.

Kaylee let out a soft moan. She slid a hand under Leo's lower back, pressing a thigh further between Leo's legs and slowly grinding her hips against Leo's. Then her mouth and both hands moved downward, passing Leo's navel and the jut of her hips, her black curtain of hair leaving a trail across Leo's stomach. Leo released her grip on Kaylee's hair—she couldn't help it—and she raised her hips just enough for Kaylee to pull her thin underwear quickly down and off.

The girl pushed Leo's thighs apart, and when she slipped her tongue between Leo's legs, it felt nothing like the biting-cold grasp of her freezing hands on Leo's hips. Kaylee's fast breathing brushed Leo's thighs between hot waves of soft, quick movement, and Leo couldn't decide if the chills running up her sides came from the girl's icy hands or her burning mouth.

Leo grabbed her own hair, her chest heaving as she

fought not to move. It didn't take very long, and even after she shuddered in release, Kaylee didn't pull back for a few more seconds. "Fuck…" she breathed, not caring if that one word broke the rules. Kaylee bit the inside of her thigh with another growl; it carried far less frustration than the last. Leo tipped her head back, breathing heavily with her eyes closed, and waited for Kaylee to lay down beside her when she felt the girl withdraw.

She heard the doorknob to the bedroom door turn, heard the door open and then click quickly shut. Leo raised herself up on her elbows, wondering who the fuck else would come into her room without knocking. But there was no one there. Not even Kaylee. The sound of Kaylee's bedroom door shutting across the hall was the only indication of what had actually happened. Stunned, she glanced at the floor and found the girl's Metallica t-shirt still crumpled by the bed.

Throwing her head back down on the pillow, Leo glared up at the ceiling fan again and felt an odd mixture of amusement and confusion. "What the fuck?"

32

...OVER THE LAST eight months, five other government testing sites across the Midwest have been targeted by the radical terrorist group after their first attack on the Salco Genomics buildings outside of Decker, Montana. Federal officials have yet to identify and apprehend anyone associated with this extremist group, and anyone who may have knowledge of these peoples' whereabouts or information regarding the attacks is asked to report to their local police department, or call this hotline number...

...The story about the man with some kind of magical ability to make people think they're hearing fighter jets originally aired on Donald Havish's World-Wide Conspiracy show on KWMR Springfield, Missouri. Yes, the radio host is

an eccentric man who encourages outlandish stories of UFO sightings, New Age practices, and underground tunnels spanning across the globe. His listeners, though, pay attention, and the word has spread. Apparently, the number of people experiencing this strange phenomenon of being psychologically affected by the words of passersby and acquaintances has quickly grown. We receive new reports every day of people feeling like they've lost time out of their day, only to find...

...Rising numbers of Pointera *dependency have been reported throughout the northeastern states of the US, and some just slightly less in the Midwest. And yet, Laleopharm's stocks continue to skyrocket, with a shocking 567% increase in the last six months...*

...and still, no one can seem to decide on what to call these people or what it is they can really do. The religious community has heralded them unbelievers who have been touched by the Devil himself, sent forth to tempt the righteous into wicked ways.

Groups like the Coalition of Reality have another hunch about this, having always fought against the rising dominance of Social Media and the Information Technology industry in today's economy, especially since the advent of the one-minute Infodeo years ago and the Association for Social Technology's partnership with the FDA. They insist the abilities harnessed by this small population of people stem from the growing prevalence of "plugging in", as they call it— the inability of society to function normally without logging in to their Topper or MindBlink accounts. The Coalition of Reality has specifically called these people "the higher evolution of the human species."

Some practitioners of Eastern and alternative medicine claim that these "special abilities" are just another undocumented and undisclosed side effect of the drug Pointera.

And we've all heard the wailings of conspiracy theorists across the nation, who insist that the government has been kidnapping civilians and performing illegal experiments on them, enhancing their DNA with these new powers in order to manufacture an army of superhumans.

Of course, we have no evidence to confirm or deny any of these...

"Turn that shit off."

Leo heard Karl's gruff voice echo from the kitchen as she walked downstairs. When she stepped out of the hallway and into the living room, it seemed she was the last one to wake up. She glanced into the kitchen to see Karl, Brad, and Randall gathered around the tiny box TV on the counter next to the fridge. The twins stood by the island, stirring their coffees in tandem, and Mirela closed the oven door, having just pulled out fresh muffins. They smelled amazing, but Leo wanted to know what had made Karl so angry. It had sounded like a bunch of corny newscasters, and she opened her mouth to ask about it.

"Good morning, sunshine."

She turned to see Bernadette on the couch, her head wrapped in a fresh bandage above a mostly lucid smile.

"Morning," Leo said, and she couldn't help but smile

back. "Good to see you awake." It surprised her to hear those words from herself, but it didn't feel wrong. That was how she felt.

"Oh, is it?" The woman winked at her, then winced a little as she adjusted herself on the couch. "Nice of you to say so."

"Leo, do you want some coffee?" Mirela called, slapping her oven mitts down on the counter. "Just made a fresh pot."

Leo's eyes fell on Cameron, sitting alone on the bench in the living room. The smirk on his face seemed completely out of place among the expressions he'd given her so far, and she was only too happy to turn away from him and head into the kitchen. "Thanks," she told Mirela, skirting past the twins to get to the coffee. They didn't pay her any attention. "What time is it?"

"Almost eight." Randall turned to her with his arms folded, giving her an amused smile. "Not used to waking up early, huh?"

"I guess," she said slowly, grabbing a mug from the shelf and pouring herself a cup of coffee. She nursed it for a few seconds, amazed by the fact that Mirela seemed to make coffee and some kind of breakfast every morning. "What were you guys watching?"

Karl turned to face her, rubbing the side of his face through his beard. Then he reached out and grabbed his own mug off the counter. "Just some bullshit on the news. These people are idiots."

"They're talking about us," said one of the twins.

"They're saying we're the spawn of the Devil," the

other added, throwing horns with his hand and brandishing them at Leo.

"Remind me which one of you is which," Leo said. She found it impossible to tell the difference, their identical appearance distracting her from what they'd just said and creeping her out a little. Their mirrored smiles faded simultaneously, and they stared at her blankly for a few seconds before shrugging at the same time and walking out of the kitchen. Leo heard Brad laughing behind her, and when she turned to him with a questioning glare, he just mocked the twins with an exaggerated shrug and flashed her a gleaming grin.

A door closed in the hallway by the front door, and Kaylee rounded the corner into the living room, dressed in another all-black outfit. Leo watched her, completely unsure of how to handle seeing her now. Striking up conversation with her seemed completely absurd, even if Leo had had any semblance of her own social skills, but part of her felt like Kaylee's actions the night before would have made it at least a little easier for them to communicate. Right?

Kaylee approached Bernadette on the couch and handed her a book. Bernadette looked up at her with an exclamation of gratitude.

"Thank you, sweetheart," she said. Kaylee bent down to kiss Bernadette on the cheek, then she headed toward the kitchen.

Leo managed to catch the girl's eye, and she wasn't quite able to squeeze out the half-smile she'd intended to give her. Kaylee walked up to her, expressionless, holding her with those brown eyes like they'd never met before. She stopped inches from Leo, staring up at her, and said in a low voice, "I want my shirt back."

What the hell? Leo blinked, completely fucking confused by the girl's amorphous collection of signals. Kaylee knew exactly where her goddamn shirt was. Leo didn't even think about it—she completely forgot all the changes of gratitude and community she'd started to feel within herself since meeting these people and reverted right back to her old self. "Then go get it," she said, distinctly feeling the frown of annoyance that flashed across her face.

Kaylee stared at her for another second, her eyebrow hiking up in almost a twitch like it had the night before during their less-than-brief exchange. Then she stepped passed Leo and grabbed herself a muffin.

No one else seemed to have noticed; they all ate their breakfast, drank their coffee, talked to each other. They almost acted like Kaylee wasn't there, like the ridiculous shit she pulled wasn't weird at all. Leo took another sip of her coffee, and when she looked up, she found Cameron staring at her from the bench. Instead of his normal attempt at intimidation, he now just grinned at her. What the hell was wrong with the guy? She headed quickly toward the sliding doors in the kitchen, feeling remarkably better once she stepped out into the fresh air.

The rest of the day passed like some weird, dream version of reality. Karl exuded nothing but vibrating tension, and while Brad still flashed Leo his gleaming, double-take-worthy grin, it seemed dulled by the unanswered questions. Who had come after Bernadette? Did they know she'd been brought to this house, where Sleepwater just so happened to make its home? And if they did know—whoever 'they' were—would they come busting down the door here, too, looking for them?

Leo smoked half a pack of cigarettes on the porch that morning, watching the river rushing by below her. No, this kind of 'waiting for the other bomb to explode' way of wasting time wasn't new to her, but she'd never felt it mirrored back to her by so many others before. The combined, forced-away anxiety floating over everyone in the house seemed to triple its power. She couldn't decide if she wanted to approach someone and talk about it, or if she should just shut herself up in her room for the rest of the day. Neither option offered a real relief.

When she stepped into the kitchen for lunch—a huge pan of lasagna Mirela had seemed to whisk out of nowhere and in no time at all—Leo noticed the door to the room by the staircase hanging open just a little. It was the room by the front door, the one she'd seen Randall chuck two giant duffle bags into before she'd met everyone, and she thought maybe he slept there when he didn't take the twins home. Holding her plate in one hand and scooping forkfuls of food into her mouth with the other, she slowly turned the corner from the kitchen and into the hallway. The sound of zippers being forced open and closed, heavy things bouncing against each other and clacking, and a muffled curse seemed to echo around her. She could only see a little through the door, but she managed to glimpse … yup, two black duffle bags, at least, and a bunch of what looked like cable wiring.

"Hey!" Randall's face popped up behind the door, his

huge glasses slipping down the front of his nose.

Leo nearly stabbed herself in the mouth when she jumped, and she leaned back against the hallway. "Fuck, man," she breathed, then stuffed another bite of food in her mouth so she wouldn't say anything else nasty.

Randall slid the glasses back up his nose and grinned at her. She couldn't help but return the smile while she chewed. "What's up?" he asked.

"Nothing," she mumbled around her food. "Just heard noise in there. You okay?"

"Yep, we're all set," he said, sliding through the doorway just enough so he could pull the doorknob closed behind him. Before Leo had a chance to ask him what was in there, he leaned toward her plate. "That lasagna? Fantastic! I'm starving." And he skirted past her toward the kitchen, his long arms pumping at his side when he tripped briefly over his own shoe.

Frowning, Leo gave a final glance to the closed door, then turned and followed him. What, more fucking secrets? For now, she figured she'd had enough illumination shed on Sleepwater's doings from the night before. It could wait.

Kaylee and Cameron were upstairs, maybe in the same room, maybe not. Doing who knew what. Leo didn't know what to think of whatever weird, protective, silently angsty relationship those two had going on. She also didn't know if she cared. She'd considered following Kaylee upstairs to maybe talk to her about the night before until she saw Cameron following close behind, and she shut that idea down. Brad and Karl had gone out briefly to the 'General Store', they called it, for groceries, and Mirela went to take a nap after making lunch. Randall had taken his plate of food out-side, and she didn't know where the hell the twins were. They still creeped her out, popping up all over the place like they seemed to do.

So it was just her standing in the living room, and Ber-nadette, who lay on the couch reading the book Kaylee had brought her that morning. Leo went to sit on the other end of the couch, picking at the last pieces of lasagna. Bernadette seemed to know a little bit about everyone, and she won-dered if the woman wouldn't mind being the first to fess up and let Leo in on what the hell kinda weird shit Kaylee pulled. It made her feel really stupid, then, realizing she ac-tually wanted to know more about the girl and that she found it so hard to bring it up.

"What can I do for you, Leo?" Bernadette asked. She glanced over the pages of her book at Leo, her reading glasses sitting at the tip of her nose.

"Hmm?" She only noticed then that she'd been staring at the woman while her brain dragged her around in circles.

"You've been staring at me, pushing your fork around on an empty plate." The woman's smile told Leo everything she needed to know—if anyone was going to tell her about Kaylee, Bernadette would.

"Sorry," Leo said. Sorry? She hardly ever apologized for anything, and here she was, acting all awkward and shy like an idiot.

Bernadette laughed. "Don't be." She dog-eared the page she was reading, closed the book, and set it down on the coffee table. "I know your few days here haven't exactly been stress-free." Leo smirked. "What's on your mind?"

Bernadette pushed herself up just a little on the cushions, readjusting her arms.

"Can I help you with that?" It just fell out of her mouth.

"No, no. I'm fine. Go ahead."

Leo took a deep breath, caught Bernadette's blue gaze, and managed a half smile. "What's up with Kaylee?" Jesus, that sounded stupid and ignorant all at the same time.

Bernadette chuckled. "What do you mean?"

"She's just… uh…" The words eluded her. Yeah, Leo knew what Bernadette could do with her words, how strangely having listened to the woman's beat seemed to tear down the wall of necessary politeness, but she really couldn't bring herself to tell a woman old enough to be her grandmother what had happened the night before.

"Did you try talking to her?" Bernadette asked, saving Leo from the embarrassment of having to come up with something.

"Well, kinda." She blew out a half-assed chuckle. "But that didn't really work out… the way I expected." Rubbing the back of her head, she looked up sheepishly at Bernadette.

The woman only raised her eyebrows and gave a smile that said, 'I completely understand.' "And you want to know…"

"Just… where she comes from," Leo answered. Making eye contact with Bernadette and keeping her gaze seemed infinitely easier now, and it seemed maybe she'd get a break. "She's the only person who seems like she *really* doesn't want me here, and nobody else seems to notice. And then… well, she's done a few things that say the exact opposite."

Bernadette nodded slowly, like she knew everything already, and Leo felt a flush rise at the top of her ears. No way could the woman know what had really happened.

With a big sigh, Bernadette lowered her head and stared at Leo, giving her the same look she had on the day they met—the day she'd told Leo about having to make a choice to join Sleepwater. "You know we don't tell people about any beat but our own," she said slowly.

"Yeah," Leo said and closed her eyes. She clunked the fork on her plate a few times.

"But I'll tell you," Bernadette added, "because I have a feeling I might be the only one who will. At least for a while. It might even help you out a little."

Leo looked up again and caught the hint of a dubious smirk on the woman's face. "Help me?"

"I saw you two this morning." The older woman's smirk turned into a grin when she raised her eyebrows a few times.

This morning? When Kaylee had stared her down and demanded her shirt back? Leo hardly thought anything in that short-lived interaction counted as even remotely close to what Bernadette seemed to insinuate, and just thinking about it kind of pissed her off. And then she thought about the night before, about Kaylee in her bed, and while that had pissed her off too, not to mention completely confused her, she couldn't hide a tiny smile. "I don't think—"

"You don't have to say anything else," Bernadette added, cutting her off. "This stays between you and me." She eyed Leo over her reading glasses. Leo nodded. "You of all people know what I mean when I say that girl has really had it rough." Yeah, she'd figured that much. "And Kaylee wasn't spared a lot of truly negative attention that came her way. Her father worked at MindBlink."

Leo had been staring at her jeans, but her eyes flicked up to Bernadette's face at those last words. "At—" The rest of her sentence stuck in her throat.

"With your father," Bernadette added, giving a tiny nod in response.

Leo slumped back against the couch cushion and blinked. No fucking way. Kaylee had mentioned Leo's dad the night before, but it made no fucking sense then, had seemed like some weird thing about dads before seducing chicks in their bedroom. Goddammit, if her own good-for-absolutely-nothing father was the only reason the girl had even looked at her in the first place—if he wasn't already dead, Leo would have killed him. She'd spent too much time getting the fuck out from beneath him and his name, his fucking debts, and his pathetic junkie life.

She took a deep breath. "So, that's the only reason she…" It was impossible to get the rest of the sentence out, but she didn't feel like she had to anymore. Bernadette seemed to have some kind of mind-reading abilities in addition to her beat, unless Leo was so transparent, all her thoughts flashed in neon letters through her skin.

"Leo," Bernadette called, tilting her head to get Leo's attention. "It has nothing to do with you." Leo looked back up at her. "I think, more than anything, that serves as an extra connection between you two. At least in her mind," Bernadette added. "You know what it's like to grow up under the hand of a man who pioneered the Information Technology

Industry."

Leo felt like her eyeballs would burst from her head, and when she squeezed them shut, it only doubled the feeling. "Fuck." It was all she could whisper. She'd thought she'd done everything possible to completely erase that man's meaning from her life altogether, and apparently, she'd been wrong. Apparently, his work—and his name—would keep haunting her. And if the mention of his name had brought Kaylee into her bedroom and out again just as quickly, what value did it have here for these other people? For Sleepwater? Did they keep her here because of who her father had been? She clenched her fists into the cushions and leaned back to look at the ceiling.

"She's gotten a lot better since she and Cameron found Sleepwater," Bernadette said, the sound of her voice a welcome distraction.

"Are she and Cameron…" Leo couldn't finish that sentence, either. What the hell had happened to her ability to speak?

With a tiny chuckle, Bernadette shook her head. "No, not at all." She smiled. "They came to Sleepwater at the same time, together, and I'm sure they have more of a history than even I know. But Cameron's seen himself as the only person who would protect her for so long, I don't think he'll give that up any time soon."

Leo couldn't decide if that was a good thing or totally fucked up. She could handle this information about Kaylee, could maybe think about talking to her eventually and disregard what she knew and what had happened. But the image of Cameron's scowling face kept popping back up. Either way, she felt a little surer that whatever they were doing upstairs, if they were even in the same room, they weren't fucking. And that thought made her feel like she was back in fucking high school.

"If you choose to… look further into that connection," Bernadette continued, catching Leo's gaze again, "be careful. With her. Kaylee's only ever been used to hurting people, and it's taken its toll on her more than you can imagine."

Was Bernadette really concerned about that tiny little girl hurting her? Leo would have laughed if Bernadette's expression, serious as all hell, didn't make her insanely curious. "What do you mean?"

Bernadette frowned. "That's what she does, Leo. That's her beat."

33

AFTER HER CONVERSATION with Bernadette, Leo went out for a walk by the river. She made sure to stay far enough away from the water and close enough to the house that she could either run or scream if she had to. Both of these things felt oddly appropriate, but really, she had a nagging feeling that the river was a lot more dangerous than it made itself out to be. Kind of like Sleepwater, and funny how the name seemed so fitting for them both.

She didn't have a clue where all this was headed. Finding Bernadette on the side of the road with Karl had been enough. Hearing Karl's story and that Sleepwater was apparently some rebel group terrorizing labs and their research around experimenting on people like them? Even better. For a brief moment, between all the information the night before and waking up that morning, she'd thought that maybe something simple and distracting would come along. With Kaylee. But even that had a fucking disclaimer beneath all the confusing wrapping paper and erotically violent little bow on top.

If Karl's place hadn't been completely destroyed, she'd want to just go back there, get wasted on the couch. But then none of this would have happened.

She hiked up a small hill on the riverbank, climbed over a boulder, and just stood there, staring. The water rushed below her, screaming out its own tense energy, and it made her dizzy to watch the rapid movement. Leo kicked a fist-sized rock into the river and watched it get sucked under by the white, foaming mass, wiping away the spray of freezing water that splashed back up at her face in response. The same thing would happen to her if she wasn't careful—she'd be washed away by all the chaos. And for what?

There wasn't a single other choice she was even remotely willing to make.

Among the groceries Karl and Brad had brought back for them were a couple of rotisserie chickens, a salad Mirela had concocted with vegetables and a dressing Leo had never seen before, and a giant gallon of tea. Of course, there was beer if anyone wanted it. Leo took one.

Tony and Don said they wanted to watch some old black and white film, and they grabbed the tiny box TV from the kitchen counter, setting it up on an entry table against the wall so anyone sitting down could see it. To Leo's surprise, Cameron wordlessly walked upstairs and came back down with a set of freakishly large speakers and a ridiculous coil of wiring, offering it to add to their viewing pleasure. It seemed like a silly thing, really—to have just learned some-one had gone after both Karl and Bernadette, without know-ing who they were or if they'd try again, and to now be sit-ting around the living room with the remains of their dinners in their laps, watching a movie. But Leo appreciated the ef-fort on the twins' part, and it made sense. The day had been unbearably awkward, watching people move in and out of the house, sharing tense glances, whispering short, tight con-versations in passing. No one wanted to talk about what was going on, and with both the movie and Cameron's proven sound system at work, they had an excuse not to.

Mirela filled a few giant bowls with popcorn she'd cooked on the stove, handing one of them to Leo with a smile. "Thanks," Leo said, surprised by the gesture. She hadn't had popcorn in a long time.

"Looks pretty good," Mirela replied, giving Leo a slow wink. "Anybody else need anything?"

"Lights," one of the twins called, and the other made a quick flip-the-switch motion with his hand.

"Right." Mirela turned off the living room lights, then walked to Brad, who was sprawled out in his armchair with another bowl of popcorn and a beer. "I'm gonna turn in early," she said, leaning over the chair to kiss him briefly.

Brad lightly put a hand to Mirela's cheek. "You okay?" he asked with a frown. She gave a slow nod, closing her eyes. "Love you," he added.

"Love you."

Leo watched the exchange and felt a flutter around her

diaphragm. Something didn't seem quite right in Mirela's eyes, her slow smile tinged with what looked like pain. Leo hadn't seen that expression before and, knowing Mirela had slept almost entirely between lunch and dinner, felt the long-unfamiliar sensation of concern for someone else. Real concern.

Mirela stood and walked across the living room toward the front hall and the staircase, followed by a barrage of murmured good nights along the way. Leo glanced at the couch next to her, shared by Randall and Bernadette, who gave each other a look that left Leo entirely out of the conversation. She figured if no one else seemed particularly concerned, maybe she didn't have a reason to be, either. Though that wasn't necessarily how these people worked, was it?

Karl had just stepped through the sliding glass door from the porch and placed a hand on Brad's shoulder, giving a little squeeze, before he sat in his own chair. The twins had taken up the far couch, which really gave them the best view of the TV, and Cameron sat alone on the bench below the window. Kaylee wasn't there.

Then the movie started, and Leo let her attention drift back there, as she figured it was supposed to do. The twins had chosen some ridiculous film about Soviet Russia, and Leo couldn't remember ever having to focus so hard just to figure out what was going on in the first fifteen minutes. At first, she thought it had something to do with the twins constantly distracting her with their whispers and sniggers as they pointed at the screen.

"Quiet, children," Cameron hissed, and while Don—or Tony—only turned around to flip him the bird, Leo found herself smiling. Apparently, that was another one of the twins' quirks. Apparently, this was movie night. She didn't know those existed, in any house, anymore.

It hardly registered when the couch cushion moved just a little under an added weight and the popcorn bowl was lifted deftly from her hands. Leo turned to see Kaylee sitting there, her legs crossed beneath her, the bowl of popcorn resting in her lap. The girl just stared straight ahead at the TV, the images flashing blankly across her face and reflected back in her eyes. Kaylee grabbed a fistful of popcorn and crumpled it into her mouth.

Leo's automatic reaction was to say something shitty and take the bowl back, but she stopped herself. If this was Kaylee's way of doing things, fine. She let herself relax against the couch, more than aware of the pressure of Kaylee's bent knee against her thigh. She reached out herself for more popcorn.

"Do you know what the fuck's going on?" Kaylee whispered, never taking her eyes off the screen. Leo could barely hear her.

"Something about missiles and vodka," she murmured. She tried so hard not to turn her head to look, but she caught the barely visible flicker at the corner of Kaylee's mouth.

"Do you like it?"

"The movie?"

"Vodka."

Leo all but snorted. "I guess. If that's all there is."

Kaylee grabbed another handful of popcorn. "I think it's all shit."

While this was technically their third conversation, and

the longest by far, it definitely seemed the strangest. Maybe Kaylee wasn't just a bitch all the time. Maybe she found talking just as difficult as Leo did.

Kaylee handed the bowl back to Leo, lifted one of her knees just a little, and scooted backwards to lean fully against Leo's side. Leo froze. Was this chick trying to cuddle with her and watch a movie? She quickly flicked her gaze toward the others. No one was watching them, and she had no clue if this was another one of Kaylee's freaky games she hadn't learned the rules to yet. Trying to ignore it, she reached for the popcorn, but then Kaylee grabbed it again and put it back in her own lap.

Leo tried so hard not to laugh. Okay. She put her arm around the girl instead.

She might have imagined it, but she thought she felt a tiny shudder run through Kaylee's shoulders after the girl leaned back even more into her and seemed to finally relax. If Leo had given a fuck about the movie before, she didn't now. Kaylee's hair felt like feathers on her arm. The girl was so small.

Something about this seemed incredibly wrong, tugging at a few tight strings of nostalgia when Alex flashed briefly through her mind. Leo hadn't done anything like this with anyone else, had never wanted to, and had never thought she would. But she pushed that out of her head, swallowing, when the other part of her thought it felt … right. And that was okay, wasn't it?

Kaylee barely turned her head so Leo could hear her. "Do you—"

A loud echo of knocks came from the front door, startling just about everyone. "Uh, I'll get it," Brad said, standing slowly. He jumped a little and moved faster when a few more hurried knocks rapped against the wood. Leo couldn't see the front door from where she sat, but she noticed Cameron staring down the hallway instead of at the TV. She heard the creak of the door opening.

"Karl here?" The voice was way too loud for the guy to have even noticed the dark, quiet house.

"Who are you?" Brad framed the question in a nice-enough way but with an undercurrent of warning.

"He's here, right?" the man answered, completely ignoring Brad. "I need to talk to him."

Karl pushed himself up out of the chair and headed toward the door. Everyone had pretty much stopped paying attention to the movie. He disappeared around the corner and into the hallway, then said, "Evan. What are you doing here?"

"Jesus Christ," the man said, sounding almost relieved. His voice was familiar—Leo knew an Evan, didn't she? "I busted my ass to get here as fast as I could, man." The terror and guilt in his voice drowned out the noise of the movie, which, Leo noticed, sputtered away with poor gunfire sound effects.

She sat up then, took the bowl of popcorn from Kaylee's lap, and set it on the floor. Yeah, she knew an Evan. She'd worked with him for exactly a week in Louis' back room at the Purple Lion—the guy who made a shit-ton of money spinning himself into animals. Something was wrong. She saw Cameron out of the corner of her eye, leaning forward on the bench and poised to jump up.

"Hey, calm down," Karl said.

"You don't have time for that, man. I'm so sorry. I think someone's coming."

The room exploded into action. Randall almost flew across the living room toward the room by the front door, Cameron close on his heels. Kaylee stood to follow them, yanking the TV's power cord right out of the wall. Leo was grateful to not have the sounds of fighting continuing in the background, but she still had no idea what was going on. Brad's footsteps pounded on the stairs as he ran up toward his bedroom.

"Who?" Karl's voice boomed from the hallway.

"Fuck, I don't know," Evan answered, his voice broken by the sound of the twins sliding the coffee table into the center of the living room.

Leo skirted around them and into the hallway. The door to the extra room was wide open now, and she saw Kaylee, Randall, and Cameron hunkered down around the black duffle bags and wires, moving quicker than she could follow. Through the sounds of zippers and heavy things moving around, she barely caught Evan's words of "just talking" and "wasn't thinking" and "some kinda military."

"What's going on?" she asked.

Karl whirled around to face her, fire behind his eyes. "Leo, go help Bernadette up. We need to go." In a second, she glanced past him to see that she'd guessed right about Evan. He caught her eyes, and his face drained of color. Then she turned and thudded across the wooden floor toward the couch and Bernadette.

"That was fast," the woman said, trying unsuccessfully to push herself all the way up into sitting.

Leo leaned over with a hand behind the woman's back to help her up. "Careful," she said, feeling the blood pounding in her neck. What the fuck was going on? Bernadette groaned, leaned her elbows on her knees, and closed her eyes. "What can I get you?" Leo asked.

"Just that glass of water." Bernadette cleared her throat and waved a hand toward the side table. Leo thought she was going to spill the water all over the woman's lap before she handed it to her. She heard more footsteps enter the room, something being tossed onto the coffee table and rustled through, but nothing clicked in her head.

"Want one?" one of the twins asked.

Bernadette opened one eye through the water glass, then swallowed. "Tony, you know I don't touch those things." It came out as almost a growl, making Leo turn around.

He held a fucking gun.

"What the fuck?" Leo shouted and almost fell backward on her ass.

Tony shrugged and stuck the gun in the waistband of his jeans. Leo's eyes flickered from the weapon to the coffee table, and she almost choked. Two of the black duffle bags lay spread wide open, revealing more fucking guns than she thought was allowed in a single house. The third was on the floor, and in it she glimpsed a thick, sturdy-looking laptop and a bunch of other technical shit she didn't understand.

Brad and Mirela ran down the stairs, Leo's backpack flapping against Mirela's long sweater. The woman also carried two smaller bags, and she set them down beside Cameron and Kaylee before delivering Leo's.

"This one's yours," Tony said, offering Leo a pistol and grinning. Well, she could fucking tell the difference between them, now.

"I don't—" she started.

"We're going out the kitchen," Karl ordered. The black bags were zipped up, cinched, and slung over shoulders.

"Karl, I—" Evan said before Karl whirled on him.

"You're coming with us." Then he looked at Leo and raised his eyebrows. "Take it."

Leo swallowed, and Tony dropped the pistol in her hands. It was heavy and cold, and she didn't realize how hard she gripped it until she stood and watched the others heading toward the sliding glass door.

The twins moved to either side of Bernadette and helped her off the couch. They both held her up with one of their own arms, carrying what looked like machine guns in the other. "Jesus," Leo whispered. She grabbed her backpack from the floor and strapped it over both shoulders.

"Go wide around the house to the van," Karl said. "Bernadette gets there first."

Leo stepped in line after Randall, the gun slippery in her sweating hand and her heart pounding.

It seemed too quiet outside in the darkness, the river just to their right far too loud. Leo hoped it was the river and not the blood all going to her head. Tony and Don moved quickly with Bernadette between them and obviously knew exactly where they were going; they didn't have flashlights or any light to guide them. She realized then just how stupid of a move that would be.

She heard tires crunching on the gravel lot, doors opening swiftly, and she gripped the gun even tighter. How was she supposed to see if anybody fucking came at her? They moved along the riverbank and between the few thin trees before the forest thickened, and Leo couldn't decide if she should be watching out for whoever was after them or trying to keep up with Randall in front of her. Something crunched back by the house, probably the front door being kicked in. Her breathing came heavy as she jogged to keep up, the light of the stars streaking sporadically through the branches like a strobe light across her face.

A shout from behind, a dull whip in the air, and the tree trunk in front of her exploded. "Shit," she shouted and ducked, though it wouldn't have done her any good if the bullet hadn't missed.

"Go!" she heard Karl shout. The tapping of gunfire behind her intensified and grew louder, and she just fucking ran. They'd already started moving back to the left, where they'd come up to Randall's van by the road, and she briefly caught a glimpse of the twins helping Bernadette into the back before another bullet hit the ground next to her foot and she skidded into the dirt.

Scrambling to her knees, she glanced back toward the house and saw what looked like a bunch of headlights bobbing in and out of the darkness. They were everywhere. Then she saw Kaylee running up toward her, Karl and Evan close on her heels, and one of the bobbing lights way too close behind them. She didn't even think—she raised the pistol and squeezed off a shot. The unexpected force of it knocked her backward, and she shouted in surprise.

Then a figure barreled out of the forest and into her, sending her sprawling across the ground. She thought she heard Karl shout something else, but her ears were ringing. When she turned to look, she found the person who had run into her wearing dark fatigues, the headlight broken and dangling from the side of his head. The man stood, paused, and she knew he'd seen her. Leo scrambled to her feet and froze. All rational thinking left her, and for the first time in her life, she couldn't even move as the man leveled his own gun at her chest.

Through the sound of gunfire, she heard someone talking. And then Kaylee stepped up from behind her, walking slowly toward the man with the gun.

"Once upon a midnight dreary, while I pondered, weak and weary…"

Was that Poe? The psycho chick was reciting poetry while they were being run down!

The man in front of her went rigid, and his weapon slipped out of his fingers and into the dirt. Then the most excruciating pain Leo had ever felt gripped her entire left leg, and she crumpled. It burned beneath her skin, through her muscles and bones, roiling and exploding in every form imaginable—not contained in any one spot but consuming any other possible thoughts Leo could have had. She coughed into a spray of dirt beneath her cheek, choking, struggling to suck in air. She hadn't ever been shot, but she figured if a bullet hurt, this was a hundred times worse. Her leg felt like it was being twisted around a pole of spikes, and when she clutched it with both hands, wracked with spasms on the ground, she couldn't even really feel it anymore. All she felt was pain.

She opened her eyes just long enough to see the man's face on the ground, feet from her own, his eyes wide and staring blankly at her. Dark streaks slithered from his ears and nose toward the dirt, and something shimmered on the ground beside his head. Only when a pair of boots appeared beside Leo's head, their owner's shadow blocking out the light reflected in the shimmering pool, did Leo realize it was blood.

"I…"

She heard Kaylee's voice, but she couldn't say anything. The pain had died down only a little, but it still shot through her like a ravenous muscle cramp, and she squeezed the tears out of her eyes.

"Fuck, get her up," came Karl's voice, and Leo felt hands digging painfully into her armpits, lifting her from the ground. She screamed when her left leg took a little of her weight. "I got her," Karl said, and she got a quick glance of Kaylee running away from them toward the van. "Sorry, kid," Karl grunted as he half-carried, half-dragged her. "That was my fault."

She didn't know what the hell he was talking about, but she wanted the pain to fucking stop. They must have been close, because it seemed only seconds before they made it to the open door of the van and hands reached out to pull her inside.

"What happened?" someone asked.

Leo thought it just a little odd that she felt the van jerk into motion, swerving a little in the gravel, before she heard the door sliding shut.

"Forgot to give her a headset."

"Oh, fuck," came another voice, followed by a chuckle.

Then she passed out.

34

THE VIBRATION OF the van's engine made Leo want to go right back to sleep when she felt herself waking up. She was warm, her head lay on something soft, and the pain in her leg was gone. That last thought made her open her eyes, and the first thing she saw was the underside of Kaylee's chin—she was lying in the girl's lap. Then she realized the tickling sensation she felt at the top of her head was Kaylee's fingers brushing through her hair. Leo would have relaxed into it, would have enjoyed the sensation and the weirdly intimate gesture on Kaylee's part, but the image of the pool of blood by the man's head flashed through her mind, and she sat up as quickly as she could manage.

Kaylee pretty much flinched out of her seat when Leo

moved, quickly folding her arms and turning her head farther than necessary just to stare out the window. Leo groaned when she finally sat up all the way in the seat, her head feeling like it was about to split open. "What happened?" she asked, her voice scratchy.

"Hey, look who's alive," one of the twins said from behind her.

Leo turned in her seat to look back—the twins, Evan, and Cameron sat in the middle row, Randall, Brad, and a sleeping Mirela in the back. Cameron looked a bit more than mildly uncomfortable squeezed next to the twins and Evan, but they'd laid Leo out in the first passenger row so she could lay in Kaylee's lap, and that was all the room they had.

"How you feelin?" Karl asked from the driver seat, and she turned around again to meet his gaze through the rearview mirror.

"Fine."

Karl nodded once at her, and she turned to look at Kaylee, who acted like she hadn't even noticed anyone else was in the van. Leo wanted to talk to her, to say something, but she had the distinct feeling that she'd just caught Kaylee in a deep, dark secret and that the last thing the girl wanted to do was talk about it in front of everybody.

Leo rubbed the back of her head and looked out the other window. It took a minute to figure out why the view seemed so strange—mountains stretched on either side of them, the morning sun just barely peeking out over the summits outside Kaylee's window. They were even more in the mountains than Brad and Mirela's house had been.

After just a few minutes, they slowed down at an intersection seemingly dropped in the middle of the highway and turned off in front of a General Store. Leo frowned; from the front, it really didn't look much bigger than a convenience store. Cameron stepped up from the middle row to open the door, and pretty much everyone filed out. Leo stayed back for a second and turned to Kaylee again, who still stared out the window. "Are you okay?" she asked, thinking it a better time to ask now that not everyone could hear them. Bernadette still sat in the front passenger seat, and Karl had just stepped out and shut the driver-side door.

Kaylee turned her head so fast that her curtain of hair lifted and almost hit Leo in the face. She glared at Leo, eyes shimmering, and two tears slipped down her cheeks. Leo swallowed, the pain she saw in Kaylee's eyes almost as intense as the pain she'd felt from Kaylee's words. Because she knew that was what had happened to her leg—Kaylee's beat meant for the man who'd aimed his gun at her. Leo took a breath and opened her mouth to speak, but Kaylee's lip curled. "Get the fuck out," she spat.

Leo's automatic reaction was to glance up at the rear-view mirror—she thought she felt eyes on her reflected there. But Karl wasn't in the van, and Bernadette seemed to be asleep. Sighing, Leo crawled out of the seat and hunched over to step out of the van, closing the door behind her. Whatever Kaylee's fucking problem was, she didn't want to deal with it right now. She had absolutely no idea what was going on in the first place.

Karl had stepped around the back of the van to meet her, and he fixed her with an expectant stare. Hands in his pockets, he kicked a patch of dirt in the parking lot and lowered his head toward her.

"What?" Leo asked, shoving her hands into her own pockets as she walked off toward the General Store's front steps. She didn't have the energy for any more guessing games—for running around in any more circles.

Karl followed closely by her side. "That really was all my fault back there," he started, then cleared his throat.

"Which part?" she asked. She distinctly felt his eyes boring into her, but she didn't look up at him, even as he held the door open for her and she stepped inside.

"You getting hurt."

She would have loved to hear more, but Cameron approached them on his way to the checkout counter, then slapped a hand down on Leo's shoulder. "Mornin', champ," he said with his off-putting grin. "Looks like you earned your stripes. Glad you made it." He nodded a bit too sarcastically and pushed past them with an armful of potato chip bags.

"What the hell is he talking about?" Leo asked. It was so tiring trying to figure out what everybody meant instead of just hearing what they wanted to say.

Karl made a noncommittal noise in his throat. "Want some coffee?"

"I guess." She followed him to the counter of coffee and creamer packages, staring at the weird stains on the carafe even though it was stainless steel.

Karl pulled out a Styrofoam cup for both of them and started fixing his own. "Remember when I told you the beat doesn't work through technology?"

"Like recordings." She stared down at the coffee he absentmindedly poured in her cup as well.

"Yeah." He reached into his pocket and pulled out a fist, opening it by his waist to reveal a small, foldable headset—just an earpiece and an extendable microphone. "It's my fault because I never gave you one of these." He looked up quickly to glance around the store like he was showing her a handful of drugs instead of technology.

Leo would have laughed if they were talking about anything else. Instead, she let out an overly long sigh and rolled her eyes, opening five of the creamer containers into her coffee. "I'm too tired to guess," she said, surprising herself by how annoyed she sounded.

Karl fiddled with the earpiece in his hand. "We all wear one of these," he said in a low voice. "It's how we… protect ourselves from each other, if we have to. Some of our beats can get distracting when we're... working."

"You mean like blowing shit up?" Leo spat at him.

He quickly glanced over his shoulder, then gave her the most demeaning stare she'd ever seen. "Come on," he whispered. "I explained that."

"Yeah, but apparently you forgot to give me the magic headgear," she replied, pointing to Karl's fist. She stirred her coffee a little too hard, leaving a puddle on the counter before almost slamming the lid on the cup. "And you forgot to tell me that Kaylee's beat kills people." Feeling a headache coming on, she brushed past him and grabbed a package of crackers, almost running up to the counter. The guy manning the store just stared at her impassively, and she felt her blood boil when she realized she had to wait for Karl to join her— she hadn't brought her money in with her.

The cashier's eyes rolled lazily to rest on Karl when he stepped up beside her, and Leo glared at the neon Open sign in the window. When they stepped outside, Karl wordlessly handed her one of the two packs of cigarettes he'd bought, and they lit up by the picnic table next to the sidewalk.

"You can't blame her," Karl finally said, turning to look at her. Leo chewed on the inside of her cheek. "You two have a lot in common."

Leo couldn't help the sarcastic laugh. "Except for she's got serious problems."

"Oh, that's right. I forgot you're perfect."

A flush of anger and embarrassment hit Leo in the face, and she quickly huffed down the last of her cigarette. He was right, she knew. Leo was just as fucked up as the next guy, but if Kaylee had that much power to hurt someone with her words, how much pain had the girl caused with her beat? Leo had a hard enough time trusting people in the first place, mostly because she could make anybody believe any of her bullshit if she really wanted. She couldn't imagine what it must have felt like to just hurt people all the time.

That thought seemed to explain Kaylee's last ... nighttime visit. Maybe all the girl wanted was to make someone else feel *good* for a change, and fuck reciprocation. Leo gulped her coffee and headed back toward the van. Maybe there was a way to figure the girl out, after all.

The others had all gotten what they needed from the store and returned to the van, joking with easy smiles like nothing had happened—like they hadn't been chased by men with guns in the middle of the night. As she watched the others getting back in their seats, Leo stared at Evan—the bearer of all their bad news.

She stopped Randall before he could duck back into the van's side door, putting her hand on his shoulder. "Is this guy staying with us the whole time?"

"Evan?"

She nodded.

"Yeah. We're stopping by a place in Red Feather Lakes. Town in Colorado. And then we'll figure out where we're going from there." He gave her a simple smile, then jumped like he remembered something and reached into the pocket of his green windbreaker. "Just in case." He opened his hand to reveal another headset.

Leo took it, gave a nod, and raised the headset in a salute. "Probably a good idea."

Randall chuckled and ducked to step into the van, and Leo followed, sitting next to Kaylee again. It looked like the girl hadn't even moved, but she munched on a bag of chips—probably from Cameron. Leo toyed with the plastic package of crackers she'd made Karl buy, not hungry in the least bit and wondering what the fuck else was waiting for them in Colorado.

Karl got back into the driver's seat, hoisted a thumbs-up without turning to look back, and started the van. The second they turned back onto the highway out of the General

Store lot, it felt like they were right back in the middle of nowhere, in the mountains, with nothing around for miles. Leo wondered how people could live like that, so far away from absolutely everything. When she really thought about it, though, that seemed exactly what she was doing herself now, with Sleepwater, and she realized she wouldn't have it any other way.

After a few minutes of silence, Brad called out from the back, "Anybody mind some tunes?"

The general consensus was a complete lack of opinion, so with a cheer, Brad issued a CD case and told Leo to pass it up to the front. Metallica. Leo stared at it for a few seconds, then passed it up to Bernadette's waiting hands. She noticed Kaylee's snort of amusement and couldn't help her own tiny smile. The sounds of the first track's slow guitar harmonies filled the van, and even though no one had been talking before the drums started, the silence seemed just a bit more communal with the heavy metal blasting through the speakers. Leo couldn't believe that Bernadette didn't seem to have an issue with the music—even seemed to nod her head a little with the rhythm.

How had this become her life?

Leo reached over and grabbed Kaylee's hand from the girl's lap. She didn't even think about it, didn't give herself enough time to wonder whether or not it was a good idea here. Kaylee didn't turn, didn't look at Leo, didn't return the gesture with a squeeze or any form of acknowledgment. But she didn't pull her hand away, either.

35

KARL HANDED DRIVING duty over to Randall the next time they stopped for gas, and they finally pulled up to what looked like an old warehouse a few miles outside of downtown Sterling. It was just past midnight, and the only light came from a flickering Open sign in the front window of a dive bar a few blocks down the street. Nobody said a thing as they filed out of the van, exhausted and cramped. Leo glanced at Mirela, who seemed to have slept the whole drive, and noticed the grimace on the woman's face as she bent over and twisted, stretching her body.

When Leo lit a cigarette and took a fresh breath of the thin air, Kaylee approached her and held out a hand. "Lemme have a drag of that."

Leo glanced at her own cigarette and frowned. She'd never seen Kaylee smoke before, but she handed it over anyways. Kaylee stared at her, unblinking, as she took a few long drags. The girl took her time and didn't offer a smile or a word. But something about her seemed a little less hardened toward Leo—only slightly more inviting.

They shared the rest of the cigarette as the twins unloaded bags from the back of the van. A woman dressed in only a tank top and short shorts, with a huge, meticulously groomed growth of dreadlocks, stepped out through one of the warehouse doors and called out Karl's name. Brad and Mirela seemed to recognize her too, and they gathered in semi-hushed voices to hug the woman. Leo wondered if she had any idea that this many people would be showing up in a van in the middle of the night, not to mention the fact that they were most likely being followed. That thought alone made her light another cigarette, which Kaylee also silently shared.

The woman with the dreadlocks waved them over, and after grabbing their bags from the pile outside the van, everyone filed in through the warehouse door in weary silence. Most of the lights were off, but a few work lamps clamped to the rafters lit their way. Leo thought something looked a little off about the layout inside until she realized they were weaving their way through box-like rooms built inside the warehouse, made of two-by-fours, wood paneling, and cheap-looking doors. Then they passed a series of untreated shelving that reached all the way to the warehouse's tin ceiling, stuffed almost to overflowing with books, furniture, clothing, odd bits of household appliances, and even a few mannequins. Full-sized kitchen appliances lined the wall ahead of them, and then they entered what felt like an open living room. A mish-mash of couches, chairs, beanbags, and pillows were scattered about the space, and Leo noted the first standing lamp with an actual lampshade in the far corner, lighting up the crowded-feeling area.

"My name's Shannon," the woman with dreads said, finally addressing them all. She smiled warmly and waved a hand for them to sit. Leo flopped into the closest beanbag and had to keep from laughing too loud when Kaylee just about jumped on top of her. They did a bit of awkward rearranging in the giant cushion, not looking at each other, but Leo finally got her arm around Kaylee's shoulders and wondered just how much she might get away with now. Brad flashed them another huge grin as he sat behind Mirela to rub her shoulders, and when Leo quickly looked away, her gaze fell on Evan's terrified expression. He didn't seem too excited to be here, but if their near capture at the mountain house had been her fault, she wouldn't have been too happy to spend more time with other beat-spinners, either.

Karl helped Bernadette onto one of the couches, and a few seconds of strained silence hovered around them. "So, you guys made it to the Red Feather House," Shannon continued. "And just in time, too. We've got kind of a shindig planned for the day after tomorrow, and luckily, you guys get the first pick of our rooms." Leo wondered who else the woman was referring to, as Shannon had been the only one to greet them.

"Rooms?" Evan asked.

"Right inside the back door," Tony called, pointing over his brother's head in the direction they'd come.

Shannon grinned. "Yup. They're all empty right now. I think we have twelve."

"So… this is a hotel?" Don asked. Karl grunted a laugh.

"Sort of," Shannon said. "We also host a lot of music shows. And, of course," she added, turning to smile at Bernadette, "Sleepwater's always welcome here." Bernadette nodded sleepily and shifted her weight around in the couch. "Feel free to help yourself to anything you find here. Food, clothes, whatever. We have a lot of stuff and it's here to be used." Then Shannon stood and scratched her head through her dreadlocks. "I'm at the top of these stairs if you need anything," she added, pointing to a set of raw stairs leading up to a platform that had been built against the warehouse wall. "But you guys should be fine. You've been through a lot, I'm guessing, so I'll leave you to it." She exchanged tired smiles and more warm hugs with Karl, Brad, Mirela, and Bernadette, and all the others who'd showed up in the van stood from their seats with audible groans and sighs.

Grabbing her backpack, Leo headed back toward the box-like rooms, taking her time to soak up the weirdness of the way the warehouse had been turned into a space resembling something livable. The only thing she hadn't seen so far was a bathroom, and she wondered if Shannon kept it hidden on purpose. She watched the twins grab two of the ramshackle rooms themselves and didn't wait to see what everyone else had done before she opened the next door. The thin mattress on the floor was covered only by a wool blanket and pillow, and a lightbulb hung from the rather low ceiling hammered to the top of the box. She pulled on the string to the light and almost tore a hole in the wall as she backed into it. A half-naked mannequin stood in the corner, its head bare except for a few patches of colorless fuzz, its left arm missing at the shoulder.

Cursing under her breath, she turned around and almost stepped on Kaylee standing in the doorway. "What the fuck?" she blurted.

"I like this one," Kaylee said, her expression as deadpan and unreadable as ever. Slowly, she looked over Leo's shoulder to briefly eye the mannequin.

"Great. You can have it," Leo said, but when she tried to step out of the room, Kaylee slammed her hand up against the doorframe, completely blocking the doorway with her tiny body. The lightbulb swung gently.

"All the other rooms are taken."

If Leo didn't know better, she would have thought the girl was attempting a pouting face. "Seriously?" she asked but couldn't keep the corner of her mouth from twitching up into a tiny smile.

Kaylee stared her down without blinking. "Can I stay with you?" The way she said it, coming from anyone else, would have made Leo think it was the absolute last thing the girl actually wanted.

Leo turned away from her and dropped her backpack at the foot of the mattress, letting a barely larger smile flicker when she heard the door close behind her. When she turned back to face Kaylee, the girl was reaching out to pull the string of the lightbulb. Moving just quickly enough to stop her, Leo stepped toward her, slid a hand along her cheek, and kissed her. Kaylee stiffened and stepped back, but Leo followed the short distance to the wall until she had Kaylee pressed up against the paneling. The girl kissed her back, her heavy breath betraying the apathy expressed in her stillness.

Finally, Leo pulled back and hooked a finger through a belt loop of Kaylee's jeans. She noticed Kaylee squinting, and where before she would have thought it was in anger, it now appeared with the shimmering at the corner of the girl's eyes, the flush just at the top of her cheeks. Was she about to cry?

"I'm not mad," Leo said, remembering the tears Kaylee had wiped away when she'd woken up in the van. Yeah, the girl's beat hurt like hell, but Leo couldn't blame her for that.

"You should be," Kaylee hissed, glaring at her like she had the first time Leo stepped into Brad and Mirela's mountain house to meet Sleepwater.

Only now, Leo realized the glare meant something else entirely. It wasn't animosity. It wasn't hatred or some perpetual state of being pissed off. The girl was daring her to get closer and begging her not to run away. Nothing but pain and loneliness and only having hurt people existed behind those eyes, and Leo's sudden recognition of it clarified Kaylee's odd behavior like a giant magnifying glass. She wondered how long it had been since anyone had made this girl feel anything beyond miserable.

"Fuck that," Leo whispered and quickly kissed her again, wrapping an arm slowly around the girl's waist. Kaylee gave another sigh, then seemed to give in, collapsing into Leo's body pressed against her. She wrapped a fist in Leo's hair, pulling her closer, and then Leo was throwing the girl's shirt across the tiny box of a room—kneeling to unbutton Kaylee's jeans and bite the hot skin just beside the sharp curve of a hip. She yanked down, loving the way the sound of slightly ripping clothing mixed with the gasp of surprise before Kaylee's head fell back against the flimsy wall. Then Leo stood, pulled the girl to her again, and led her to the tiny mattress. When she ran a hand across Kaylee's collarbone, tasted both the sweetness of skin and the tang of a metal nipple piercing in her mouth, she realized the girl was trembling. She couldn't be sure it was entirely out of excitement, that fear didn't in some part drive the tightness of Kaylee's closed eyes. But when Leo stopped to look at her, the girl opened her eyes, either unaware of or ignoring the few tears slipping out.

She wanted to say something but remembered the last time they'd been in this situation; Kaylee had told her to shut the fuck up. And maybe that was the best way to handle whatever the girl was feeling right then, because while for the first time Leo actually cared enough to want to say something, she had no idea how to do it the right way. But she knew how to do this.

When she pulled at the band of gray cotton just under Kaylee's hips, the girl grabbed her face and kissed her with something far less like anger and bordering on gratitude. Determined not to let their last encounter repeat itself, Leo slipped a hand between Kaylee's skinny legs and decided she'd do whatever it took to make sure neither one of them felt more pain than pleasure.

36

IT SURPRISED HER a lot less than she expected when she woke up to find that Kaylee hadn't left this time. What did surprise her was the softness of the kiss the girl gave her when she opened her eyes, followed by the extra half hour they gave themselves on the lumpy mattress before putting their clothes back on. When they stepped out of the make-shift box of a bedroom, the first thing Leo saw was the twins, hauling the black duffel bags out of the boxes in which they'd spent the night. Tony glanced up at her as he zipped up one bag, flashing her a huge grin and raising his eye-brows. Don slung his own giant bag over his shoulder and hit the side of his fist against the thin wall of his box-room, letting out mock moans in the same rhythm.

Leo glanced at Kaylee beside her, feeling like an idiot when she noticed her mouth hanging open but unable some-how to shut it. Okay, so they hadn't been quiet, and she had no idea how to gauge what Kaylee might think of it. But the girl only shoved her hands into the pockets of her tight jeans and headed toward what served as the warehouse's living room. She didn't look at the twins, didn't look at Leo, but the tiny flicker of a smile at the corner of her mouth was unmistakable. Leo couldn't tell if the tangle worming its way through her gut was from anxiety or relief; it had a been a long time since she'd had the need to distinguish between the two.

Tony snickered, and she turned from watching Kaylee to fix him with a glare and flip him the bird. But she couldn't hide her own tiny smile before she walked to the front of the warehouse too.

Everyone else was already awake, standing around a table that hadn't been in the front room the night before but was now loaded with coffee, muffins, and a box of donuts. There was little conversation, yet again, but the tension of the last day and a half had morphed into something closer to excitement—anticipation. Leo grabbed a paper cup and filled it with coffee, pausing halfway through a bite of muffin to watch the twins deliver the duffel bags in the center of the room, grinning like idiots. Everyone from Sleepwater stepped away from the table and found seats. Leo glanced at Evan, who stood against the far wall, looking so uncomfortable it made her want to punch him in the face. Somehow, he seemed to know more about what was going on right then than she did, and she doubted he'd had very much to do with Sleepwater other than showing up in the middle of the night with a warning that gave them barely enough time to get out. She glared at him, and as the others gathered around the duffel bags, Leo also noticed that Shannon found some particular interest in Evan as well. The woman sat on the stairs leading up to her lofted bed, eyes narrowed, looking like some hungry animal about to pounce on the guy. Leo understood the feeling, but she didn't know what reason Shannon would have for aiming that kind of obvious disdain.

"Let's get this fuckin' show on the road."

Leo looked away to find Cameron lying back in the giant beanbag, a thick, indestructible-looking laptop perched in his lap. His perpetual scowl went unchanged, but some light she hadn't seen before flared behind his eyes. Was this how the guy showed excitement?

"I'm ready too," Randall added, and when Leo turned to look at him, she saw a slightly larger laptop in his lap. This one looked like it folded into a crash-proof suitcase, an odd collection of antennae poking wildly from the top. A handful of thick cables ran from the machine to two smaller black boxes Randall had placed on the floor beside his chair, giving his already alien-like physique a cyborg twist.

Turning to meet Karl's gaze, she realized her mouth was hanging open and felt her teeth clack together when she closed it. Karl gave her a tiny smirk in response, and the bite of muffin stuck in her throat, suddenly dry. She half expected one of the twins to hand her another gun out of the duffel bag and shove her out the door again. But nobody was rushing around this time, and there were no strangers in night gear banging down their door. No, this felt more like a fucking meeting, and Leo still had no fucking idea what was going on. Go figure.

"Well, while we're here," Brad started, sitting backwards on an uncomfortable-looking chair and resting his chin on his folded arms, "we might as well get some work done in Colorado." Then he grinned, bouncing his eyebrows.

"Fuck yes," Don shouted.

"It's been too long," Tony added.

"Longer if you two don't shut the hell up," Cameron muttered.

"Name of the place is Vanguard Industries," Brad continued, his grin mellowing into a coy smile. "They've been off the grid for a while, apparently, but we got some information on them last night that set us up perfectly."

"Who made the call?" Bernadette asked softly, nursing

her coffee.

"Louis," Karl replied. He remained standing behind Brad, feet set squarely and arms folded. "As a... show of good faith." Bernadette nodded slowly. Leo glanced at Evan again, feeling something off about him being in the room at the mention of Louis. The man just stared at the concrete floor.

"Place is in North Park, middle of nowhere. Simple enough to get to. Low security. Same routine for us."

"When?"

Leo almost choked on her coffee when she heard Kaylee ask the question. The interest in the girl's voice was entirely new.

"Tomorrow night," Brad answered. "After Shannon's little shindig." Shannon smiled and nodded, though Leo thought the smile looked awfully tight on the woman's face. "We'll have some fun before we get down to business. Should get to Vanguard Industries' lab between two and three in the morning."

"So should we go over the fucking inventory, or what?" Cameron asked, completely expressionless as he tilted his head but for that gleam in his wide eyes.

"I got the layout down last night," Randall said, typing away at his sturdy machine. "Pretty easy, actually. I'll have photos printed for everyone later today."

"They've got almost zero security," Cameron added. "An entrance gate, handful of cameras. Piece of fucking cake. And if by some fucking freak of nature I can't turn their systems off while we're there, we've got enough ammo to get this done twice." He exaggerated typing the final key on his own laptop and almost slammed it shut, settling back self-righteously into the giant beanbag.

Leo stared at the black duffel bags in the center of the room, nauseous from the memory of Tony casually handing her a handgun at the mountain house. Then she glanced at the twins.

"Yeah, dude," Don said, bobbing his head like someone had just turned on his favorite song. "We're gonna blow up a fucking lab."

37

SHE SAT OUTSIDE behind Shannon's warehouse hotel, staring at the printed photo Randall had given her the day before. He'd given everyone their own, actually, and Leo wondered why they hadn't just printed up some giant poster of the damn image instead, mounted it to the wall of the warehouse, and connected the dots of their plan with extra-thick markers and pieces of string. That was how ridiculous the whole thing sounded, like some low-budget spy movie. How the hell was this image of some cement building supposed to help Sleepwater in any way? It looked more like a prison than a research facility, piling on another layer of her already simmering doubt.

Sucking down the last sour drag of her almost-finished cigarette, she swallowed, stubbed the butt out, and blew yellow smoke across the image. She would have liked to see the photo wither under the haze. Apparently, Randall's indestructible computer set also came with a portable laser printer; Sleepwater had the resources to hand out the life-saving headsets that kept them from destroying one another in action, but they couldn't provide holographic layouts of their next target, or handheld devices with step-by-step instructions on how to blow up government labs. But who was she kidding? Sleepwater wasn't a back-room empire of top-level hackers playing Robin Hood against the One Percent. They were a bunch of freaks, with no idea how or why they'd become that way, fighting for their lives against some faceless institutional beast that had them running for their lives. Blow up labs or be kidnapped and tortured. Right?

The hesitation and disbelief she'd felt when Karl had exposed her to the beat-spinning world, to others more like herself than she could have ever dared imagine, felt like a bee sting compared to the rabid dog of fear clawing its way up her back and down her throat. These new people in her life, with whom Leo felt more comfortable than she had in a long time—maybe ever—offered her now a way to do what she'd always yearned and feared to do. She could fight back. She could take up arms against the fucked-up world which had always cast her aside. She could make a home for herself with Sleepwater and actually belong. It called to her, it terrified her, and the only thing to which her chaotic mind returned was the question of what it would take this time for her to really fuck this up. Specifically how she might fuck up their *operation* with Vanguard Industries more than anything else. The awkward escape from their pursuers at Brad and Mirela's had really taught her nothing; she knew fuck-all about shooting guns, trespassing in stealth, or explosives of any kind. And Sleepwater hardly ran a boot camp for such hobbies, so it wasn't like she was going to get any one-on-one training for this shit.

So was she really going to do this?

The sound of multiple car doors shutting took over the silence, followed by voices coming from inside. Leo stuffed the photo into the pocket of her jeans and stood, waiting to find out what everyone's definition of 'shindig' was. Apparently, more beats would be spun tonight, and while she figured the mood might be a little lighter than her first unofficial *interview* with Sleepwater, she wondered if anything about this was going to be fun at all.

Loud bass music pushed through the door as she opened it to step inside. She had to walk through the rows of bedroom boxes, joined shortly by one of the twins who stepped out of his own room. She didn't have the patience to focus on figuring out which one it was; she could only think about how, after this gathering of Shannon's, they'd all be off to go do some shit infinitely more nerve-wracking. And she hoped something with these other beat-spinners might give her enough courage not to want to shoot herself instead on their way to Vanguard Industries' facility.

A few strangers passed her, walking slowly through the maze of plywood and paneling to supposedly drop off their bags in one of the tiny rooms. One skinny man wore a neon purple sweater, and his white pants looked like they must have been stolen off a ten-year-old. He glanced at Leo and flashed her a smile; even though she felt the look of discomfort on her own face, she couldn't wipe it off.

She hadn't participated in the day's work of decorating the damn place for this get-together. But others had brought in the necessities—more tattered pillows placed around the main living area, joined by a few rocking chairs that looked precariously like they'd been pulled out of a fire. Either one of the newcomers had brought art with them, or someone else had found it in the incomprehensible selection of personal knickknacks stuffed into the warehouse's industrial shelving. Either way, Leo stopped to stare in what was almost appreciation at a canvas painting of a green woman peeling off the skin of her own face.

She caught Mirela's eye as she walked past the painting, and the woman gave her a calm smile, nodding toward the table by the front garage door, which now held a few giant pizzas. The easiest way to feed a bunch of people who were less interested in food than in the reason they were all there. Leo noticed there wasn't any beer laid out; part of her panicked at the thought of heading out in the van later that night completely sober, and the other part of her knew it was a good idea. If presented with the opportunity just then, she would have gotten shitfaced. So she grabbed a piece of pizza and a bottle of water, trying not to make eye contact with anyone while still attempting to figure out how many people outside of Sleepwater had showed up.

A tiny blond woman with one eyebrow perpetually raised sat next to a bald man with a face covered in acne scars, chatting away with Randall. A redheaded woman leaned in close to Bernadette, speaking into her ear above the beat of the music playing. Then the guy in the purple sweater returned from whatever room he'd chosen, almost skipping his way to a rocking chair set against the wall. Leo half expected him to start singing Zippity Do Da. The twins laughed at something Randall said, Cameron occupied his typical brooding position in the giant beanbag, and when Leo locked eyes with Kaylee, the girl actually smiled. It was close-lipped and small, but a smile. So Leo joined her on a pile of pillows, saying nothing. But she couldn't ignore the heat of Kaylee's crossed legs pressed up against hers, or Kaylee's fingers just barely slipping under the waistband in the back of Leo's jeans. That did nothing to kill the churning anxiety in her gut.

Leo only noticed Shannon when the woman turned down the music playing on the speakers, then returned to her seat on the stairs by the front of the room. She didn't look particularly happy—maybe the turnout hadn't been what she'd hoped. Then again, they were almost in the middle of nowhere. What else did the woman expect?

"Glad everyone could make it," Shannon said, knocking a few dreadlocks back over her shoulder. "It's been a while since we've had this many here." The bald man moaned in agreement; Leo almost expected him to throw out an 'Amen' or a 'Hallelujah' as he rocked back and forth, nodding. "It's good to see people coming back. Good to see new faces." Leo could have sworn Shannon looked right at her for the sliver of a second, not liking what she saw on the woman's face. Suspicion? Disdain? What the hell had *she* done? "You're always welcome last-minute."

"Fuck yes," Brad said, wrapping his arms around Mirela's shoulders.

The cheerful sound of Brad's comment struck a nerve in Leo, and it took her a second to figure out that that was what pure trust sounded like. Everyone who had come here with her seemed completely comfortable, completely at ease in this place, even after everything they'd been through in order to get here. Even Karl had shed his outer layer of defensive skepticism, sitting back in his chair with his arms folded, watching the gathered circle with bright eyes. Then she glanced at Evan, who somehow had still managed to find a seat completely removed from the others and stared at Shannon like his life depended on it. She swallowed a hard lump. Something didn't feel right, but no one else seemed to think the same.

"So can we get this thing started?" Purple Sweater asked. It was amazing that he pulled off such a languid pose on the pillows in those white pants.

"Sure, Zach," Shannon said.

The guy spoke first of the beach at sunset, and the more he described it, the more the room around her began to fade. She sat on the sand, felt the breeze, smelled the salt and fish as he detailed them. She reached out to stroke the sand and glanced over at Kaylee. The girl's head was thrown back, a thin smile upturned toward the cloudless sky. The beach receded as the teller changed his description. The sky fell toward her, the waves building up and solidifying into slick, black rock. She smelled the decay, the wet, metallic slickness of the cave around her. She was suddenly very cold and held herself, shivering. There was no light, no sound but the speaker's voice as it echoed quietly off the rock. Water dripped from the ceiling, and the repetitious puncture of the silence grew louder and louder until it was suddenly soft. A clock, ticking in the corner of the room. She felt the rough fabric of the chair below her, smelled the disinfectant, the sterilized counters and tools. The linoleum tiles stretched forever in front of her, overlooked by a dark green sign that read 'Hospital Visitor Sign-In'. Leo's stomach clenched, and she gripped the arm of the chair hard to steady herself.

Her hand dropped to her side as Zach finished his beat, and the buzz of the music behind them punched through the silence of the hospital room. The others around the room had mixed expressions on their faces. Fear, discomfort, a few with contented nostalgia. Then the fog cleared, and some of them started laughing.

"Fantastic," the red-headed woman exclaimed, grinning. "Can you do that with any place?"

"If I've been there, or at least seen a picture, yeah." Zach looked around the circle. "Can never see it myself, though."

The redhead pulled her legs in to cross them and said, "I'll give it a shot." Bernadette gave her a pat on the shoulder, and then the woman began. Her voice was soft and calming, very pleasant to listen to, but after a minute or so, Leo let out a barking laugh. She found it ridiculously funny. Listening to the girl's words, the story of how she found out her mother had cancer, she knew it was a sad story. She knew it was completely inappropriate, but she shouted a laugh again and covered her mouth. Looking at the others, she saw their mouths quirking, trying so hard to contain it. Giggles escaped, then grew into mountains of guffawing and laughter continuously feeding on itself. The redhead kept spinning her beat.

Through streaming tears, Leo glanced at Karl. His forehead was slumped into his hand, shoulders jerking silently. The twins were almost rolling on the floor, pointing at each other, and Kaylee hid her mouth with both hands. Even Cameron snickered, snorting into his arm. Then she looked at Shannon and laughed even louder. There was nothing funny about it—she knew it was the redhead's beat—but Shannon wasn't laughing at all.

Then a loud bang came from the other side of the garage door at the front of the warehouse, and Leo cracked up again. As long as the redhead spoke, no one could stop laughing. Another bang came at the door, followed by shouts, and then Shannon turned and met Leo's gaze full-on. Leo had enough time to recognize, between each gasp of breath in the beat-induced hilarity, that the woman wore one of the tiny headsets covered by her thick dreadlocks.

Shannon was the only person not affected by the redhead's beat.

Then the garage door jolted, slammed upwards, and half a dozen men in indiscernible black uniforms swarmed into the room. The redhead stopped her beat immediately, shouted a loud, "Fuck!" and stood. Leo noticed their headgear—the same set of electronics as the men who'd raided the mountain house, only this time their night-vision goggles and the small green lights seemed a lot less threatening. Laughing still, she wondered if that had anything to do with seeing them in the light, or if the redhead's beat still had her. And there was only a second for that thought.

She met Karl's gaze. His mouth was still slanted in an uncharacteristic smile, but his eyes made the hazy change from blissful carelessness to terror. The others stood from their chairs or pillows, trying to fight off the fog of the red-head's words. Leo felt slow, sluggish, and when Karl dodged past her toward the back of the warehouse—toward the exit by the bedrooms—she wondered why he didn't try to take anyone else with him. She heard the twins' laughter cut off abruptly, followed by a shout, then she turned to see Shannon again, just standing there, staring at the growing chaos.

"Fuck you!" Kaylee shouted.

Leo felt the smile on her face, though she knew the effects of the redhead's beat were wearing off quickly now. She turned, almost as if through mud, to see one of the men in uniform doubled over, holding his face. Then she saw Kaylee kick the guy, all one hundred pounds of fiery force, and three others seemed to materialize next to the tiny girl. They tried to restrain her, tried to grasp at her flailing fists and feet, and Leo felt a long-dormant rage well up within her.

The sound that came out of her throat was more growl than shout, and she launched herself at the nearest intruder, bringing her knee up into his groin. Only briefly was she aware of Randall guiding Bernadette towards the back of the warehouse, of Brad knocking one of the men in uniform against the wall and pinning him there by the neck while Mirela managed to get away. Cameron dragged one of the twins in the same direction—she couldn't tell who. Where was the other one?

Someone's fist connected with her stomach, and she lost all her air, almost gagging. The sounds of surprise and fighting seemed to grow weaker until Kaylee called out for her. She watched three of the men carry the girl off, grunting and cursing while she fought like a wild animal. Leo felt a pair of hands on her shoulders, and she lashed out, flinging her fists in all directions and trying to get to Kaylee.

"Jesus Christ," came a low voice from behind her,

struggling to hold her in place.

"What the hell are you waiting for?" This new voice came from the garage door.

"She's fucking fighting me."

"Well we need her too. Make it work."

Leo had just enough time to wonder why these assholes weren't shooting at them this time. Then she heard a crack, followed by white pain radiating down her spine, and she dropped.

38

SHE WOKE IN a bright room—too bright. Her head hurt like hell, and when she tried to move it, a wave of nausea accompanied the burning in her neck. Willing her eyes to focus, she noticed the bleach-white tiles of the ceiling, then of the walls. Looking down, she recognized the starched sheets and plastic frame of a hospital bed.

"You're awake," someone said. "Just in time."

Something snapped inside her, some panicked thing that had always been kept at bay beneath her stoic acceptance of the cards she'd been dealt, and it leapt from her. This, Leo had to fight.

A man in a white lab coat approached her, holding some device with one hand, and Leo swung her fist into his face. He staggered backwards, dropping the device, and she whipped the sheets off to throw herself out of the bed. Vertigo overwhelmed her for a second, and she blinked like she was wasted before managing to focus on the other end of the room. A sliding glass door served as her exit, and she barreled toward it, her shoes squeaking on the tile.

"Carter," the man shouted. "I need you in here."

Leo was almost to the door, and then a short blond man with a pitiful excuse for a mustache appeared on the other side. They stared at each other for a brief second before he slid the door open and took a step inside.

She felt the words burning in her chest, rising up out of her throat with more urgency than she'd ever used them. When her fists didn't do the job, her words always did, and she pulled every bit of force she could muster behind her beat. "You need to let me go, now." The words flowed slowly, giving her time to notice the tiny flesh-colored implant in the blond man's ear.

"Nice try," he said, giving her what looked like a grimace of pity. "Sorry."

The sting hit the muscle of her shoulder just barely before she saw the needle in his hand. She blinked again, overwhelmed by another wave of warm, swimming nausea, and then her legs gave way beneath her.

It seemed she was destined to repeat the episode when she woke again, but there was no voice to greet her and no man to punch in the face. The room was empty. Leo swallowed in a bitingly dry throat and tried to push herself up again. The soft clink of metal stopped her as much as the rather tight grip of restraints around her wrists chained to the sides of the bed. She tried to call out, but her throat felt too dry, and when she jerked automatically in protest, she found her ankles bound as well. Then she noticed her bare feet, the loose, white pants she wore, and kicked furiously. The motherfuckers had undressed her, taken her clothes, and who knew what the hell else.

She didn't know if that pissed her off more than the fact that she'd let herself get caught, but she knew she had to get out. That was more important than finding out where the fuck she was and who these assholes were. At this point, she didn't think it mattered. Shouting and struggling, she called out for someone to come and fucking let her out. While sweat beaded on her brow and her ankles chafed against the straps, she thought she was going to have to scream her throat raw—which she'd never done before—in order for anyone to notice.

But then someone in a white coat walked down the hall toward the glass door and slid it open—the man with the blond mustache.

"Fuck you," Leo spat.

"That's understandable." He closed the door behind him and pulled a tablet from the front pocket of his lab coat. "I might have given you too large a dose." Stopping to tap something into his tablet, he looked back up at her as if she'd asked a question. "Just a sedative. You were out longer than I expected."

"What the hell do you want?" Leo pulled harshly at the straps around her wrists, trying in vain to loosen them.

"To show you what exactly it is we're doing here. I'm Dr. Carter—"

"I don't care who the fuck you are." The words burned up through her throat of their own accord, and though Leo knew the man had the implants, that her beat wouldn't work through that technology, she couldn't stop it. "You need to untie me and let me out."

Dr. Carter tilted his head with the same pitying expression. "I thought you'd already figured out that that won't work here." Then he blinked rapidly, looking nervous and more than a little uncomfortable. "I'd hoped I'd be able to introduce you to everything here quickly and easily, but you really didn't give me much choice." He closed his eyes, frowning, as if making some vital decision, then stepped closer. "You're making my job harder than it has to be, and

I know *you're* a lot more uncomfortable now than you have to be. Can we agree to be more civil to each other moving forward? You don't freak out again, and I won't sedate you. We're running a little short on time, and we haven't even started."

Leo hated his brown eyes, wanted to pluck them from his head. He wanted to talk to her like she had a choice in the matter, while the asshole had her strapped down to a hospital bed like a mental patient? "Let me the fuck out of here," she said, straining against the restraints and raising her head toward him. "I'm not doing anything for you." She jerked again, tugging and rattling the chains connected to the bed.

"This isn't how I wanted—"

Leo screamed, cutting him off and feeling her face grow hot. She'd never been trapped like this, had never been in a situation where her beat didn't work at all. Every time, she'd managed to talk and walk her way out of whatever trouble she got herself into, and this felt like the most blaring dead-end in the history of dead-ends. What the fuck was she supposed to do? That thought struck home, and her anger toward the man turned to panic. Screaming again, this time she felt hot tears prick at the corners of her eyes, and breathing felt oddly difficult.

"I tried," Dr. Carter mumbled, typing something into his tablet again and flinching. Then he turned without another word and left the room.

She tugged and pulled at the straps, feeling her wrists chafing against the thick material, feeling her stomach churning with fear and frustration. What the fuck was this place? What did these people want from her? Leo tried to pull some explanation from her memory. The only thing she could think of was that the people who had chased them from the mountain house had caught up with them somehow, holding her here. But those men at Brad and Mirela's had shot at her—at them all—and seemed to hardly care who they hit. The men who had burst into the warehouse hadn't raised a gun to anyone.

That made her think of Shannon then, and she seethed. If she didn't know any better, she would have said Shannon was the one who had sold them out, who had told these people where they were all hiding. At this point, Leo didn't think she knew any better at all. Someone had already sold Sleepwater out once, and it seemed the fucking woman with the stupid dreadlocks had done the same. Or maybe it had been her the whole time.

And now Leo lay here, on a hospital bed in what was obviously not a hospital, chained up and without a clue as to what they wanted from her—without a clue as to how to get the fuck out.

Muffled voices came from the direction of the hallway; she couldn't see anything through the glass door but the opposite wall just outside. The voices grew louder, and she struggled again, jerking against the bed and letting out a string of curses. No matter how many needles that blond fucker decided to stick in her arm, she wouldn't go down without a fight.

But the person who rounded the corner to slowly slide open the glass door wasn't Dr. Carter.

Leo froze, thinking with some small, objective part of her brain that this was the only person in the world who could make her stop fighting. If only for that moment.

The blue eyes were unchanged, though her blond hair was pulled back in a tight bun, making her face strikingly angular. The smile, though—that was all wrong. Nothing like the boundless, joyous expression from so many years ago, this was more like what Dr. Carter had offered. This smile was made of empathy, curiosity, and more than a little pity. This smile said, *I knew you once, and now I have no idea who you are.*

"Hi," Alex said. It came out just barely louder than a

whisper.

Leo felt her chest rising and falling, felt like a caged animal staring down the barrel of a shotgun, and all she could do for a second was swallow again in her dry, sticky throat. Her eyes bounced around in her head, taking in every part of the room, of the hallway outside, of the bright floor tiles, and it seemed impossible to focus on the woman standing before her. Alex was gone, a ghost from a different life, and looking at her now would make this more real than Leo had been willing to accept. So she finally closed her eyes and cleared her throat with a weak cough.

"What are you doing here?" she asked, hating how dried-out her voice sounded.

"What am I doing here?" She thought she heard Alex trying not to laugh. "You don't even know what *you're* doing here."

The glass door slid shut with a rustle and a click, and when Leo opened her eyes, she found them focused on the pair of plain, practical sneakers now standing beside her bed. They seemed oddly out of place here. "Then tell me." Maybe if she spoke normally, pretended like this was anyone else, it wouldn't turn out to be as shitty as it felt.

"To start," Alex said, making eye contact with the strap around Leo's wrist, "you're in a research facility. And we… need your help."

"Who's we?" What Leo really wanted to ask was how the fuck she could help anybody, chained up like this—and why the hell they'd think she'd cooperate at this point.

"That's not something I can talk about with you right now."

When Leo looked up, she met Alex's gaze and that odd expression of discomfort. What had everybody so bent out of shape? Then she realized that even though Alex looked the same, even though they recognized each other, this was not the same person. Alex wasn't here out of love, or nostalgia, or a need to prove something. She only worked here and apparently had a job to do. That only made it worse, but Leo had seen the same implant in Alex's ear and knew that using her beat would remain absolutely pointless. At least Alex wasn't Dr. Carter.

"Just tell me what the hell's going on," she said, recognizing the sound of defeat in her own voice, though she tried to hide it.

"Like I said, this is a research facility. We're looking at the effects of a variety of drugs, both on and off the market."

Goddamnit, she sounded like a fucking machine. And she still wouldn't meet Leo's gaze. "And you want me to be your guinea pig?" The whole *human experimentation* thing was going a bit too far. There was no way in hell Leo would willingly give herself over to whatever science this was—especially science so fucked up they had to kidnap people.

"No, definitely not." Alex finally looked at her, taking a deep breath. "You can offer us a unique perspective on our test subjects, which would be invaluable."

"Did somebody give you a script to memorize?" The words came rushing out all at once—maybe she hadn't meant to say it out loud at all. But this didn't sound like Alex in any way. This sounded like someone she'd never met. Alex stared at her, wide-eyed, and gave a barely perceptible shake of her head. Leo grimaced. "Why do I have such a *unique perspective*?"

"Because you're like them."

Leo didn't even have to ask what that meant. She'd planned to but was beaten to it by the sound of a man screaming from somewhere down the hall. Then it came back to her—having seen only one twin escape through the back of the warehouse; Brad fighting off Mirela's attacker; Kaylee being carried away by three of the men in uniform.

"Where are they?" she hissed, jerking once against the

restraints.

"They're here. They're safe," Alex replied with a frown. Another scream seemed to directly contradict her assurances.

"The fuck they are! What the hell is this place? What are you doing?" Her mind flashed immediately to the image of Louis sitting in his back room at the Purple Lion, haughty-looking and partially amused. Karl had told her that some fucking government experiment had taken Louis' beat from him—had left him nothing more than a regular guy, surrounding himself with the one thing he wished to be again. Was that what this was? "Take these off me." She pulled again at the cuffs on her wrists.

"Leo—"

"I swear to God, if you say my name one more fucking time—"

"This isn't how I wanted to start things off." Alex looked like she wanted to reach out and touch Leo, to somehow make her feel better.

"You've got me chained up," Leo spat. "Was that part of how you wanted things?" The sliding glass door opened again, and Leo watched Alex avert her gaze nervously to the ceiling before glancing to see who had stepped inside the room.

The woman wore a slimming pantsuit of dark gray, her black heels clicking against the tile floor. Dark hair lightly framed her face around brown eyes and a quietly reserved smile. Something about her seemed far too familiar and painfully foreign all at once, and Leo found herself unable to look away. "Leona Tieffler," the woman said.

The sound of her voice sent an uncomfortable warmth through Leo's limbs, adding to the beads of sweat she felt forming at her hairline. Anger and longing battled themselves within her, and she couldn't figure out why.

"Ms. Dunn," the woman continued, staring at Leo,

"please remove those restraints."

Alex jerked into motion, as if she'd been caught day-dreaming, and approached the bed. The three or four keys on the keyring she pulled out of her pocket jangled as she moved, and she deftly released the lock on each of the four straps holding Leo down.

Leo instinctively grabbed her wrists and rubbed the sore, chaffed skin, glaring at the woman. It seemed a bit too convenient that this lady in the pantsuit knew her name, knew what she could do, had known where to find her. Leo didn't have bank accounts, credit cards, cell phone pay-ments—or any bills, for that matter. She'd disappeared off the radar the year her father had died; she'd ceased to exist as far as the rest of the world was concerned. The only com-mon denominator here was Alex, and it seemed more prob-able by the second that the blond ghost from her past—the girl who used to be everything to her—had been the one to make this happen. How the hell had Alex found her? Leo wanted to believe that Alex's intentions ran deeper than just keeping whatever job she seemed to have here, but there was no reason that would be more likely than the reality.

"Follow me, please," the woman said, then turned and stepped out into the hall.

Slowly, Leo slid from the bed, her bare feet hot against the cold tile floor, and glared at Alex. "What did you tell her about me?" she asked, her voice low, accusatory. Alex just shut her eyes, as if the question alone hurt enough, and shook her head. Leo sneered and headed toward the door; she was right. There wasn't any other reason for Alex being here than to offer information no one else had. It had nothing to do with what they'd been through.

"You're the one who left," Alex finally said, and Leo stopped before the open door at the sound of her voice. "You don't get to be angry."

She wanted to turn around, to have something to say

that would make this worth it, but she had nothing. Part of what Alex said was right—Leo *had* left her, along with everything else she'd hated about her life six years ago. She'd been terrified of what would happen if she stayed, of what else the world would be able to take from her. And she'd gotten the hell over it. Now, finding out what the hell was going on in this place was far more important than reminiscing with someone who obviously didn't care that much about her. How much *could* someone care if they worked for the same people who'd had Leo kidnapped, drugged, and chained up in a room? So she turned into the hallway and kept walking.

39

LEO HALF EXPECTED the hallway to feel just as much like a nightmare, lined with flickering lights and bodily fluids smeared along the grimy walls. But it was the opposite—clean, professional, sterile-looking. Everything a research facility ought to be. Except for the screaming.

The woman in front of her walked with a straight spine, looking neither left nor right into the identical rooms with sliding glass doors. But they weren't exactly identical; Leo noticed that the lights in these rooms were particularly bright, far brighter than the soft lighting in the hall. She stopped to look through a door on her left and saw a man she didn't recognize strapped to a hospital bed as she'd been. Sweat glistened on his forehead, neck, and upper lip, and he clenched his eyes tight as if in pain. Then he jerked against the restraints, and his eyes burst open to settle on her.

Leo swallowed hard, feeling the shock of his stare burn through her. Then the man's eyes roamed lazily from her face to the ceiling, registering nothing about her presence outside his prison.

"They can't see you," the woman said from behind her.

Leo turned to face the woman, who gazed into the room with the blank mien of impassivity. If ever there was an embodiment of callousness in the name of science, she thought, this was it. The woman looked like she was watching someone fill out paperwork.

"We find that it affects our data if they can see out of their rooms."

The glass doors must have been two-way mirrors, then—except for the door to the room in which she'd been kept. Leo blinked, feeling the fear and the anger rising, wanting to unleash it on everything around her but lacking the proper excuse. Was it curiosity that kept her silent? "What is this?" she asked, her voice a strangled croak.

The woman stood still and silent for a few seconds, then turned and walked off again. Leo followed, feeling the knot which had formed in the pit of her stomach drop even further. They passed just a few more doors only to stop again in front of another. She wondered just how many rooms this hall contained, and how many *test subjects*. The woman nodded at the door, and Leo turned to look.

There was one of the twins, strapped to the bed in the same loose white pants and shirt they'd given her, monitor machines lining the wall behind him. An IV tube connected him to the stand holding what looked like an oddly high number of fluid bags. She couldn't tell which twin it was at first. The chorded muscles of his neck and the throbbing vein in his forehead didn't make it any easier, nor did the hard clench of agony in his jaw. Then his body lifted from the bed as if on its own, held down only by the four restraints, and he let out another piercing scream. She caught what seemed to be the shimmer of scar tissue on his right hand—the hand with which he'd offered her the gun—and knew it was Tony.

Leo stepped up to the door, placing her hand against the

glass, and felt the hot sting of tears. What was this? Then the grip of surprise and horror opened and let her go, and she fumbled against the handle to slide open the door. The woman put her hand on Leo's shoulder and gently guided her back.

"What are you doing to him?" Leo cried, trying to fight against the woman's hold. Something about watching Tony in that much pain turned her muscles to jelly, left her with barely enough strength to remain standing.

"He'll be fine," the woman cooed, disturbingly reassuring.

From around the corner, another man in a white lab coat approached them, pausing only briefly to nod at the woman and murmur in businesslike greeting, "Dr. Kerrigan."

The woman nodded back, and Leo watched the man enter Tony's room, closing the door behind him. He noted something on his own tablet, checked the IV bags and monitors, then added something to the IV. Almost instantly, the tension of agony eased on Tony's face, and he sank back into the bed, closing his eyes in relief.

"What we're doing here is incredibly important for people like you," the woman—Dr. Kerrigan—said in a soft voice. "We're trying to make you stronger."

"You just drugged him," Leo whispered.

"It's to combat the pain. Each test we perform has its own… personal side effects, which can be quite uncomfortable. But Tony has already told us what we need to know about him, and we're working on finding his unique signature."

Leo finally turned to look at Dr. Kerrigan—those brown, stoic, determined eyes—and felt a chill roll down her spine. "You're talking about his beat."

"His beat, yes." The woman gave a thin smile. "His *ability*. We've just recently found that not every chemical makeup has the same effect on every one of our subjects who are… like you."

"If you know what I can do, why am I not still strapped to that bed?" None of this made sense. The whole thing felt like an oddly-staged performance, some macabre presentation just for her.

Dr. Kerrigan gave her a confused smirk, as if it surprised her that Leo didn't already know what was going on. "Because I need your help. Come along." This time, she waited for Leo to fall into step beside her as they resumed their journey down the hall. "I know you must be thinking this is a horrible place, that we do terrible things to people. Experiment on them. Torture them. I promise you that's not true." They turned the corner only to enter another identical hallway. "There have been a few facilities over the years dedicated to finding people with these abilities, like yours, in order to remove the genetic markers which lead to the *beats*, as you call them. Some of the subjects return to their former lives changed. Normal. Others haven't been as lucky. That has led to quite a bit of animosity, as I'm sure you well know."

Leo immediately thought of Louis again, of how he'd had his beat taken from him. Of how Sleepwater had rallied behind their captured fellows to destroy the facilities doing this to them. Of how so many of them had been on the run from people just like Dr. Kerrigan for so long.

"Our aim here at Vanguard Industries is completely different."

Leo stopped in the hall, staring at the cold tiles beneath her bare feet. Vanguard Industries—this was the place Sleepwater had planned to attack the night she'd been captured. She had no idea how much time had passed since then—if it was the same night or a week later—but at least she knew she was close. She hoped the others had stayed close as well, that they'd gotten away from Shannon's warehouse and had stayed enough away to be able carry out their plan anyways. Maybe they knew that she and Tony were here.

"Not too much farther," Dr. Kerrigan said, interrupting her thoughts. "Just let me make my point."

Leo swallowed, trying to keep her expression impassive, and resumed walking.

"Some have wanted to remove these incredible abilities in the name of science, using that as an excuse to mask their fear of you. But in this Information Technology age, with the advancements we've made both in information uptake and pharmaceuticals, I believe those who can do what you can do are a boon to society, not a plague." They stopped at a large metal door, and the woman punched in a five-digit number on a coded keypad. With a click and a hiss, she pulled the door open and gestured for Leo to step in ahead of her. "The U.S. Department of Defense has seen a lot of benefits after their partnerships with companies like Laleopharm, who, coincidentally, is funding the research I'm so excited to show you. And we're trying so hard to find a way to make this work for everyone."

They ascended a short flight of stairs in a dimly lit hallway, stepping out at the top into a viewing box. Two men sat at the control panels at the front of the room, monitoring a variety of data Leo found incomprehensible. Behind the monitors was a wall of glass which seemed to look out over a large, domed room below them.

"We want to isolate the source of your abilities and enhance them, give you the power to control the effects you have on others. Aim at specific *targets*, as it were. Lengthen the effect time on your listeners. The White House is incredibly interested in the potential of these enhancements, and they've been renegotiating some of their key roles in order to incorporate people like you into their teams for foreign policy, defense, and military strategy. Personally, I find it incredibly exciting. That is, of course, assuming our research here has something to offer."

Dr. Kerrigan leaned over one of the men at the desk to peer at a data screen, nodded in pleasure, and turned to fix her piercing gaze again on Leo. "You could do so much to help this country. You, John—that's the first man you saw today. Tony. All it takes is a little cooperation in return."

Leo felt her mouth run dry, waiting for the other shoe to drop. This woman was obviously insane, just like the rest of the world, and who fucking knew what she was going to ask in return for bestowing what she thought was this magnificent gift? It seemed far more like just another set of shackles.

"We need to know where to find you," Dr. Kerrigan continued. "All of you. Who knows what kinds of gifts are out there, how many people possess these abilities? And who better to help us find them than you?"

"You want me to give them all up?" Leo asked, feeling her palms slick with sweat. "So you can experiment on them and hand them over to the government?"

"Don't look at it that way." Dr. Kerrigan stepped up to the wall of glass. "Look at it as giving those like you an opportunity, something far better than the types of lives most of you seem to lead. A chance to make something of yourselves instead of hiding from those who hate what they don't understand." She turned back toward Leo. "But that can wait for a while. Right now, I need your help with something much more at-hand. Take a look."

Leo stepped up toward the glass, her heartbeat pounding in her ears. When she looked down, she almost choked.

They had Kaylee tied down to a half-reclined exam chair, her hair swept back dramatically behind the electrodes placed on her forehead, temple, and down her throat. Her fists were curled tight atop the armrests, knuckles white below the nylon straps holding her there. Even from where Leo stood, she could see the sheen of sweat on Kaylee's skin, the hard clench of resolution in her set jaw. She imagined the girl was grinding her teeth together, though Kaylee made no noise and barely moved. Only the rapid rise and fall of her chest in labored breathing showed she was still alive—that she could still move at all. She looked like she'd been fighting some invisible foe, like she needed rest and nourishment but couldn't take the chance. Then Kaylee's eyes shot up toward their viewing room, burning hatred and defiance through the glass window, and Leo knew this wasn't a two-way mirror. Though she didn't show any sign of recognition, Kaylee knew she was there—knew Leo was watching her.

"This one has been particularly difficult," Dr. Kerrigan said, giving her head a tiny shake to clear the hair from her face. "Nothing we do or say gets any results. She won't tell us what we need to know, and I can only imagine the strength of her resistance to these tests. While she neither screams nor speaks, the spikes in her vitals show she must be in extreme pain, which is unfortunate. Without her cooperation, we've had to administer every compound we've formulated just to see what works. She doesn't even respond to the sedatives afterward." She turned her attention to picking at her already clean fingernails. "So I need you to tell me what she can do."

Swallowing hard, Leo couldn't take her eyes off Kaylee's burning gaze. It seemed like so long ago that she'd met Bernadette for the first time, but she distinctly remembered what the woman had said to her. *The ownership of the beat goes both ways. It is for each of us to show at our own discretion.* Bernadette had stressed the importance of this, as had the others in Sleepwater, though no one ever said specifically why. Back then, Leo didn't know that anyone was being hunted down by the government, that anyone was being experimented on because of what they could do. She had no idea what any of it meant, and now she seemed to grasp the weight of what Dr. Kerrigan had just asked her to do. An incredible amount of control, it seemed, came from knowing what someone's beat was, and this fucked-up doctor expected her to give it up just like that—to give Kaylee up just like that.

"I can't…" she whispered, staring through the glass.

After a few seconds, Dr. Kerrigan turned to look down at Leo. "I've been looking for you for a long time, Leona."

That made Leo look up. The way the woman said her name made her skin crawl.

"I was a little too late when I came to find you after Marcus' death. But you left quite an impression on a few people when you… disappeared. One of them being Miss Dunn. She wanted to find you just as badly as I did, and in exchange for her being so forthcoming with information about you—to help find where you might have gone—I offered her the internship that led to her position with us here. She's *very* good."

Alex—she was talking about Alex.

"I was surprised to find you harbor these same abilities, Leona, but it makes your role here that much more fitting. It helped me to follow you, knowing you'd be with others who can do something similar. It took a lot longer than I anticipated, but now I have you here to help me in my research—in *our* research. We can do this together. So will you tell me what I need to know?"

Leo felt the blood drain from her face, felt the tips of her fingers grow instantly cold with disgust and fear, and she blinked, hoping this wasn't true. Hoping this really was some twisted fucking nightmare. Then she could wake herself up. "Who *are* you?" she asked, the words sticking in her throat like static.

Dr. Kerrigan frowned, pausing for a moment before the impact of realization softened her features again. "You really don't remember." She blinked. "I know you were young when I left you and your father... but I really hadn't expected you to completely forget me. I suppose you didn't have much in the way of—"

Whatever the woman said next, Leo never heard. Blood rushed to her head, drowning out everything else in a whirring pulse of rage. She'd thought the woman's strange hold on her might have been a beat or some promise of information to come; the last thing she had expected was to find that that voice, those eyes, came from a part of her so buried beneath her own survival she couldn't dig it up herself.

This bitch had the fucking balls, after discarding her like an ugly sweater when she was young enough to remember nothing else—after leaving Leo with her *father*, the goddamn drug addict—to ask for her help? She'd brought Leo here, under the pretense of kidnap and torture, assuming that all would be forgiven and they'd experiment on people together? Even still, these people—those whose lives had been overturned by the abilities of their own beats—were more of a family than any of Leo's flesh and blood, and they deserved far better than what was being asked of her. She couldn't wrap her mind around the reality as the pain she thought she'd peeled off and thrown away like dead skin came rushing back in an instant. She stared down through the glass at Kaylee, roiling and empty all at once, at a complete loss.

"Leona? Will you help me?"

The sound of her mother's voice broke her from the numb void of her revelation, and she lost it. Screaming, Leo launched herself at Dr. Kerrigan, hands outstretched towards the woman's throat, and pinned her violently against the wall of glass. The woman let out a choke of surprise, her head banging against the window, and even if Leo had been fully aware of the fact that she was choking the woman who had birthed her, she wouldn't have tried to stop herself. Then the two men in lab coats jumped from the seats at their monitors and struggled to remove Leo from what would have been her murder victim. They held her by the arms as she kicked and fought, lashing out still.

Gasping, Dr. Kerrigan gently held her throat and fixed Leo with a gaze more impassive than any she'd bestowed upon her other test subjects. "I'm going to assume your answer is no."

Leo almost managed to break free from the men holding her, lunging toward Dr. Kerrigan again with all the hatred she could muster. But then she felt the sharp sting of yet another needle in her arm, and the warmth spread. She glanced down into the room at Kaylee, who still stared up at her, watching the whole thing. Before Leo passed out, she thought she saw the tiniest hint of a smile prick the corner of the girl's mouth.

40

"I'LL GIVE YOU another chance."

Leo recognized the voice, but her eyes weren't working, the lids weighted down by heat and pain. When she managed to open them, she found Dr. Kerrigan at her bedside, peering down at her with a blank expression. Her mother.

No. That woman was gone. This was someone else entirely, someone hoping to prey on Leo's emotions to get what she wanted—what she shouldn't have.

"I want you to be a part of this," the woman continued, "and I want it to be on good terms."

Leo closed her eyes again. The back of her hand itched.

"Help me, Leona. Tell me what I need to know, and I'll help you out of this."

She wanted to tell Dr. Kerrigan that she wouldn't be *in this* if it wasn't for the psycho woman—that she wouldn't need help at all if the woman hadn't come looking for her in the first place. That was the last thing she'd ever wanted.

"Leo."

That made her eyes fly open. She hadn't started calling herself Leo until years after her mother had left. The woman couldn't possibly have known about the nickname on her own. That meant it was part of the package of information obviously offered willingly by Alex. Leo swallowed the lump in her throat, her cheeks burning with anger.

"Go to hell," she rasped.

Dr. Kerrigan just looked down at her for a long time, blinked rapidly, and sighed. "That's that, then. I can't do anything else for you." She motioned toward the sliding door, which opened to let in two other people in white lab coats. One of them pushed a stainless-steel cart, and Leo tried as hard as she could not to look at what it carried. "That doesn't mean I don't want you to know what's happening. I'm still going to tell you everything, starting at the beginning, and I'll try to be as honest as possible."

Leo felt her breathing quicken against her will when one of the nameless assistants wheeled the metal tray toward the bed, and Dr. Kerrigan picked up a syringe of thick yellow fluid.

"Marcus and I worked together in the beginning, you know." The woman held the syringe upright and tapped it, gently pressing the plunger until a thin stream oozed from the needle. "That was how we met. Laleopharm's partnership with MindBlink brought a lot of people together in the name of science and technology. I was on the team that helped develop Pointera, nasty little drug that it became." Dr. Kerrigan lowered the syringe toward Leo's side, and Leo realized why her hand was so itchy. Looking down, she saw the medical tape strapping an IV into the back of her hand. She bucked against the restraints, and Dr. Kerrigan only glanced up briefly. "Hold still." The command was given without any real consideration, as the woman merely picked up the injection site on the IV tube and emptied the syringe into it.

"Your father was a brilliant man," she continued. "Completely dedicated to his work with those little Infodeos he created. God, was he brilliant. And for a while, Pointera only increased his brilliance, and I don't think I've ever been so in love... with a person or a product."

The itch in Leo's hand crawled up her arm, burning like nothing she'd ever felt before. She squeezed her eyes shut and told herself she wouldn't cry out as the pain quickly spread.

Dr. Kerrigan replaced the syringe on the steel tray and leaned over to press a few buttons on the monitors behind Leo's bed. "He was also, tragically, one of the first to experience the drug's hidden pitfalls. Oh, of course, my team had seen the potential for abuse quite clearly from the beginning. That's what made it so brilliant. It touched places in the human brain no chemical had ever glimpsed before. We figured that, under medical supervision, that potential for abuse would be minuscule. And we were paid an unbelievable price not to publish our findings in that regard."

Leo choked back a grunt of pain, heat searing through her chest. She blinked rapidly and glared at the ceiling.

"I should never have let myself get so emotionally attached." Dr. Kerrigan sighed and glanced at the ceiling, rolling what seemed an imaginary kink out of her neck. "That has always been my first rule. Never get too involved in any project. But Marcus and I took our work together to a whole new level. Then the genius of a man went too far. The drug that intensified his brilliance eventually killed every intelligent brain cell he ever had."

Leo's father had been a junkie most of her life, but she'd loved him—in some small part that didn't resent him for stealing her childhood. It was more love than she'd ever held for the insane woman pumping god knew what into her veins. She grunted, realizing she clutched the bedsheets in tight fists.

"It was either stay and clean up his mess, or leave and save my career. And after Pointera's effects went public, I had to start working on something new. This, here, will redeem the mistakes I made back then."

"Wh—what did you give me?" Leo croaked. An invisible hand closed around her throat, and her eyes seemed glued to the steel cart as the two men in coats wheeled it out of the room, leaving her alone with Dr. Kerrigan.

The woman leaned in close, studying Leo's face without meeting her eyes. "We're calling it Formula S-12, for now," she said matter-of-factly. "Something I've used once or twice on subjects with similar abilities to your own."

Sweat poured down Leo's face, stinging her eyes. "Similar..." she rasped, unable to finish the sentence.

"Tell me what you're experiencing right now."

"I can't—" Leo gasped, her blood on fire, a deep, aching pain burrowing into her lower back. Her breath ran shallow, and the image of a fish flopping around on dry land entered her mind. She bucked against the restraints, the bedsheets sticky against her body, and lost consciousness.

"...might not be it."

Alex's voice brought her back to consciousness. Panic flared in Leo's chest, and she heaved in agony.

"I'll be out in just a moment." Alex sounded worried, forced. A brief silence was followed by footsteps and the sound of the glass door sliding open and then closed. Leo felt her near the bed, and then Alex's face peered over her, brows drawn down in concern. "How are you feeling?" The question sounded pathetic.

Hatred. That was all Leo felt in the moment, briefly overshadowing the unbelievable throbbing behind her eyes and the tight aching in her joints. She glared back into those blue eyes, wanting to scream at her betrayer but only managing a choked-off grunt.

"Just give her what she wants," Alex said. "Then this can be over. This is the last thing I want for you."

Leo moaned, sounding to her own ears like a frightened child. She squeezed her eyes shut, feeling the hot trail of tears run from beneath her lids. There was no way in hell she was going to acknowledge Alex now—no way she was going to give Alex or Dr. Kerrigan anything they asked for. Not after what they'd done—to her, to Sleepwater, to Kaylee.

"Leo… please…"

She turned her head away, laying a clammy cheek against the already sweat-stained sheet beneath her. The sound of Alex leaving the room seemed to take all her tension out with it, and she fell gratefully back into darkness.

"…up to one hundred twenty units per liter, please. Oh, you're back." Dr. Kerrigan leaned over her, eyes bright with excitement.

Leo didn't bother fighting against the restraints this time. She felt exhausted, wasted, like someone had pulled the string of her own vitality and completely unraveled it.

"We're trying something new today," the woman said, the mad arousal in her voice betraying the cold, calculating way she scanned Leo's body. "It's called Birofin. Been on the market a few years already. It's used to treat seizures, but we'll be giving you substantially larger doses. It hasn't worked very well on many other subjects, so I wouldn't get your hopes up, but I think you have remarkable potential as an exception." She pushed down the plunger of another syringe and patted Leo's forearm in a failed gesture of reassurance. Leo didn't even have the energy to flinch.

"This looks promising." Dr. Kerrigan fiddled with the monitors again and left the room without another word.

Leo woke to the sound of screaming. She wondered what poor fucker was getting tortured in a room next to hers until she realized the screams came from her own throat—dry, cracking. Her brain said it was unnecessary to keep the noise going; the logical part of her felt fine. Her body had other ideas. In a moment of surreal realization, she noticed the separation there between the physical and mental. As if from outside herself, she watched her body buck against the straps holding her to the bed, saw the rash-like flush crawling down her neck and the damp rings of sweat soaking through her white uniform. She still couldn't quite understand the rush when two assistants burst through the sliding glass door, pushing a metal tray toward her bed as if her life depended on it; it might have. Then she understood how bad it was when the men spoke to one another and she couldn't process a single word of it.

She mentally catalogued the relief her body must have felt when they delivered more drugs to stop the agony.

Time became only an idea. She had no clue how long she'd been here—couldn't remember how many different drugs they'd pumped through her. How many tests. They must have added liquid feed to her IV, because she hadn't eaten anything since she'd gotten there, and she didn't remember being force-fed. Of course, her throat hurt all the time now, but she remembered the raw, frantic sounds of her own screams. They hadn't changed her clothes, though, after the first time. She stank of sweat and something with which she was all too familiar—desperation. That end-of-the-line, what-the-fuck-do-I-do-now stench bordering between body odor and rankness. And for the first time in her life, Leo began to really believe there was no way out of this.

Dr. Kerrigan entered the room, and Leo stared blankly at the ceiling. The woman hadn't accomplished her main goal yet, that much was clear, but breaking Leo's defiance seemed to be the secondary objective, and Leo was on the verge of giving it to her. She was done.

"This *has* been quite the trial," the woman said, hands stuck into the pockets of her lab coat. She peered at the monitors. "I have to be honest with you, I felt about ready to give up last night. It bothers me more than I can say to have to put you through this."

Bullshit. Leo's eye twitched.

"But then I started thinking of Marcus again, and the idea struck me. We've never used Pointera for this particular research. I was so ready to put that failure behind me that I never considered it a viable option in the present. Why not target the superior temporal gyrus one more time? Oh, Leona, I wish I could open your brain and pinpoint exactly where your gift comes from." She sighed with a noncommittal hum. "But that would end our work, and I still need you." Dr. Kerrigan pulled one hand from her coat pocket, revealing yet another syringe.

God, it looked just like the needles Leo's dad had emptied into his own veins—thick, white. Volatile. The shit came in little white pills at the pharmacy, but on the streets, it got crushed and boiled and injected. And it looked like this. She could almost smell the vinegary, astringent stink, having breathed in the same fumes during the years she'd cut and hawked it herself. But she never touched it. Not once.

Dr. Kerrigan handled the syringe with more tenderness than she'd ever shown toward her own daughter. "If only for nostalgia's sake," she said, adding it to the IV. She smiled, and Leo's blood ran cold.

41

WHEN CONSCIOUSNESS RETURNED, Leo couldn't figure out what was wrong until she realized she felt fine. Nothing hurt. The sweat had cooled and dried on her skin and clothes. The soreness of her muscles came from previous tension, not current fatigue. Her throat burned only from having screamed it raw, missing the fiery sting of drug-induced agony. And it was so quiet.

The quiet unnerved her. She'd grown used to the screams from down the hall—to the sliding of the glass door, the susurrus of movement beyond, and the whispers of scientific observation. They still had her strapped to the bed, though; had they even noticed her change?

She could have sworn she heard a clock ticking somewhere, but she'd never seen one in her room. It seemed one of the ticks was louder than the others, oddly misplaced, but what could she do about an odd sound? What did it matter here?

Then she heard a new sound, one that made her heart

leap with a glimmer of excitement. "Stop, please!"

It came from down the hall, but she knew it wasn't any of the other *subjects*. It wasn't John's repetitive shrieks; it wasn't Tony's siren-like wails. She never knew what Kaylee's screams sounded like—if Kaylee ever did scream—but this sound was one of the assistants. It was Dr. Carter. And with it came the familiar mumble of Kaylee's voice as she spun a beat.

Leo didn't quite understand what was happening for a few seconds—how it could happen at all. But Carter just kept begging to be relieved of the pain, Kaylee's voice never stopped, and Leo put it together. The girl's beat was working again. A jolt of hope ran through her, and she found herself laughing like a madwoman at the thought. They'd tried to break Kaylee, tried to break *Leo* to get to her, and in their desperation, they'd returned her weapon to her. Leo had never seen anyone in the building without the earpiece attached, so if Kaylee's beat was working, that meant the implants were useless.

It surprised her that no one came rushing into her room at the sound of her laughter. No one burst through the doors to check her vitals on the monitors, which beeped remarkably rhythmically and at unusually normal levels. In a place where agony was the norm, wouldn't that throw up red flags? Wouldn't they check on her if one of their other *subjects* had managed to circumvent their technology?

There it was again—the ticking through her laughter—and then the sound grew. Something shifted in the ceiling tiles above her head, pulling down a thin sheet of dust, and Leo just kept laughing. It seemed odd at first, a dull roar punctuated by a crack and another rustle in the ceiling. It took a while for her to realize that the wailing she heard next was an actual alarm system. Something was wrong at Vanguard Industries.

Dr. Carter's pleas grew louder, stronger, and then his

wail of pain was cut short. She couldn't tell what had happened—hoped Kaylee had hurt him beyond repair—and she stopped laughing to listen. A short, stout woman with a horrendous bob yanked the sliding glass door open and stumbled into Leo's room. The woman must have been an assistant; she wore the white lab coat. But she'd lost any professional air she might have held before. Now, sweat dripped from her hairline, her eyes bulged in terror, and she almost slipped on the slick tile floor as she barreled toward Leo's bed.

"You look like shit," Leo said, surprised by the return of her attitude. It had been a long time, but now she felt good enough to give this bitch some of her original bite.

"I've come to—" The woman swallowed hard, and Leo could actually hear it. "To move you to another wing."

"What's wrong with this one?"

The ceiling shuddered again, and the woman looked up at it in wide-eyed panic. "I've been instructed not to—" A loud boom resonated through the room, not close enough to seem dangerous but just loud enough to cause obvious concern. The woman fumbled with the monitors behind Leo's bed, gasping for breath, apparently unable to bring herself to meet Leo's gaze.

Then Leo had the most wonderful thought. If Kaylee's beat was working again, if something had gone so horribly wrong as to cause this woman to lose her composure entirely, maybe Leo's own beat had returned too. She stared at the implant in the assistant's head, thinking that if it didn't work, at least she'd catch the woman off guard.

She felt the words rise up in her throat and almost choked. They burned, just like they always did—oh, they burned. It felt like she'd taken a double-shot of whiskey, only this time it traveled up. And with it came the overwhelming sense of serenity and power combined. She felt unstoppable.

"Take me out of these straps."

The woman didn't stop, didn't laugh at her or tell her she was wasting her time. She looked like someone had pushed her reset button; her eyes phased out completely, she raised her head, then she redirected her attention to the straps binding Leo's wrists. Her hand produced a key-ring from her coat pocket on auto-pilot, and she brought it toward the lock on the straps. Her hand trembled violently, the keys slipping in her sweaty fingers.

"For fuck's sake," Leo spat, "calm the hell down and get me out of here."

The effect was instantaneous. The woman unlocked and released each binding on Leo's wrists and ankles in record time, her breathing calm and even, the sweat almost soaking back into her very skin as if on command.

Leo bolted from the bed and jumped down, her bare feet smacking the tiles. She took a second to orient herself, expecting the onslaught of pain or nausea that had been her recent reality. But she felt fine. No, she corrected herself, she felt fucking amazing.

Snatching the keys from the assistant's pliable hand, she headed toward the sliding glass door. Then she stopped and turned back toward the woman, who stared blankly ahead without movement or sound. "You won't follow me, you won't try to stop me, and you won't tell anyone else what's happened." The assistant made no response whatsoever, standing like a dummy in the harsh white light of Leo's *exam room*. Another quake rocked the building, sending an even heavier shiver of dust from the ceiling, but the woman didn't register a bit of it.

Leo smirked, flipped both her middle fingers at the fucking torture bed, and stepped into the hallway.

It looked like a completely different building—much more like what she'd expected the first time she'd followed Dr. Kerrigan through these halls. The lights flickered and buzzed for as far as she could see down the hallway, the rumbling coming louder and closer together now, punctuated by a tremble in the walls that brought more debris sifting down from the ceiling. It may have been the fact that Leo felt so tremendous, or the fact that Vanguard Industries looked like it was getting its ass kicked by something, but she found the whole thing hilariously invigorating. How badly had these people fucked up?

Quickening her pace, she only passed two rooms until she turned the corner and stopped. There, in the middle of the hallway, was Kaylee, strapped to a gurney and staring at the ceiling. Dr. Carter lay in a pile on the floor, unmoving.

"Hey," Leo said.

Kaylee raised her head from the gurney, fighting against the restraints holding her down until she recognized Leo. Then she grinned. "How'd *you* get out?"

"How'd *he* end up on the floor?" Leo countered, nodding at Dr. Carter's body. She would have bet the fucking lab-rat clothes on her back he was dead. Kaylee only fought down her smile, and Leo rushed to the gurney, thankfully only having to go through two keys on the keyring before she found the right one. "How you feeling?" she asked, standing back as Kaylee sat up. The girl stared at her with a smirk, and that was more than enough of an answer. "We gotta get outta here," Leo added.

"No shit." Kaylee rubbed her wrists.

"We have to grab the others first," Leo said, pointing down the hallway and taking a step.

"Others?"

Leo stopped and turned around, hating the fact that she had to explain the next bit—and now, of all times. "They fuckin' grabbed Tony." The smile immediately left Kaylee's face. "And another guy named John. I'm not gonna leave them here."

"Yeah. Where—"

Two men and another woman in their goddamn white coats practically slid around the corner, stopping just feet from Leo, Kaylee, and Dr. Carter's body. A combination of fear and hatred played on their faces, and they glared at her, their breath coming ragged and heavy as the lights flickered in the hallway. Leo didn't understand the hatred part; *she* was the one who'd been practically tortured for who the hell knew how long, not these assholes.

"Hey, you can't do that," one of the men shouted.

Such a stupid statement. The neighborhood was going to shit all around them, plus they already *had* done whatever *it* was. Escape from their beds? Kill a doctor? Did it matter? After everything she'd been through, the sentence was particularly obnoxious, and Leo rolled her eyes. "Oh, drop dead," she said, resorting back to the scathing, angsty tone of annoyance so often used in her teenage years. That was all it was—a knee-jerk reaction to an impossible situation—but the words came out feeling like she'd just swallowed a lit cigarette.

The assistants stared blankly back at her for a brief second, their eyes foggy and empty, and then they did. They dropped dead. Each body crumpled to the floor like a puppet cut from its strings—no cries of pain, no shouts of fear. No resistance.

"Holy fuck," Leo breathed, feeling the aftertaste of her beat and wondering how the hell she'd just managed that. Had she just killed three people, or was that considered suicide? She and Kaylee just stared at the bodies on the floor until an explosion wracked the building.

She knew it was an explosion this time, because one side of the hallway a few rooms down collided into the other. Plaster and insulation pelted against the standing glass doors, showering them with debris. Power lines dangled from the ceiling, sparks lighting up the curtain of dust behind them. Leo worked her jaw a few times, trying to cut out the ringing in her ears as she straightened from her crouch and looked around. Where the hallway dead-ended, she recognized the key-code panel on the door; Dr. Kerrigan had led her through there when she'd shown her what they'd done to Kaylee. That meant Tony and John's rooms were back the way she'd come.

Unable to hear her own voice, she grabbed Kaylee by the arm and yanked her back down the hall. It could have been the adrenaline, but she thought she felt an unnatural heat at their backs. Explosions *and* fires—fucking perfect.

Fortunately, the sliding doors were glass, and they could see into each room from the hallway. Finding the others was easier than she imagined, and she only briefly registered how calm she seemed when she picked the right key on the first try and unlocked Tony's restraints. She'd never seen him so serious, so fucking unamused. But it made sense; she couldn't blame him for it. He followed them quickly, wordlessly, and when they reached John's room, the man stared at them with wide eyes.

"You the ones blowing this place up?" he asked. It wasn't fear in his voice, more like a cynical hope, manifesting in his deep frown above an accidental smirk.

"No," Leo said shortly as she unlocked the last strap on his ankle.

"Then who is?"

"No fucking clue."

The four raced down the hallway, rocking explosions echoing behind them. They turned another corner in the fucking maze of a *research facility* and stopped short. Dr. Kerrigan stood in the center of the hallway, the only thing blocking their path to the set of steel double-doors which presumably led outside. Not *really* blocking their path, though, Leo thought; there were four of them against one hated doctor. Dr. Kerrigan seemed to calculate those odds at the same time, and it brought a sickened grin to her face. It wasn't a grin that said, *I will stop you at any and all costs.* It was a grin that said, *I was right.*

Time seemed to stretch on into eternity as they stared at each other, and nobody moved amidst the chaos. Leo was fully aware of the fact that she could open her mouth at any second and make the bitch do whatever she wanted. She could tell her to drop dead. She could tell her to go crazy, to go home and slit her own wrists, to turn herself in and shut this place down forever. But she didn't. She didn't know why—couldn't name the invisible hand holding her back, telling her to wait—but she held in the beat threatening to spill out and kept her mouth shut.

The world started moving again, and Dr. Kerrigan pivoted to the side, clearing the way toward the door, nursing that disgusting, self-satisfied gleam. Leo walked toward the door, followed by the others, and feeling the woman's eyes on her back was more disturbing than the gaze of any man who'd ever catcalled her on the streets.

42

LEO DIDN'T KNOW what she'd expected to see when they stepped outside, but it sure as fuck wasn't this. It was dark out, the moon high in the sky, and that part made sense. She'd been brought here in the middle of the night; now someone was busting them out in the dark. The chain-link fence surrounding the huge property flickered in a rosy glow, and she realized it came from the fire now consuming half the building behind them. Another explosion burst from the way they'd come, and it sounded louder out here somehow. Leo thought she heard laughter from around the side of the building, and then a figure burst around the corner, running at full-speed in all black. He passed the four escapees standing just outside the exit doors, then stopped.

When he turned to look at them, Leo almost choked. It was Cameron. He stared at them, wide-eyed, the cut-off laugh still hanging from his grin. "Goddamn, Randall's good," he said.

"Fuck yes," Kaylee added.

Leo turned to see a smirk on the girl's face. Tony just stared at Cameron. John's eyes were wide white orbs in the dark, reflecting the burning, exploding chaos.

"What are you doing here?" Leo asked. Immediately it sounded stupid, and she expected Cameron to give her shit for it.

Instead, his eyes lit up with more enthusiasm and—yes, it was—joy than she'd ever seen in him. "Blowing shit up," he said, like she should have known that was his sole purpose in life. Then he nodded at Tony and tossed him a bottle of spray paint. "This is what we do."

Tony stepped away from the doorway and turned toward the brick wall of the building. He shook the spray can vigorously, then held his arm up, the sound of the released aerosol strangely loud for the circumstances. Five broad strokes across the wall, and he left a simple blue double-helix against the bricks. Leo stared at the sign, overwhelmed by déjà vu. Then the whirring chop of a helicopter barreled toward them.

A searchlight found them, temporarily blinding Leo and erasing the image of the sign on the brick wall in front of her. "Come on," Cameron called and took off running again toward the fence. They followed him, the flashing lights behind them growing brighter as military issue Jeeps raced around the rubble toward them. Leo chanced a glimpse backwards and almost tripped over her own feet. One of the Jeeps had stopped by the wall of the building, and a handful of men in all black, wearing the same fucking headgear with the blinking green lights, rounded the corner from a different direction. Another explosion wracked the building, and a flock of people in white lab coats spilled from another exit door, gawking about. In the darkness ahead, she saw another group of people in black running towards them, and she wondered how the hell they were supposed to get out of this mess, being cornered on three sides. And Cameron was leading them right toward the new group.

Gunshots rang out, strikingly dull against the helicopter overhead and the roar of the burning building. She couldn't tell what direction they came from, and it seemed odd that the people in black running towards them were waving frantically. Shouts accompanied the gunfire, and then Leo heard a familiar voice.

"The van's behind the fence!" It came from in front of her, from the man waving his arms, and then she recognized Karl. Sleepwater had shown up after all.

All parties converged on one another—the men with blinking headgear and guns, the Vanguard Industry scientists and assistants, Sleepwater, and the four lucky fuckers who apparently were being rescued. Then Leo found herself completely unable to follow it all. She saw Brad dodge an attacker, ducking and rolling across the ground before shoving an elbow into the man's face. She saw Mirela, grim-faced and unnaturally pale, aim a handgun with both hands, her feet positioned squarely in the dirt. Don scrambled through the bodies, dodging white lab coats and finally punching one woman square in the face in his desperate attempt to reach his twin. Leo noticed the woman was Alex, and she felt an odd mixture of anxiety and vindictive pleasure.

More gunfire rang out in the valley, cracking against the shouts and scuffles, and Leo heard Karl's battle cry as he squeezed off multiple shots in a row. Then he lashed out at another man running toward Brad, striking him in the temple with the butt of his handgun and shoving him hard onto his back. Running was the only thing Leo knew she could do, and she did it well, heading toward the chain-link fence and dodging out of the way when Karl kicked at whoever it was chasing her. Dirt and debris dug into her bare feet, but the pain only made her move faster.

Kaylee's voice rang out behind her, much louder than it should have been—almost like she was playing it over loudspeakers. "I have been one acquainted with the night…"

Leo didn't recognize the words, but they echoed behind her with the same cadence she'd heard in Kaylee's beat before. The girl obviously liked poetry. Leo smirked even through the burning in her lungs as she ran. A woman screamed behind her, then a man, followed by more cries of agony than she expected to hear. The gunfire stopped with the sounds of fighting, and Leo skidded to a halt. When she turned around, her stomach dropped a thousand feet.

They all lay on the ground, writhing and screaming, clutching their own arms or legs or heads. Everyone—the government men with the blinking headgear, the white-coated employees of Vanguard Industries. Then Leo noticed Brad crawling along the ground on his belly, gritting his teeth in anguish and reaching desperately for Mirela. Tony and Don stared at each other with terror on their faces, hunched into themselves. Karl let out a loud, "Fuck!" grappling for his dropped weapon but unable to steady his hand enough. And in the center of it all stood Kaylee, staring up into the stars and reciting whatever fucking poem she'd chosen for this beat.

"Shit," Leo breathed, then took off running back toward the girl. She only briefly processed the fact that she wasn't affected by it at all, that John stood behind Kaylee with a gaping mouth, also seemingly immune. "Kaylee!" she yelled. "Kaylee, cut it out." The girl brought her gaze down to look at Leo, a confused frown darkening her brow. Leo finally reached her, shaking her head wildly. "Their earpieces don't work," she said, stooping toward Mirela to help lift her up by the arm. "We gotta go."

"What the fuck?" Cameron screamed, clenching his eyes tightly and rubbing his forehead.

Those in Sleepwater who had come to join the fight

quickly got a hold of themselves again, scrambling up from the dirt to head back toward the fence and the van. The men in black and researchers in lab coats stirred as well, and Leo turned back to Kaylee. "Seriously, we gotta go," she said.

An odd look of excited realization dawned on Kaylee's face, and she grinned. Then she turned away from Leo and the fence and started her beat again. It sounded even louder than before, however impossible that seemed. Leo wheeled around and followed the others, wondering how the hell they were still standing upright and moving toward the van. The cutting whir of the helicopter came closer, almost overhead, and Leo watched her shadow grow incredibly long before her. Kaylee's voice got even louder, defying the capabilities of normal vocal chords, and then something about the helicopter above them changed. It sounded wrong—a high-pitched whine, but Leo didn't want to waste time in turning around to look.

She didn't have to. Another explosion sounded close behind them, and the chop of the helicopter blades through the air was replaced by the metallic ping and thud of scattered shrapnel hitting the ground around them. Leo stumbled toward the fence, feeling the searing heat at her back, and finally jumped up over the chain-link after Cameron. Her feet hit gravel on the other side, and she turned to gaze through the metal. Amid the fading screams of those still left on the Vanguard Industries grounds, from within the blazing chaos of ruined buildings and vehicle carcasses, Kaylee walked calmly towards them through the smoke. A fierce excitement burned in her eyes above a barely contained smirk, and Leo felt an odd mixture of pride and fear. Whatever the girl had just figured out how to do, it was fucking huge.

Kaylee took her sweet-ass time getting to the fence, but she climbed it like she hadn't just spent a seeming eternity inside a research lab, tortured for the secrets to her beat. She stopped briefly in front of Leo, raised and lowered her eyebrows, and followed the rest of Sleepwater into the van. Leo blinked, her eyes stinging from the smoke and maybe some emotion she couldn't name. She stared at the wreckage on the other side of the fence, still unable to completely believe everything that had just happened and wondering if she'd have some kind of breakdown further down the road. Right now, it felt fucking right.

Then she turned and climbed into the middle seat of the van. Karl gave her a quick look from the front passenger seat, then turned around as Bernadette put the van into gear and headed out toward the highway. Sirens wailed in the night, but they were far away.

43

THE VAN WAS too quiet. Not like it had been when they'd left the mountain house—full of expectation and a wary sort of excitement. This silence had formed from disbelief, a what-the-fuck type of shock, and it seemed most of them still tried to hide the receding pain from Kaylee's beat. More than anything, though, a pregnant fear swelled around them.

Kaylee sat next to Leo in the van's middle row, her head tilted back, eyes closed above a close-lipped smile. She looked like she was lounging on the beach, not fleeing from torture. She hadn't said a word—no one had—but she looked happier than Leo had ever seen her. Nobody looked at Kaylee; they made a point to look away, actually, and Leo felt like something even worse than blowing up Vanguard Industries—than watching Kaylee take down everyone around them with her words—was just around the corner.

"Thank you," John said from the other side of Kaylee, addressing everyone. "Thanks for taking me with you." His eyes were bright, alert, and he might have been the only one oblivious to the tension. "My name's John—"

"Shut up," Don spat from the back seat. He had his arm around Tony, who still hadn't spoken since Leo unlocked his restraints, staring blankly out the window.

Leo took a deep breath, her insides churning, wondering what the hell was going to happen next. What *could* happen next, after all this?

Another ten minutes of painful silence passed. For all her age, Bernadette drove like a professional, racing around the curves of the passes through the Rocky Mountains. Leo had no idea where they were going, and even if she'd cared more about it, asking still would have felt wrong somehow.

"Fuck!" Cameron shouted from the back seat beside the twins. "Is nobody gonna say a goddamn thing about it?"

In the row in front of her, Leo watched Brad smooth his hand over the back of Mirela's head, and Randall only straightened in his seat, rigid and tight where he was normally languid and confident. He pushed his glasses up the bridge of his nose.

"Seriously?" Cameron continued. His screaming made Leo's head pound, but she couldn't build up the nerve to tell him to take it down a notch. "Kaylee, what the fuck was that?" He gripped the back of the middle seat, pulling himself almost into their row.

Kaylee turned to look at Leo with a smirk, rolling her eyes in Cameron's direction as if Leo was in on it too. As if Cameron were the odd one out here and everyone else knew exactly what was going on.

"Hey, I'm talking to you!" Cameron shook the back of the seat vigorously. "What the *fuck* did you just do to us?"

"Cameron," Karl called from the passenger seat up front. He didn't turn around, his voice calm and even, but there was no denying the tension in his shoulders, the obvious energy it took for him to keep his cool.

"Fuck you, Karl. You can't just shove this under the

355

rug. What happened—"

"Cameron, I need you to calm down—"

"No! I need to know what the fuck we took out of that lab!"

That did it. This wasn't about Cameron's physical pain, about having had to blow up a research facility. This wasn't even about the extra effort it took to break Leo and the others out of Vanguard Industries. This was all about Kaylee, about Cameron's fear *of* her, and something inside him had apparently broken because of it.

"Can you pull over as soon as there's room?" Karl asked Bernadette, his voice low. Luckily, the shoulder reappeared on the highway just a few moments later, leaving enough room to park the van on the gravel beside a sign labeling this a 'scenic overlook'. Leo doubted anyone would be paying attention to the view.

"Asshole," Cameron hissed, slamming his unbuckled seatbelt against the seat. The twins avoided meeting his gaze too as he crawled past their knees from the back seat and headed toward the door. Leo pushed the automatic door handle, and it took way too long for the door to slide open. Everyone waited to see what Cameron would do before getting out of their own seats.

Karl took a deep breath, let it out, then unbuckled his seatbelt and opened the door. Cameron paced in the gravel turn-off, vigorously rubbing the top of his head over and over. "Cameron…" Karl started.

"We're just gonna keep driving? Not ask a fucking question?" Cameron fumed, gesturing wildly.

"We just broke them out of a *lab*," Karl replied, his voice raising in volume now just a little. "We don't know what happened in there—"

"We don't *need* to know, Karl! You can't ignore it. Her beat's a fucking weapon, now. Went through our fucking headgear—" He tapped on the earpiece still clinging to his ear, then ripped it off and chucked it down the canyon into the darkness. "What the hell do we do with that? What else can she do that we don't know about?" Cameron spun around, glaring at everyone else in the van like a madman. "Does nobody else give two shits?"

Nobody said anything.

Then Kaylee stood from her seat, almost not having to duck at all as she stepped out of the van. She paused only to grab a hoodie left on the floor before putting it on and stepping out toward Cameron.

"What are you doing?" Leo whispered, but of course, Kaylee didn't pay any attention. When Cameron saw Kaylee move, he froze, staring at her with wide eyes and the look of a man trying not to piss himself.

Kaylee gave him a chilling smile. "I'm just gonna go," she said, nodding.

"Kaylee, you don't have to go anywhere," Karl said, though he didn't move toward her and didn't offer any other solution.

"No, it's fine. I'll just walk. Hitch a ride. Nobody's gonna hurt me." She raised her eyebrows, her grin widening. She headed away from the van like a martyr headed for the noose, only she had nothing to fear.

"Don't fuck with me," Cameron growled. He fumbled in the pocket of his black jacket and took out a pistol, aiming it straight at the girl. The van's yellow interior lights glinted off the steel.

"Woah, woah," Leo said, throwing off her seatbelt and scrambling out of the van. "Cameron, you don't need to do that." She heard Brad cursing behind her. Kaylee stopped, but the smile never left her face.

Cameron only glanced at Leo briefly. "You saw what she can do. What she did to us." He shifted uneasily on his feet, his hand trembling. Leo had a feeling his hands never trembled. "Did you see exactly what they did to her in there?

Were you with her the whole time?"

"No," Leo said and threw up her hands. "But they did the same thing to me." Cameron spared her only another quick glance, and when she looked at Karl, his lips were pressed tightly together. He gestured with his eyes for her to keep going, but he didn't move.

"W-what the hell *did* they do?" Cameron stuttered, quickly losing the courage it had taken him to start down this road in the first place.

"My beat's… stronger… too," she said. The image of the three assistants crumpling to the ground in the hallway streaked through her mind, and she couldn't come to terms with whether or not it had been her fault—whether or not she'd killed them.

"Bye, Cameron," Kaylee said, giving him a condescending nod and moving to leave.

He raised the gun to the sky and fired a shot, his hand shaking wildly. Everyone ducked at the sound—everyone except Kaylee—and Leo braced herself for the worst now. Kaylee's eyes flicked to Cameron's, who swallowed and stared at her like he *had* shot her. Tears welled in his eyes even before Kaylee spoke, the pain on his face comparable to the pain just beginning with her beat.

"Only reapers, reaping early…"

Leo heard the words—another fucking poem, it seemed—and braced herself. Kaylee's beat hadn't worked on her when they were escaping, and she didn't expect it to this time, but she didn't think it was fair for Kaylee to hit everyone else. She whirled toward the van, wondering who might need her help first, but nobody moved. Everyone stared at Kaylee and Cameron, completely unaffected by the girl's words.

Cameron, though, got the full force of it. He gritted his teeth and met Kaylee's gaze, trying to fight an uncontrollable beat. She stared at him blankly, reciting the poem, her eyes burning with something Leo had never seen before. Then Cameron broke, his set jaw wilting into a grimace, and he fell to his knees. He dropped the gun, arching his back in agony before letting out a scream.

"Kaylee," Leo said, taking another step closer.

The girl kept spinning her beat. Cameron stayed down, knees splayed, bending almost completely backward as if someone held him up by invisible strings. He screamed again.

"Cut it out." Leo lunged at Kaylee to step between her and Cameron, as if that would stop her. She grabbed the girl's shoulder, feeling the words burning up through her throat. "Stop. Kaylee, that's too much." But, of course, her beat had no effect on Kaylee, either. Cameron's hands curled into claws, rigid in torment, his whole body shaking.

Finally, Kaylee stopped. Cameron collapsed in release, rolling onto his side with a moan and gasping into the dirt. Then Kaylee turned her gaze on Leo and tilted her head. "You coming with me?"

Leo blinked, completely caught off guard, and she looked wide-eyed down at Cameron on the ground before meeting the girl's dark gaze again. She'd liked Kaylee, she really had. Things had seemed as normal with her as Leo thought they were ever going to get, but this she couldn't do. Whether or not Kaylee's beat was stronger now, whatever they'd done to her at Vanguard Industries had fractured any sanity she might have had left. The girl was completely psycho. "No," Leo said, scoffing and then correcting herself. Her insides churned, her legs felt weak enough to let her drop right there, and she tried to hide it by frowning at the girl in disbelief.

Kaylee shrugged, then grabbed Leo's face in both hands and kissed her. Leo only half struggled to pull away, wondering why it was still so hard to do. Then Kaylee stuck her hands in the pocket of her hoodie and headed back down the highway the way they'd come. It didn't take long for her to fade out of the van's headlights and into the darkness of the mountains, but Leo watched her all the same until she disappeared.

Then she turned to Cameron. He'd finally managed to sit up, and now he rested his elbows on his knees, holding his head.

Karl had squatted down beside him, reaching out a concerned hand but hesitating to touch him. "Are you okay?" he asked.

Cameron closed his eyes. "Just... just give me a minute."

Leo looked up at the stars, still feeling small in a world that made even less sense now than it ever had.

44

THEY DROVE ANOTHER eight hours straight, and it was almost midday by the time they stopped at a shitty-looking motel in Las Vegas, New Mexico—not Nevada. With the shared name, Leo had expected it to be far more than what it was, but she'd learned not to get too disappointed.

Apparently, the plan had been to make a stop in the town anyways, even before Kaylee had lost her shit. Mirela had a sister in San Antonio who had agreed to let them all stay while they figured out what to do next, but that was a lot more driving than any of them were willing to commit to without some rest. If they hadn't been chased from the mountain house in Wyoming, they could have gone back there, Randall told her. But they'd never been chased down like that before, and this was a whole different game now. Leo wondered what the hell it would take to get these guys to quit doing what they apparently loved so much—terrorizing government-funded research labs, busting out captured *subjects*, and hunting down other beat-spinners to join their ranks. With everything she'd been through in the last few days, though, she couldn't imagine doing anything else when she actually thought about it. It was chaotic and fucked-up, but part of Sleepwater's world fit her perfectly.

She and John headed back across the street from the gas station where they'd bought a case of beer. The man had pretty much not left her side since she'd untied him from the hospital bed, and for all his muscular bulk, he really just acted like a lost puppy. He had obviously tried and failed in making friends with the rest of Sleepwater; maybe he lacked the proper skills, but if that were the case, Leo couldn't figure out for the life of her why he'd chosen her as his new anchor.

Making sure the street was clear before jaywalking, Leo squinted against the midday sun and lit a cigarette. She offered one to John, but he just shook his head, cradling the case of beer under one arm. When she took that first drag, though, it didn't quite feel or taste the same. They'd bought the beer with money Brad had given them, and Leo was surprised to find that a pack of smokes hadn't been the first thing on her mind. But she'd picked one up with the extra cash, realizing that, within Vanguard Industries, she might have expected never to smoke again.

She took two more drags and scowled, dropping the cigarette and crushing it under her shoe. Sleepwater had brought her clothes, too, and she'd silently commended them on being so prepared—mostly. Karl had given John a pair of his jeans and a white undershirt, which clung to John's torso like a second skin, obviously way too small. The guy didn't seem to mind. As long as they were out of that building and out of the white scrubs, things felt way more normal. That was what mattered—some form of normalcy right now.

They stepped up onto the sidewalk from the street and headed toward the van parked behind the motel. "So…" Leo started, feeling somehow responsible for acclimating John to their new world. "What did you do before... being experimented on, and all that?" She suddenly wished she hadn't put out the cigarette, but it wasn't a strong enough urge to make her light another one.

"Oh," John said lightly with a little smile. "I'm a nurse."

Leo did a double-take and craned her neck to look up at him. He gave her a shrug and a smile, which she couldn't help but return. "Really?"

"Yeah. Doubt I have a job to go back to, though. I don't know how long they kept me in that lab, but it was definitely more than just a few days." His brow darkened then, and his hand tightened on the case of beer.

Leo sucked on her lower lip. She didn't want to go back down memory lane with him so soon after leaving that place, and she figured he felt the same way. So she just didn't say anything else.

The others waited for them at the back of the motel, not really talking at all, but Brad's face lit up a little when he saw them return. "Well, we got all our rooms figured out," he told her, as if somehow that would make her happy and making her happy was a good thing.

"Cool," she said, bobbing her head, and a little smile followed.

"You and me get the girl's room," Bernadette told her, waving the key card.

"That would mean something *way* different if Kaylee were still here," Don said. It came out like every other joke he and Tony had made together—cocky, self-assured, a little over-the-top in delivery. But this time the joke fell flat on its face and stayed there. If it hadn't been too soon to mention Kaylee, even if things between her and Leo—whatever they'd been—hadn't died when the girl left, the snide comments were only funny because they came from the twins. Tony, though, said absolutely nothing. He didn't even look at his brother, didn't crack the faintest hint of a smile, and that seemed to make things even more awkward than they had a right to be.

"Beer," Karl said, breaking the silence. It wasn't a question, but it served perfectly as an invitation to leave the tension behind and maybe blow a little steam. Everyone else nodded and started moving again, following Karl into the three-bed room he unlocked.

Brad had gotten four rooms for them—one for Leo and Bernadette, a single for Brad and Mirela, and the guys broken up into the other two rooms, each with two beds and a couch. The entire group filed into Karl's room, which he told John they'd be sharing with Randall, and Leo had to keep herself from laughing in relief. She had a feeling that John and Cameron in the same room overnight wasn't a good idea at all. Cameron and the twins, on the other hand, had always seemed to carry a decent friendship, though she wondered how that would go over now; Tony still seemed to be back at Vanguard Industries, strapped to the hospital bed. If nothing had brought him out of it by now, she didn't know what would.

They filled the room up almost to the brim, sitting beside each other on the beds. Randall had grabbed the chair in front of the tiny desk in the corner, and they passed around the beers. Even Bernadette took one, grinning when Karl popped the top off with his lighter and handed it back to her. Randall passed two toward Brad and Mirela, who sat beside each other on the floor.

"No thanks," Mirela said, a slow smile creeping over her face.

"Brad," Randall said, leaning over even farther to hand one to him.

"Nope. Me neither." Brad held a hand up, his eyes filled with some emotion just bursting to get out.

"What?" Cameron said, his mouth hanging open.

Leo hadn't known anyone here but Karl for very long—and she'd only known him a few weeks—but she'd never seen Brad turn down a drink. He seemed to have one in his hand almost all the time, except for when they were driving or working at blowing up research buildings, of course.

"What's going on?" Randall asked, his own beer half-way to his lips.

Mirela looked at Brad, anxiety, excitement, and what Leo thought looked like embarrassment raging across her face. "Well…"

"We're pregnant!" Brad shouted, throwing his arm around her and grinning from within his flaming-red beard.

Mirela rolled her eyes at him and sighed, then looked at each of them in turn. "We thought our stop here would be a little more… lighthearted. Maybe we should've waited—"

"We needed something to fucking celebrate," Karl said, raising his beer. "Congratulations."

Everyone offered some form of congratulations, and a toast went around the room. Only Tony didn't say anything, but at least he looked Mirela in the eye, and at least he was drinking his beer. Leo figured that might be all he was capable of at the moment.

"How far along are you?" John asked. It seemed such a weird question coming from such a hulk of a man.

"Ten weeks," Mirela said.

Leo couldn't help it; she snorted a laugh through her nose. "John's a nurse."

That was met with complete silence, and they all stared at the man in Karl's too-tight undershirt.

"Get the fuck out," Cameron said.

John turned to look at him, lurching from the bed with a confused expression. "Oh, uh… Okay." He stood fully, but Bernadette put a hand on his shoulder and gently guided him back down.

"He's messing with you," she said, and Brad and Randall burst out laughing.

Leo looked up to see the tiniest smile creep onto the corners of Tony's mouth, almost indistinguishable, and when she locked eyes with Don, he was grinning. When she laughed, John turned to look at her, and through his confused frown, he chuckled. She realized then that this must have been what it was like for the others when she'd first met them, when Sleepwater had decided whether or not they wanted to keep her. They'd fucked with her just like this, and now... Now, she knew what it felt like to really be a part of it.

It didn't surprise her at all that she couldn't sleep. If they'd stopped at the motel in the middle of the night, she would have found it just as difficult. So Leo sat out on the curb of the motel parking lot, watching the fading late-afternoon sun and debating whether or not she actually wanted to light a cigarette.

It hadn't taken the group long at all to kill the case of beer, and it took even less time for the celebratory air to die down before they all decided to break up the party and get some rest. If Leo had known Brad and Mirela longer than she had, she probably would have been more excited for them. Babies for people who wanted them were a good thing. But she couldn't get the image out of her head of Brad and Mirela writhing in pain on the ground at Vanguard Industries, or the vision of Mirela running through the woods away from her house, men in black suits and gunfire at her back. Leo had started to think that *she'd* do a whole bunch of things for Sleepwater and the individuals who made it what it was; she'd endured far more pain than she had to under Dr. Kerrigan's guise of research in order to keep Sleepwater's secrets. Brad and Mirela, though, took it to a whole new level. They were pregnant, and it didn't stop them from doing what they'd always done in Sleepwater's name.

That thought made Leo frown, and then she heard a door opening and closing. Turning around, she saw John leaving the room he shared with Karl and Randall, but he was alone. He met her gaze and gave her a little shrug, and she found herself returning his slightly awkward smile. The guy seemed to know exactly when she was alone, and so far, he'd come to join her every time. She was about to ask him what he wanted, but another door opened. Don snuck out of his room, the first time she'd seen him *without* Tony, and he closed the door silently behind him.

The guys nodded at each other and walked together down the balcony to the staircase, coming to join Leo on the curb. They came to sit on either side of her, comfortable in the silence until Leo felt she had to do something. She finally lit that cigarette.

"Can't sleep?" She breathed smoke at the asphalt parking lot, letting them decide who she was asking.

"It's Tony," Don said quietly. He picked up a pebble and chucked it, letting a few more seconds pass in silence. "*He* can't sleep. I know he's tired, and I know he's pissed, but he won't sleep. He won't talk to me. Just sits there on the bed staring at the wall, and it's driving me crazy." Don turned to look at her. "What did they do to him?"

Leo swallowed. "Same thing they did to us, I'm pretty sure." She tried to convey the regret she felt over Tony having come out of it the way he did, but the expression felt more like a squint.

"I think... I think they took his beat," Don said, his voice cracking on the last word.

"Fuck." Leo instantly thought of Louis, of the things he'd done just to stay in the beat circle even though he could no longer spin one himself. That man had some serious fucking issues, and she couldn't imagine the twins being broken up by something like that—even though she had no idea what either of their beats were in the first place.

"I think I can help with that a little," John said, leaning forward to meet Don's gaze.

"I don't think your nursing skills are gonna do anything for this," Don said. Again, it felt like it was intended as a joke, but it didn't have the same ring to it anymore.

"But my beat can."

Don looked at Leo, who only shrugged. She didn't know what John could do; it wasn't her place to ask. But he was about to show them, apparently.

"All right. Why not?" Don stood and turned toward the stairs, Leo and John following close behind.

When they opened the door, Cameron was still passed out on the closest bed, snoring. Tony sat on the farthest bed, his knees drawn up to his chin, staring at the blank wall across the room. Leo watched him for a bit. His eyes were glassy and rimmed with red, but he didn't even seem to blink. He didn't turn to look at them when they entered, and he didn't move when John sat next to him and Leo and Don shared the couch.

John didn't waste any time with introductions or small talk. It sounded like small talk; he described his work at a hospital in Pueblo, the kind of patients he worked with, the things he'd done during his career that had made him proud. But there was the unmistakable focus in his gaze, the slight tension of the muscles in his neck, and Leo knew immediately that everything he said was part of his beat. Tony got that glazed, foggy look, and then he blinked ever so slowly. His eyes flickered toward John just once, and then all the tension melted out of him.

He didn't quite pass out; it was more like dissolving into himself and the bed. Tony's body lost its rigidity, and he leaned back into the mattress, his eyes closed before he hit the pillow. Don jumped from the bed beside Leo, eyes wide in fear.

"It's okay," John said, holding up his hand. "He's just asleep." As if in response, Tony rolled onto his side and snored loud enough Leo thought he'd wake Cameron.

"That's your beat?" Don asked, the corners of his mouth twitching. Leo figured he itched to make another joke, but he had enough sense to keep it to himself this time.

"Yeah," John said with a tiny chuckle. "I'm a really good nurse." Leo snorted, then covered her mouth with a quick glance at Tony.

"How come I'm not asleep?" Don asked, concern creeping back into his frown. "If that was your beat... I'm still awake."

John gave Leo a glance that seemed to say he thought he'd fucked up. She gave him a tiny nod to go ahead. "I know it's weird," he said. "I just kind of felt that I could... aim it, somehow. Apparently, it worked."

"Kaylee could do that too," Leo said, shifting to face Don next to her. "I'm pretty sure that's how we even got off the lab's property in the first place." The images of roaring flames and black swirling smoke mixed with the clanging of crashing helicopters in her head. That had all been Kaylee, in the end. "Our beats are... stronger, too." Strong enough to kill three research assistants by accident. And the only other person who'd been there to see it wasn't here with them anymore.

"You tried to use yours on Kaylee," Don said, shaking his head. "It didn't work at all."

"Yeah, whatever they did to the three of us—" Leo nodded toward John "—we're not affected anymore. By any beat."

"And whatever they did to him left him like that," Don said, looking at his brother.

Leo didn't say anything. What *was* there to say to that? Don got up and grabbed the thin wool blanket folded at the end of his bed. He laid it over his brother lovingly, using the only comfort he knew how to give at that moment. It seemed to be enough for him.

"What happened to that Evan guy?" Leo asked after a few minutes.

Don finally smirked and glanced at the lump of Cameron's sleeping form on the bed behind them. "Cameron almost killed the guy. He didn't buy that it was just shitty luck, especially when those assholes broke into the warehouse and—" he swallowed "—took you guys."

"He thought Evan ratted us out?"

"Yeah. Him and Shannon."

"That chick with the dreads?" Leo asked. Her stomach turned.

"Yup." Don nodded, a tiny frown knotting his brow. "Brad and Karl made a bunch of calls. Blacklisted Shannon's place. Nobody's gonna be helping her for a while. The rest of us left the warehouse that night and stayed at another safe house until we… came to get you." He laughed. "I think you guys might not have needed us at all."

"It was good that you showed up," Leo said. The reassurance came out so quickly, she didn't have time to really process how oddly normal the sentiment felt. Was comforting people just part of what she did now? Even so, it seemed a necessary balance to the chaos she'd lived for the last few weeks—something she *could* offer. "And *he* was glad you showed up," she added, nodding toward Tony.

"Yeah…" Don's frown returned. "I don't really know what to do with him now. What to do *for* him."

"Have you met Louis?" Leo didn't know if associating with the owner of the Purple Lion would help Tony or just make things worse for him, but maybe the man's story would give Don some context—for what not to do, if anything.

"No, but I heard the stories." Don picked at his finger-nails. "Bernadette called him after that night at the ware-house. His place isn't safe anymore, either. Somebody's been hitting it, too. You know, taking people." The look he gave Leo when he glanced up at her held more fear than she'd ever seen in another person's gaze. She swallowed.

"Where's this Louis guy?" John asked.

Leo realized how confused the guy must have been by their conversation; he hadn't been a part of anything before Vanguard Industries. "He owns a nightclub in Wyoming," she said. "Had his beat taken away from him, like Tony."

John's eyes went wide. "So I guess it's not just people getting kidnapped in Colorado, is it? It's bigger than just where they held us."

"Yeah," Leo said. "I guess so. And Sleepwater's been fighting these people for a long time."

"What's Sleepwater?" John asked.

Don and Leo exchanged a glance and another smirk. "You're lookin' at it," Don said. "Part of it, anyways. You came in at a pretty *awesome* time."

Rolling her eyes, Leo gave John a nod. "I thought *I* had a shitty introduction. You'll figure it out as we go along." She grinned, thinking this might have been how Karl felt when he dragged her into this what felt like forever ago.

45

THEY'D DECIDED IT was a better idea to stay at the motel through the night before leaving early the next morning. Now that Brad and Mirela's secret was out, it seemed in poor taste to shove everyone in the van again with nothing more than a few hours of sleep behind them and nothing less than ten more hours of driving ahead. Why not give everyone the chance at a full night's sleep, especially after everything they'd just been through?

Leo found it a little odd that the rest of Sleepwater was so calm, so casual about taking their time in this town. They'd blown up a government-funded research facility, hurt who knew how many people, and downed a helicopter. Apparently, they considered themselves professionals at it—minus the getting paid part—and Randall had told her there was nothing to worry about. He'd set up some system tuned into the police radio dispatch, both surrounding Vanguard Industries in Jackson County and where they stayed now in San Miguel County. She didn't understand how he got into both channels at the same time, especially so far away from northern Colorado, but Randall got it done. He'd assured her both channels were quiet on the issue of the burning building and the *vandalism* they'd committed; weird, yes, but so far, a relief. He had his bulky computer set up in his motel room, the volume at a low buzz while the police dispatch droned on in the background. Just in case.

Karl had told her he wanted to talk to her about something, essentially planning her dinner for her at the diner just a few buildings down from the motel. It wasn't like she had anything else to do; Brad had gotten takeout, the others had decided to stay in, and it was getting dark.

They sat at a cheap laminate table, the booth upholstery peeling beneath her fingers. Leo was hungrier than she expected to be when she ordered and even hungrier when their burgers showed up on off-white plastic plates. The bun was soggy and stuck to a tomato that could have passed for ripe a week ago. Leo let it drop to the plate with a smack and cut into the single patty. Food poisoning still wasn't necessarily ruled out.

"This place is shitty," she mumbled through the meat.

Karl sipped on his coke, dipped a fry in ketchup. "We can do so much better."

She glanced up at him from the rings of drink stains on the table. "What do you mean?"

"You and I." Frowning at his plate, he ate a few more fries. "When things calm down. I've put aside a little bit of money. I've been wanting to stop working for Louis for a while. Doubt he'd want me at the Purple Lion now anyways. I want to open a bar."

She stared at him, painfully swallowing the dry hamburger. "You want a bar?"

"It would be half yours. I'm sure you could make a better burger."

Leo chugged her water and waited for him to look up at

her, but he didn't. "That's what you wanted to talk to me about?" He still didn't answer, smothering his burger in more ketchup. "I don't know shit about bars... or burgers."

Then he did look at her, and a tiny smile twitched beneath his tomato-stained mustache. "You could figure it out."

She gave him a wry smile, forgetting about her food. "You're fucking with me."

"Nope."

Sitting back against the booth, she took a minute to really think about what he'd said. It seemed fucking ridiculous. She looked up at the tiny TV mounted in the corner of the diner and suddenly lost her appetite. Karl looked up at her again, frowned, and turned around to follow her gaze.

It was Dr. Kerrigan, being interviewed by some news station. Leo hadn't heard the TV before as they sat in the diner, but now she couldn't tune out the sound. Part of her wanted to tell the waitress to turn it down.

"The recent malfunctions at Vanguard Industries in North Park, Colorado have left some Jackson County residents a little rattled. Dr. Megan Kerrigan is here with us today to explain what happened last night and to help put these concerns to rest. Dr. Kerrigan, you said this was an electrical issue that got out of hand?"

"Hi, Brenda. Yes. Parts of our building are quite old, and we'd been aware of some electrical issues in the east wing of the complex for a few weeks now. We thought we'd contained it, but the damage went a bit further than our inspectors had foreseen. A small power shortage occurred inside one of our storage rooms, where we unfortunately had been temporarily keeping a good portion of our flammable materials. We finally had just received approval for a new addition to the building, and we'd moved things around a bit at the wrong time, apparently. We suffered a bit of damage, but we've managed to contain it, and there's nothing to

worry about."

"There sure did seem to be... a lot of damage—"

"Yes, well, accidents happen, and we're rectifying the issue now. All of our research was preserved, and there was no exposure of any of our compounds, so there's absolutely nothing to worry about. The important thing is—" Dr. Kerrigan turned to look directly at the camera and grinned *"— we will find out exactly what happened, and we'll make sure the mistake does not repeat itself."*

Leo felt the blood drain from her face. "What a load of shit," she whispered. Who in their right mind would see the short footage of the burning research facility and actually believe it was an *electrical malfunction*? That last part, though, came like a punch to the gut. It felt like Dr. Kerrigan had been looking right at her, talking right *to* her, and she knew there wouldn't be any reports filed or police involvement. That psycho woman wanted to find Leo—to find Kaylee and John—all on her own and repeat whatever success she felt she'd apparently made with them.

Karl turned back around to look at her.

"Do you know who that is?" she asked, her voice scratchy. He nodded. "Did you know that she's my..." She couldn't say it.

"She doesn't have to be if you don't want her to." His calm, dark eyes bored into hers.

"Does everyone know? Cameron, Brad, Bernadette? Everyone?"

"Yeah."

Leo felt her heart sink—something like guilt, relief, and gratitude mixed into one. Her eyes stung. "You knew she'd come looking for me."

"And we knew a bigger risk came with it. But you're one of us." He didn't give her sympathy, didn't try to make her feel better. He said it like it was, the complete truth, and Leo choked back words she didn't think she could say.

Karl's eyes flicked behind her toward the front window of the diner, then widened. His whole body went rigid, and his hand shot to his hip. He seemed frozen for a split second—either in rage or fear, she couldn't tell—and then he jumped from the booth, jostling the table with a loud bang.

"What?" Leo asked, turning to look through the window. All she saw was Karl lunging past her, headed toward the door. "Karl?"

She got up after him, tossed a twenty on the table, and almost jogged to catch up with him out on the sidewalk. His long legs carried him quickly, with a purpose, and he stared across the street at a man strolling along. He craned his neck forward, his jaw set tight, fists clenched at his sides. Almost like he was hunting the guy—stalking him. They passed the motel, and Leo looked up to see John stepping out of his room. She met his questioning gaze and gave him a shrug as she jogged just behind Karl. John must have noticed the strangeness of the situation, because he hurried his pace too and raced down the staircase.

"Hey!" Karl shouted, his voice a hoarse growl. The man across the street turned at the noise, and when he caught sight of Karl, he bolted. Karl gave another wordless yell and darted across the street.

"Karl!" Leo thought the car barreling down the road was going to run him down. It narrowly missed him, and the driver laid on the horn. "Karl!" she called again, making sure the street was clear before running after him. She heard John following not far behind.

The street lamps flashed past her in the twilight, and she could barely keep up. The man vanished around the back of the gas station, Karl close on his heels, and when Leo rounded the corner of the brick building, Karl already had his hands on the back of the man's jacket. He spun the man around and swung a knock-out right hook to the guy's jaw, sending his head flying back. The man would have crumpled to the ground if Karl didn't have such a tight grip on his collar, holding him up by adrenaline alone.

"Karl, what are you doing?" Leo shouted. He pummeled the man's face again, blood spraying onto the concrete. "Karl, stop!"

"This sonofabitch murdered my wife!" Karl bellowed, sending his fist into the man's stomach. Then he grabbed him by the collar with both hands and slammed his head against the brick wall, fuming.

Leo barely had time to register what happened. The stranger's face—dark, hollow, and covered in blood—contorted in terror and desperation. His hands fumbled in the pocket of his jacket, so close to Karl's heaving body, and the shot rang out just as John rounded the corner to join them. At the same time Karl went down, John was at the stranger's throat, slapping the gun from his hand and immediately carrying on the beating Karl had started.

"Fuck!" Leo ran to Karl's side, praying to anyone who would listen that he was okay. The red stain blooming on his chest told her otherwise, as much as she didn't want to believe it. Karl's body jerked on the concrete, his chest heaving, blood spewing from his lips as he coughed and wheezed. "Karl..." Her hands shook when she placed them on his chest, and she didn't even have to try to ignore the warm stickiness beneath her palm. She was vaguely aware of John's grunts behind her as his fist connected over and over again with the person who'd just shot the man now lying in her arms.

"Call Louis," Karl whispered, his wide eyes locked onto hers. "Ask for the key." A fit of spasms wracked him, and he coughed again.

"You're gonna be okay," Leo whispered, trembling. "You're gonna be fine."

"Use it to... make a safe place for them."

Leo shushed him, noticing his hand groping at something inside his jeans pocket. She quickly fished it out for him and almost cried out when she unfolded the wrinkled photo of his wife—the same one she'd held when she'd first stepped into his home. She placed it in his hand, helped him clutch it, and automatically wiped away the blood he coughed into her face with her sleeve. "Don't say anything," she told him. "Look at your wife." She wasn't a doctor—didn't know shit about gunshot wounds—but there was no way he was going to be okay. There was too much blood, too much wheezing in his breath, and she groaned as she looked him up and down, searching for a way to fix it. She had to do something.

She felt the words burning up through her throat, stronger and fierier than she ever remembered them. She aimed them at him more desperately than she'd ever spoken any words, any beat she'd ever told. "Everything's okay." Her voice cracked, but she carried on, even though Karl convulsed again and his breath pushed through a wet gurgle. "She's waiting for you. You're going to see her soon, and she can't wait to be with you again." Karl stared at her, his eyes glazing over from her beat. The pain and panic drained from his face, and a smile cracked his blood-splattered lips. "She loves you so much," Leo said, unable to keep back a tiny sob. His eyes wandered, as if he could see what lay ahead of him, and then his breath hitched in his throat and didn't come again.

"Leo," John said, his voice greeting her as if through syrup.

"No." She couldn't take her hand from the wound in Karl's chest, even as the picture of his wife fell from his lifeless fingers. "I can't." For the first time in a long time, tears streamed freely down her face.

"Leo, we have to go. We have to get the others out of here too."

"No!" She felt John's firm hand on her shoulder, and she jerked away from it. He grabbed her arm and yanked her to her feet, but not before she snatched the picture of Karl's wife, her heart breaking over the smile still on his face.

46

THEY DIDN'T END up staying at the motel overnight, and they couldn't go back for Karl's body. Even if they weren't still technically on the run after what they'd done at Vanguard Industries, John said he was pretty sure he'd killed that man behind the gas station. For all his kindness, for having worked to heal people as a nurse, he didn't seem remotely bothered by that fact. If Leo had been able to get the image of the blood thick in Karl's beard out of her mind, she would have admired John for the confidence he seemed to have in his decision.

They'd rushed out of the motel, no one bothering to question what had happened or suggest they double back and make sure. Sleepwater was used to split-second decisions— life or death situations—and they moved with the same sure swiftness they always had. When Brad had asked where Karl was, John had been the one to step up and explain. He'd spoken quickly, efficiently, telling them he was sure Karl was dead and that the cops would be there any minute. He relayed the whole thing as if he saw that kind of thing every day—as if it didn't even bother him. And why should it? He didn't know Karl. He hadn't been through what they'd been through. Karl hadn't given *him* another chance to finally mean something in this world. To John, it was just one more body—a guy he'd only known for less than twenty-four hours.

Though the van had been completely full on their drive into New Mexico, it seemed empty and hollow now, despite only missing one man. But that man was Karl; his presence had been bigger than anyone's. Bigger than Leo had ever realized. She clutched the photo of his wife as Bernadette held her in the back seat. The old woman's embrace was comforting, maternal, and it only made Leo cry even harder. No one said a word as they made their way to Texas.

Mirela's sister Zoe and her husband lived in a decent-sized ranch house in the suburbs of San Antonio. They greeted those in the van with more excitement than was appropriate—no one had had the chance to call them and let them know what happened. The somber mood was infectious, and Mirela's family quickly acclimated to the situation. They'd made up beds for everyone—one extra than necessary, now—and Zoe's husband Aaron went to the store to turn what had been their breakfast for two into enough food for almost a dozen. Almost.

Leo didn't eat anything. Her last bite of food had been a nasty, charred bit of hamburger with Karl, and the idea of ever eating again made her stomach hurt. She hadn't even washed Karl's sticky blood off her hands, rusty specks still clinging to her face. Bernadette was the only one who tried to talk to her, and she finally managed to get Leo into the shower once everyone had settled down for the night. Leo felt like they were all watching her, waiting for her to do something—whether it was to dust off her hands and pick herself back up or completely fall apart, she couldn't be sure. She seemed stuck in between, unable to move, unable to process. She kept expecting him to walk through the front door any minute with that stupid smirk on his face, telling her she was an idiot for not trusting him.

When she finally opened up to Bernadette in the stillness that night, telling her everything that had happened, the old woman made a point of honoring what had been Karl's last request. With tears in her eyes, she dialed Louis' number on the landline and handed the phone to Leo.

"Karl's dead," she said into the receiver, knowing that if she tried to say anything else, it would never come out. "He told me to ask you for the key." The words sounded so callous in her own ears, so blasé. Like a written script.

"Do you have an ID?"

The question surprised her, and she glanced at Bernadette as if the woman could hear the conversation and somehow give her some guidance. Bernadette only gave a nod of reassurance. "No…"

"I'm buying you a bus ticket. Tell Bernadette to check her email." Then he hung up.

Two days later, she stood at the Greyhound station in Casper, Wyoming, waiting for the ride Louis had said he'd send for her. She shifted her backpack on her shoulder, feeling uncomfortable and shifty even after she'd already made the trip. Apparently, she *had* needed an ID to go with her bus ticket, and apparently Louis had drivers who even worked for him across the country. The driver of her bus took one look at her ticket, asked if she knew Louis, and didn't give her a second glance as he nodded toward the back of the bus. Almost thirty-one hours on the road back had made her stiff and sore, but she welcomed the feeling. It reminded her that she wasn't dreaming, that she wouldn't be waking up from what seemed like the worst nightmare.

A silver Lexus pulled up, remarkably out of place, and a thin woman with a hooked nose rolled down the driver-side window. "Leo?" Leo looked at her with a frown and nodded. "Get in. Louis is waiting for you."

Leo rolled her eyes and opened the back door, sliding in with a sigh. She bet Louis was really enjoying this mafia-don bullshit, wherever he was. That, or he was too scared to look her in the eye. The last time she'd seen him, he'd black-mailed Karl into spinning a beat and getting him high. Whether or not Louis felt any guilt over having orchestrated that shitty scenario, Karl seemed to be getting even with him now in making him meet with her. Whatever this key was, it obviously wasn't just something Louis could have dropped in the mail.

If the woman driving the Lexus had been the talkative type—which she definitely wasn't—Leo wouldn't have said a thing. The forty-five-minute drive flew by, even in silence, and they pulled up in front of a self-storage building. The driver didn't say anything or give Leo another glance, but she turned off the engine. Leo let out a snort of contempt and stepped out of the car.

He made her wait another ten minutes, but finally, Louis pulled up in a black Range Rover he'd decided to drive himself. Leo stepped away from the wall she'd been leaning against and shoved her hands in her pocket, fighting the wild anxiety brought on by the sight of Louis' gelled hair and probably designer sunglasses. She didn't know if she was angry at him, grateful for his help, or completely terri-fied of what Karl had left her.

She was surprised, though, to find the man dressed in all black when he stepped out of the SUV. His normal flam-boyant, colorful flare had been exchanged for a dampened version, and Leo swore to herself that if he was mocking her pain by wearing black—if he even so much as mentioned

Karl's name in the wrong tone—she'd beat him right there in front of the storage units, security cameras or no. But when he stopped just inches from her and removed his sunglasses, there was no mistaking the bags beneath his red-rimmed eyes. His grief was obviously as real as her own.

"This is yours," he said, pulling a keyring with one key from his pocket and dangling it before her from his index finger.

"Thanks," she said and gently grabbed it from him.

He looked her up and down for a moment, his lips drawn tight, then pulled her in for an extremely tight, extremely close hug. Leo was too shocked to return it, and by the time she got her arms moving, Louis had already released her and taken a step back. Breathing deep, he brushed the front of his shirt as if she'd left something on it and stared down the row of storage units, blinking rapidly. "Some-day... eventually... you'll have to come tell me everything that happened." He looked back at her then, and she nodded.

Looking at him now, knowing what he'd gone through at the hands of people like Dr. Kerrigan—knowing what that *felt* like—she saw a completely different person. Soft, trying to be callous, with an undying need to remain a part of the world that had been so horrendously ripped from him. But he still carried the basic sense of what Sleepwater had tried to do all along—to help others like them.

He gave her a curt nod, then turned on his heel and headed back toward the Range Rover. "But don't expect me to pay you for that story," he added, turning slightly to look at her over his shoulder. Then he slid his sunglasses back down from his forehead. "I hope you know you're fired."

Leo tried to laugh, which came out sounding more like a confused sigh, and she watched him drive away. Then she looked down at the black letters scribbled on the purple plastic—629—and searched for the matching unit.

It was a small unit at the end of the row, closet-sized.

She half expected the key to not fit the lock; that seemed more appropriate somehow than everything working out the way it was supposed to. Because how could this be real, Karl leaving her something? How could anyone want to leave her anything? She glanced nervously up and down the concrete rows of the complex, both wanting to be left alone and hoping someone would come along to stop her—to save her from being disappointed. But then she swallowed, told herself to grow a pair, and opened the door.

Definitely the size of a closet. She flipped the light switch, stepped inside, and closed the door behind her. Her immediate thought was that it was empty, but there was actually just one thing there, lying neatly on the ground. The bright blue cooler starkly contrasted against the grey cement floor. Leo almost laughed at the ridiculousness of it. Who paid for storage units to hold a drink cooler? She thought of Karl's place and the minifridge he kept stocked with beers. For a second, she expected this to be his one last joke—he'd left her a cooler full of beer.

But then she opened the white plastic top, and she barely registered the hollow sound of it hitting the floor. The cooler was filled with cash. Not like piggy-bank cash—stacks of twenty- and hundred-dollar bills, held together with rubber bands and neatly piled. The stacks almost filled the cooler completely, and on the very top sat a scrap of lined notebook paper with just a number scribbled in the center—499,980. It took her a minute to realize it was the total count. Karl had left her twenty bucks short of half a million.

She sank to her knees and grabbed the piece of paper, staring at it as if it were more valuable than the giant pile of cash in front of her. Then she burst into tears.

With no one there to see her, to hear her or comfort her, Leo must have cried on the floor of that storage unit for at least half an hour. When she felt it had been long enough, her wracking sobs turned into sudden giggles. She threw her head back and howled with laughter at the ceiling light, cracking up over the whole thing. Wiping her eyes, she folded the notebook paper and stuffed it into her jeans pocket.

Karl had wanted her to use the money to make a safe place for them. That was exactly what she'd do.

47

LEO WALKED TO the window to plug in their neon Open sign. She'd had it connected to the lit sign above the entrance, and she smiled as the blue reflection spilled onto the wooden counter. Even upside-down, that reflection looked great.

When she'd bought the place, it had come with only four tables, seven chairs, and two stools; the bar was chipped, peeling, and looked like some animal had bitten a chunk out of the corner. But it was hers. She'd run a hand underneath one of the hanging lamps that day eighteen months ago, curling the spider web and dead flies around her fingers. It had taken a lot of work, tens of thousands of dollars in repairs, and more time than she'd ever given to any one thing. Karl would have thought it was shitty and too expensive—a fucking mess—and he would have loved it. She'd named the bar *Tracey's*.

"You gotta remember to turn the sign on when you open," she said, leaning over the bar and tapping the wooden counter to get his attention.

John looked back at her from the beer tap and shrugged with a wincing smile. "I know. Sorry."

Tuesday nights had been a little slow recently, but it was only eleven—plenty of time still for things to pick up. Leo sat at the table by the kitchen door and lit the last cigarette in her pack, enjoying the fact that it was her fucking place and she could do whatever the fuck she wanted.

A kid walked in and went straight to the bar, maybe nineteen. He got John's attention right away and spoke in hushed tones. John only shook his head slowly and shuffled farther down the bar. "Hey!" the kid hollered, and the other patrons eyed him warily. John turned, biting his lip and frowning. "Hey, I could really hurt you if I wanted to, you know. You have no idea—"

"Listen, kid," John started, and the kid took a big, exaggerated breath.

"Woah," Leo called, and in a few strides, she was at the bar, leaning on it next to the threatening, skinny terror to all bartenders. The kid glanced at her, his eyes wide, fists clenched at his sides. "Is your throat burning?"

His face went white. "How—"

"Good. Kill it." She dragged on the cigarette, blew in the other direction, and smiled at John. "Will you go get me a pack of cigarettes?"

John moved slow, playing dumb. "Sure thing, boss." He didn't try to hide his sarcasm, but he dropped the rag on the bar and headed toward the door.

Leo looked at the kid under raised brows. "What's your name, killer?"

He was still shocked, still white, but he stuck his hands in his pockets and eyed her suspiciously. "Travis."

"All right, Travis. You gotta be subtler than that, yeah?" He didn't reply. She walked around the bar and grabbed two beers out of the cooler. "You're not twenty-one, are you?"

she asked, holding the beer in suspense.

"No." His frown darkened in suspicion.

"Right." She popped the tops off both bottles and set one in front of him. "I get points for guessing." She drew on the bottle, winking as a smile finally crept onto Travis' face. He followed her lead, and she crossed to his side of the bar to take a stool next to him.

"You Tracey?" he asked.

Leo blinked at the question, turning to look at the framed photo of a smiling redhead in the sunshine hanging behind the bar. "No," she said and finally snorted a laugh. "Listen, Travis. I know exactly what it was you were about to do to poor John, and I know it's incredibly stupid to cause a scene like that in public nowadays."

Travis took another sip of beer, frowned, and stared behind the bar like a kid caught eating too much candy. "I thought I was the only one."

Leo laughed. "There's federal laws against it, and you thought you were the only one?" He gave a pathetic shrug and stared at his jeans. "There are other people out there who can do what we do."

His eyes were wide as they met hers. "You?"

She smirked, and John sauntered through the front door, tossing the cigarettes onto the bar. She packed the box and unwrapped it. "Yeah," she mumbled, cigarette sticking briefly to her lips as she lit it.

"How many are there? What can they do? Do you know them?" Travis pulled on the beer again, attention completely captured.

"I know where to find them," she said through the smoke and offered one to the kid.

Thank you, Dear Reader, for grabbing this book. If you enjoyed it, please consider leaving a review on Amazon and/or Goodreads. It is *the best* way to thank any author!

Looking for More?

Visit KathrinHutsonFiction.com for news and updates on more Thrillers and Fast-Paced Sci-Fi Adventures. You can also sign up for my newsletter, where you get some exclusive dark surprises not seen anywhere else.

Do you like Dark Fantasy?
Check out my other series:

The Unclaimed Trilogy (NA Dark Fantasy)
Sanctuary of Dehlyn
Secret of Dehlyn
Sacrament of Dehlyn

Gyenona's Children Duology
(Dark Fantasy)
"The Jungle Meets Kill Bill... with dragons!"
Daughter of the Drackan
Mother of the Drackan

"And the Great Drackan resumed its place upon the stone." The child's eyes sparkled with delight. Honai rolled the parchment again and set it back on the shelf. The child jumped on the bed, her dark curls bouncing between her shoulders as she pulled the skirt of her nightgown as far out as it would go. Honai laughed. "What are you doing?"

The smile the girl gave her wet nurse was fierce and wild. "I want to be a drackan."

Honai smiled and walked to the bedside. The girl jumped high, landing blindly on her knees as the nightgown whipped over her head. Honai giggled with her, tickling the child's body, then straightened her out on the mattress. "But I'm sure the mighty drackans are not so careless as to let their wings cover their heads?" The girl grinned, wiggling under the quilts. Honai situated her in bed and knelt. "Why do you wish so much to be a drackan?"

"They're the greatest things that ever lived."

Honai smoothed a lock of dark hair from the child's face, frowning in mock consternation. "These are the same drackans I know, yes? The terrifying, ruthless brutes, who destroyed villages, ate livestock, and burned forests with their firebreath?"

The girl patiently shook her head. "They only killed people who scared them. They only ever wanted to fly and protect their babies. And they saved the one boy who would not run from them. He believed in them, and I believe in them." She held up her hands, casting shadows upon the bed, and pulled a face at them. "I wish I could hear their stories."

Honai stood and straightened her skirts. There was no point in arguing with a child's vibrant imagination, especially before bed. Especially this child. "Well, I'm sure they have their stories, my dear, but they are not for tonight. Sleep well, and perhaps you may dream of your drackans."

"Yes," the girl sighed, squirming in tired excitement. "And they will tell me everything."

Honai kissed the child's forehead but paused at the doorway to the chamber. The hairs on the back of her neck prickled, and the wrongness she sensed quickly became a sound. It mocked the flapping of Lord Kartney's banner in the wind, posted high above the watchtower. Many nights, it was the only sound outside the castle. But this noise was no banner. It was louder, thicker, splitting through the air with intent. In a matter of seconds, a calm night of normalcy shredded into terror. It had finally come.

She turned toward the window, knowing the truth and fearing it all the more. There hovered a great red drackan from the High Hills, head stretched out tight on its neck, body hovering with the rhythmic beat of its wings. The drackan's armored scales shone in the firelight—brown with a tinge of fiery, metallic red. The broad wings almost scraped against the cold outer stone of the tower as it pushed a dignified head through the opening almost too small for it. The length of its neck crossed the room toward the child's bed.

The girl had pushed herself up, wide-eyed and glowing with excitement.

The seconds stretched long and thin before Honai's wits scattered, and she screamed. A voice, much louder than it should have been, echoed through the room. It came from the beast itself, though the bone-crushing jaw never moved, the eyes never left the child's face. A bodiless, sexless voice, dark and ancient.

'You do believe in us, fledgling. I think it high time you had your wish.'

Honai stared in mute horror as the beast's ridged snout hovered above the child's legs. The girl reach out a tiny hand, steady and calm. Glassy, intelligent eyes passed between the hand and the small face. Judging. Waiting.

"I am not afraid," the child stated boldly and lightly touched the creature.

When finally Honai could move again, her terror rushed her out of the chamber and through the castle. She ran down the stone halls, bumping against the corners as she turned through the corridors.

She finally reached the dining hall where Lord Kartney sat drinking with his men. "Milord," she gasped.

The dark-haired lord turned from the table to look at her with a half-smile still playing across his lips. He noted her concern and stood abruptly, the smile fading into a worried frown. "What is it, Honai?"

The woman stumbled and fell to her knees at his feet. "Milord, a… a drackan… in the child's room…"

He whispered his daughter's name and brusquely turned to his men. Wordlessly, they followed him through the castle halls. The drackan's diminishing tail vanished through the open window just as they burst through the door. Kartney unsheathed his sword and rushed to the window, wildly slashing out, but the bare steel caught only the frigid night air.

A scream of fear and misery echoed from the tower of Brijer Turret, lasting almost as long as it took for the child's bed to grow cold.

About the Author

Kathrin Hutson has been writing Fantasy and Sci-Fi since 2000. She can't get enough of tainted heroes, excruciating circumstances, impossible decisions, and Happily Never After.

In addition to writing dark and enchanting fiction, Kathrin spends the other half of her time as a fiction ghostwriter of most genres, as an Independent Editor through her company KLH CreateWorks, and as Fiction Co-Editor for Burlington's *Mud Season Review* literary magazine. She finds just as much joy and enthusiasm in working closely with other fiction authors on their incredible novels as she does in writing her own.

Kathrin lives in Vermont with her husband, young daughter, and two dogs and is constantly on the lookout for other upcoming authors, great new books, and more people with whom to share her love of words.

Sign up at kathrinhutsonfiction.com for exclusive access to fiction deals, Advanced Reader Copies, and dark surprises you won't find anywhere else.

Author@kathrinhutsonfiction.com
www.facebook.com/kathrinhutsonfiction
www.kathrinhutsonfiction.com
www.instagram.com/kathrinhutsonfiction
www.twitter.com/exquisitelydark